Zero Sum

An Alexis Parker novel

G.K. Parks

This is a work of fiction. Names, characters, places, events, and other concepts are the product of the author's imagination or are used fictitiously. Any resemblance to actual persons, living or dead, places, establishments, events, and locations is entirely coincidental.

No part of this book may be reproduced in any form or by any electronic or mechanical means including information storage and retrieval systems, without express written permission from the author.

Copyright © 2022 G.K. Parks

A Modus Operandi imprint

All rights reserved.

ISBN: 1942710348
ISBN-13: 978-1-942710-34-9

Thank you for reading this book and making this series possible. I wouldn't be able to do this without your support.

BOOKS IN THE LIV DEMARCO SERIES:

Dangerous Stakes
Operation Stakeout
Unforeseen Danger
Deadly Dealings
High Risk
Fatal Mistake
Imminent Threat
Mistaken Identity
Malicious Intent

BOOKS IN THE ALEXIS PARKER SERIES:

Likely Suspects
The Warhol Incident
Mimicry of Banshees
Suspicion of Murder
Racing Through Darkness
Camels and Corpses
Lack of Jurisdiction
Dying for a Fix
Intended Target
Muffled Echoes
Crisis of Conscience
Misplaced Trust
Whitewashed Lies
On Tilt
Purview of Flashbulbs
The Long Game
Burning Embers
Thick Fog
Warning Signs
Past Crimes
Sinister Secret
Zero Sum
Buried Alive

BOOKS IN THE JULIAN MERCER SERIES:

Condemned
Betrayal
Subversion
Reparation
Retaliation
Hunting Grounds

BOOKS IN THE CROSS SECURITY INVESTIGATIONS SERIES:

Fallen Angel
Calculated Risk

ONE

I held my breath and pressed against the wall, waiting for the guard to pass. This was a bad idea. Correction, it was a terrible idea. Possibly the worst idea ever. I knew better. Yet, somehow, I let Lucien Cross talk me into this.

The guard moved through the lobby, heading toward me. I counted his steps. Thirty feet. That's how far it was to the locked door from which he'd emerged. Fourteen. I pressed my palm against the large pillar which concealed me from view while I fumbled in my jacket pocket for my phone. Ten.

Glancing at the screen, I watched as the final number continued to shift and morph at lightning speed. *Come on*, I thought. What was taking so long? As soon as I was close enough to pick up the wi-fi signal, I logged onto the secure server through a backdoor. By now, the software should have cracked building security and spit out the door code, but it hadn't. Six. Now was not the time to improvise.

Soundlessly, I slid around the wide pillar as the guard moved past. His continuous footfalls reassured me he hadn't noticed anything amiss. I let out a breath. But he wasn't the only obstacle.

As soon as the double doors clanged, I knew he'd moved

on to the stairwell. Now I had to get across the lobby without triggering the motion sensors or getting caught on camera. The sensors were easy enough, as long as I stuck close to the path the guard had taken. But that led me directly into the camera's line of sight.

After taking another breath, I peered around the pillar, finding the oscillating camera headed in the opposite direction. As quickly and silently as possible, I dashed across the open expanse to the next nearest pillar and plastered myself against the back as the camera swept toward me.

I'd wanted to disable the camera with a quick EMP burst, but Lucien warned that would cause more guards to check out the disturbance. They wouldn't believe the camera was on the fritz or a wire had gotten loose. Most security guards I'd encountered weren't nearly that dedicated to their jobs, but these were the crème de la crème. Just like this damn security system.

The camera swept from one end to the other. I couldn't wait another cycle. I had to move. The guard would be back soon. Waiting wasn't an option.

I slipped behind the final pillar, maneuvering around the back until I made it around the side. From here, I could glimpse the number pad. The red light at the top told me the door was locked. Despite the chic design, I'd seen the specs. Unless I had the code or something to burn through the door, I wasn't getting past the reinforced steel.

The camera swiveled again, and I froze, hoping it couldn't spot me. As soon as the camera ticked by, I peered around the side of the pillar, making sure the guard wasn't returning, and beelined for the panel.

"Dammit," I hissed. The final digit still hadn't been found, so I punched in the five numbers I knew and checked again. Nothing. I studied the keys, but I didn't notice any smudges or fading. The camera clicked as it reached its limit and started turning back in my direction.

I had three chances to get it right before the alarm sounded. With ten digits, I had a thirty percent chance. That was better than zero. I made my first guess and got a beep. Quickly, I reentered the first five digits. *Hurry,*

Parker, my internal voice urged. Nine? Four?

Before I could decide, my phone let out a chime. Seven. I punched it in, hit the pound key, and depressed the handle the moment the light turned green. Sliding through the doorway, I pushed the door closed. Did the camera catch the door closing? I didn't want to wait around to find out.

The elevator banks covered both walls, but I wasn't stupid enough to fall for that trap. Instead, I pushed open the door to my right. The metal push bar let out a loud grunt followed by a resounding thud as the door closed behind me. If anyone was close, they definitely heard that.

I waited, listening for footsteps while I surveyed the area. The stairwell wasn't that much different from the one the guard had gone into on the other end of the lobby. Concrete steps, cinderblock walls, and metal railings. In the dark, I couldn't tell if the paint was chipped, but the air smelled musty. Only guards and thieves took the stairs.

After thirty seconds in the deafening silence, I decided it was safe to proceed. The schematics hadn't shown any motion sensors or cameras here. But that didn't mean new additions hadn't been installed.

I crept slowly up the steps, watching for red lights or odd devices along the walls. When I reached the top floor, I knelt beside the door handle. The stairs continued upward, but the only thing above me was the roof. The emergency exit sign was a joke. That wasn't a means of escape. That was a death wish.

Taking out my phone, I held it close to the keypad on the wall. The unlock code varied for each floor. But unlike the other levels, this one had yet to be deciphered.

I checked the time while I watched the numbers populate. Maybe I should back out now. It wasn't too late. Lucien could do this job himself, if it was that important. Once I opened this door, I wouldn't have a choice but to see this through to the end.

As if on cue, the unlock code appeared on my screen. I didn't believe in signs, but I spent days studying the security system before breaking into the building. And that didn't factor in the hours of research and the work the techs put in to crack these door codes. I might be a lot of things, stupid came to mind, but I wasn't a quitter.

I punched in the code and pushed the handle down. The door let out a squeak. Cringing, I held it cracked open and waited. When no one came to investigate, I crouched down and slipped inside.

Bright overhead lights assaulted my senses. As soon as my eyes adjusted, I moved away from the door. The receptionist's desk was a large semi-circle built into the floor. I moved behind it, aware of the camera on the wall to my right and the other one farther down the hallway.

With the open floor plan, cover positions were few and far between. The freshly waxed floors shone brightly beneath the lights. Again, I considered what a terrible idea this was. Best case scenario, I'd be arrested. Worst case scenario, I'd be killed, probably by one of the armed security guards. I'd left my nine millimeter in the car, figuring that might increase my chances of survival. But given the givens, I couldn't be certain of anything.

Come to California. It'll be like a vacation. You'll love it. Ha. I rolled my eyes. No one mentioned anything about this. And if they had, I never would have gotten on the plane a few weeks ago. Right now, I could be three thousand miles away, at home, watching TV, or, more likely, camped out behind my desk, running background checks, not testing out our client's security by breaking into his office.

I wondered what the jails offered for lunch. This was Los Angeles, so it might be something better than a cheese sandwich. Maybe I'd get avocado toast and almond milk, but I doubted it. Also, I wasn't particularly fond of either. Who thought smearing unflavored guacamole on burnt bread was a good idea? Dammit, now I wanted nachos.

After I finished this job, if I finished this job, that'd be my first stop. The paperwork could wait. I deserved a break.

The receptionist's computer had been powered off. Any incoming calls had been forwarded to the answering service, so I didn't have to worry about anyone being drawn to my location. But the guard would be back at some point, and I didn't want to miss my window to sneak out. So I had to move.

Removing my lock picks from my jacket pocket, I duck-walked to the door, concealed from view by the curve of the desk and the plant placed in the crevice between the desk and wall. Unlike the rest of the doors in the building, this one didn't require an access code.

Fifteen seconds later, the tumblers slid into place, and I turned the knob. Once I was safely inside the copy room, I locked the door. That would slow down any guards who decided to investigate.

Before I stood up, I spotted the camera on the other side of the room. I hadn't expected that. The schematics didn't show a camera here. Was the head honcho so paranoid he had it installed to discourage his employees from stealing office supplies? Or had he caught his workers in scandalous positions? Weren't copy rooms supposed to be turn-ons? I never had any desire to get freaky in front of a warm, humming machine or to print out copies of my butt. But maybe I was the exception, not the rule. I'd have to ask Martin about it when I got home.

Except this camera wasn't making that any easier. Unlike the one in the lobby, this one remained stationary. The only way to avoid getting seen was to get underneath it, but how could I do that from here?

Making it up as I went along, I crawled beneath the table in the center of the room. For all I knew, the camera had already spotted me, but since guards hadn't barged inside, I had to assume it hadn't. However, now I was stuck beneath the table. If I emerged, the camera would see me.

I pressed my palms against the top of the table, testing to see if it could be lifted. The thing weighed a ton, but two legs raised off the ground. Hoping whoever monitored the security feeds wasn't paying close attention, I inched the table forward. The back legs dragged, letting out a rumbling screech, loud enough to wake the dead.

With any luck, the sound couldn't be heard from the back offices. However, I wasn't sure the people on the floor below couldn't hear it. As soon as the end of the table was beneath the camera, I lowered the table onto the floor, took a breath, and crawled out from underneath it. Hopefully, the camera hadn't seen me, even though the footage would show the table moving when security reviewed it, preferably at some point in the future.

I remained under the camera and opened the door which led to a large room filled with workstations. The camera to my right faced the other way, so I didn't have to worry about that. The only one left to worry about was posted at the end of the large community work area. Given its range, I should be able to skirt around it by sticking to the walls on the opposite side. So I did. But the moment I turned the corner, I knew I messed up.

Muffled voices came from within one of the nearby offices. I couldn't quite make out the words, but they sounded angry. Something heavy slammed down. Now would be a great time to retreat, but I had to assume my breach had been discovered and security was on the way. If I turned around now, I'd run right into them.

Instead, I dashed toward the inviting glow of the vending machines. I took up a position against the outer wall of the alcove, knowing that whoever came out of the office wouldn't be able to spot me without turning around to grab a snack.

But my relief was short-lived. Wedged against the soda machine, out of view, was a security guard. Blood dripped from the hole in his chest.

I crossed to him and checked for a pulse. But his open, lifeless eyes answered my question before my fingers verified it. He was dead.

The spatter against the wall and the coins on the floor indicated whoever shot him must have snuck up behind him when he was getting a drink. His ID card and gun were gone. I pulled out my phone to call 9-1-1, just as I heard two loud pops come from one of the offices. The shooter was still here.

TWO

Before my call connected, two men emerged from the back hallway. My research showed at least four offices belonging to top executives situated just past this area. Only the most dedicated would go to work on a Saturday, so the casualties should be at a minimum. But the shots fired told me the guard I found wasn't the only victim.

I kept my back against the wall as they moved past my position. The shooters wore business suits and carried semi-automatics with suppressors. One of them had a thick, metal briefcase in his hand. I held up my phone and began recording, knowing it'd be nearly impossible to identify them from behind. But it was worth a shot.

As they approached the community work area, the one with the briefcase stopped and turned. I stepped deeper into the alcove and slid to the floor. Without a weapon, I didn't stand a chance.

"Wait." Briefcase peered in my direction.

Don't breathe. Don't move. I ran through every self-defense lesson I'd ever had. My best chance of survival would be at close range. But I'd have to act fast, and I'd need the element of surprise.

"What is it?" the one without the briefcase asked.

"I'm not sure. I thought I saw someone," Briefcase said.

"A guard? I thought you took care of him."

"I did."

"Did you make sure?" The one without the briefcase came two steps closer. "Or do I have to do that too?"

My heart hammered in my chest. What did I walk in on?

"No, he's dead," Briefcase said.

"You're certain?" The other man took another step toward me.

"Yeah. The glow from the machine must have caught my eye. Let's move. Our window is closing."

I lifted my phone and caught a glimpse of their faces as they turned back around. The two men continued into the community work area. Not wanting to risk speaking, I hung up on the operator and sent a text to 9-1-1. *Two active shooters, at least one dead, possibly more wounded.* Followed by the address.

Every instinct told me to go after them, but the two pops I heard had been gunshots from a silenced weapon. Someone was dead or dying. I had to find out which.

Hoping for the latter, I crept out of the alcove and scurried down the hallway. The shooters might not be alone, but I couldn't let someone die if there was a chance I could render aid.

The first office I checked was empty. The room hadn't been tossed. Nothing was out of place. Moving on, I pushed open the door marked *Vice President, Fenton Roundtree.* Blood pooled around the body. One shot to the head and one to the heart.

I felt for a pulse, but there was no point. I snapped a few shots of the scene and scanned the room. The drawers in the filing cabinet were open. The entire middle drawer was empty. No files. No office supplies. Nothing.

Given the shooters' heavy artillery, their calm demeanor, and the way I'd found the guard and this victim, I could reach only one conclusion. Those men were professionals. Was this a hit or a robbery?

I quickly checked the other two offices, but they were empty. No bodies. Nothing amiss.

I needed a weapon, but the executive offices didn't offer

much, not even a glass liquor bottle. However, I found a golf club in Mr. Barber's office. I gripped it in both hands, kept my back against the wall, making myself as small a target as possible, and moved quickly and silently to the shooters' last known location.

By the time I reached the community workspace, the men were gone. I looked up at the camera, which appeared to be functioning, but aside from the lone guard, who'd met a horrible fate, no one responded to the present threat. How could that be? What was going on here?

For the briefest moment, I wondered if this was an elaborate hoax. I'd been tested before by Martin in a fake armed robbery. But the guard I found and the body in the office weren't fakes. Those had been living, breathing people, and now they were fresh corpses.

I moved at a faster clip down the hallway. I didn't care how many members of building security spotted me. They had guns. They needed to respond.

When I reached the reception area, I studied the elevators, but the shooters hadn't taken any of them. That left only the stairs.

Shouldering my way into the stairwell, I held the club tighter, prepared to swing at the first sign of trouble. It was stupid to bring a knife to a gunfight, which didn't bode well for my current weapon of choice. But I didn't spot the shooters.

I listened for noises—footsteps, dress shoes against the concrete steps, talking, anything. I didn't hear a single sound. They couldn't have made it to the lobby that quickly.

I peered over the railing, but I didn't see anything. The floors below were shrouded in shadow. I called building security while I headed to the roof. While seemingly farfetched, I wanted to make sure Briefcase and his friend didn't have a helicopter waiting.

But this wasn't an action film. The bright afternoon sun beat down on me as I stepped outside. However, the monotonous ringing in my ear meant building security couldn't answer the phone. How many guards did those two bastards murder? Was anyone left alive?

Racing back the way I came, I hurried down the steps, jumping the last few of each flight as I made my way to the ground floor. Since I couldn't hear them, I had to assume they couldn't hear me. I had to stop them, but I didn't have a solid plan or any plan. The best I could do was delay the bastards from leaving and hope the LAPD's response time was better than advertised. If not, the police might have another homicide to add to the growing list.

Once I reached the lobby, I peered out the tiny glass window. Shadows on the floor swayed back and forth. The men were no longer in the building. They'd just left through the front door.

An exit like that should have tripped the main alarm, which meant they had the door code or they disabled the entire security system. That would explain why the guards hadn't responded, assuming they were alive. Would that explain why no one in the security office answered my call?

I ran outside, but I lost sight of the shooters. The few people on the street didn't seem flustered or perturbed, which meant the men concealed their guns. At least the body count wouldn't rise.

I'd spent more time than most scouting the building. I should be able to figure out the best escape routes from here. But it was hard to think straight with the adrenaline, fear, and anger coursing through my veins.

I had parked in a garage a few blocks away and passed at least half a dozen cameras. The shooters would want something more remote. Something with easier access. They needed to disappear before anyone noticed them. That meant parking in an alley or lot.

I jogged down the block, glancing down every opening, but I didn't spot them. Across the street was a gas station and repair shop. Several cars were parked along the side fence while six other vehicles took up positions at the pumps or waited in line to refuel. The man with the briefcase unlocked the door to a black sedan.

Armed only with the putter, I did the only thing I could and yelled, "Gun." My warning carried across the busy intersection. Pedestrians scattered, looking nervously over their shoulders and across the street.

Someone else shouted, "Over there."

I had no clue what he'd seen, but that led more people to panic and flee in every direction. Several people called the authorities. Between the text I'd sent and the calls being placed, dispatch would have to send additional units. Closer units. Maybe every available unit.

However, unless patrol was a block away, they wouldn't arrive in time. I charged across the street, causing more angry beeps from confused and annoyed motorists who didn't understand why pedestrians were jaywalking in droves, and smashed in the rear window of the getaway car just as the backup lights illuminated.

The man without the briefcase turned, pulled his piece, and aimed at me while Briefcase stomped down on the accelerator. I dove out of the way as the car slammed into one of the stopped cars on the street before lurching forward. The man in the passenger seat rolled down his window and unloaded his weapon in my direction.

Bullets flew, causing people to scream. I took cover behind an old pile of tires and some empty oil drums. The bullets pierced the rusted drums and impacted against the repair shop, rattling the shutter doors. I didn't move. Of all the days not to have my weapon. He continued to fire, aiming at the stack of tires which concealed me from view. The rubber thumped with every shot, puckering toward me and threatening to expel the lead.

When he stopped firing, I cautioned a glance over the tires. The driver desperately turned the wheel, ramming the car in front of him and pushing it out of the way. When he couldn't push it far enough to allow his escape, he reversed, grinding the bumper against the side of the car he'd previously hit. By now, that car was empty. The owner had abandoned it as soon as the gunfire started.

If the shooters were out of bullets, now was my chance. I couldn't count on the cops. I had to do something. If I could get close enough, I might be able to incapacitate the driver before his buddy could retaliate. That'd give the cops more time to arrive.

I edged around the tires, moving in a crouch behind the parked cars. Just as I reached the last one and prepared to make my move, flashing lights and sirens arrived.

Two police cruisers approached the scene, laying into their horns and ordering the stopped cars to get out of the way. Briefcase gunned the engine as he reversed. He slammed into the car behind him, hard enough to send it into the second lane. But it didn't make enough of a hole for him to punch through, so he put the car in drive, his wheels spinning.

I broke cover and ran for the car, golf club at shoulder height. I hit the front driver's side window as the car jolted forward. The window shattered. The tip of the putter caught on the doorframe and was ripped from my grasp as the car rammed the other vehicle out of the way and broke free from the parking gridlock.

One of the two police cruisers found a hole and maneuvered around, chasing after the fleeing black sedan, but the second car was stuck. "Hands in the air," came over the speaker.

Could this day get any worse? I raised my hands, my palms blistered from my grip on the club. I lowered to my knees, glancing in the direction the shooters and the police cruiser had gone. L.A. was known for high-speed chases. Surely, those bastards wouldn't get away.

One of the officers got out of the car and approached me while the other attempted to deal with the ongoing chaos. The cop kicked the bent golf club farther away from me. "What's your name? What's going on here?"

"Alexis Parker," I said. "I sent the text message about active shooters to 9-1-1. I followed them out of the Barber Productions building," I jerked my chin toward it, aware how this probably looked, "and tried to stop them from leaving. At least two men are dead on the top floor. A guard and possibly the company's VP. I'm not sure about the rest of building security. They didn't answer when I called them for help."

"Did you see what happened?"

"No, but I heard the shots. The shooters had silenced semi-autos. The two pops I heard came from Mr. Roundtree's office. When I went to check it out, I found a man dead on the floor. The guard had been killed before that. I'm not sure when. He was already dead when I got there."

"What were you doing at Barber Productions on a Saturday? Do you work in the office?" the cop asked as he circled around me.

"Not exactly."

"What exactly?"

"You wouldn't believe me if I told you."

He didn't like that answer. "Stand up. Keep your hands on your head. I'm going to pat you down. Do you have any weapons on you or anything sharp in your pockets that might stick me?"

"No. My ID is in my front pocket. Left side."

He pulled out the case of lock picks, snorting as he confiscated them. "You're a thief."

"No."

He held up the case. "Explain what these are for."

"I forget my keys a lot."

He didn't buy it. Once he was done, he opened my wallet. "You're not local, so maybe no one told you, but breaking and entering is illegal in the state of California."

"I wasn't breaking and entering. Mr. Barber hired me to assess building security for threats."

"Yeah, right." He glowered at me. "Who are the shooters? Are you working with them?"

"I've never seen them before." I nodded at my phone. "I took video and photos. That should help you ID them, assuming the other patrol unit can't run them down."

"We'll see." He didn't bother looking at my phone. Instead, he rifled through the rest of my wallet. "You're a private eye?" He took out my license and held it up to the sun before flicking it with his finger, as if it might be fake. "You're far from home and out of your jurisdiction. What case are you working?"

"Like I said, Mr. Barber hired me to check out building security. Right now, you need to send officers inside to assess the situation. One guard is dead. The condition of the others remains unknown. They might need assistance, medical intervention. You have to help them. I don't want anyone else to die today."

He grunted my request to his partner, who barked orders to the other two patrol units which had just pulled up on the other side of the street. "They'll check it out. In the meantime, you're going to walk me through everything, starting with why you were in that building in the first place."

THREE

Every interrogation room looked the same with its drab walls and metal furniture. But unlike the others I'd visited, this one had a window. However, permanent blinds had been placed over it and tilted upward, making it impossible to see outside from a seated position. But the light coming in told me it was still sunny, so I resisted the urge to look at my watch.

The responding officer had handed me over to Detective Dean Petrocelli who'd seemed a little full of himself during the introduction when he flashed his badge. Robbery-homicide division. He scratched the back of his head, just behind his ear as he read over the notes he'd made during our conversation.

"Fleas?" I asked.

He looked at me over the paper. "What was that?"

"It was a joke. A bad one."

"Kind of like the statement you provided." He dropped the pad onto the table. "Level with me. If you come clean now, we'll work something out. You weren't carrying a firearm. Given the surveillance footage we obtained from the gas station, your actions could be construed as self-defense. It doesn't have to go down as ag assault or assault with a deadly weapon. I'll make that go away. You have my word, but only if you cooperate."

"It wasn't a deadly weapon. It was a putter."

"You ever play mini-golf and see a five-year-old throw a tantrum? Deadly weapon."

"I've told you everything I know."

"Somehow, I doubt it." He stood up, shoving his hands in his pockets and attempting to appear less threatening. "It's simple. All I need you to do is tell me who those men are."

Had he listened to a word I said? "I don't know. But you're a detective. Figure it out. I gave you their descriptions, video footage, and a license plate number. That's all I know."

He stood in front of the window, casting his chiseled features in shadow. "Why were you in that building? You aren't an employee. You don't have an ID card. How'd you get inside? Keep in mind, we have your lock pick set and this nifty app we found on your phone."

"I didn't break in. Okay, technically, it might look like that, but legally, I didn't break in. I had permission to enter the premises and be inside the building."

"Explain that to me. Who gave you permission?"

"Why don't you ask my lawyer?"

He chuckled at Mr. Almeada's card which sat on the table in front of me. "Your lawyer's three thousand miles away. We might be waiting a while. Are you sure you don't want to handle this yourself? It'd save us all some time and trouble. It's a simple question."

"With a complicated answer. Mr. Barber hired Cross Security to perform an assessment on his office building. As part of the assessment, I was told to infiltrate Barber Productions and subvert the existing security protocols in order to point out weaknesses in the system."

"Aren't there easier, less illegal ways to do that?"

"Yep."

Petrocelli cocked his head at me. "So what? You did it this way for kicks?"

"It wasn't my call. It was my boss's. In fact, you should talk to him because I made the exact same point you did. I'm aware of how this looks. But it's the truth. Call Mr.

Barber. He'll tell you."

"We'll find out soon enough. Someone's checking with Mr. Barber now. We'll see what he has to say." Petrocelli came back to the table and sat down. "Why are you operating so far from home? As far as I can tell, you have no reason to be here."

"Again, we agree." I gave him a winning smile. We weren't enemies. We both wanted the same thing, even if Mr. Robbery-Homicide didn't realize it yet.

"That's not an answer."

"Lucien Cross, my boss, is expanding Cross Security. Half our clients live or work in L.A., so he thought opening a satellite office here made sense. We go where the work is."

"Officers went to your alleged office. No one's there. In fact, the entire place was empty. No furniture. No workers. Nothing. You don't even have a working telephone."

"That's getting installed Tuesday. And I don't know what they're talking about. There's furniture, a coffeemaker, a whiteboard, and some markers. The rest is getting delivered next week."

"You don't even have your office set up and you're breaking into someone else's?" He cocked an eyebrow at me. "Were you looking for decorating tips?"

"Yeah, sure."

"What about your coworkers?"

"It's just me, for now."

"You're the only one Cross sent to open this new office? I find that hard to believe."

"What can I say? I'm employee of the month. Hell, I'm employee of the whole freaking year. So he figures I can run the place myself."

"You're not helping yourself, Ms. Parker."

I exhaled. "Cross thought I could use a change of scenery. It'll save on overhead to wait until everything is set up before staffing the place." No wonder the detective didn't believe it. I barely bought Cross's crap. The reason he sent me here was to get into Martin's good graces and weasel his way back onto Martin's research project. If I made the company a few bucks in the process and saved my boss some time from doing monotonous tasks, that was just a bonus.

Petrocelli scratched his head again. "You understand why I'm not buying this, right?"

"If I were lying, I'd have a much better cover story. Maybe something involving ninjas."

We sat in silence for a few minutes. Petrocelli thought it'd loosen my lips. But I had no problem waiting him out. Except the longer this went on, the worse things would get.

"Did you apprehend the shooters?" I asked. "A patrol car went after them, but I didn't hear anything over the radio."

"What if I were to say they're in the room across the hall, confessing to everything and saying you masterminded the whole thing?"

"We both know that's a lie. Were they apprehended?"

He shook his head. "Any idea where they might have gone?"

"I don't even know who they are."

"So you keep saying."

"How many dead?"

"Why do you care? The two you reported are more than enough for me to charge you with felony murder."

"I didn't commit a felony."

"Breaking and entering."

"Again, you can't prove that."

"I can prove it."

"How? Do you have surveillance footage or eyewitness testimony?"

"You admitted to being inside the building. We found the tools you used to gain unlawful entry on your person. You gave us your phone willingly. If it quacks like a duck." He pointed to the camera in the top corner of the room. "Plus, you confessed to breaking in, remember?"

"I didn't confess to anything. I was hired to enter the building. It was part of my job. Cross Security has a contract. Mr. Barber is the building's owner. Performing my duties in accordance with the contract he signed does not violate any state or federal law that I'm aware of. Neither of us are lawyers, at least we aren't acting in such a capacity at this particular moment, so let's leave that for others to decide. Right now, your goal is to locate the shooters and arrest them. Stop wasting your time asking me stupid questions and let me help you, Detective."

He picked up the pen. "How about you start by telling me their names?"

"Oh my god, would you freaking listen? Do I have to ask for a translator?"

He held up his palms. "Fine. You don't know who they are. You've never seen them before today. You said you gave me everything you could. How exactly do you want to help?"

"For starters, you could let me go."

"You're lucky I haven't charged you yet."

"Since you're so sure I'm involved, why don't you?" Lucien kept some of the best criminal defense attorneys on retainer. I never liked thinking about it or why that might be, but I knew whatever circumstantial evidence the police might have would be dismissed as soon as Almeada contacted his West Coast associates and got them up to speed. But that took time. Frankly, I was surprised someone hadn't already barged into the room. Cross would advise me not to speak at all without counsel, but that wasn't how I worked.

"Don't tempt me."

When our staring contest continued for too long, I gave in. "We should assume the guard I found near the vending machine was killed to prevent him from alerting the others or causing trouble. From the way his body was positioned, I'd say the guard was surprised when the shooter came up behind him. He probably never even saw his killer." I told the detective what I'd heard the men discussing as they left. "The guard wasn't the target, which leads me to believe the dead guy in the VP's office was, unless they just wanted whatever was inside the filing cabinet and eliminated potential obstacles to make their escape easier. Unless you found other bodies and other potential motives."

Petrocelli didn't even blink.

"The shooters gained access to the building before I arrived. Have you checked the security footage? You might find a clue."

Again, he answered my question with unwavering silence.

"Well, you should check." I crossed my arms over my chest and leaned back. "I can wait."

"Is there a point to all this? Or are you hoping to be a big enough pain in the ass that I just let you leave?"

"You should be rounding up the dead guy's enemies. Have you even IDed him yet?"

"Fenton Roundtree."

That matched the name on the door. "Was he tortured? When I found the body, his fingers were broken."

That earned a blink. "You expect me to believe you weren't part of it?"

"Ugh." I ignored the sudden wave of queasiness. It didn't matter how many bodies or how close I'd come to death. Some things never got easier. "The two shots indicate the shooters are professionals, just like the clothes they wore and the way they behaved, at least until everything blew up around them."

"You mean the gas station."

"Yep."

"Which is the incident you caused by allegedly chasing after two armed men with nothing but a putter."

"I called 9-1-1, but since patrol took their sweet time showing up, I didn't have a choice."

"You expect me to believe two professional hitters allowed you to walk away unscathed."

"They didn't allow anything. It just happened."

Petrocelli drew an arrow on his notepad, making his notes look more like a rudimentary timeline. "Do you realize how crazy that sounds?"

"I used to be a federal agent. Given the shit I've seen, it's not that crazy."

"Fine." Petrocelli didn't believe me, but it didn't matter. "How did you know they had an escape vehicle waiting?"

"Lucky guess. Pros would have scouted ahead. They probably drove several routes to and from, figuring out the best path based on day and time. You should pull DOT footage over the last couple of weeks and see if you can spot them."

"Will I spot you?"

"No."

He stifled a snort. "I find that hard to believe."

"My only interest was evaluating building security."

"And you just happened to be doing that the same day two men break in and murder Barber Productions' vice president. That's convenient."

"That's my luck."

"It's a hell of a coincidence."

"SSA Mark Jablonsky always says coincidences don't happen."

"Are you finally confessing?"

"I don't have anything to confess." Could someone in Barber's employ have gotten word about the assessment and figured they'd take advantage? "My security check was unplanned. It was supposed to be a surprise. Mr. Barber stipulated we couldn't act during normal business hours. He didn't want the check to interfere with day-to-day operations. That left late nights and weekends. Acting in broad daylight minimized the chances of a random person seeing me sneaking into the building and calling the police." A million theories formed inside my head, but sharing them would only stoke the coals of suspicion. "I don't think anyone was following me. I tend to keep an eye out for things like that."

"Paranoid?"

"You can probably see why."

A knock sounded at the door. Petrocelli got up and opened it. He stood in the doorway, keeping his back to me while he scanned the tablet, swiping left every thirty seconds or so. "All right. Schedule an interview for when he returns and have someone follow up with the head of security. I want to know what's going on." He handed back the tablet, listening as the officer whispered something else to him. "When's he supposed to get here?" Petrocelli nodded. "Have someone pick him up in the morning." He stepped back into the interview room and pulled the door closed. "Your story checks out."

"I told you it would."

"You did." But Petrocelli forgot to give his face the good news. "You're free to go, Ms. Parker."

"Great." I picked my phone up off the table.

"I looked into your background, but that led to a lot more questions than answers. I'm not sure who you are or what you think you're doing in Los Angeles. But you should know, this is my city. I'm not looking for some former Fed turned private eye to stick her nose in where it doesn't belong. You might want to play Nancy Drew and consider every possibility as to who the shooters are and what they want, but no one hired you to do that. If you get in my way, I will arrest you for obstruction, and no amount of fancy lawyers or rich businessmen can stop me from doing that or sending you back where you came from. Do I make myself clear?"

"Not my case, not my problem." I smiled. "You have nothing to worry about, Detective. This is where we part ways."

"I'm glad we're on the same page. However, since you remain the only witness to these murders, don't leave town."

"I thought you said you wanted me gone and if I didn't comply, you'd escort me to the airport." I held up my palms when my quip was met with a hard glare. "All right. Fine. I just have one last question."

"What is it?"

"Where's the best place to get nachos?"

FOUR

"I was getting worried," James Martin said. He'd covered the pool table in graphs and projections while he tapped against a tablet, comparing the data on that screen to the laptop on the other side of the table. "You didn't answer any of my texts. I even used that find-my-friend app to make sure you hadn't fled the state. Do you want to tell me why you spent a good portion of the day at the police station? I called to make sure you weren't dead, but other than assuring me you were alive, the police wouldn't tell me anything."

I dropped my bag on the closest chair, kicked off my shoes, and headed for the wet bar. "It's been a day. Are you hungry? I brought nachos home. Actually, fajitas. Well, nachos fajitas. They're basically loaded nachos."

"I know what they are, sweetheart." He glanced in my direction, noting my disheveled look. "Are you okay?"

"More or less."

"Come here." He snaked his arms around my waist, forcing me to put the food on top of the bar before brushing his fingers through my hair and giving me a kiss. "What's wrong?" He lifted me onto one of the bar stools and pressed his forehead against mine. "Talk to me, Alex.

What happened?"

"I'm okay." I stared at the takeout containers I'd picked up from one of the taco trucks on my way to my car. "Where did we land on dinner?"

"I had that working dinner tonight, so I already ate."

"Great. More for me." I popped open one of the boxes and snagged a chip, soggy from the melted queso and sauteed peppers and onions. "What about a drink?" I asked around a mouthful.

He kissed my cheek, letting his lips linger for a moment. Martin wasn't stupid. He always knew when something was wrong. "What are you in the mood for? I'd say tequila or margaritas would pair well, but I know your stance on that." He cocked his head at the open container, grabbing a chip from the edge and crunching down on it. "Lemon drop martini?"

"Sounds good."

He gave a generous pour, filling the shaker by sight alone. "I'll get some ice."

"I don't need ice. Warm is fine."

He poured it into the glass and pushed it in front of me. "Maybe a straw would be better."

"Only if you have a fun, twisty one. I like those."

"I'll add it to the shopping list."

After a few more bites and several gulps from my drink, I didn't think I could stomach anything else, especially the questioning look on Martin's face. He didn't have to ask or pry. All he had to do was be attentive, and he could break me. I pulled my phone out of my pocket and checked my messages, but Lucien hadn't returned any of the calls I'd made to him since getting released.

"Can I borrow your phone? I'm not sure mine's working."

"That would explain your lack of responses." Martin plucked his off the pool table and handed it to me. I scrolled through his list of contacts and dialed Lucien's cell. He answered on the third ring.

"Screening your calls?" I asked.

"I don't have time to talk."

"Did you get my messages?"

"Yes."

"Don't you think you should make time? We have a problem. A big one."

"Are you still in police custody?"

"No."

"All right. Good. The rest can wait. I'll talk to you tomorrow. Until then, don't do anything."

"What about Barber? He hasn't answered my calls either."

"There's a reason for that. We'll talk tomorrow. It's late. You should get some sleep." Cross hesitated for half a second. "I'm sorry."

"Sorry?" But he'd already hung up. I let out a frustrated growl and handed Martin back his phone. "Bastard."

He read the name on the screen before putting the phone on the bar. "Sweetheart, what's going on?"

"I found a murdered security guard while I was conducting my assessment. The shooters were still there. They killed the company's vice president and stole whatever was in his office. The police thought I was involved."

"Shit." Martin reached for my hand, but I pulled away. "What can I do?"

"Would you mind putting these in the fridge?" I closed the takeout container. "I'm not hungry anymore. I just want to take a shower."

"Sure."

I didn't want to shut him out or hide from him, but I didn't want to talk about it either. I didn't know what I wanted, other than to figure out what the hell was going on. And Cross was no help.

I went into the bedroom suite and stripped down. Since Martin signed a six month lease, I was supposed to consider this place home. But it wasn't. Today proved it. My detective pals, O'Connell and Heathcliff, wouldn't have sweated me inside an interrogation room for nearly eight hours.

After shoving my clothes, which felt dirty and gross, into the hamper, I stepped into the shower and closed my eyes. Images of the dead guard came to mind, followed by the rapidly growing pool of blood surrounding Roundtree's body. His eyes remained open, staring at the ceiling while blood trickled across his forehead. Based on the blood, the exit wound had taken out a good portion of his skull.

Letting out a growl, I blinked a few times and reached for the shampoo. I wasn't going to let this get to me. The police didn't want my help, and Cross wouldn't want me going near this. He had that stupid rule about homicides, so I had to let this go. I just didn't know how.

I lathered my hair and stepped under the spray, letting the soapsuds wash away. I repeated with the conditioner before reaching for the body wash. Of all the days, why did it have to be today? Why did the shooters strike today? The only person who knew I planned to infiltrate the building ahead of time was Lucien Cross and whoever he told. He wouldn't have set me up like this. Cross was a lot of things, but he wasn't a cold-blooded killer.

Sliding open the shower door, I leaned out and grabbed my phone off the vanity and sent my boss a text. We had to talk about this. I had to know what he knew, who he told, and what to do now. Tomorrow was too far away. I needed a plan tonight.

He ignored my text, like the rest of my messages. I stared at the screen, hoping to see the three circles indicating he was typing a response, but they never appeared. I tried calling again, but it went straight to voicemail. Considering the three hour time difference, he might have gone to sleep. Little things like having one of his employees arrested wouldn't keep him up at night, at least not when it was me. By now, he was used to this.

I put the phone down, stepped back into the shower, and finished scrubbing the day off of me. When I opened the shower door again, Martin was standing on the other side, holding a towel.

"I thought you might be missing the towel warmer we have at home, so I put this in the dryer for a few minutes."

"You didn't have to."

He dried me off and wrapped the towel around me before grabbing a second one for my hair. After scooping the long, brown strands into the towel and securing it on top of my head, he enveloped me in his arms. "You look a little green."

"It must be the food."

"You didn't eat enough for that to be the case."

"Maybe I ate before I got home."

"I'm not buying it." He nodded toward my phone. "When you didn't answer any of the texts I sent you, I knew something was wrong. I should have sent a legal team to storm the police station."

"My knight in shining armor." I squeezed him hard. "I'm okay. My client cleared me, or someone in his company did. I'm not sure. I can't get a hold of him either. I drove by his place on my way home, but no one answered the door. That's weird, right?"

"He might have been speaking to the police or dealing with company issues. He just lost his vice president."

"Yeah, I guess." But something didn't feel right. Everything about this situation was off.

"Do the cops have any suspects besides you?"

"I told them everything, but Petrocelli plays his cards close to the vest. I don't know if they caught the guys. I don't know anything."

He rubbed my back through the towel. "What can I do?"

"You're doing it." I stood on my tiptoes and kissed him. "Why don't you join me in the shower? I can't seem to scrub the ick off."

"That's in your head."

"Fine." I tugged on his hand. "Distract me instead."

His bright green eyes told me he was considering the offer. "You look like you need to lie down."

"I get it. You'd rather take this into the bedroom."

"Alex, I'm serious."

"So am I, handsome." I stole another kiss, stepping backward and leading him toward the shower.

"Alexis, stop," he said breathily.

I held up my palms. "Your mouth says no, but your eyes say yes."

He gave me a sexy grin before he could stop himself. "Answer my question first. Do you feel okay? Or are you just trying to shut me up?"

"I'm angry and confused, but that's nothing new." I glared at my phone. "I would say Cross told me to back off the assignment, but he didn't say anything. He told me he'd talk to me tomorrow. That's it. None of this even matters to him. So I don't want to think about it anymore tonight." Even though that's all I'd been thinking about.

Martin fought to keep his expression neutral as he tugged the hairdryer free from the cabinet. "I have a quick call to make. I'll meet you in bed." He slipped his hands around my waist and nuzzled against my neck. "I'm glad you're all right."

"You're reconsidering the shower, aren't you?"

He laughed, but it was for show. "Temptress." He kissed along my neck until I was practically humming. "I just have a few things to finish up. Dry your hair. I don't want you to catch a cold."

"Make sure the security system is armed."

"It is, but I'll double-check."

"Thanks."

He stopped in the doorway. "Are you sure you don't want to eat first? I know how you get. Have you eaten anything today besides a few chips and a martini?"

"Not since breakfast. But that was more than enough."

Instead of arguing, he crossed to me again, as if he couldn't get enough, and kissed me hard. "Ten minutes. I promise." And then he was gone.

FIVE

I woke a few hours later. It was too dark to see much of anything. When I tried to turn, I found myself pinned to the mattress. Martin had me in a death grip, acting like a human shield, protecting me from the world.

"You're doing that thing again." I pushed against him until he eased off of me. "A girl needs to breathe."

"Is this better?" He tugged on my side, pulling me flush against him, and combed his fingers through my hair.

"A little." I blinked, glad he couldn't see my facial expressions.

Instead, he heard it in my voice. "You're still thinking about what happened to those men."

"I can't help it. I don't know what to do. There's nothing I could have done to save them. There's no action I could have taken or tactic I could have employed that would have resulted in a different outcome. The guard was dead before I got there, and before I had time to process what I was seeing, they'd already shot Roundtree." My words sounded practiced, measured, like the exact recitation I would have given to a superior when I was a federal agent or written in my report and handed to Mark.

"I know. You did what you could. The police will find

them," Martin said.

"I just wish there was more I could have done. If I'd been armed, I might have been able to prevent their escape. But breaking into an office building with a loaded nine millimeter would have been a stupid decision. I needed more intel. Do you think Cross knows something? Maybe that's why he's ducking my calls."

"I doubt it. Why would he do this?"

"He wouldn't." I moved to get out of bed, but Martin held me tightly.

"Where are you going?"

"Crazy."

He chuckled. "I hate to break it to you, but you're not a superhero. You can't save everyone."

"If only I had super powers." I settled against his chest, thinking about the most popular comic book heroes. Not all of them have super powers. Some of them just happened to be rich and had tons of gadgets. "Actually, you could be my super power. Why don't you make me a fancy utility belt?"

"I'm working on making you bulletproof. Isn't that enough?"

"I thought you gave up on that."

"Not entirely." Martin drew random shapes on my back with his fingertip. "Since I'm the millionaire genius, I'm pretty sure that makes me the superhero." He kissed my forehead. "Do you want me to show you my super power again? It'll take your mind off things for a little while."

"Raincheck?"

"You should go to a meeting."

"You took the words right out of my mouth." From the way he'd been clinging to me, I wasn't the only one who needed therapy. "If you let me get up, I'll see if I can find one since my regular one only meets on Tuesday nights."

"Sweetheart, there are no grief counseling sessions at three a.m. It can wait until morning."

"I know, but I might as well look now, while I'm looking at everything else."

"Let me know the time and place. Wherever you want to go, I'll make it work."

"I wish we could go home."

"Soon. I promise." He found my hand and brought it to his lips. "Until then, I'm here for you. Whatever you need."

"Are you sure that's not your super power?"

Even though the room was dark, I saw him grin. "It's just one of many."

I stumbled out of bed and headed down the hallway. Where to begin? At this time of night, I wasn't exactly thinking clearly, but the questions I had needed answers. And since phoning Cross had led to nothing but frustration, I'd do it myself.

Powering on my laptop, I squinted against the bright screen. After my eyes adjusted, I turned on the side lamp and grabbed my notepad. I jotted down the few known facts. Only two likely scenarios came to mind. One, Fenton Roundtree had been targeted. Two, the murders were consequences of the break-in to steal whatever had been inside the filing cabinet. But since none of the other offices had been visibly ransacked, Roundtree must have been the target, unless that was a coincidence, and those didn't exist.

That left me with another question. Was Roundtree's murder due to a personal vendetta or a professional one? As usual, I started with the basic background check.

Fenton Roundtree had an ex-wife and a current wife. His monthly alimony payments were in the mid-four figures. The mortgage on his current house made me cringe. He wasn't quite underwater. He was managing. His current wife, Sonya, contributed a significant amount of income to the family, which included her two children from a previous marriage.

I scanned her background. She and her ex were seismologists. They shared joint custody of their children and otherwise appeared to have split amicably. I looked into him, but he had no reason to want Fenton Roundtree dead.

I never found a single report or suggestion that the children had ever been abused or endangered. The court didn't find Milton Sneed, Sonya's ex, to be unfit, and Sonya never contested that fact. Since Milton had never filed any claims against Roundtree, I didn't think his murder had to do with his family life. But I'd revisit that if nothing else surfaced.

Fenton Roundtree didn't have any felony convictions. No DUIs or instances of public intoxication. I dug deeper, but the databases indicated he was clean, so I switched to social media.

Since Roundtree worked as the vice president for Barber Productions, which created, edited, and mastered a lot of scores and sound effects used in games, movies, and other forms of media, I figured he'd be a tech geek with a budding social media presence. But I didn't find him on any of the major platforms. His only presence was in an online gaming community.

I scanned the posted comments he'd made and the responses he'd gotten, but the conversation was light and non-threatening. The few questions he asked appeared related to his job, and the respondents were more than happy to assist. This was getting me nowhere.

My fingers itched to phone-a-friend for help, but even with the three hour time difference, it was still too early to call Mark Jablonsky or my detective pals, especially on a Sunday morning. If I made calls like that, I probably wouldn't have any friends. And since Detective Petrocelli hadn't been enthused by the prospective of becoming my new best bud, I couldn't afford to lose the ones I had.

Instead, I called Cross Security and had the service connect me to Lucien's executive assistant, Justin. Even though he was Cross's righthand man, Justin would get me what I needed, unless the boss gave him specific instructions not to, and if that was the case, I needed to know.

After seven rings, Justin picked up the phone. "What do you want, Ms. Parker?"

"I need the Barber files, specifically whatever Cross has on Brent Barber."

"That should be in the database. Are you having problems remotely logging in?"

"I've already read what's been uploaded. I want Cross's files. The original ones. The ones in his filing cabinets."

"Ms. Parker—" Justin began, but I cut him off.

"Look, we both know Cross keeps a lot to himself. That's already been established. Last time, it bit him in the ass. I don't want this to happen again, especially when my ass is on the line here. Brent Barber was one of the clients Cross signed when the company was still getting off the ground. That means he didn't do as much vetting."

"Lucien knew Brent from before," Justin said. "We both did."

"Tell me about him. At least one security guard and the vice president of his company were killed yesterday. Any idea why that might be?"

"You'd have to ask Lucien."

"I did. He told me we'd talk tomorrow. It's tomorrow. Should I call him instead?"

"I'm surprised you haven't already. Let me guess. He didn't answer. It's not like he can be reached right now, anyway."

"Where is he?"

Justin ignored my question. "Brent trusted Lucien to invest his money wisely. After eighteen months, Brent had high enough returns to break away from the family business and do what he loved, which was working on music. Digital manipulation mostly. Cut to Brent starting a small sound production company which worked freelance for a lot of indie films and smaller advertising firms. The warehouse he used as his studio contained a lot of expensive equipment, so he hired Lucien, who at that point had left Wall Street and had gone into security, to safeguard his investment. That's about it. Brent has used Cross Security ever since to make sure he's protected and his operations run smoothly."

"They didn't yesterday." I thought about the job I'd been given. "Why did Brent want the assessment and upgrade? Did something happen? Was he threatened?"

"I really can't say."

"You can't?"

"I don't know, Ms. Parker. Lucien didn't loop me in. This is a West Coast problem, something the West Coast branch should deal with."

"I'm the only Cross Security employee on the West Coast, and I'm technically not even an employee. I'm a private contractor."

"First, you're not the only employee. There are dozens of security teams operating in the area. Second, you're contracted to work for Cross Security. Hence, you're an employee."

Deciding it was too early in the morning or late at night to pursue this argument, I asked Justin to see if he could find anything out and forward it to me. I didn't care if the records were eight years old. Anything he could give me would help. At the very least, it couldn't hurt. He promised to try, but that would depend entirely on Cross not squashing my request. As usual, my boss was intentionally keeping me in the dark.

After hanging up, I stared at the clock. Despite all the work I'd done, it hadn't taken particularly long. Maybe I was finally getting good at this. But it didn't feel like it. It felt like one of those interminably long nights that would drag on, denying me the one thing I desperately wanted—answers.

Against my better judgment, I dialed an all too familiar number, surprised when someone answered. "Go for Jablonsky."

"That's how you answer the phone?"

"It is when I've been behind my desk all damn night." Mark exhaled. "Are you okay? Is Marty okay? It's like four a.m. there."

"Martin's fine. I'm...okay." I snorted. "Well, it's me, so that's probably debatable, even under the best circumstances." I filled him in on everything that happened and my extensive conversation with the detective from robbery-homicide. "I can't believe this is happening."

"Are you sure they aren't charging you?"

"Petrocelli said my alibi checked out. Cross Security has signed contracts, so I should be in the clear."

"Why do these things keep happening to you?"

"I've been asking myself the same thing."

"This is why you shouldn't be working for a son of a bitch like Lucien Cross." Mark muttered a few other things under his breath. "Did you find any dirt on Roundtree or Barber?"

"Nothing official, but I thought you might be able to dig a little deeper. See if there are any open investigations into either of them or the company."

"You want me to look for complaints too, right?"

"Against them or made by them?" I asked.

"Both."

"Well, since you're offering, how can I say no?"

He grumbled again. "All right, let me see what I can pull up."

I listened to the clacking of keys. When the sound abruptly stopped, I asked, "Did you find something?"

"I'm not sure what I'm looking at. It looks like Barber's on the periphery of some RICO looking thing. I need to do more digging. Have I mentioned I've been up all night working on actual OIO business?"

"Which is why I thought you needed a break." I paused. "You shouldn't be pushing yourself so hard."

"Then stop asking for so many damn favors." He inhaled audibly. "Let me make a few calls and do some checking. I don't want to give you the wrong information. I'm not sure who the target of this investigation is or how Barber connects."

"What are you seeing?"

"Honestly, Parker, I'm not entirely sure. I'll call you as soon as I get a hold of someone who can tell me something. But it's Sunday morning, so it might be a while."

"As soon as you can."

"Yeah."

After we hung up, I tried a few more searches, but I couldn't find a thing. Without access to federal law enforcement databases or the LAPD's network, there wasn't much I could do. Annoyed, I got up to pace, wondering what Mark had found.

With my mind reeling, I wandered into the game room, turned the volume off on the pinball machine, and pulled the plunger back. I had to do something with my pent-up energy. I barely noticed when the table lamp turned on.

Familiar footsteps sounded behind me. *Martin.*

A moment later, he grabbed my hips. "Careful. You keep that up, you might tilt."

"Didn't I say that to you once?"

He laughed before sliding his hands down my arms and placing them over mine. "You looking to score?" His breath tickled my ear.

"Just two thousand more points, and I'll be on top."

"You want some help?" He flexed his fingers over mine while nipping gently at my earlobe.

"Stop playing dirty."

"That's the best way to play. The dirtier, the better."

"Martin—" I hit the flippers again, sending the silver ball shooting up the ramp and earning a hundred thousand point bonus.

"Satisfied?" he asked.

"Yes." I hit the flippers a few more times, but keeping the ball in play wasn't nearly as important now. When I got the game over message, I spun in his arms. "What are you doing up?"

"You said you wanted to be on top. Why don't you show me?" His green eyes darkened. "Come back to bed."

SIX

I wriggled around to face him. Confused as to why he was still asleep, I glanced at the clock. It was almost nine. We'd had quite the late night, both with work and play. Still, he usually got up at the crack of dawn to surf, swim, or run on the beach. Sleeping this late was out of character, so I poked him.

"Are you okay?"

He opened one eye. "Huh?"

"Are you okay?" I repeated.

He smiled sleepily, his eyes closing. "I'm incredible." Whether that was meant as a compliment or a boastful comment was anyone's guess. "Are you?"

"I'm fine. Go back to sleep." I gave him a gentle kiss and slid out from under his arm. "You earned it."

"It's a super power, sweetheart." He opened both eyes, watching me pull a hoodie on. When I didn't grab my nine millimeter from the nightstand drawer, he decided it was safe to leave me to my own devices and shut his eyes again.

On my way to the bathroom, I spotted his tablet on the floor beside the bed. At some point, he'd gotten up to work while I slept. "What time did you finally go to sleep?" I asked.

"After eight."

"Martin," I gave him an exasperated look, but with his eyes closed, he didn't see it, "you can't go on like this."

"Have we been introduced? I'm Kettle." He lifted his hand off the bed in a weak wave, his eyes still closed.

I hated his work schedule as much as he hated mine. Yet, neither of us would ever quit. At least our dysfunctions matched in this instance.

After washing up, I went to the kitchen to make breakfast. But cooking was Martin's thing, not mine. Instead, I took out one of the takeout containers from last night, emptied the contents onto a baking sheet, and stuck it in the oven to warm. Did coffee go with nachos? I wasn't opposed to finding out, but working the demonic espresso machine wasn't how I wanted to start my day, or any day. Deciding I'd wait for Martin to get up and make the coffee, I turned the oven off and circled the kitchen a few times before walking through the rest of the house.

Looking out the window, I spotted a police vehicle parked halfway down the block. Either Petrocelli didn't believe I wasn't involved, or he assigned a unit to deter me from investigating or provide protection. That sent a shiver through me. Professionals didn't leave witnesses. I'd seen their faces, but I had no idea who they were. Did they know who I was?

It was time I got back to work, if not for my sanity then for my safety. Since I already looked into Roundtree, I shifted my focus to the dead guard. I didn't know his name, but Cross Security had the employee files. I'd see where those led and take it from there.

Unfortunately, they didn't lead me anywhere. Justin sent over a few of Cross's files, but it was basically the same as what I'd already reviewed. My boss kept a lot of things private. But I knew he kept dirt on our clients. He said it was to be proactive. I figured it was so he could blackmail them should any of their requests jeopardize Cross Security. But Justin didn't send any salacious details concerning Brent Barber.

Taking a break, I changed my mind on the nachos, put the oven back on, and wandered into the game room.

Martin had removed his files and papers from the pool table. They now sat in a pile on top of the air hockey machine. I moved them to the wet bar, figuring they'd have less chance of blowing away and ran my fingers against the buttons on the pinball machine, smiling as thoughts of last night came to mind.

I circled back to the living room and paced in front of the sliding glass door, watching the waves crash on the beach and the water in our pool ripple from the breeze. Sure, everything looked pretty and peaceful, but it never stayed that way. At least not for me.

I picked up my phone and called Lucien again. During the week, he'd usually be at work by seven, sometimes earlier. But since it was Sunday, getting a hold of him proved impossible. My call went directly to voicemail, so I left another message.

"Cross, this is Parker. Again. I haven't been able to get a hold of Mr. Barber. His assistant told me he'll be unreachable for the next few days. I don't like it. The police said he verified my story, but they didn't speak directly to him either. I find his absence odd. Maybe it's just bad timing. The cops are keeping tabs on me, though. I think it'd be best to get ahead of this thing. Call me back."

Powering on my laptop, I opened my work e-mail, hoping to find something else from Justin. But my inbox was empty. Mark hadn't called back either.

The timer dinged, and I pulled out the tray of nachos, poured a glass of juice, grabbed a fork, and sat on top of one of the stools to eat. Detective Petrocelli had been right about one thing. These were damn good.

I was halfway through devouring the tray when the proximity alarm went off. Someone was approaching the front door. I grabbed Martin's tablet, unlocked the screen, and tapped on the doorbell camera. A luxury sedan had parked in the driveway.

Cops didn't usually drive cars like that. The dark tinting made it hard to see inside. Could those be the shooters from yesterday? I had no idea how they would have located me, but since I wasn't sure who they were or what they wanted, I couldn't dismiss it. At least backup was close.

Dashing into the bedroom, I grabbed my nine millimeter from the nightstand, just as the doorbell rang. Martin blindly reached for his phone, scooping it up and glancing at the display.

"Stay here." I tucked some spare ammunition into my pocket and held the gun at my side. "If you hear gunfire, call 9-1-1."

"Sweetheart–"

"I'm serious. Actually," I searched the room, frantic to find a safe place, "lock yourself in the bathroom and hide in the tub."

"Alex–"

"We don't have time to argue."

He gave me a sideways look and rubbed his eyes. But he didn't move from his spot on the bed. The doorbell chimed again, followed by loud knocking. Martin held up his phone so I could see the screen. "I know you despise Lucien, but shooting him won't help matters."

"Lucien?" I squinted at the screen, watching my boss pull out his phone and make a call. A moment later, Martin's phone rang. He didn't even bother looking at it before handing it to me. I pressed the green button. "Why didn't you answer any of my calls or texts?"

"Are you home?" Cross asked.

"Yes."

"Then open the damn door." He hung up before I could say a word.

I handed Martin his phone. "You don't have to hide in the bathroom, but if you hear gunfire, find a shovel and tarp."

"You don't need a shovel. We can toss his body into the ocean."

"It could wash ashore."

"Not if we stuff him with ball bearings."

I raised an eyebrow. "How much thought have you put into this?"

He shook off my question, pulled the covers up, and rolled over. Apparently, that was how to end a pointless conversation.

When I opened the door, Cross sauntered inside without

so much as an invitation. He'd been here before, visiting Martin prior to my cross-country move, so he didn't stand on formality. He tucked his sunglasses into the collar of his shirt. "Coffee?"

"What are you doing here?"

"You didn't exactly give me much of a choice." He turned his nose up at the sight of my juice glass and made his way to the cabinet nearest the espresso machine. "I hopped on the first direct flight, which was the red eye. As soon as I landed, I was met by police officers who wanted to have a word with me." Finding the canister, he worked the coffeemaker with practiced ease, placing a mug underneath the spout before the coffee brewed. He took a long sip, set it to make another one, and turned around to face me. "Between airplane mode and being questioned by the authorities, I haven't had much time to take or make calls. The few I did make were vital." The second cup brewed, but he left it underneath the spout before helping himself to a fork and joining me at the counter. "Do you have any idea who the shooters are?" He eyed the gun which I hadn't bothered to put down.

"You sound just like Petrocelli." I left the heavy artillery beside the fridge and picked up the second cup of espresso he'd brewed, which he must have made for me as an apology. "I've never seen them before. I didn't notice them casing the place, either."

"Do you think they noticed you?"

"I'm not sure. They seemed surprised to run into me."

"I checked the security footage. They set the cameras to loop before they entered."

"What about the other guards? Could one of them be involved?" Maybe that's why the shooters murdered the guard, but nothing in his file indicated he affiliated with criminals or could be convinced to assist them in the break-in. "What did the police say to you?"

"Nothing." Cross used the fork like a shovel to pick up a section of nachos. He examined the toppings, unsure if he should put it in his mouth or down the disposal. "I didn't inquire as to their progress."

"Of course you didn't."

He gave the chips a sniff and took a small bite. After chewing carefully, he finished what was on his fork and helped himself to more of my breakfast. "You know company policy when it comes to homicides."

"That's easier said than done. You should listen to your voicemails, that is, if you can stop eating my nachos for two seconds."

"In that case, don't drink my coffee." He nodded at the tiny mug halfway to my lips.

Instead of arguing, I took out a second baking sheet and the other takeout container while Lucien listened to the dozen messages I'd left him. By the time he was finished, the rest of the nachos were hot. I divided them into two portions and slid more onto Lucien's tray. "Did Mr. Almeada make the trip with you?"

"No, he isn't licensed in California, but his firm has a branch here. The top defense attorney, Jason Ganz, met me at the station. We've provided the police with enough documentation that they can now focus their attention in the right direction and stop trying to pin what happened yesterday on you." He jerked his chin toward the front door. "Hopefully, your shadow will get reassigned to harass someone else."

"I don't think that's why they're here. I think Petrocelli's afraid the shooters will make a move on me."

"That seems unlikely. He probably assigned a unit to keep tabs on you. The police don't know anything about us. Cross Security's physical presence in the area is rather unknown. We can't afford bad publicity, which is why I made this trip. Even though I've had security teams functioning across the globe for years, having an office here is different. It's important the LAPD knows we aren't crooks or hired guns. They need to trust we'll stay out of their way if they stay out of ours. Did you give them any reason to think otherwise?"

"No."

Cross looked like he didn't believe me. "Did your messages cover everything, or is there more to the story?"

"I told you what happened."

He glanced toward the bedroom when he heard a noise.

"When's the last time you tried to get in touch with Brent Barber?"

"An hour ago."

Cross scraped the melted cheese with the side of his fork. "Petrocelli told me our client had a family emergency and would be gone for a few days. He wondered if I knew anything about it." He sipped his espresso. "I haven't found any travel arrangements in Brent's name. No flight plans have been filed. No tickets purchased. As far as I can tell, he hasn't left town."

"Do the cops know that?"

"I'm sure they do."

I studied my boss. "Do you think something happened to him?"

"I'm not sure."

"Could he be involved with the shooters?"

"No." Cross's gaze hardened. "I'm worried about him."

"Have you spoken to him?"

"Not directly. He had his assistant, Sylvio, pass a message to me. For now, Brent thinks it'd be best if we back off. He'll be in touch once things settle."

I didn't like the sound of that. "Back off of what?"

"The investigation, I assume." Cross ran a hand through his hair before picking up his cup and returning to the espresso machine. "Brent could have been the intended target. It sounds to me like he's overwhelmed. I'm sure he'll come around once he catches his breath."

But I'd worked for Cross long enough to know he didn't believe that. "Has anything like this happened before?"

Cross shook his head, his back to me.

"Do you have any reason to think Brent might be involved in drugs or some other illicit activity?"

"Why in the world would you ask me that?"

"Those men had all the markings of professionals. They got in and out of the building without disrupting any security systems. Killing the guard in a secluded area was tactical. I have it on good authority they tortured Roundtree for information before killing him and emptying out whatever he kept in the middle drawer of his filing cabinet."

"Interesting theory. Is it yours or Detective Petrocelli's?"

"Mine."

He rested his hips against the counter, tucking his hands into his pockets. "It sounds like Roundtree pissed off the wrong people."

"It doesn't read like it. I already looked into him. Do you know if anyone else was hurt or killed yesterday?"

"I don't believe so. Petrocelli only mentioned two victims."

"Good."

"Not good. At Cross Security we have a duty to protect our clients. Right now, we don't know much of anything. Brent has gone radio silent, so we have to piece some things together on our own."

"Admit it. You think he's in danger."

"That depends on what the shooters wanted. I've never known him to use a go-between. I don't know why he didn't call me himself. Something's up." Cross picked up his cup and took another sip before clearing his throat. "If Brent is in danger, we have to do something about it. I have a reputation to uphold. I can't let our first West Coast job get botched."

SEVEN

Finding Brent Barber had become our new priority. Cross didn't want to step on the LAPD's toes by allowing me to investigate the double homicide. Instead, we had to skirt around the periphery while trying to figure out why our client was MIA, what was taken from Roundtree's office, and why Roundtree and a guard had been killed.

"I thought you vetted your clients," I said. "I guess you didn't go back and retroactively check into the first few who hired you."

Cross's eyes went ice cold. "Brent Barber's a good guy. He never had any run-ins with the law. He doesn't have a criminal record. He's not married, but he has a live-in girlfriend, Adrianna Keys, who he's been seeing for several years. She moved in with him three years ago. As far as I can tell, her past is behind her."

"Past?"

"She used to strip on weekends when she was in college."

"Anything more recent?" I asked.

Cross shook his head.

"What else do you have on Barber and his company?"

"He comes from family money. After he received his inheritance, his father wanted him to go to work at the firm, running political campaigns, but Brent wanted nothing to do with the family business. He wanted a way to stand on his own two feet. One day, he showed up at the investment firm where I worked. Upper management didn't want to have anything to do with him for fear of angering his father, so they passed him off to me."

"A match made in heaven."

"Something like that." Cross leaned back, cringing when his back popped loudly. "Once Brent had made enough, he took off on his own, bought a warehouse, and retrofitted the place with sound stages and recording studios. But since it was in a sketchy neighborhood, he needed protection."

"Which is when you came back into the picture." I thought about the things Mark had said. "Do you remember if he had any problems with anyone around there? Maybe he paid protection in order to be left alone or saw something go down that he shouldn't have."

"Brent never mentioned it to me. We installed top-of-the-line systems and lots of brute force preventative measures. Bars, razor-wire, triple bolts, and twenty-four hour security. Brent always portrays himself as a professional. Even out here, you won't find him in board shorts or hoodies." Cross gave my outfit a pointed look, which I ignored.

"I never met him face-to-face. We spoke on the phone once. Twice, maybe. He never mentioned any problems or areas of concern to me, except optimizing building security. There must have been a reason he wanted a security overhaul."

Cross looked uneasy. "I'm not sure. I figured he just wanted an upgrade. Maybe his request should have sent up a red flag. The last time we met for drinks, he didn't seem like himself, but I didn't give it much thought."

"People without problems don't hire security consultants, and their employees aren't shot in the office." But it was too soon to jump to that conclusion. For all I knew, Roundtree could have been targeted for something entirely unrelated to Brent and Barber Productions, even if I found that hard to believe.

Cross reached into his bag and pulled out his laptop. Opening it on the counter between us, he scanned for a particular video file and hit play. I recognized the interior as the lobby of Barber's office building.

"Where did you get this footage?" I watched the shooters from yesterday enter through the front door. The one carrying the briefcase had a keycard. That's why the alarm didn't sound.

"I planted pinhole cameras when Brent took me to tour the building after he signed the contract."

"That was over a month ago, before I even got here. Why didn't you tell me this?" I stared at my boss. "Were you checking up on me?"

"Not everything is about you, Alex." Cross cleared his throat, a sure sign he was uncomfortable. "If you must know, I did it to cover our asses. We're building a reputation here. I set these cameras up to show Brent how thorough we are and to illustrate any holes you found in his security."

"Did you show this to the cops?"

"This is protected under trade secrets."

"I'm pretty sure it's not."

"Regardless, it doesn't provide a better look at the shooters' faces than the video you took. Facial rec hasn't gotten any hits yet, but we're not dialed into the California criminal databases the same way we are at home."

"It's a shame the LAPD didn't ask you to design their computer system."

"Perhaps one of these days, but for now, we work with what we have and avoid getting tripped up in a police investigation."

"How exactly do we do that?"

"I thought you might have some ideas. By now, you've probably befriended half the department. Why don't you ask for a few favors?"

"Petrocelli didn't want to be BFFs. I even offered to braid his hair, but it's so short, that was a nonstarter."

"Alex," he hissed.

"I offered them my help and expertise, but they didn't want it. I was told not to leave town but to stay out of the way." I didn't want to bring up my conversation with Mark. I didn't know enough yet.

Cross scratched at the thick stubble on his cheek. "And you actually planned to listen?"

"Like you, I don't have any sway with the department." I glanced toward the bedroom, surprised Martin hadn't joined us yet. Hopefully, he'd gone back to sleep. He'd been burning the candle at both ends for so long he didn't have anything left. And whatever he did have, he spent on me.

"Does James?"

I turned my focus back to my boss, anger burning in my eyes. "After everything you put him through, he can't afford more bad publicity, which means I won't ask and I sure as shit can't get locked up. We have to be careful here. Robbery-homicide division seems keen on labeling this exactly what their namesake would have us believe. But Roundtree was tortured. I don't know the extent. All I know is those two men wanted whatever was inside the filing cabinet. Once they got it, they left. So the questions couldn't have gone on that long. The murdered guard hadn't been dead long. He was warm when I found him."

"Are you sure you found everything on Fenton Roundtree?"

"Pretty sure."

"If Roundtree didn't give them everything they wanted, they might have gone after Brent."

"You don't think this is about whatever was inside that drawer?" I eyed him curiously. "Do you know what they want or what they took?"

Cross scanned the footage he'd taken using his pinhole camera. Roundtree had arrived at the office building a little after nine a.m. He was dressed for business, but he didn't carry anything with him. No briefcase. No computer bag. Nothing.

Cross sped through the rest of the footage, but no one else showed up for work. A group had straggled in a few hours before Roundtree. They each had passes and were assigned to work on the third floor. They went straight to their offices and never stepped foot on the executive level. Roundtree had the entire floor to himself, except for the twenty-four hour security guards. Cross backed up the feed, checking to see if Roundtree ever came to work with anything small enough to fit inside the briefcase, but he usually showed up with a messenger bag. So it was anyone's guess.

"Whatever was inside that drawer must have been work product," I surmised.

"Not necessarily. It could be anything. Maybe Brent had Fenton stash something for him."

We watched the footage again, paying attention to everything Brent brought into the office. Each day he came and left with the same briefcase. "Do you have any other cameras?" I asked.

"No, I just set up the one in the lobby."

"This doesn't help us."

"No shit." Cross called Justin and asked him to run a full background on Roundtree, along with a security assessment.

"Roundtree worked late a few nights, but he never went to the office on Saturday. Yesterday was a first. Why do you think he did that? Do you think he intended to meet those men? Maybe that's how they got the keycard. Do you have access to the security logs? We might be able to link the card to an employee," I said.

"It was a master key. It wasn't coded to any specific person. It could have come from anywhere. It could be a clone, or the shooters decrypted the system and created the card themselves."

"Is that possible?"

"Yes. I'm just not sure how likely it is." Cross rewound the footage of Roundtree entering the building, noting the timestamp.

"Brent could have gotten an extra card made and gave it to them," I suggested. "That might explain why he's gone into hiding."

"Our client didn't have his VP murdered."

"Are you sure?"

"I've already examined Brent's phone records and

financial statements. Nothing tracks."

"That doesn't mean he didn't find a workaround."

"He didn't. He wouldn't. I would have found it." Cross sounded certain. "We don't have a large enough timeline to work with. For all we know, Roundtree could work one Saturday every month."

I washed the dishes, needing something to do while I processed everything. "What about Roundtree's phone records?"

"Justin will get them," Cross said. "Those could be telling."

"Did you ever meet Roundtree?"

"No."

I tried to think, but everything that came to mind resulted in more unanswerable questions. I dried the dishes and put them away. "I don't know how to take Brent's absence. I could argue either side because we don't know enough or have any proof of anything. But there's one thing I just can't shake. Why would Brent lie about going out of town if he has nothing to do with any of this?"

"He wouldn't."

"Are you sure he hasn't left town?" I asked.

"I can't be a hundred percent positive, but everything indicates he's still here. The last trip he took was six weeks ago. He, Fenton, Sylvio, and a few other members of the staff attended an award ceremony, where they were honored for the sound effects they'd done in a movie. They signed some clients. It was all good." Cross showed me the travel itinerary, credit card bills, and phone logs. "As you can see, there's nothing here. No new charges. If Brent's traveling, we'd see it. We can't ping his phone because it's off. But the last call he made pinged the cell towers near his house. His credit cards haven't been used. His car's anti-theft system shows that it's at his house. No money has been withdrawn from his account. He hasn't skipped town. We'd know."

"What about his girlfriend? She must know where he is."

"She's on a business trip."

Some of the tension melted away. "He probably went to

see her. Let's give her a call and see what's going on."

Cross rubbed his chin. "Justin tried her cell, but she didn't answer. He tracked down her business line and left a message with one of the PAs, but Adrianna hasn't called back yet."

"That doesn't necessarily mean anything." That familiar itch gnawed at the back of my brain. "Have you checked her credit cards and financials? She might have shelled out for Brent's trip. That would explain a lot of these oddities."

"Nice try, but her cards haven't been used either. However, her phone is turned on and shows she's where she's supposed to be."

"Have you pulled her phone records? When's the last time she spoke to Brent?"

"Not since Monday afternoon." Cross checked his messages and e-mails again. "I know we could interpret that either way, but—"

"It's suspicious as hell. I don't like this."

"Me neither. Brent might just be scared and hiding out. That's why I keep hoping he'll reach out. I told his assistant Sylvio I'd assign Brent a team of bodyguards, figuring they might be in communication, but I haven't heard back. According to phone records, Brent's maintained radio silence since his final communication with his assistant. If Sylvio knows where Brent is or they have another means of communicating, Sylvio will tell him I'm here and offering to protect him. That should be enough to get him to reach out if he needs help."

"What was Brent's last communication?"

"He called Sylvio to tell him he had a family emergency and would be gone for a while."

"Was that before or after the murders?"

Cross brought up the information. "After the murders but before the police notified Sylvio about the incident."

That could go either way. "Don't you think Brent would contact the police if he believed his life was in danger?"

"Brent doesn't always act in his best interest. He has issues with cops and paranoid tendencies."

"Sounds like someone else I know."

Cross looked at me. "Yes, I'm aware of your position on

such things."

"I was talking about you."

He tilted his screen toward me. "These are Brent's phone records. According to this, the only call he made yesterday was to his assistant. Other than that, he didn't receive a single call or text until after the shooting, and he didn't answer any of them."

"What about e-mails?"

"I haven't had a chance to do a deep dive on his internet history, but a quick scan of his inbox didn't reveal anything either."

"He must be psychic to know to go to ground right before the police come calling."

"It could be a coincidence," Cross said.

"Not possible."

He scowled at me. That was one thing we'd never agree on.

"Here's the sticking point," I said. "Brent has no reason not to answer our calls. He knows you. He knows your position on police matters. So why isn't he responding? Has he done this before?"

"I don't think so."

"We need to question the assistant and see what he knows. We should set up a face-to-face."

"Agreed. But before we do that, I'm going to check out Brent's place."

"I went by last night. It didn't look like anyone was home."

"Did you go inside?"

"I didn't think breaking and entering was a good idea after spending eight hours arguing with Petrocelli that I'd never do such things."

"All right. I'll check it out."

"I'll go with you."

"Not with the watchdogs outside. I don't need you rocking the boat. Until they're gone, you cannot go anywhere without risking being followed."

"What about you? I'm sure they're suspicious why you crossed the country on such short notice."

"I doubt it. I made my intentions clear." He yawned.

"Now, if you don't mind, I'm going to see how much I can find out while I wait for Justin to get me what I need."

"What do you want me to do in the meantime?"

"Whatever you can think of to figure out where Brent might be or what those men wanted badly enough to kill over. I suggest you build new profiles on everyone involved in case we missed something." He scanned the kitchen. "I'll need to borrow some equipment. Do you have your gear from yesterday handy?"

EIGHT

Forty minutes later, my phone rang. It was Cross.

"Did you find Brent?" I asked.

"No. I didn't get a chance to check inside his house. The police are poking around outside."

"Did they find anything?"

"I don't think so. I've been watching them for the last fifteen minutes. They haven't gone inside, but they did a thorough search around the property. I'm not sure what they are hoping to find."

"Brent," I said.

"Knowing the cops, they're scouting for aluminum briefcases and firearms. But since they haven't busted down the door, I'm guessing they don't have a warrant yet."

"Do you think they have grounds?"

"Since when does that stop them?"

"Lucien," I berated.

"They're leaving Brent's property. Now they're talking to the neighbors. I'll have to come back after it gets dark." He yawned again. "I guess I'll check in at my hotel, take a shower, and maybe squeeze in a nap, unless you found something."

"Not yet."

"All right. Call if that changes."

"Are you going to answer?"

"I haven't decided yet."

Rolling my eyes, I put the phone down. I'd just finished putting together everything I could find on Fenton Roundtree, which wasn't much. He was a California native. He'd worked several different jobs in the entertainment industry before signing on as Barber Productions' VP.

Roundtree had plenty of connections to studio execs, which might have been what kept Barber Productions in business. From what I'd found, Brent Barber's original business—inside the converted warehouse—squeaked by until they mastered the audio for an independent film that gained critical acclaim and national recognition. That's when Brent's business took off.

After that, Brent relocated, figuring he'd find more work and opportunities in Hollywood. The first thing he did was approach Roundtree. Roundtree had the necessary connections. Without him, Barber Productions wouldn't have been anything more than a small fish in a big pond.

Now, with Roundtree gone, I wondered if the company would survive. But since Barber Productions had been around for almost five years, I had to assume Brent had made enough connections that he'd have a steady following. Maybe he didn't need Roundtree anymore, so instead of firing him, he had him killed. But I had no basis for thinking that.

The police had plastered photos of the shooters on their website, requesting information regarding their identities and whereabouts. I saved the images to my computer and stared at them. "Who are you?"

Before I could send another ridiculous request to Justin, my phone rang. This time it was Mark.

"How bad is it?" I asked.

"Brent Barber doesn't appear to be the target of the RICO investigation."

"So why is the FBI interested in him? Are they hoping to use him as an informant?"

"That'd be my guess."

"Who do they want him to inform on?"

"Did Cross tell you Barber's uncle is Luther Bianchi?"

"You're kidding."

"What have I told you about staying away from organized crime?"

"I didn't know any of this." My fingers flew over the keys. I scanned the headlines. "Didn't the Bianchi family go legit?"

"If that were true, why is the FBI working a RICO case involving them?"

"Is this about drugs?"

"Most things are. I haven't actually gotten a straight answer out of anyone yet, but the Bianchis got on our radar due to a tip the DEA received."

"Racketeering could be any number of things, from extortion to fraud to trafficking contraband to engaging in union corruption. Maybe it's not drugs and that's why the DEA handed it off. Bianchi had a lot of pull with city workers. I always thought he was about controlling unions, not selling drugs."

"Should I buy you a map? You're close to the border."

That didn't necessarily mean anything, and Mark knew it. "Luther Bianchi," I repeated, typing his name as I said it, "has he even made the news in the last two decades?"

"That doesn't mean he went legit. It just means he got smarter."

"Who's hoping to use Brent as an informant? I'll need the name of the agent in charge of the op. He must have eyes on Brent." That might explain why our client had gone missing. I pulled up his bank statements and credit card records, hoping for a clue as to where he might hide.

"I already talked to the agent in charge. He can't help you. Brent Barber's been approached a few times, but he refused to cooperate. He claimed he didn't know anything and that his uncle's business was his uncle's business. The agent couldn't get anything to stick, so he let him slide. That was a dumbass move, if you ask me."

"It's probably true. Cross said Barber cut ties with the family and branched out on his own, roughly eight years ago."

"I'd think that would be easier said than done."

"What about Brent's father? Is he involved in any of

this?"

"I don't know. Brent Sr. isn't a Bianchi by blood, and you know how that goes. Your client's mother was never accused of anything, but family is family. I bet Thanksgiving at the Barber-Bianchi house is quite interesting." The drawer in Mark's filing cabinet squeaked. "I've called the L.A. field office. They agreed to send me their files after I mentioned working with Sam Boyle. His name still carries some weight around there."

"They see his name on their wall every day. They should recognize it." I didn't want to think about him or Michael.

"His name's on our wall, not theirs."

"It should be on both. Actually, it shouldn't be on either."

"As soon as I get the files, I'll see if they have anything else on Barber that might prove useful. I'll call you back."

"Hang on," I said before he could hang up, "what did the LAPD say?"

"They don't have any leads at this time."

"Do they know about the RICO investigation or Barber's relationship to Luther Bianchi?"

"Petrocelli didn't mention it to me, but he wasn't very forthcoming. I wouldn't put much stock in that."

After hanging up, I did another quick search of Brent's hangouts and made a few calls. No one had seen him. I looked into his friends and recent contacts, but he didn't have much of a life outside of work. The people he socialized with were the same ones he saw in the office every day.

Deciding that wouldn't lead anywhere, I created a profile for Luther Bianchi. Bianchi had once controlled several unions and thus a good portion of city employees. He'd strong-armed his way into a position of power and had intimidated anyone who tried to stand up to him. That included government workers, but he only operated on the East Coast. Unlike his nephew, he'd never expanded his business westward.

Bianchi hadn't been accused of any violent crimes in nearly three decades. The last time he'd been arrested, he'd served eighteen months after several bodies belonging to his opposition had been recovered from a riverbed. Even then, he'd only been charged with abuse and desecration of a corpse, and he'd won the appeal.

Instead of sticking with controlling the city from the inside out, he moved on to the horse tracks and took over several book-making ventures. At the height of his empire, he'd run most of the underground gambling scene and all that went with it.

But when power started to shift as the old guard died off, Bianchi turned over a new leaf and went legit. At the present, he owned and operated a few dozen bars, clubs, and restaurants. None of which were in L.A.

His sister, Brent's mother Marilyn, stayed as far away from the family business as she could get. She became a pediatric nurse who worked for a small private practice. I scanned the rest of the details surrounding her life, but I never spotted any overlap. She never waitressed in any of the bars or restaurants her brother owned. She and Luther never crossed paths professionally. And Brent had never worked for him in any capacity.

Brent's father, Brent Sr., came from an affluent background. He operated a political campaign organization. I couldn't quite figure out what it did or why it was so important, but I could understand why Barber had wanted to distance himself.

Blowing out a breath, I grabbed a notepad and wrote out several potential motives for Brent's unexplained absence. My thoughts remained on threats and revenge. Bianchi must have enemies from before he turned his life around and plenty of current enemies if he was still up to no good, as the RICO investigation would have me believe. Brent Sr. had more than his fair share of enemies too. Brent Barber and his production company might be the easiest exploitable weakness one could use against these two powerful men. The theft and murders could have nothing to do with Brent and everything to do with his family.

Cross must have known this. He couldn't have missed it, not after spending so many years getting to know Brent. I tried calling him, but after five rings, I hung up. That answered my earlier question.

Frustrated, I called Justin. "What do you know about Brent's family?"

"A few things."

"Do you think that's why he might have been taken or killed?"

"Taken?" Justin's tone sounded off.

"Yes, like the movie."

"I don't know. I'm not sure I see the relevance. Brent has nothing to do with the things his father and uncle do."

"Find out for sure," I insisted. "I don't want to miss anything. The last thing Lucien needs is a dead client on his hands. Oh, and when you talk to the boss, since I doubt he blocks your calls, tell him this cone of silence thing isn't working for me. I need to know what's going on and what I should do."

"Didn't he tell you?"

"He told me to stay put, build profiles, and figure out how to find our client."

"That sounds like enough instruction to get you started," Justin said.

"I get bored easily."

"I've noticed that. If you've hit a roadblock, I can send you some unrelated background checks to perform. Since you're working remotely, we've gotten backed up on things around here."

"That's all right. I'll manage."

He laughed. "I figured as much. By the way, Barber Productions' financial statements are waiting in your dropbox. I didn't see anything amiss, but feel free to double-check."

"Great. Thanks." Hanging up, I perused the company's financial statements. Money didn't appear to be a motive for the shooting, at least not on a corporate level.

I looked at the notes I'd jotted and the profiles I'd put together. Taking it a step further, I compiled a list of Bianchi's potential enemies. Most of those names were outdated. Some of them had died of old age and others retired to Florida. I tried making a list of enemies for Brent Sr., but that list seemed endless. Plus, I didn't see why a

Barber-Bianchi family issue would result in Fenton Roundtree's demise. Roundtree had no connection to either man or their enemies, unless his murder was meant to hit the point home.

As a last ditch effort, I scrolled through every photo I could find that connected to Brent Barber's extended family, but I didn't see the shooters in any of them. I called Amir, but facial recognition hadn't gotten any hits yet.

When I couldn't stare at the computer screen for another moment, I climbed off the stool. Every bit of research led me in a circle. This wasn't the way to locate a person. I needed to be out looking for him.

Going out the back door, I followed the walkway to the side of the house, contemplating ways of ducking the cops. But they'd already left. Apparently, they'd decided I was too boring to monitor. Now I could do something. I just wasn't sure what that something should be. If I were at home, I'd hang out at the precinct and pester my cop friends to let me assist on the homicide investigation. But Petrocelli made it clear he wouldn't go for that.

"What to do? What to do?" I headed back inside, searching for another set of lock picks. Cross hadn't gotten any answers by going to Brent Barber's house, but I sure as hell would.

NINE

I kept my eyes on the mirrors. No one was following me. Still, I couldn't help but wonder why the police car had been called off. Did Detective Petrocelli find the shooters?

As I approached Brent's house, a modest three-story in a reasonably priced neighborhood, I kept my eyes peeled for a police presence. Cross said they'd searched outside the house before canvassing the neighborhood. What were they looking for? Was that just part of their due diligence in the homicide investigation?

Deciding that I'd make myself crazy trying to answer these questions, I let it go. All that mattered was the cops were gone now. I continued past the house and turned onto a side street before looking for a parking space. I pulled my hair back and put on my sunglasses, my ponytail swinging back and forth as I strolled down the street.

Brent had a doorbell camera and two security cameras on each side of the house. One camera faced the front, while the other faced the back. In the event Petrocelli came back with a warrant, I'd have some explaining to do, but I couldn't think about that now.

The first thing I did was try the doorbell. With any luck, Brent or Adrianna would answer. When that didn't work, I rapped against the door. “Mr. Barber,” I called, “I need to speak to you. May I come inside?”

I felt around the top of the doorframe and studied the décor on the front porch. After checking beneath the potted plants, I lifted the welcome mat. No key. Cross had taught his client well.

Between the storm door and the screen door, I counted at least five locks. And I thought this was a nice neighborhood. Moving away from the door, I peered at the windows. The lights remained off. No one was home.

After making sure none of Brent’s neighbors were watching me, I went around the side of the house. The flowerbeds contained fresh footprints, courtesy of L.A.’s finest. What were they looking for?

A trellis ran up the house beside the back door. Small, dark pink flowers had grown along it, reaching almost as high as the second story window. I examined the white wood, but no one had attempted to climb it. None of the windows or locks appeared tampered with. If Brent had been abducted or worse, whoever did it covered his tracks. The professionals I’d encountered yesterday came to mind.

Cupping my hands against the back door, I pressed my forehead against the cool surface and peered inside. The tinted glass and dark interior made it hard to see. I examined the lock on the back door and removed my picks. In twenty seconds, I’d unlocked the sliding door, but when I tried to push it open, it only moved a few inches.

“Dammit.” A metal bar ran along the inside, preventing the door from opening. I shut the door and tried the nearest window. Locked. So I tried the next one. And the next. “Fourth time’s a charm.”

I looked behind me, but the next-door neighbor’s privacy fence acted as a barrier, shielding me from view. Sliding the window up, I kicked the screen in and climbed through the opening. Now if Petrocelli wanted to charge me with breaking and entering, he’d have a case.

The security panel on the wall should have registered the break-in, but nothing beeped. I approached the panel and removed my cell phone. The app I’d used to get inside Barber Productions would work here, but the green indicator on my phone insisted the system was deactivated.

Brent wouldn't have left his house without arming the system. Donning a pair of gloves, I tucked the sunglasses into the pocket of my hoodie and unzipped halfway so I could reach my nine millimeter, then I moved methodically through the house.

Brent and Adrianna had a landline and answering machine but no messages. I checked the caller ID. Aside from telemarketers, no one had called the house in the last thirty days. The fridge remained stocked with the basics and some leftover sushi. The receipt was taped to the top of the box, but the date had smeared.

I opened the box and gave it a sniff. It hadn't spoiled yet. Brent must have ordered it Friday night or Saturday afternoon, but I hadn't seen that in his phone records. Perhaps his assistant had placed the order before he left work. Making a mental note to ask Sylvio about it, I shut the fridge door. From the looks of things, Brent hadn't planned to disappear.

Aside from a coffee cup, the sink was empty. The dishwasher had a couple of plates and a few utensils, but that was it. None of the glasses had lipstick smears, so Adrianna hadn't been home recently.

Moving on, I searched the living room and dining room, but I didn't find anything amiss. The guest bathroom remained stocked. If Brent had taken off in a hurry, he hadn't disturbed anything downstairs.

The edges of the steps showed scuff marks. Had someone been dragged? I took a few photos, just in case, and jogged up the steps. The second floor contained the master suite. Unlike the first floor, which had been neat and tidy, the bedroom was a disaster.

Crumpled sheets hung from the unmade bed. Dirty clothes had been tossed in haphazard piles. A pair of men's running shoes were sideways on the chair, the laces dangling over the arm. Despite the mess, I didn't think the room was a crime scene.

The closet door was cracked open, so I nudged it wider with the toe of my shoe. A suitcase-sized space was carved out of the clutter. After analyzing the way the closet was organized, I realized the bulk of the empty hangers were on Adrianna's side. The missing suitcase must have been hers. After all, she was supposed to be out of town this week.

Several other suitcases had been opened and left unzipped on the floor. I checked each of the pockets, but they were empty. The largest one had a hanging tag with Brent's flight information from six weeks ago. Obviously, this was his bag. If it was here, he should be too.

Even after searching the dresser drawers, I still couldn't tell if Brent had packed any of his things. The drawers appeared full. This was getting me nowhere. I searched the rest of the room for anything damning—documents, burner phones, anything that would indicate Brent had something to do with murdering Roundtree. But the bedroom didn't contain any clues.

I cleared the rest of the second floor, finding Adrianna's appointment calendar in her office. She had written San Diego in bold letters for this week and the next. Beside the calendar, she'd left her hotel information and work details.

I tried calling her hotel. The desk clerk connected me to the room, but Adrianna didn't answer. Cross had tried to contact her too, but she'd gone radio silent, just like her boyfriend. I tried her cell phone, hoping she might answer the unfamiliar number. When it went to voicemail, I asked her to call me back and hung up. I even tried calling her from her house phone, figuring she'd definitely answer, but that didn't happen either. Cross was right. Something was wrong.

Brent's car remained in the garage. If it were missing, I would have thought he went to surprise his girlfriend. A romantic weekend away would explain a lot, but that didn't appear to be the case. Adrianna's lack of response remained troublesome. Where was Brent, and why wasn't his girlfriend answering her phone?

The stairs creaked as I headed up the final flight. When I made it to the top, I froze. A steady beeping sounded to my left. Was that the security system? It sounded too faint to be the alarm.

Hurrying toward the noise, I hit the light switch and entered the room. A red light blinked in time with the beeping. The shredder had a paper jam. I moved closer to the contraption and unplugged it. The machine felt hot to the touch. How long had it been beeping?

Deciding it might be best to make sure whoever had been in the midst of shredding wasn't hiding nearby, I cleared the top floor. Aside from a few dust bunnies, I didn't find anyone hiding under the desk or behind the treadmill.

Brent had made the top floor his mancave, complete with office and a home gym. Everything was leather and chrome, unlike the rest of the house which had softer, warmer tones. Brent even had a soundproofed recording studio and several musical instruments. Given how he lived and his obvious priorities, I didn't think he'd abandon work unless he had a damn good reason.

Once I was sure the area was clear, the first thing I did was try to access the security system. With all those cameras posted outside, one of them had to have seen something. But every time I clicked on a video file, I received an error message. Since I was unfamiliar with this particular system, it'd be easier to copy everything and let Cross figure it out.

While I was at it, I wondered what other information Brent had stored, so I gave his hard drive a look. His computer contained thousands of sound files. He also had a full calendar with half a dozen meetings scheduled every day this month. Nothing looked off or suspicious. He and Roundtree had a presentation to make at a major studio on Thursday. Even though I didn't have proof, my gut said Brent wasn't involved in yesterday's incident. That left only two possibilities. He got scared and ran, or someone else was responsible for his absence. The sushi in the fridge made me think it wasn't the former.

I plugged a USB drive into Brent's computer to copy his hard drive. While that ran in the background, I knelt beside the shredder. Lifting the cover, I expected to find the bag underneath filled with paper shreds. But there were only a few strips.

Examining the blades, I unlatched the top cover and pulled out the crinkled paper that had gotten stuck sideways. A dark reddish-brown stain covered half of what remained of the page. Blood.

I smoothed out the deep wrinkles, wishing the page hadn't been chewed up by the shredder. *Last chance. You've been war...* had been written in black marker. The shreds contained the rest of the message, but I got the gist.

I went through the house again with fresh eyes, afraid I'd missed something. But I didn't find any bloodstains or signs a struggle took place. The house appeared pristine. After examining the ceiling and crawlspace, I phoned Cross, surprised when he answered.

"We have a problem," I said. "I'm at Brent's house. The security system's been disarmed. I found a note in the shredder. It reads like a warning, and it's coated in blood." I told Cross what it said.

"Are you sure it's blood?"

"It looks like it."

"We'll have to find a lab to analyze it. What about Brent? Any sign of him?"

"I don't think he packed a bag, but he's gone."

"He could have left in a hurry."

"Left? I was thinking someone hauled him out of here." I told Cross about the scuff marks on the steps.

"Check the security cam footage. See what that shows."

"I can't access it. I keep getting an error message."

"It should have backed up to the cloud." Cross tapped on his phone. "I can access his cloud account. It'll just take time. It'll be faster if you check the hard drive. I'll walk you through it."

After following my boss's instructions, I found the recorded surveillance footage saved on a partitioned off section of the hard drive. "You're not going to like this."

"Did someone break in? Was he taken?" Worry dripped from his words.

"Worse. The cameras were disabled. The last forty-eight hours of footage is nothing but a blank screen."

"The picture is blacked out?"

"That's what blank screen means." I played the last few minutes of recorded footage. A car drove down the street about twenty minutes before the footage blacked out on

Friday afternoon, but since the cameras were angled toward the house and not away, I couldn't get a plate. "It looks like whoever cut the camera feed did so before Brent returned home from work on Friday. Could he have turned them off remotely?"

"Only the doorbell cam but not the others." Cross cursed. "Grab the shredder and whatever's in the trash. I'll meet you at your place."

TEN

Cross watched as I carefully brushed fingerprint powder over the torn note. The powder stuck to the smudges around the edge of the page, but it failed to reveal any whirls. The paper didn't contain any usable prints.

"Were you wearing gloves when you pulled it out?" he asked.

"What do you think?"

"I don't know. That's why I'm asking."

I glared at him. "Yes, boss, I wore gloves."

He yanked the ripped sheet off the pool table and held it up to the light. "This feels like copy paper."

"Is that important?"

He shrugged, placing the page down on the green felt and lifting up the motor and blades from the top portion of the shredder. "This should have cut right through it. I don't know why it got jammed." Picking up a tweezer, he gently tugged a crumpled strip of paper free from the contraption.

"Do you think it was wet or sticky when it got fed into the machine?" I carefully unraveled the removed strip and laid it on the table beside the larger portion of the note.

"Possibly." He pulled out a few more strips, sorting them by size. "I contacted a private lab. They'll run the note and determine what the unknown substance is."

"Can they reconstruct it too?" I narrowed my eyes at the uniformly cut strips. This was the world's least fun jigsaw puzzle.

"It's not that kind of lab." He watched as I flipped one of the strips around. "If we can't figure it out, we'll scan it and send it to Amir."

"Why are we wasting our time on this?" I placed my palms on the edge of the table. "I can tell you what the note says. *Last chance. You've been warned.*"

"Is that all it says?" Cross plucked out another strip. This one had marker scribble over some much smaller printed text. He pulled out a few more pieces of paper before handing me the tweezer. "We need to know what the threat was written on. It might give us some clue as to who wrote it. I'd like to have it pieced together before I hand off the top portion to the lab."

"Yes, sir."

He took a seat at the wet bar and plugged the USB drive into his computer. "How did the house look?"

"I already told you."

He climbed off the stool and picked up my phone to examine the photos I'd taken. "These scuff marks don't look like much. Did you find any broken glass? Splintered wood? Anything at all?"

"We've had this conversation four times. You should have met me at Brent's house instead of coming here. Then you could have checked everything out for yourself."

"We can't risk it, not when the police might return."

"Don't you think we should update them on what we've learned?"

"What have we learned? For all you know, that stain is chocolate milk, and Adrianna left Brent the note when he forgot to put the toilet seat down."

"And people say I have an active imagination." I looked up from my task, studying my boss. "The first twenty-four hours are crucial in missing persons cases, and we're already beyond that point."

"You know my history, Alex. You know what we just went through. I don't want to make the same mistake again. But you're right. Time is of the essence." He scanned the info from Brent's copied hard drive. "He never received any threatening e-mails. His internet history doesn't show any oddities. Neither does his financial statements."

"We know he didn't receive any odd phone calls." I tugged the final piece of paper free from the blades. "The lab should analyze the shredder for the same unknown substance."

"Agreed. Bag it up. I'll drop it off as soon as we make some headway on those strips." Cross scanned the information on the screen.

"Justin sent over Barber Productions' financials. I went over the employee list three times. Whoever threatened Brent did so without making any noticeable waves." Again, the thought that professionals were behind this came to mind. "Why do you think he tried to shred the threat?"

"If Brent did that, it was probably his way of hoping to make it disappear."

"That's not exactly how these situations work." I stared at my boss's back, but he didn't bother to turn or make eye contact. "Why didn't he come to you with this? He pays you to provide security. This is a security issue."

"I don't know, Alex."

"*Last chance*," I repeated as I maneuvered one of the pieces beside another one. The black marks lined up. Finally, some progress. "That would imply the threats were ongoing. Whoever wrote this wanted Brent to do something or stop doing something. It doesn't look like Brent made any significant changes. Everything's been business as usual."

"Not everything. He asked us to reevaluate his company's security."

"So he didn't think this was a personal issue." I moved another strip beside the other ones, but it didn't quite fit. I placed it to the side and picked up another piece. "I found the note in his home. That seems personal."

"Maybe the men you encountered yesterday went to Barber Productions in order to find Brent, and when they didn't, they went to his house."

"That might explain Roundtree's broken fingers. Does Brent usually work weekends? The top floor of his house makes me think he's a workaholic."

"He doesn't normally go to the office on the weekends. You saw the footage." Cross tapped his fingers against the bar. "But with Adrianna out of town, he'd have no reason to stay home. You could be on to something. Brent might have been the target."

"Which means Brent might be dead, except I didn't see any evidence of that inside his home, except for the unknown substance on the threat."

"Fuck." Cross tapped more fervently at the keys. "Whoever deactivated his security protocols bypassed them remotely. That shouldn't be possible."

"Do you think he's dead?" I asked. "The police stomped all around the flowerbeds. Do you think they were looking for freshly dug earth?"

"They were looking in his windows. Stop jumping to conclusions. The cops wouldn't have reached that conclusion without a solid lead. If they had that, they would have searched inside his house too."

"Lucien," I said as patiently as possible, "we're wasting time. We're not going to find anything. The security system was turned off, just like at Barber Productions. None of the doors and windows appeared to be tampered with. The house didn't look like a crime scene. But no one would leave a paper jam in his office, fresh sushi in the fridge, and flee without at least grabbing some provisions."

"You said the doors and windows were locked."

"All except one." I shuddered. "That must have been how they gained entry."

"I doubt it. More than likely, Brent let them inside."

"Dammit." I reached for another paper strip. "Why would he do that if he was receiving threats and so frightened he'd leave his shredder beeping?"

"I'm simply making the points the police will if we bring this to them." Cross jerked his chin at the shredder. "I wonder if there's any way to find out how long the system was jammed."

"You think Brent disappeared right after feeding it the threatening letter?"

"The beeping would have made him unplug it if he'd

stuck around."

"I still don't get why he'd shred it. That's destroying evidence. He could have taken the note to the police or to you."

"Unless he didn't want anyone to know about it." Cross stepped away from the computer and lifted the shredder. After pulling the serial number, he returned to the computer. After watching a few tutorials, he examined the shredder until he found a port. "Do you have any cables I can use to hook this up?"

"Hang on." I went into the living room and searched Martin's briefcase. After finding the proper cord, I returned and handed it to Cross. He plugged the shredder into his computer and executed a few rudimentary commands, pulling up the log. "How did you do that?"

He ignored the question. "It looks like the blades came to an emergency stop at 14:21:39."

"That was 2:21." I read the second string of numbers, which appeared to be yesterday's date. "That was less than an hour after Roundtree was killed. That can't be a coincidence."

"I never said it was." Cross stared at the screen, his face much paler.

"What are we supposed to do now? The shooters from yesterday are probably the same guys who made Brent disappear. The police need to issue a BOLO. They need to do something."

"They won't."

"How can you be sure?"

"I spoke to Mr. Ganz about the current situation. Given that the police were snooping around Brent's house earlier, he's already a person of interest. Unless you found a body or clear signs an abduction took place, Petrocelli won't even entertain the possibility Brent's another victim. He'll say Brent got scared and ran, and the reason he's scared is because he hired those men to break in to his company."

"We have this." I gestured at the partially shredded threat. "That proves he's not involved."

"Does it?" Cross asked. "Think about it, Alex. He hired us to break in to his office. Why wouldn't he hire another team to do the same thing or much worse?"

"That's bullshit."

Cross rubbed a hand down his face. "I don't want to leave this up to the cops. Brent's a friend. Do you think he's alive?"

"I don't know. But if he is, we have to find him."

"Have you figured anything out with those shreds?"

"Working on it."

"Work faster," he said. I lined up a few more strips, matching the ragged tear at the top and the black marker lines on the page. The other scraps were beyond my capabilities. Cross finished evaluating the computer while an E and the back portion of the D took shape. He came over to help. "If Brent was taken, shouldn't a ransom demand have been issued?"

"It depends on the reason for the abduction." I kept working on the pieces, feeling the tension radiate off Cross. "Brent's uncle and father have plenty of enemies. Do you think one of them is the reason this is happening?"

Cross slid another strip between two other pieces, hoping to line up the writing. "I've already reached out to Brent's mom and dad. Neither admitted to knowing anything about this." After a few more tries, he moved the strip to another section and repeated the process. "I haven't contacted Luther Bianchi yet. Once I do, things will get messy. That's why I want to be sure we've exhausted all other possibilities first." He finally slid the strip into place.

"Bianchi might already be aware of the situation, if he's the reason this shit is happening."

"Perhaps." Cross glanced at me. "Isn't the FBI keeping tabs on Luther Bianchi? Wouldn't they have noticed any suspicious behavior?"

"Possibly."

Cross nodded as I stuck another piece in the right place. "Men like Bianchi take care to avoid the usual methods of surveillance. We can't spy on him through our usual remote means. No pinging his phone. No checking his call logs. He's too smart and careful for that. That's why you might have to reach out to Jablonsky for answers."

We finished reconstructing a small section of the note.

Cross pointed at the printed text beneath the thick handwriting. "This looks like an order slip." He reached for his phone and photographed the front. "We need tape."

I went into the kitchen to grab some, hearing a few unfamiliar voices coming from the bedroom. Then I heard Martin speak. He'd probably just woken up and was already on a conference call.

Shaking the thought away, I returned to the game room with the tape. After we secured the pieces together, Cross flipped over the section of the paper. "This is a fax order."

"Who still faxes?" I asked.

"Food delivery will sometimes fax in orders they receive from customers since a lot of kitchens find that easier than having to check computer orders and text messages."

"You're joking."

Cross shook his head. "It's similar to how they function with order pads."

I grabbed the magnifying glass I'd been using and held it over the taped-up strip. "This was Brent's sushi order." That explained why he hadn't eaten the food. He probably thought it was poisoned. "We need to find the delivery guy."

"Get started on that. I'll take the rest of this to the lab."

"Results could take days."

"Not for the price I'm willing to pay."

ELEVEN

Cross had been right. Brent didn't order his own dinner. He had Sylvio do it for him. Sylvio sent me the information from the order, including the delivery driver's information. After a few minutes, I found the driver's last name and address.

I was waiting outside his apartment when he returned from work. He barely noticed me as he locked his car. Before he could pull the metal gate open, I slid in front of him.

"Tim Purcell?" I asked.

He stepped back, his hands coming up in a defensive stance, like a boxer the moment he hears the first bell. "What do you want?" His palms were scraped and covered by large, flesh-colored bandages.

"I'm Alex Parker." I gave him a friendly smile. "I have a few questions about a delivery you made."

"What delivery?" He shrunk backward, like a scared, abused animal. "I really shouldn't talk to you. Use the contact us button in the app if you have any questions or complaints."

"Tim, please, I need your help." I raised my hands in surrender but held my ground. "A friend of mine has gone missing. You brought him dinner Friday night. I was hoping you could tell me something about that."

He swallowed, shifty-eyed. "The rainbow roll, right?"

"You remember?" I hadn't expected that.

He lowered his hands, but the unease remained. "I don't want any trouble. I don't know anything. I'm sorry." He reached for the gate, but I didn't budge. "C'mon, get out of the way. I've had a long day."

"What happened Friday night?" I nodded at his hands. "Are you okay? Did someone hurt you?"

Startled by the question, he stopped dead in his tracks. "It's not every day I get mugged making a delivery, and the few times it's happened, no one ever wants the food, they just want my money."

"I'm sorry that happened to you. Can you describe the man who mugged you?"

"I don't know. A little taller than me. Fit. I'm not sure what it was, maybe his tone or the look in his eyes, but he was the scariest son of a bitch I've ever seen. He had a gun with um...what's it called?" He spoke with his hands, holding them close together and spinning them in separate directions.

"A silencer?"

He nodded. "I've only ever seen those in movies and video games. That's almost what he looked like, a real-life hitman. He just needed to shave his head. He had the suit and everything." He looked around again.

"Did he say anything to you?"

"He wanted the food. He wanted to make the delivery for me. At first, I thought it was a joke. I told him if he thought that was his life's calling, he could apply for the gig on the app. They take just about anyone. When I tried to go past him, that's when he grabbed me and shoved the gun into my side."

"What did you do?"

"What do you think? I gave him the bag. He said it'd be best if I forgot all about it and about him, if I knew what was good for me."

"How'd you get roughed up? Did you fight him?"

Tim made a snorting, whistling noise. "He yanked the

bag away from me and shoved me backward. I hit the pavement pretty hard. After that, he headed toward the house, and I took off. I wasn't about to wait around to see if he'd change his mind."

"Did you see anything else?"

"I'm trying to forget all about it, y'know. Discussing this is the one thing I'm pretty sure I'm not supposed to do." He tugged on the bar. "C'mon, you're gonna get me killed. I really gotta go. I can't risk being seen talking to you, not if you're connected to the guy who ordered the food."

I reached into my pocket and pulled out a wad of cash. "Will you accept hazard pay? I need to know if you saw anything else."

He eyed the bills, unsure if he should take them. "I didn't see much. I was in a rush to get out of there, but as I was driving away, I saw the guy in the suit leave the delivery on the doorstep and walk away."

"Do you know where he went?"

"He got into a black car." He took the two hundred dollars and stuffed it into his shirt pocket. "I didn't get a plate or anything. I don't know what kind of car it was. I don't know why he did all of that just to leave the box on the doorstep. But I don't want to know." His eyes grew gentler. "You said the guy who ordered the sushi is missing now. I hope you find him and he's okay. But I can't help you."

"Are you sure the man with the gun didn't say or do anything else?"

"I don't know. He was crouched down near the door for a while. I thought I saw him writing something, but I can't be sure."

"Thanks. Watch yourself," I said. "And you might want to consider filing a police report."

He waved off my suggestion, pulling the gate open the moment I stepped to the side. "I'm not doing anything except keeping my head down and minding my own business. This," he gestured between us, "never happened. Don't come around here again."

Unsure if Tim was telling the truth, I watched his place from the confines of my car. The only way to figure out if he'd been honest was to question Brent's neighbors, but according to my boss, the police had already done the heavy lifting. I wondered what they'd learned.

Once I was convinced Tim wasn't involved and whoever had roughed him up on Friday wasn't going to return to finish the job, I headed to the police station. The place seemed much friendlier today, probably since I wasn't walking in with handcuffs. The officer working the main desk was inundated with an elderly gentleman's questions. After she got him squared away, she let out a frazzled breath.

"May I help you?" she asked.

"I hope so." I gave her a sympathetic look. "I hate to bother you. I can see you're having one of those days."

"You could say that." She rolled her shoulders back. "What can I do for you, ma'am?"

It'd be best to let that one slide. "I noticed officers were out in force earlier today. They were asking about Brent Barber. Is something going on in the neighborhood? Did something happen to him?"

"What's your address?"

"I don't live there. I was visiting a friend."

"It's nothing to worry about." She narrowed her eyes. "Can you wait here a second?"

I wasn't planning to stick around long enough for Petrocelli to question me again. "I'm kind of in a rush. I was just concerned. My friend said she thought she saw an unfamiliar black car parked on the street and a weird guy hanging around. He had on a suit, but she thought she might have seen a gun. I don't know. Her imagination sometimes gets the best of her. She didn't want to say anything because she didn't want to sound like a nutcase. She hasn't seen Brent or Adrianna in a few days. I told her I'd see if anyone reported any of this. If no one has, I'll try to convince her to come down here to do it herself."

From the look on the officer's face, she wasn't buying my bullshit. "What's your name?"

"I'd prefer not to say."

"Ma'am, please step to the side and keep your hands where I can see them."

I knew that tone. "Really, that's not necessary. Detective Petrocelli and I had quite the conversation yesterday afternoon. He warned me to stay out of police business, but it's kind of my job." I held up a hand. "I'm going to reach into my pocket and remove my wallet so you can see my ID."

"Slowly."

I pulled out my wallet and held it open. "I'm a private investigator. Brent Barber hired me to evaluate the security in his office. I reported the shooting. But since I haven't been able to get in touch with my client, I went by his place and saw the police cars. I wondered if you knew something I didn't."

She looked torn. "My father became a private eye after he retired, so I get the position you're in. But we are not allowed to discuss ongoing investigations with civilians. And that license doesn't give you the right to investigate anything in the state of California."

"I know. My status here is pending, but I'm working private security in the meantime. I just want to know if you think Brent is a suspect or a potential victim. He's my client. His abrupt disappearance is unsettling, particularly given what happened yesterday."

"You'd have to ask Detective Petrocelli."

"I'd rather not."

She chuckled. "Not that anyone can blame you for that." She slid my wallet toward me. "You're on the right track. Someone was seen loitering outside his home on several occasions. The next-door neighbor thinks he saw a black sedan Saturday afternoon. The only reason he remembers the car is because it had a broken rear window. Two men in suits were hanging around near the car. He didn't pay them too much attention, but when he heard a commotion outside, he went back to his window again. He's not sure what was going on, but the guys were having a hard time getting something into their trunk." She raised an eyebrow. "Any idea what that might have been?"

"No, sorry." But it had to be Brent. I just didn't know what condition he'd been in when it happened.

"If you figure it out, let us know. These men are killers.

They're dangerous. We know how to handle these types of situations. We have the law on our side. You don't."

"I got it. Thank you."

As soon as I made it back to the car, I phoned Cross with an update. "The police think Brent was taken against his will. The next-door neighbor described a car, just like the one the shooters drove, outside Brent's house right after they got away from me. The neighbor saw them stuffing something cumbersome into the trunk. I'm guessing they forced Brent to go with them. Given the blood and scuff marks, he probably put up a fight."

"How do you know what the police think?"

"Don't ask questions you don't want the answers to."

"Let me guess. You waltzed inside and offered up everything you knew in exchange for whatever they were willing to tell you."

"I didn't waltz. It was more of a two-step. Actually, it was a jig."

"Alex," he hissed.

"I'm heading back to Brent's house to speak to the neighbor and get a firsthand account. We should speak to Sylvio too. Maybe if you sit down with him, he'll come up with something useful, some clue as to who these men are or why they want Brent."

"That's my next stop."

"How are things going at the lab?"

"They're still analyzing the upper portion of the threat for foreign substances. They should have answers for me within the hour."

"Do we know if it's blood?" I asked.

"It is." Neither of us spoke, the implication hanging heavy in the air. "Could it be the delivery guy's? You said his palms were scraped."

"The man with the gun had already taken the delivery from Tim before he shoved him to the ground. But it's possible, I guess."

"Do you believe Tim's story? It sounds pretty farfetched. He could be working with them."

"I doubt it. He appeared genuinely shaken."

"Run his background, anyway."

"I already have. He committed a few minor offenses as a teenager, but nothing violent and definitely not in the ballpark of murder or possible abductions. He has a lot of positive reviews on the delivery app, so whatever happened Friday evening isn't normal behavior for him."

"Did Brent leave a review?"

"He couldn't have. Sylvio placed the order. It would have been on his account, and unless Brent called his assistant to complain about his meal, Sylvio wouldn't know anything about this."

"I'm not buying it."

"Which part?"

"Sylvio."

"Do you want me to talk to him?"

"I'll do that myself, but I want some ammunition I can use to bluff before I confront him. You've already run background checks. So I'll have to figure something else out."

We disconnected, and I headed back to Brent's house. It looked just as it had when I'd left. I parked in his driveway and followed the sidewalk to the next-door neighbor's house. Unfortunately, most of what he said was what he'd told the police.

"When did you first notice the black sedan?" I asked.

"I don't know. It was a few days ago. It kept coming back. I thought maybe it was a friend or relative visiting someone in the neighborhood. The people across the street have a teenage girl. I figured it might belong to one of her friends or her boyfriend, but when I saw the man in the suit leaving Brent's house and getting into the car, I knew I was mistaken."

"Are you and Brent close?"

"Not really. We're all very busy. He and his girlfriend keep to themselves and don't throw loud parties. That's all that really matters." Unfortunately, that meant he had no idea how long Adrianna and Brent had been gone or who would want to threaten or harm Brent.

Before returning to my car, I walked around Brent's house one more time. The security system had been disabled. The cameras were shut off. The house had no obvious signs of a break-in prior to my dramatic entrance. The shooters must have knocked on Brent's door and ambushed him. We needed to establish a better timeline. That would narrow things down. Doorbell and traffic cam footage could be used to track the black sedan. But with no known ransom demand, I couldn't fathom why those men had taken Brent or what they wanted. Until his body was found, we had every reason to believe he was still alive. I just wasn't sure how long he'd last.

TWELVE

Even from three thousand miles away, Cross Security was able to access traffic cam footage, but it wasn't enough for us to figure out where the black sedan had gone after paying Brent a visit. I'd asked Brent's neighbors if they'd let me see their security cam footage. After hearing about the situation, they had willingly allowed me to make copies.

I typed the black sedan's plate into the database. It had been reported stolen two weeks earlier. The owner was a sixty-eight year old woman who lived in the Valley. She never married and had no children. I looked into her extended family, but I didn't think the shooters turned kidnappers connected to her. They probably chose her vehicle because it was an easy target.

"All right, Parker, think." But ordering my brain to work never helped matters. It only frustrated me.

I played the footage Brent's neighbors gave me again, hoping to figure out what the men placed inside the trunk. But no one's security camera covered Brent's driveway. I hadn't noticed any bloodstains or drag marks outside the house. The only possible ones had been inside, on the edge of the steps.

I reached for my phone and called Cross again. "Did the lab find blood on the shredder?"

"Some. They said it looked like someone wiped it off. It wasn't visible to the human eye."

"Was it Brent's?"

"It looks that way, but I can't fathom how it got there."

The house didn't look like a crime scene. Nothing had been disturbed. "His computer gave me an error message."

"But you pulled the files from the partition."

"That's where it backs up, right?"

Cross hesitated. "You think the shooters deleted or corrupted the home security system's information."

"They turned the cameras off remotely, but the system logs other things, like when it's shut off, when the codes are punched in, and what doors and windows are opened and where they are."

"They didn't want anyone to know they came inside."

"That'd be my guess. Brent soundproofed part of the top floor because of the recording booth. If he didn't let them in, he might not have heard them come inside the house."

"Not if he was working with those damn headphones he always wears," Cross said.

"I'm guessing he received the threat, possibly dismissed it or did something he thought would take care of it, and continued on with his normal routine."

"Or he decided to take a few extra precautions and avoid the office, just in case."

"Possibly."

"The shooters didn't find him there, so they went to his house and broke inside." Cross paused. "Except you didn't find any signs of a break-in."

"Maybe they're that good."

"Or they had a key."

"Also possible." I waited to see if Cross would say anything else, but he remained silent. "They found Brent in his office and got the jump on him. They forced him to make those calls and say he had an emergency and would be incommunicado for the next few days. They must have found the threat they left and decided to shred it to get rid of the evidence. At some point during all this, Brent put up a fight or resisted."

"Hang on a second." Cross spoke to someone in the background. After some back and forth, he came back on the line. "They hit him with the top of the shredder."

"Really?"

"The lab found cracks on the underside of the plastic housing and a misalignment of the blades. The shredder was damaged, which is what caused the jam. The tech speculated someone had dropped it or knocked it over. But it could have hit against something."

"Like Brent's skull."

"They might have been mid-shred when Brent made a run for it. That would explain how the blood got on the upper portion of the note while the lower half remained untouched."

"They dragged him down the stairs. I'll send the photos of the scuff marks to you." I hit a few buttons and made sure I got the image sent notification before I pressed the phone back to my ear. "Did the lab find any brain matter or cerebral fluid mixed in with the blood?"

"No. Brent's skull wasn't bashed in. The amount of blood on the document and shredder isn't enough to indicate a severe injury. Did you see any spatter or stains in his office where you believe the attack occurred?"

I thought back, but I'd examined everything. "No."

"Then we approach this on the assumption he was alive when they took him. Our next step is to get him back." Lucien Cross used that tone only a few times before. Normally, Justin would attempt to intervene and Almeada would show up or call a few minutes later. But no one was around to talk Cross down from doing whatever stupid thing he'd set his mind to.

"Is this something Cross Security is equipped to handle?" I asked.

Cross ignored me.

"Doesn't this violate the rule about involving ourselves in a police investigation?"

"They aren't investigating this, at least not yet. They want to find him, but they don't know what we know," Cross said.

"We should share our intel."

Again, he ignored me. "Sylvio's meeting me in a few minutes. Together, I'm sure we'll figure this out."

"Yeah, but—" A million questions ran through my mind. Sylvio knew every intimate detail of Brent's life. So did Adrianna. Either of them could be involved, or they could be working together. It was also possible they had nothing to do with it. But that seemed unlikely. Sylvio must know something that could help us find Brent.

"Take the night off, Alex. I'll call you in the morning."

"Are you fucking kidding me? I'm all you have out here."

"Which is why I need you to stay away from this for now. The police are keeping tabs on you. Let's not give them any more ammunition to use against us. I have teams on standby who can assist, if necessary. I've already reached out to some local fixers. I'm not sure who's involved in Brent's disappearance, but once I find out, they'll handle it. I don't need you to help me with that. Once we determine who has him, we can negotiate his release."

"You're talking about conducting a negotiation on your own. You aren't a hostage negotiator. You have no idea what you're doing or who you're up against. You don't even know what they want or how to get it."

"That's why I'll hire professionals to assist. I've been here before. It doesn't matter what they want. I'm gonna make damn sure they get it." He hung up before I could get a word in edge-wise.

I tried calling back, but it went straight to voicemail. I put the phone down, picked it up again, and called Justin. Tattling wasn't something I enjoyed doing, but Cross wouldn't listen to reason, and he'd blocked my number. So I called the only person I knew who could save him from himself.

After I explained the situation, Justin let out an anxious sigh. "It's a good thing you called. Lucien gets like this sometimes. He forgets he's not as untouchable as he likes to believe. Given his most recent brush with death, he probably thinks he's unkillable. I'll get him off the warpath. In the meantime, you should heed his advice. No reason for you to get caught up in his insanity. I've been there. It never leads anywhere good. You don't want whatever this is to come back and bite you in the ass."

"No, I don't. And I don't want to have to bail out his ass eight years from now either."

"Don't worry about that. You heard him. He'll hire professionals to handle the situation. I'll make sure of it," Justin promised. "If you find something, let me know. Everyone here has made this case a priority. We have the data you sent us. You and Lucien aren't alone. Every single member of Cross Security is backing you up."

"Again."

"That's what family does."

Family. I never thought of Cross Security that way, even though I probably should have. This was a live or die business. I'd laid everything on the line for Cross not that long ago. I just hoped he wasn't letting the past repeat itself. He should have learned from his mistakes. Then again, Brent Barber was one of Cross's friends. They had a history, which obviously meant more to Lucien than his rules and guidelines.

I had to help. This must have been how my friends felt when I went running into the middle of something they wanted me to avoid. After this, maybe I'd take their concerns to heart and not be so reckless. Maybe.

Based on the few facts we had and the giant leaps we'd made, I called Mark Jablonsky. "Hey, before I say anything else, I want to apologize for all the dumbass things I've ever done."

"Are you dying?"

"I hope not."

"Continue."

"I think Brent Barber's been abducted." I laid out everything we'd gleaned from witnesses and surveillance footage and concluded with the threatening note and blood evidence.

"The girlfriend could be in on it," Mark said. "Cross is right to question the assistant. Sylvio should have known something was wrong immediately. You pick up on things when you work that closely with someone. He must have realized something was off when Brent contacted him. Sylvio could be hiding something or covering something up."

"Everything I've found indicates this is an abduction. Cross is hoping it's a kidnapping, but it looks more like murder. No one's received a ransom demand, as far as we know."

"I wouldn't be so sure about that."

"Why?" I asked.

"In the last six hours, Bianchi's accounts have lit up like Christmas trees. The agent in charge of the RICO investigation thought Bianchi got wind of what was going on and decided to move some things around to make it harder for us to track, but Bianchi could be putting together a ransom demand."

"What do his phone records show? I'm guessing there's an open wiretap."

"No one's heard anything related to a kidnapping or ransom, but Bianchi doesn't do business on any line we know about. We've got ears on several of his associates' phones, but nothing popped there either."

"How would the kidnappers reach out to him?"

"That depends on who they are. You said the shooters were professionals. They could have been hired to do the job. They might not be the brain trust behind it. A local rival could have orchestrated it. The demand could have been delivered in person."

I let the words sink in. "Someone needs to pay Bianchi a visit, throw some words around about Brent being abducted, and see if Bianchi opens up. The last time I checked, kidnappings are within the FBI's purview and offering our assistance might be a great way to gather more intel for RICO."

"I'll do what I can, but I'm gonna need something from you."

"Anything."

"Marty got me courtside seats to see the Lakers. I want a signed jersey too."

"How about I buy you an entire outfit to wear and you ask for the signature yourself?"

"Does this outfit include a big foam finger?"

"I'll give you the finger."

Mark laughed. "Fine, but only if you throw in snacks."

"It'd be cheaper if I signed my car over to you."

"You drive a piece of shit. Why would I want that?"

"Fine. Snacks too."

"One other thing."

"What's that?"

"I doubt Luther Bianchi's going to let the FBI handle a negotiation for him. If Cross really wants to help Brent, he'll have a team ready to assist who won't resort to unnecessary bloodshed."

"Cross said he has people on standby."

"Good."

"Yeah."

"You don't sound convinced."

"Cross is taking this one personally. I'm not sure how interested he is in talking things out."

"My suggestion, steer clear. You don't want more blood on your hands. I'll do what I can. I'll be in touch if we get a green light on this."

THIRTEEN

I watched every bit of security footage I could find. The men in the black sedan had been keeping an eye on Brent's house for the last week. They never approached the house or made a move until Friday night when one of them assaulted the delivery driver.

Every move they made was concise, as if it had been carefully planned. Since they'd done their homework, there shouldn't have been any collateral damage, but Fenton Roundtree and the lone security guard appeared to be just that. The shooters had a keycard to enter Barber Productions. They'd subverted that security system too. And to think, I wasted all that time creeping across the lobby. If I hadn't wasted so much time avoiding the cameras, I might have been able to stop them.

I drummed my fingers on the table, knowing that wasn't true. I didn't have a weapon. They would have killed me too. They tried at the gas station. Frankly, if I hadn't intervened, they would have gotten into their car and drove away without anyone being the wiser. They wouldn't have been in such a hurry to get Brent and escape. Who knows what they would have done then. Maybe I would have found his body next to the shredder.

The phone rang. It was Mark. "What's the verdict?" I asked.

"A team went to see Bianchi. They told him we heard his nephew had gone missing and offered to assist in the recovery. He told them to leave."

"Did he know Brent had been taken? Maybe he was afraid the authorities would compromise Brent's safety."

Mark snorted. "That's why he had his lawyer show up to tell us to get off his property and stop harassing him."

"Damn."

"I hate to say it, but this looks like it might be Cross's show. Do you know what he's planning?"

"Probably something stupid."

"Be careful," Mark said. "I'll let you know if anything pops off here."

"Thanks."

I put the phone down and stared at the home screen. Why hadn't Cross called with an update? I hated being in the dark. I sent him a text, asking for a progress report.

Working on it.

That didn't tell me much. Frustrated, I turned my attention back to the computer, but it didn't know who the men were who kidnapped Brent, what they wanted, or where they took him. Since I was convinced they were professionals, I searched for listings, hoping to find someone who'd been hired to conduct a job like this. The dark web had all sorts of players on it. But no matter how hard I looked, I couldn't find these assholes. Cross Security's tech experts would have better luck than I would, and they were already on it.

Martin emerged from the bedroom. He rubbed a hand down his face, confused as to why I was kneeling on the stool while I worked at the kitchen counter with my laptop screen nearly horizontal.

He placed his hands on either side of me and gave my neck a kiss. "You're back."

"How was your conference call?"

"Which one?"

"Any of them. All of them."

"I don't know. It's easier to read the room in person. It's

also much more dramatic when I stand at the front of the table and take charge."

"You can use the kitchen table next time."

"It's not quite the same." He emptied the used grounds from the espresso machine and refilled it.

"Isn't it a little late in the evening for espresso?"

"That never stopped you."

"Did you get any sleep last night or this morning?"

"I must have since I had the strangest dream."

"Yeah?"

"I thought Lucien was here and you wanted me to get a shovel."

"That wasn't a dream." I tried to get off the stool, finding myself stuck since my legs had gone to sleep.

Martin grabbed me before I lost my balance and helped me to the ground. "What did he want?"

I gave him a breakdown of everything I'd learned and how I'd been spinning myself in circles ever since. "Cross told me to keep my distance while he figures this out. I'm afraid he's going to do something stupid. Mark's looking into it too, but he also told me to avoid getting involved."

"Are you planning on listening?"

"I'm here, aren't I?" That didn't mean much, and we both knew it.

"You should consider leaving this to whoever Cross hires. It sounds unnecessarily dangerous, especially since the two men you encountered appear to be guns-for-hire. I don't want you mixed up in that, especially when your client has some questionable family ties."

"Why would an enemy of Brent's family want to interrogate Fenton Roundtree and steal whatever was in his filing cabinet?"

"To make a point or send a message. Maybe Roundtree had a spare key to Brent's house or something else they deemed vital. Roundtree had plenty of knowledge about the company. They might have intended to use that to force Brent to comply."

"You might be right." I scanned the company files Justin had sent over, but I didn't see what could have been so important to kill over. "I still don't know what they took from his office."

"Barber specializes in sound production. Could that have anything to do with anything?"

"I don't know. I doubt this is because someone didn't want a movie or game to be made."

"It'd have to be something else. Recordings or," Martin shrugged, "I don't know. All I know is that I'd prefer if you weren't within a hundred yards of a professional killer. I want you to stay safe. Do you think you can do that for me?"

By Martin's standards, most things I did were unnecessarily dangerous, which made his newfound obsession to teach me to surf confusing. "I'll be fine. I promise. Well, unless a shark attacks. Then that's on you."

"Sweetheart, there are no sharks."

"Do you want me to quote shark attack statistics to you? I have the page bookmarked."

"No."

"Okay."

"That doesn't mean the discussion is over. I'll keep you safe from the sharks if you promise to avoid the men with guns. Deal?"

"I'll do my best, but that's the job. You knew this about me when you signed up." I pointed to the ring on his finger. "Now do you see why I refused to do the whole marriage thing? Just think what our vows would have been like."

"I'd like to find out one of these days." He brewed a cup of espresso and rolled his neck from side to side. "Did you find a meeting?"

I'd gotten distracted, not that grief counseling was ever one of my top priorities. "I'll go to the usual one on Tuesday."

Martin blew on the steam wafting up from his cup, eyeing me over the rim. His expression said otherwise. "There's one in Venice Beach at nine o'clock tonight. We'll be cutting it close, but if we hurry, we can make it. Traffic shouldn't be too bad. I'm not sure about parking. I'd ask Marcal to drive us, but by the time he gets here, that could be another twenty minutes or more, so I'll ask him and Bruiser to meet us there. Worst case, I'll leave the car with them while we go inside."

"Do you hear yourself?"

"What?"

"You're being ridiculous."

"You mean proactive." He went to the fridge and stared at the shelves. "You finished the leftovers."

"Cross helped with that." I glanced at the clock. "You haven't had anything all day. You should eat something. The meeting can wait."

He pulled out the container of eggs. "I can scramble these up really quick, and we can get dinner afterward."

"I don't want you to starve or rush off on account of me."

He peeled a banana and took a bite. "I won't make you go, but I think you should."

"Fine. We'll go. Do you want me to scramble those while you get changed?"

"Do you know how to make scrambled eggs? Pro tip, the shell stays outside the mixing bowl."

I grabbed a whisk. "Really? I thought you liked them crunchy."

He grinned. "You don't have to cook for me."

I eyed the espresso in his hand. He'd been working so much he hadn't had a moment to breathe. He needed a break. "You do it all the time. It's my turn to do something for you."

"If I remember correctly, you did something pretty damn amazing earlier this morning." He put his cup down, resting his forearms on the counter while his green eyes stared into my soul. "In case I haven't mentioned it, I'm glad you're here. I missed you, despite the gunmen."

"I didn't like it when we were apart. I just wish this," I waved the whisk at my laptop, "wasn't happening."

I grabbed a bowl and cracked the eggs while Martin changed out of his power suit and into something appropriate for sitting in a converted gymnasium or church basement. By the time he emerged in jeans and a fitted t-shirt, I'd finished scrambling the eggs and had popped a few pieces of bread into the toaster.

He wolfed down the food and grabbed the keys to the

sports car he leased. Despite my best efforts to delay things, we still made it on time. Unlike most meetings I'd been to, this one was in the back room of a wine bar. I couldn't help but think it made perfect sense. It saved everyone the trouble of finding the nearest bar to drown their sorrows and forget about the stories others had shared.

However, the discussion at this meeting was just like all the rest. I couldn't stay focused. My mind kept wandering back to everything that had happened over the last two days.

I checked my phone at least a dozen times, relieved when it finally buzzed. Martin took my hand and gave it a squeeze. I met his eyes, nodding. *I'll be right back,* I mouthed before leaving the room.

"What's going on?" I asked.

"A lot. I won't get into it on the phone," Cross said. "Sylvio received a few encrypted texts from the kidnappers. I've contacted a professional negotiator. But Sylvio already reached out to Luther Bianchi, making this more complicated."

"What do you want me to do?"

"There's nothing to do. We don't have an open line of communication. We're still trying to figure out who these men are and what they want. Have you made any progress on that?"

"No."

Cross cursed. "All right. Once we find a way to contact them, we'll ask what it's going to take to have Brent returned and go from there."

"Where are you? I can meet you."

"No. The police were outside your door this morning. I don't want them showing up here and ruining whatever chances we have."

"I'm not being followed."

"Are you sure? You went to the station and reminded them to keep an eye on you."

That hadn't been my intention, but I understood why he didn't want the authorities around. Depending on what the kidnappers wanted, they might not be pleased if the police got involved, especially after what happened yesterday afternoon. "Fine."

"I'll call you later."

After we hung up, I returned to the meeting, feeling even less in control than before. I hated not being able to do anything. Martin raised a questioning eyebrow when I retook my seat.

"Nothing yet," I whispered. He wrapped an arm around me and kissed my temple.

The meeting concluded with a prayer, which was something I wasn't expecting. But it couldn't hurt. We didn't hang around to chat with anyone or try the gluten-free scones.

"Is everything okay?" Martin asked as we slipped into the back of the town car. "What did Lucien say?"

"They're working on it. I should keep my distance for now. He's afraid the cops might follow me to their secret location, which I'm guessing is probably his hotel room." I rolled my eyes and checked my phone again.

"I didn't hear it buzz."

"It's on silent."

"Is he calling again?"

"No, but I wanted to make sure to turn my ringer back on. I don't want to miss a call from him or Mark. Kidnappings and ransoms are the worst. As far as I know, we haven't been able to contact the kidnappers, and they've only sent a few cryptic messages. Without a ransom demand or proof of life, I don't know how we'll ever locate Brent. We're not even sure what any of this is about. His odds aren't good."

"I'm sure Cross knows that."

"Brent's his friend. It's hard for him."

"We've been there, Alex. Cross and I. We've been on that side of it."

"I almost forgot." I squeezed his hand. "I'm sorry."

"I'm just glad we got you back."

My mind returned to the things I knew. "I'm still not sure what to make of Brent's assistant or his missing girlfriend. The men who took Brent had access to his office and home. At least, it looks like they did. Someone close to

Brent has to be involved."

"Not necessarily." Martin leaned forward, giving Marcal instructions on where to take us.

I arched an eyebrow, confused. "Why aren't we in your car?"

"Bruiser will drop it off at the house. This way, we can drink without worrying about driving home."

"Not tonight. I want to stay sharp."

"Do you mind if I'm not?"

"Whatever you want, handsome."

He looked shaken, but after spending an hour with that group, I understood why.

After hitting up an outdoor grill where I ate half of Martin's cheeseburger and all of his fries while he worked his way through a flight of whiskey meant for the two of us and two glasses he ordered afterward, we went home. Sleep didn't come easily that night. Instead, I continued coming up with theories, one more outlandish than the last.

When morning came, Martin loosened his grip and ran his thumb across my cheek. "Morning, beautiful. How are you feeling?"

Group therapy always took its toll. But for the first time, I was okay. Preoccupied with the current situation, but otherwise okay. If anything, I was worried about Martin. This situation brought up some baggage for him.

"I'm fine." I snuggled closer. "Are you?"

"I'm perfect."

"And so very humble." I ran my fingers through his dark brown hair, which was spiking out in every direction. His eyes didn't sparkle like they usually did. "Why are you still here? By now, you're usually buried in work or flirting with anyone wearing a bikini." I picked up the sheet and looked down. "In case you haven't realized it, I'm not wearing a bikini."

"It doesn't matter. I always flirt with you." He gave me a gentle kiss. "The waves looked disappointing this morning, and I don't feel much like swimming."

"That's probably for the best on account of the sharks."

He rolled his eyes. "Do you want to go for a run?"

"Do you have time?" I reached for my phone and

checked my messages. No one wanted to talk to me which meant nothing new had surfaced or I was intentionally kept out of the loop. Either way, I didn't like it.

He combed his fingers through my hair, getting my attention. "I can make some time."

I took his face in my hands and kissed him again, unsure if I should push him to talk about whatever was on his mind. Normally, I let things go until he brought them up, but something told me he might need a sounding board.

He moved closer. "On second thought, we can forget the run. You can do with me as you like."

"That's a terrible pick-up line."

"Only if it doesn't work." He traced a line up and down my forearm. But he didn't have time for a leisurely morning, and neither did I.

I planted a kiss on his chest and climbed out of bed, searching the dresser for shorts and a tank top. "Do you want to run along the beach? We could probably get two miles in."

"That works." He got up and stretched while I ducked into the bathroom to get ready. When I came out, we switched places. "What did you think of Venice?" he asked.

"Italy?"

"Smartass. We didn't get to see much of anything last night. I'd like to go back, grab a bite, stroll along the canals, and check out a few of the shops. I saw the way you eyed the bookstores we passed."

"I didn't see any canals. Then again, you did drink quite a bit last night. You might have been hallucinating. Are you sure you aren't talking about Italy?"

"We should go there too, but that's a discussion for another day. I just realized, since you've been here, we haven't done anything on the list."

"That's not true."

"What have we done?"

"We saw the Hollywood Walk of Fame."

"That's only because I had that work dinner nearby and you decided to meet me afterward."

"It counts."

"Venice Beach looks fun. We should go back when it doesn't involve a therapy session." He emerged from the bathroom, using the doorframe as support while he stretched his calves and hamstrings some more.

"Add it to the list."

He grabbed his phone off the bedside table and pecked at the screen with one hand.

"You have a literal list?" I asked.

"Do you want to see?" He flashed the screen toward me, revealing a lengthy list of bulleted points.

Before I could answer, my phone chimed. I glanced at the nightstand, afraid of who it might be or what he had to say. It chimed again with a second text. I scooped it up to read the waiting messages. Cross wanted to meet at the office. Before I could reply, he sent another message. *Ten o'clock.*

"Is our run canceled?" Martin asked.

"No, but we might have to run a little faster."

FOURTEEN

Despite the situation, my muscles remained loose and relaxed as I drove to the office. The run had helped tamp down the nervous energy. Surely, if something terrible had happened, Cross would have called with the news last night. Maybe Brent had been released or rescued. Like they said, no news was good news. And since Mark hadn't called with any details and the police hadn't come knocking, I had to hope for the best. But in my gut, I knew to prepare for the worst.

Lucien Cross had rented a small office in a building downtown. The previous tenant had used it to operate a phone sex hotline. When I first took over setting up the West Coast office, there was nothing inside, not that there was much space to fill. The office contained three small rooms, each soundproofed, and a tiny reception area. Compared to the main office building back home, this wasn't even big enough to be our break room. It reminded me of my old private eye office at the strip mall. It was quiet and cozy, the kind of place I could hide away to work or do online shopping.

Since I started getting the office into shape, I supervised the furniture delivery. Now we had a few filing cabinets, desks, and four chairs. The rest would arrive next week. Cross probably wouldn't be thrilled by the amount of progress I'd made, but something was better than nothing, and I'd have a comfortable place to sit while he yelled at me.

I tucked my sunglasses into my collar and headed down the hallway. A few men in cheap suits waited for the elevator. Two of them chatted away. When they saw me, they smiled.

"Good morning," the one on the left said.

"Morning," I mumbled.

"Haven't I seen you around here before?" he asked. "1D, right? The detective agency?"

"Yeah," I paused near them, "is something wrong?"

"You just missed the delivery guy. He brought you a package, but no one was there to claim it. He asked if it was okay to leave it outside the door. I told him it was. I hope that's not a problem."

"Thanks." Maybe the printer arrived ahead of schedule.

"Hey," the other one called as I moved past them, "do you want to grab coffee sometime?"

Before I could say no, the elevator doors opened. The one who told me about the package clapped his friend on the shoulder. "This is Jett. I'm Eric. We're in 4L–Risk Management. Stop by anytime you want. It gets kind of lonely up there. Maybe you could dazzle us with some detective stories."

"We'll see. Thanks again for the heads-up on the package."

"Anytime."

As I headed down the hall, I spotted the large, square cardboard box on the ground beside the door. It had been sealed with extra layers of packing tape along the seams. I glanced at it while I unlocked the door. The address had been handwritten, *Cross Security, Office #1D,* but I didn't spot any shipping or mailing information.

I pushed open the door and crouched down to pick up the box, stopping when I noticed the bottom corner looked wet. The air smelled coppery, almost to the point that I could taste it.

Stepping back, I circled the box as a sick feeling came over me. Carefully, I used the toe of my shoe to gently nudge it. Despite the size and weight, it moved a fraction of an inch, leaving a wet, red stain on the white tiles underneath. *Blood.*

I glanced in all directions, but I didn't see anyone. I stepped into the office, keeping one eye on the door while removing my nine millimeter from my purse and tucking it at the small of my back. Grabbing the phone off the desk, I held it to my ear. Dead. I held up the jack, which had yet to be connected to anything. The phone guy wasn't coming until tomorrow.

Dropping the cord, I pulled out my cell phone. My first instinct was to call Detectives O'Connell and Heathcliff, but they were three thousand miles away. So I called Cross. "Where are you? Why did you want to meet at the office?"

"I'm almost there. What's wrong?"

"Someone left us a box, and it's bleeding."

"Bleeding?"

"That's what it looks like."

"I just parked. I'm on my way out of the garage. I'll be there in two minutes. Don't touch anything."

Yeah, no kidding. I took up a spot near the door and peered around the side. Besides the few people using the elevators in the lobby, the hallway was empty. Security cameras covered the front door and the elevator banks. Another camera covered the far end of the hallway. Whoever left the box had been caught on video. Unfortunately, I didn't have access.

"Hey," Lucien called, practically jogging toward me, "is that it?"

"Yeah."

He maneuvered around the box and joined me in the office. "Did you open it?"

"Not yet. I only bumped it with my foot." I pointed to the growing bloodstain. "I'm hoping you ordered a box of steaks and forgot to tell them to put it on ice."

Cross gave me a cockeyed look. "What?"

"Blood like that can only come from a piece of meat. I'm hoping it's not human." But my gut knew better. "Do you think this has something to do with Brent?" I didn't see any other possibilities. "Do you think a piece of him is inside the box?"

"It's not Brent. It can't be."

"How do you know?"

"Call it wishful thinking." He stepped back into the hallway, glancing at the cameras like I had done. "Did you see who left it?"

I told him about my encounter with Jett and Eric at the elevators. "They said a delivery guy brought it. I don't see any labels or mailing information, so I'm guessing he wasn't an actual delivery guy. We need that footage to determine who he is."

"That should be easy enough to swing." He squinted toward the ceiling tiles before shaking off whatever thoughts he had. "Have you pissed anyone off lately?" Cross crouched down, eyeing the tape.

"Me? I haven't done anything except supervise furniture delivery, internet installation, and run background checks. Who have you pissed off?"

"Plenty of people." He pulled out his phone and took several photographs before sending them to his staff. "I want to see what's inside the box."

"I'm not sure want is the right word."

"Regardless." He ran a hand through his hair.

I grabbed a letter opener from my desk drawer and knelt down beside the box, careful to keep my body away from the growing pool of red. Bombs didn't bleed. Worst case, this was a biological weapon, in which case, we'd already been exposed. But that was unlikely.

Carefully, I slid the metal beneath the end of the tape and lifted it up. After several tries, I pulled every piece of tape free from one side. Then I turned the blade sideways, stuck the tape to it, and peeled the tape off the box with the letter opener.

Cross glanced down the hallway, repositioning himself to block what we were doing from view. But no one was close enough to see inside the box. And not a single person appeared interested in what we were doing.

I laid the letter opener on the ground and used a pen to

lift one of the flaps. Four cloudy eyes stared at me from within. A strange noise escaped my throat, a cross between a gasp and a curse. I didn't recognize either of the men. But with the plastic bag and blood matting down their hair and obscuring their features, it was hard to say for certain.

"Fucking A." Cross sucked in a shaky breath. "Call the police. I'll contact Jason Ganz and tell him to meet us here. Almeada would be better. Having our own lab techs would be ideal right now." He shook away the shock. "Tell me you have some contacts in law enforcement."

"Only Detective Petrocelli, and he doesn't like me much." He was going to like me a lot less after this.

"That's it? What about from your federal agent days?"

My mind raced through possibilities while I phoned the police to report the suspicious package. Aside from a couple of months I spent on loan to the DEA when Martin and I broke up, I didn't have any other friends around here who could help. And this didn't look like it fell under the DEA's jurisdiction.

"I don't care if he's in court. This can't wait." Cross tucked the phone into his breast pocket and stared down at the opened box. Then he snapped photos of the two heads.

"Do you recognize them?" I asked, my stomach roiling. The bloody smears inside the bags made the victims' features appear even more grotesque.

He stared down at them, deep wrinkles developing across his forehead. "I'm not sure, but those might be the negotiators."

"Negotiators? Did you hire them?"

"Luther Bianchi did." Cross glanced at me. "Pick your jaw up off the floor. We'll talk about this later."

"This," I gestured at the box, "violates the basic tenet of a negotiation. After what the kidnappers did to the negotiators, I'd hate to see what they did to Brent."

My boss stepped away. "Is there anything else you haven't told me about what happened at Barber Productions?"

"No."

"All right. We need to figure this out, and we don't need the police insinuating themselves into the middle of it. The stakes are too high." He nodded down at the box. "You said the men in 4L told you about the delivery. Do you think they're involved?"

"I doubt it, but they might be able to provide a description of the man who left the box since they spoke to him."

"Wait for the police to arrive. Whatever you don't want them to find or confiscate, lock in the filing cabinet. They have no grounds to search our office. The box is outside. We never took it in. But if they want to look around, let them. I don't want them to think we have anything to hide."

"Like what? The copy machine or the coffeemaker?"

"Or work product." His tone held bite. "The last thing we need is to be blamed for this. I'm going to see what Jett and Eric have to say and pull a copy of the building's surveillance footage. The police aren't likely to share with us, so I have to get access before they get here."

"Hey, Lucien," I called as he headed for the elevator, "you have some explaining to do."

"We'll discuss it later. Right now, we have to move on this while we can."

FIFTEEN

"You reported four murders in less than seventy-two hours. Tell me why I shouldn't charge you, Ms. Parker. You're the only common denominator." Detective Petrocelli rocked in his chair, his heels resting on the edge of the table. After shutting down our office, the police insisted on questioning us at the station. It was a power move, designed to show us who was in charge.

"You know I didn't commit the first two murders, so if I'm the only commonality, that would mean the two heads in the box aren't connected to the shooters from Saturday. I don't see how that's even possible. They must be connected." Cross warned me not to share too much with the cops, but Petrocelli seemed to be way off base. A little nudge in the right direction wouldn't hurt.

"How come?"

"It stands to reason since Brent Barber's the only client I have."

"We haven't IDed the heads yet. Everyone else at Barber Productions has been accounted for. I'm not seeing the connection."

"Have you found the headless bodies?"

"No reports have come in. Why? Do you know where

they might be?"

"Not a clue. Maybe they got stuck on the delivery truck and won't show up until tomorrow."

"Do you think this is funny?"

"Not at all, but if you're going to ask me ridiculous questions, I'll give you ridiculous answers."

My attorney let out a warning cough from where he sat beside me.

"Care to enlighten me on what's going on here?" Petrocelli asked. "You must know something about this. Otherwise, why would you have been sent a box of heads?"

So many responses came to mind, but now wasn't the time. Petrocelli picked at a hangnail while he rocked on two chair legs. That wasn't the most professional position for a homicide detective to take, but something about his indifference made him seem reckless, like he didn't care if he had the offender in custody, just as long as he had someone in custody and could keep his case closure rate high. Unfortunately, that meant I was on the hot seat.

"I can honestly say I've never seen either of them before. And I certainly didn't kill them."

"Why did someone box them up and send them to you?" he asked.

"The box was addressed to Cross Security. It wasn't addressed to me personally."

The wheels turned in Petrocelli's head. "Are you saying Lucien Cross knows something about this?"

Before I could answer, Ganz piped up. "Ms. Parker has done nothing but cooperate. She's simply had the misfortune of having to report these murders. You have no evidence indicating she's involved. Let her go, Dean. All we're doing here is wasting time. She doesn't know anything. If she did, she'd tell you."

Detective Petrocelli pretended he hadn't heard a word Ganz said. "Why did Cross fly across the country the moment he became aware of an issue at Barber Productions?"

"He likes to micromanage."

"Uh-huh, sure. But like you pointed out, the box wasn't addressed to you, so maybe the heads don't have anything to do with your client or your case." He reached for his notepad. "What other clients does Cross Security have in the area?"

"That's irrelevant," Ganz said.

"Not if the heads in the box turn out to be more of Cross's clients." Petrocelli gave me a wicked smile. "The lab's checking dental records. We'll know who they are soon enough. Are you sure there's nothing you want to tell me?"

"It's a workday, so I went to work. Someone dropped off the box before I got there. That's all I know."

Petrocelli dropped his feet to the floor and thumbed the screen on his tablet a few times. He put the device down in front of me. "What about him? Do you recognize him?"

I peered at the photo of the delivery guy. He wore a black and white striped polo, a pair of khaki cargo shorts, and fingerless gloves. He balanced a clipboard on top of the box. From the surveillance footage, he looked the part. "No." I pointed to his hand. "Did you pull prints?"

"They aren't in the system."

"You should check with local delivery services and see if that uniform matches any of theirs. That's probably your best bet for IDing him."

"Are you telling me how to do my job?" Petrocelli asked.

"Someone has to."

Ganz snapped the buckles on his attaché case closed. "We're done here. Unless you plan to charge her, my client is leaving."

Petrocelli leaned back in his chair. "What else should I be doing, Ms. Parker? Canvassing Mr. Barber's neighborhood for clues?"

I didn't bat an eye. "That would be a good place to start."

"What happens when I find out you've been snooping around there?"

"It's not illegal."

"Obstruction and interfering in a police investigation are."

"Ms. Parker, let's go," Ganz said, making his way to the door.

Petrocelli held me in place with the weight of his stare. "Tell me why the men around you keep turning up dead."

"I don't know."

"A word of advice, you might want to figure that out. Two heads being left on your office doorstep reads like a threat to me. You could be next, unless this is just a sick joke."

"What kind of joke?"

"Two heads are better than one. I'm guessing that's what your boss is thinking." Petrocelli jerked his chin toward the door. "You want to go, go. But once you walk out of this room, I can't help you. Tell me what you know, and I'll do my best to keep you safe."

"Thanks, but I can take care of myself." I followed Ganz out of the interrogation room and down the hallway.

The attorney led me out of the station. "The police don't have anything on you, so don't give them any ammunition. All you're doing is poking the bear. Stop that."

"I wasn't poking anyone. I just gave him a few tips."

"Tips that will bite you in the ass." He glanced in my boss's direction, making sure we remained out of earshot. "Look, if you want to discuss anything, meet me at my office and we'll figure out the best way to proceed. Obstruction is a serious offense, and one that would be best to avoid."

"Tell that to Cross."

"I've already spoken to Mr. Cross." Ganz hadn't gotten the memo that Cross was the shot caller, but he'd figure it out soon enough. "Now I'm telling you the same thing." He handed me his card. "Think about it."

"There's nothing to think about."

"In case anything changes, remember what I said. I've known Dean Petrocelli for years. He gives great testimony. Juries eat it up. The DA loves it when his cases go to trial."

"Does that mean we should be seeking better counsel?" Cross asked, peeling away from the pillar where he'd been lurking. His phone remained pressed against his ear, but he might have been on hold.

Ganz stepped onto the sidewalk. "Do what you like, but I know how to keep Dean in his place, assuming you tell me what I need to know."

"We'll be in touch, should we require your services again." Cross gave him a half-assed wave and turned toward me.

"What's going on?" I asked.

Cross held up a finger before I could say anything else. "All right, we'll meet you in two hours at that location. Once you're there, stay put. You'll be safe." He tucked the phone into his pocket. "I called a car to pick us up. We should see if the crime scene investigators are finished at the office."

"Who were you talking to?"

"An acquaintance."

I knew it was bullshit. "An acquaintance who's in need of finding a safe place to meet?"

"Not here." Cross glanced back at the door to the police station. "Wait until we're inside the car." He nodded toward the black SUV idling on the corner. A linebacker in an expensive suit lingered beside it and opened the door as we approached. "Thanks, Nero."

"Anything else, Lucien?"

"Hardware?" Cross asked.

"What do you have in mind? I have a rifle in the back, but we can always swing by the locker if you want a grenade launcher or something that makes a big boom."

"I was thinking something smaller and less conspicuous."

"I thought you wanted to have some fun." Nero handed Cross an unloaded Glock and the ammo he'd taken out of the glove compartment. "And for the lady?"

"I thought this was BYOG." I eyed him curiously. "Maybe I came to the wrong party. Who are you?"

Cross answered for him. "This is Nero. Omar's the guy driving. They're part of the team that provides protection for Miranda. But since she's currently on hiatus from her tour, her team has some downtime. So I asked to borrow them."

"Uh-huh." That was a much longer answer than I needed. "Why do you need a gun? The police didn't confiscate yours."

Cross took the offered holster and clipped it to his belt. "I left my piece in the office, same as you. But it'd be prudent for one of us to be armed at all times. And it wouldn't hurt to have a backup. Two men were killed and their heads were left on my doorstep. That requires taking a few additional precautions."

"You're expecting trouble. Is that why Nero and Omar are here? Are they going to protect us?"

"I'm sure you were taught to prepare for everything." Cross stared out the window as we passed plenty of buildings and the occasional palm tree.

I glanced from the men in the front seat to my boss, who remained so incredibly still he might have been paralyzed. "What did the police say to you?" I asked, unsure how much to say in front of Nero and Omar.

"The usual. I told them I don't know anything."

"That's bullshit. You know a hell of a lot. You said the heads belonged to the negotiators Luther Bianchi hired. Do you know who took Brent or what they want?"

"I have no idea."

That made no sense. "What do you know?"

"Not enough. Whoever took Brent sent Sylvio a message that they had Brent and they better get what they were owed or else. By the time I got wind of this, Sylvio had already contacted Luther Bianchi. Things were already in motion."

"Did you try to stop them?"

"I suggested Luther let me handle it, that I had experts waiting to help, but he refused. He said he would take care of his family himself." Cross shook his head. "Luther won't be pleased with this turn of events."

"How did the kidnappers know to leave that present on our doorstep?"

"I've been wondering the same thing." The SUV came to a halt, and Cross reached for the handle. "Thanks, Nero. When you see Miranda, tell her I'll take her to lunch to make up for the inconvenience."

"Will do, Lucien." Nero nodded to me. "You sure you don't want some personal protection?"

"It sounds like you're offering me condoms."

"Sure, I've got a few of those on hand too. Like the boss said, it's best to be prepared for anything."

"Next time." I got out of the SUV, surprised when it sped away the moment we shut the doors. A million questions came to mind, but I started with the most important one. "Is Martin in any danger?"

"I don't believe so. This matter has nothing to do with him and very little to do with you. The box served as a warning. I don't think they'd make a move on either of us unless we did something to provoke it."

"If you believed that, you wouldn't have had Nero bring you a gun." I gulped down some air as flashes of those lifeless eyes came to mind. "Do we know who sent the severed heads?"

"Someone with a flair for the dramatic and no respect for human life." Cross entered the office building while I jogged to keep up.

"What about a name? Do you have one of those?"

"Not yet. I'm working on it."

"You said the kidnappers reached out to Sylvio who passed the message on to Brent's Uncle Luther. That means we should know who we're dealing with."

"We don't. All communications have been sent via encrypted texts. Luther Bianchi won't even use a fucking phone or computer, which makes everything even harder. I had to message one of his associates in order to get them to relay my messages to Luther and vice versa. Amir's working on identifying the kidnapper, but it'll take time."

It had been over four hours since the police arrived at our office. The crime scene, if one could call it that, was limited to the cardboard box. Aside from the bloodstain on the floor, which had already been mopped up with a wet floor sign remaining in its place, the area was clear.

Despite that, Cross went to great lengths to search every fixture in our office for surveillance devices. He unlocked the filing cabinet, handed me my nine millimeter, removed his firearm, and took out three of the dozen prepaid cell phones he insisted I keep on hand. After activating them, he handed me one. "Forward your calls and use that instead."

"Fine." Better safe than sorry.

He opened another drawer, not finding whatever he was looking for. "I asked you to get this place in shape. You've been here nearly a month. I would have figured you'd have gotten more done by now."

"Seriously?" This was not the time for that conversation.

"At the very least, we need phone service."

"Agreed, but they keep rescheduling. They're supposed to be here tomorrow."

"Do we have internet access?"

"See for yourself."

He powered on the computer, entered his log-in, and checked his dropbox. "I sent the photos of the dead men to Justin, along with copies of the surveillance footage I pulled from the building's security feed." He blew up a still of the man in the polo. "The delivery guy is wearing sunglasses, but Amir thinks he could be one of the shooters from Saturday. See that tattoo," he pointed to the man's bicep, "it looks like it could be military."

"He's not one of the shooters. I would have recognized him."

"Are you sure?"

"I was trained, Lucien. Making IDs is what I do."

"Still," he narrowed his eyes as he read the intel on the screen, "we shouldn't dismiss the possibility that he's working with them."

"The police ran his prints. He's not in the system, which eliminates your theory that he was military. I'm guessing he's just a courier."

"We can't assume anything at this point." Cross clicked the mouse a few times, his eyes darting from left to right as he read the screen. "When I spoke to Jett and Eric, they told me they saw the truck the guy had driven to deliver the package. It was a white van in need of a paint job." He tapped the full screen button. "Exterior cams caught this. I had Justin run the plate. It's registered to a crisis management firm."

"Crisis management?"

Cross stepped away from the computer to circle the desk. "Mack Randall and Kevin Donzer, the decapitated negotiators, ran their own firm. They're well-known for taking care of business with the utmost care and discretion to make sure the powerful aren't targeted again. Luther trusted them to handle this."

"Did Luther ever receive a ransom demand or proof of life?"

"He wasn't much on keeping me in the loop. It was amazing I got any responses out of him, and even those were vague. Basically, Luther told me to back off and let him handle it."

"Handle what exactly?"

"Sylvio showed me the encrypted text he received. *Tell him to pay up or Brent's dead.* After he got that, he reached out to Brent's uncle."

"That's awfully vague. Did Sylvio think the *him* referred to Luther Bianchi?"

"I'm not sure, but I'm wondering how Sylvio knew who to contact or even how to contact him. By the time we met last night, Sylvio had already sent Luther the information. I should have gotten there sooner. We should have started with him yesterday. I never thought he'd intentionally keep us in the dark." Cross grabbed the cloth grocery bag which I'd left on the floor, emptied out the mini fridge and cabinet that I'd filled with snacks, and tucked the gun Nero gave him and the prepaid phones beneath the goodies.

"Did you tell the police any of this?"

"Whoever has Brent is clearly sadistic and unstable. Involving the police will get him killed, if he isn't already dead." Cross grimaced. "I don't know what's going on, but leaving body parts on my doorstep is one hell of a way to drag me into this. It's almost as if someone's testing me. Like they want to see how I'll handle it."

"Why do you think they were delivered to our office?" I asked.

"We've been snooping around and asking questions. Someone must have noticed and wanted to send us a message to stop dicking around and get them their payment."

"You don't think Luther Bianchi paid?"

"Randall and Donzer don't have a reputation for paying

out. They make people pay up instead."

"Are we getting blamed for that?"

"Cross Security always sources out negotiations. Usually, insurance gets involved and things resolve peacefully, but it's never our call."

"The police and FBI would be willing to take over. Given the heads in the box, we should let them. Luther Bianchi won't play by the rules. That's going to get his nephew killed, if it hasn't already."

"That's why I'm hoping to take control of the situation."

"But you just said—"

"Kidnappings aren't nearly as cut and dry. We need to hire a team to handle this. With Randall and Donzer dead, the fixers I have on retainer won't come near this. I don't know any negotiator who will. Bianchi isn't a mafia don. He doesn't surround himself with hitters and heavies. He's not in that life anymore. His people can't handle this either. The heads in the box prove it. We need a team. Justin's reaching out to everyone we know, but it doesn't look good."

"The FBI could provide us with a negotiator to coach you through the next steps."

"How do you think that'll go? These men aren't afraid to kill. Going to the authorities is usually a big no-no. I'll handle this myself."

"You can't, Lucien. You're too close. We don't even know what the kidnappers want. Let me make a call."

"No FBI."

"That's not who I'm calling."

SIXTEEN

This was one of those break glass type of situations. I hoped to never need to call this number again. In fact, I used it so infrequently that I wasn't sure I remembered it correctly. But when a familiar British voice answered, I knew I had the right number.

"I'm hoping this is a social call," Bastian Clarke said. "But I know you better than that. What's going on, love?"

"My boss has a situation." I told him everything I knew.

"Let me talk to Jules and the rest of the team. We'll ring you back. In the meantime, gather some better intel. Yours is utter shite. Jules will want to know who we're up against before he agrees to anything."

"Will do." I tucked the phone away, hoping I hadn't made a huge mistake. Julian Mercer and his team of former Special Air Service operatives had been in the K&R business for several years. The only other time we worked together on a kidnapping case, we'd come to blows. After that, he paid me a favor, which I returned. Since then, we hadn't spoken much.

"Well?" Cross eyed my phone.

"We need to figure out who's responsible and what they want. More importantly, we need to make sure Brent's still alive. If he's not, there's no point to any of this."

"Are they on the way?"

"Not yet. I'm not sure they'll agree to help. It all depends on circumstances."

"You should remind him you played an important role in solving his wife's murder, assuming we're talking about Julian Mercer's crew."

"How—"

"You worked on his wife's murder investigation in my lab. His name came up several times when you first signed on as a Cross Security employee. You must have crossed paths somewhere, and given his reputation with K&R, I just assumed. Am I wrong?"

"No."

"Great, so what's the problem?"

I exhaled. "Let's talk to Sylvio first. Mercer won't sign on without knowing the situation, and I won't ask him to."

Nero and Omar escorted Sylvio DePalma to one of the secure apartments Cross maintained for his celebrity clients. When we arrived, I spotted the SUV parked down the street, not too close, in case someone realized who they were and why they were here, but close enough to maintain eyes on the property and intervene in the event of an emergency.

From the moment we walked through the door, Sylvio hadn't stopped fidgeting. The nervous energy radiated off him in waves. Cross shoved his hands into his pockets and leaned against the wall while Sylvio glanced out the blinds every few seconds.

"You realize, if someone's watching the safe house, they're going to notice the window coverings swaying back and forth," Cross said.

Sylvio's already pasty skin turned even more ashen. "I'm sorry, Mr. Cross. You're right." He stepped away from the window and sat down on the couch. A second later, he popped back up, shook one of his pills into his palm, went to the fridge, grabbed a bottle of water, took a sip, replaced it, and sat down at the counter.

"Sylvio, relax. No one knows about this place. That's why I brought you here. It doesn't connect to you or your life in any way. No one can find you here." Cross nodded toward the prescription pill bottle on the coffee table, which contained Sylvio's anti-anxiety medication. "Do those help?"

"A little, but they don't seem to be doing much right now."

Cross rummaged through the grocery bag we brought, piling the snacks on the table. "No one here will harm you. You're safe. Now tell us what's going on."

Sylvio reached for a granola bar and rocked back and forth while he unwrapped it. "You know what happened on Saturday, right? Mr. Roundtree got killed." He nibbled on the bar. "That was right around the same time Brent called and said he had a family emergency and would be out of town. He left me in charge. Me. Like I was supposed to know what to do when the police came calling."

"You handled it okay." I took a seat on the couch. "If you hadn't vouched for me, I'd probably still be in lockup."

Sylvio looked in my direction. "I'm sorry for everything, Ms. Parker. I'm sure Brent feels the same way. In fact, I know he does. He's my best friend. I just...I can't imagine what he must be going through right now. I thought the negotiators would be able to help. That's what I was told, but they never reported back. Instead, whoever has Brent is even more pissed off now."

"How do you know that?" Cross asked.

Sylvio held up his phone. "It came in early this morning. I didn't even bother checking it. I thought Luther was taking care of it, that this no longer had anything to do with me."

"What does the message say?" I asked.

"It says we better not play any more games."

"Did you respond?"

"No." Sylvio's eyes went wide in fear. "What would I have said? I'm not in charge of this. Luther's supposed to be, but from what you said, I'm guessing he's not doing a good job. I don't know what to do or where to go. But I think I should do something to try to help."

"That's why we're here," Cross said. "Start at the beginning and don't jump over the critical parts this time. I want to know everything in the order in which it happened. What you told me last night wasn't nearly enough, and two men are dead today because of it."

"Right, sorry." Sylvio took a bite of granola and washed it down with another sip of water. "Saturday afternoon, the police called me when they couldn't get in touch with Brent. That was twenty minutes after I spoke to him. Before that, I hadn't really given much thought to Brent's sudden departure. Later that night, I got a message while playing one of the games on my phone. It was through the game app, but I've never heard of this user. The message said *Tell him to pay up, or Brent's dead.* Normally, I probably would have ignored it or thought someone was messing with me, but not after Mr. Roundtree and another employee were killed. So I reached out to Mr. Bianchi." Sylvio abandoned the stool in order to pace.

"Did you notice anything off at work or with Brent these last few weeks?" I asked.

"I'm not sure. Maybe, I guess."

"How about we start there?" I patted the cushion beside me. Reluctantly, Sylvio sat down and turned sideways, so he could see Cross and me at the same time.

"I don't know when it started exactly. I guess ever since we got back from the award ceremony Brent's been stressed. A lot of strange things have been happening at the office. Just weird stuff. He kept telling us it was nothing, but it was getting to him."

"Was that why he wanted Barber Productions' security evaluated?" Cross asked.

"I think so, but he never admitted that to me. When I asked, he said the building was due an upgrade."

"What kinds of odd things were happening?" I asked.

"Guards found the doors had been left unlocked while conducting their patrols. The alarm would go off at odd times. Once, it went off in the middle of the night. Brent had to check it out and called me to help him with that. Security couldn't explain what caused it. The police checked the building and everything. The security cams didn't show anything. It was so strange. Another night, when I was leaving work for the day, I guess this was a week later, I found the back doors wide open, but no one was around. The alarm didn't sound, and it never popped up on the monitors in the security office. Brent said he thought it could be a short in the system."

"Why didn't he tell me any of this?" Cross asked.

Sylvio held up his palms. "I don't know."

Cross checked the copy of the contract he'd brought with him. "Was anything taken?"

"I don't think so."

"Did anything go missing?" I asked.

Sylvio squinted as he thought. "A few things, but they always turned up in weird places. We found a soundboard in the maintenance closet and a speaker in the ladies' room. I thought someone was playing a practical joke on us. Brent sent out a memo, but we never figured out who was doing that or why. Security upped its patrols and ran a bunch of diagnostics, but nothing registered. They figured it was a glitch or hiccup."

"Did anything odd happen while Brent was away?" I asked.

Sylvio wrung his hands in front of him, fighting to keep from squirming. "No. It was a great trip. The company got some serious recognition. Everyone who went had a blast. And Brent was over the moon by all the new jobs we'd been offered, but with that came more job stress."

"Do you know if anyone in the company was ever attacked or threatened?" Cross asked.

"I don't think so."

"What about muggings or home invasions?" I asked.

Sylvio shook his head.

"Did anyone ever break into an employee's car?" Cross asked.

"Not that I'm aware. Unless it happened at the office, no one would have been obligated to report it. But I probably would have heard about it at the watercooler, and I don't remember anything like that."

"Okay, continue," Cross said.

"Like I was saying, these weird, unexplained things kept happening at work. Security always investigated. They didn't find anything or anyone. They thought it was an oversight or a mistake. A lot of artists and musicians come and go on a regular basis. They haul a lot of equipment in and out of the studio. With all our current projects and looming deadlines, we've been keeping strange hours, so it's not necessarily uncommon that doors aren't closed properly or stuff gets misplaced, but this felt like more. It freaked Brent out, and it baffled security."

Cross jotted down a few notes. "What about Adrianna? Was she ever threatened or frightened by someone?"

"Not that I recall. If she was, Brent didn't mention it to me."

"Did he talk about his personal life with you?" I asked.

"All the time. We're best friends. That's why he hired me to be his assistant. We were already hanging out all the time, so he thought I should get paid for it. He always says I know him better than anyone."

"How would you describe his relationship with Adrianna?"

"He loves her so much. He's over the moon. She's the only thing he talks about besides work. She's his everything."

"Does she feel the same way?"

"I imagine so. Whenever we get together, she's always hanging on his arm or cuddled up with him on the couch." Sylvio's face showed just the slightest bit of annoyance or jealousy. I wasn't sure which.

"Do you and Adrianna get along?"

"Sure."

I didn't buy it. "Why didn't you call her when you received that text about Brent?"

"I tried calling, but she didn't answer."

"You tried calling once," I said, recalling the phone records I'd checked. "You didn't even leave a voicemail or send a text. Shouldn't you have tried harder?"

"I figured she'd call me back. I didn't think about it. I wasn't thinking about much except Brent."

"Did Brent or Fenton Roundtree ever receive any threatening messages or weird phone calls?" Cross asked.

Sylvio scratched his eyebrow before rubbing his face. "No threats. They got tons of calls, but they were all relevant. Nothing weird."

"What about disgruntled employees or anyone who might have a bone to pick with Brent or Barber Productions?"

"Nope. Everyone's happy to be there. The studios are thrilled with our progress. No one's asking for anything ridiculous, like they usually do. Everyone's been getting bonuses for all the overtime hours. It's been great. I should have known it was the calm before the storm."

"Why?" I asked.

"It just felt too perfect. Everything was coming at us at once. High paying jobs, studio contracts, a few queries from musicians looking to cut their next album. Everything Brent dreamed of was finally happening. It's almost like he sold his soul in exchange for his good fortune." Sylvio shook his head. "This would be the part in the movie where he gets T-boned by a semi."

"Did Brent do anything shady to make these things happen?" I asked. "Did he pay off someone in order to win that award?"

"No. Brent's not like that. I just said that because, all at once, everything was happening. It all fell into place, and now it's falling apart."

"Do you know when Brent was taken?" Cross asked. "Did you receive a text when it happened?"

Sylvio moved to stand, but I put my hand on his knee. He looked at it, even more confused than before.

"Answer the question," Cross said.

"I'm not sure. I spoke to Brent Saturday afternoon. He said he had a family emergency and would be out of touch for a while and that I should make sure everything ran smoothly in his absence. The next thing I know, the police are asking me about you." He looked at me when he said it. "Later that night, I received the text from an unknown user that said to tell him to pay up or Brent was dead. They warned me not to speak to the cops or else something terrible would happen to him. I tried calling Brent, but it went straight to voicemail. I drove by his place, but no one was home. I called Adrianna, but she didn't answer either. I didn't know what to do. But since I couldn't get in touch with him, I assumed the threat was real. That's why I told you Brent said to back off and he'd contact you. I didn't want your involvement to anger the kidnappers." He licked his lips. "So I reached out to his family."

"Family?" Cross asked. "You mean his uncle."

"I didn't know what else to do. Brent said if something ever happened to him, I should call Luther Bianchi. He'd given me a number for one of his uncle's associates, so that's who I called."

"When did Brent tell you that?" I asked.

"Years ago, like six weeks after he arrived in L.A. Brent has a tenuous relationship with his father, and his mother already has enough on her plate. I thought that's why he figured his uncle was his best bet."

"Have you ever met Luther Bianchi?" Cross asked.

"No, and after all this, I'm not sure I want to." Sylvio picked up the water bottle, his hand shaking. "Luther said he'd handle as much as he could from his end, but he needed me to do some things for him. He promised whatever was happening, he'd find a way to get Brent back safely."

"What did he want you to do?" I asked.

Sylvio pulled a crinkled note from his back pocket and smoothed it out on the coffee table. If there had been any physical evidence on the note, it was gone now. "He told me to go to Brent's house and retrieve whatever was under the mat. This is what I found."

Cross turned his attention to me. "Did you look under the mat?"

"I looked everywhere. There was no note or any kind of communication."

"I found this Saturday night," Sylvio said.

"Why didn't you show it to me yesterday?" Cross fought to keep his tone neutral, but he was seething.

"Luther told me not to tell anyone about it."

"Lucien," I warned, afraid my boss might snap, "easy."

Cross circled the room, taking slow breaths. Once he was calm, he put a gentle hand on Sylvio's shoulder while he read the neatly printed words on the page. "*Pay us what we are owed, or we will dismantle your life, piece by piece. You have twenty-four hours.*" Cross frowned. "Who does Brent owe?"

"He doesn't owe anyone anything. I have no idea what that's about."

"Maybe that message was meant for Luther," I suggested. "He sent you to retrieve it. How did he know it was there?"

"I assume he contacted the kidnapper, and those were the directions he was given," Sylvio said.

"Could be." Cross examined the paper carefully. "Do you know why Fenton Roundtree was in the office on Saturday? Does he normally go in on weekends?"

"No, that was a first. I was surprised when the police told me he'd been shot inside the building."

"Do you think he was threatened too?"

Sylvio blanched. "I can't even imagine. Why would anyone do these terrible things? Brent's such a nice guy."

Cross met my eyes. "I'll have Justin phone Roundtree's wife and see what he can discover." Cross pulled out his phone but didn't dial. Instead, he tapped the device against his chin a few times. "May I see the texts you received?"

Handing Cross his phone, Sylvio gave him instructions on locating the messages. "The first one came in around seven, I think."

While Cross read the texts, I got up to examine the threatening note. It had been professionally printed on cardstock and looked like a telegraph. The watermark indicated the shop that printed it. I took a few snapshots and sent them to Amir to analyze.

"Did you receive any other communications or threats besides these?" Cross asked.

"Just one more which came in this morning." He scrolled down the screen. *Don't play games.*

"Did you reach out to anyone else after receiving the original messages?"

"Like who? The police?" Sylvio sighed. "In hindsight, maybe I should have, but I was afraid what would happen if I did."

"Next time, call me before you do anything. Do you understand?" Cross stared at him with a ferocity I'd never seen before.

"Ye-yes, sir."

"Let me see if we can determine where these messages originated or who this bastard is." Cross took Sylvio's phone and stepped into the hallway.

"Do you know what Fenton Roundtree kept in the middle drawer of his filing cabinet?" I asked.

"Um..." Sylvio closed his eyes, his brow furrowing. "A laptop, pending contracts, possibly a bottle of spirits, and his lunchbox."

"What information was stored on the laptop?"

"Company basics, payroll, employee records, our proprietary editing and recording software."

"Is that valuable?"

"I guess. It's what we use to edit and master tracks. Our programming team wrote it with input from several conductors and composers. It allows us to produce tracks at a fraction of the time. In dollars and cents, it isn't worth millions, but it's pretty cool."

"Why did he have that on his laptop?" Most VPs in a company that size didn't get their hands dirty doing technical things.

"He liked to bring it to meetings with clients to show them the progress we were making or to convince potentials of our capabilities."

"Was there anything else of value on the laptop or in the drawer?"

"Fenton kept our business information and client accounts on that computer, so he'd have whatever he needed at his fingertips. As far as what else he had in that drawer, I'm not sure. Do you think that's why he was killed? Is this what these bastards thought they were owed? Is that what the note was about?"

"I don't know." I didn't think computer software or client accounts were worth killing over, but people killed for lesser reasons every day. "Do you know if Fenton had any personal or professional issues? Did he owe anyone money? Did he steal another company's clients?"

"I don't think so. He was a good guy. I can't picture him doing any of those things."

"How did the crisis negotiators get involved in this mess?"

Before Sylvio could answer, Cross let out a grunt and hung up the phone. "Justin will look into the texts you received. The user who sent them doesn't have a registered account, which makes even less sense, but we'll figure it out. I have a crack team working on it. We've already determined the note you found beneath the mat came from a messenger service who took the order over the internet, printed the message, and delivered it to Brent's address. They'd been given instructions to leave the envelope under the mat if no one answered the door."

"Do we know who sent it?" I asked.

"It'll take time before our techs are able to figure out who filled out the form."

"What about tracking the payment details?" I asked.

"The bastard used a prepaid credit card with a bogus address. Justin's looking into where the card originated." Cross sat at the counter, keeping an eye on Sylvio, who paced near the window, making the conscious effort not to touch the blinds. "What happened after you picked up the message?"

"I called Luther back and read it to him over the phone."

"Why didn't you tell me about this last night?" Cross asked, sounding like a broken record.

"Luther made it clear I shouldn't mention a word of this to anyone, but whatever he's doing isn't helping Brent. Brent trusted you. He hired you. That's the only reason I'm telling you any of this. You came here to help him. Luther didn't. That puts you a step ahead in my book."

"You should have thought about this yesterday. Does Luther know I'm taking over the negotiation?" Cross asked.

"I might have let it slip. I kept pressing him on those points you made yesterday about proof of life and ransom demands, but he never listened. I might have said you'd be better equipped to handle this."

"Did you mention that to anyone else?"

"No. No one knows about any of this except the two of you." Sylvio looked at me. "Three of you."

"So Luther told you to retrieve the note," Cross said. "Do

you think he's been communicating directly with the kidnappers?"

"He must be," Sylvio said.

"Unless Luther put them in contact with the crisis negotiators," I said.

Sylvio pointed at me. "Or that."

"What happened after you picked this up?" Cross tapped the note.

"That's when Luther told me he'd hire a team to handle the rest. He didn't want me to get hurt. I didn't ask any questions until after we met last night. Then I had a lot of questions to ask him. He wasn't particularly receptive to them."

"Did you hear from Luther today?" Cross asked.

"Yeah, I already told you about that. This morning, he sent me another text. He said the professional negotiators he hired needed a neutral location for a drop-off. That's when I thought of you and gave him your office address, remember?"

"Oh, I remember." Cross stuffed his fists into his pockets. "Frankly, I'd rather forget. Have you heard anything since then?"

Sylvio shook his head. "I tried contacting Luther, but I can't get in touch. His associate's number is out of service or something." He took a deep breath. The anti-anxiety meds must have finally kicked in. He appeared calmer, more in control. "At this point, I don't care who I talk to, just as long as I find someone who can figure out where Brent is and bring him home safely." He met Cross's eyes. "He's my best friend. If you can help him, do it. Whatever it takes, please. I don't want him to die."

SEVENTEEN

The sun beat down on us, but I resisted the urge to roll the window down. We wouldn't be here that much longer. Cross hadn't said a word to me since we walked out of the safe house. Until five minutes ago, he'd been talking to Justin while I attempted to verify everything Sylvio said. By the time he hung up, Justin had promised to set up a meeting with Luther Bianchi.

"Do you trust him?" I finally asked.

"Bianchi?" Cross shook his head. "We don't have a choice."

"What about Sylvio?"

"Not entirely."

"That would explain why you asked Nero and Omar to keep an eye on him." I pointed as the SUV drove past the house, circled around, and parked in a different spot. "I hope Miranda won't mind."

"She'll expect me to make it up to her." Cross snorted. "Actually, that doesn't sound so bad. I could go for a little of that after a day like today."

"Hey," I nudged him, "this isn't your fault. They kept you in the dark."

"I knew it last night, but Luther said he had it under

control. I never should have believed him. I should have insisted he let me handle it."

"He wouldn't have listened anyway."

"Probably not." He jerked his chin at my phone. "When do you expect to hear back from Mercer's team? This can't wait."

"They'll get back to me as soon as they can. If they're in the middle of a job, it could be a while. Bastian didn't give me a timetable, but he would have told me if he expected a lengthy delay."

"I'll work on an alternative solution in case we need it." Cross sent a text to Justin. "He'll reach out to the insurance agencies we haven't contacted yet and see if they have any in-house negotiators they can spare or if they can make any recommendations." He put the phone down, only to pick it up a second later. "Miranda might know someone. She's been famous a long time. She's seen it all." He shot off another text. Before he could put the phone down, she responded. Whatever she said made my boss smile for the first time today. Chuckling to himself, he replied. The phone chimed again. He snickered. "Naughty minx."

"Cross?"

He glanced at me, the smile dissolving. He responded, read her reply, and put his phone down. "She'll get back to me after she has some time to ask around."

"I thought you were involved with someone."

Cross's expression soured further. "Where would you have gotten that idea?"

"Don't forget, I've seen you with Jade. Justin seems to think—"

"Jade and I aren't exclusive. Life's too hard. We go far too long without seeing each other for that to be feasible. But remind me to have a talk with Justin about spreading rumors." He pulled out of the space and waved to Omar as we passed. "If Sylvio goes anywhere, they'll follow him. We're not getting jerked around anymore. What did Jablonsky have to say about the RICO investigation?"

"The agent in charge hoped to convince Brent to inform on his uncle. But the FBI doesn't have any leverage on Brent. At first, they thought Barber Productions might be a front for cleaning Bianchi's money, but none of the forensic accountants could ever get that to hold up."

"Brent stays away from shady shit. He's careful, more than most people. Given his blood relatives, he has every reason to be cautious."

"Is that why you like to push the limits sometimes? Is that how you push back against your family ties?"

"I didn't realize this case had anything to do with me. And I don't recall psychotherapy being taught at Quantico, nor were you ever a behavioral analyst, so keep the therapy lecture to yourself, unless you want me to turn it around on you."

"Message received." I clamped my mouth shut. Normally, I didn't buy into that stuff, but Cross had brought it up in such a way I couldn't help but think he must be projecting. Damn, grief counseling was getting to me. I'd have to cut that out before I completely lost my mind.

"This still makes no sense," Cross said. "From what Sylvio told us, it sounds like Luther Bianchi was in contact with the kidnappers from the very beginning. He knew the note had been left under the mat. They could have contacted him first, and the unknown texts Sylvio received came from one of Bianchi's guys as a test of loyalty or something like that. After all, Brent could be used as leverage against the old man."

"We don't have any evidence to support that," I said. "But given the package we received today, I'm guessing Bianchi didn't comply with the kidnapper's demands, so I don't see how this is a test."

Cross stared out the windshield. "Bianchi won't talk on the phone. Even when he communicated with Sylvio, it was through encrypted texts via an app using an unknown associate's account and phone. I'll have to fly home to meet with him. Once we sit down face-to-face, I'll have a better sense of what's going on."

"Do we have time for that?"

"Do you have any better ideas? Sylvio said he'd loop us in, but since he failed to tell me most of this when we spoke last night, he could be withholding more details. Even if he's not, he might in the future."

"Why didn't Brent come to you with whatever this is? Cross Security had that system installed in his office. You should have been his first call when things went wonky."

"I don't know. It makes no sense. Maybe I should have pushed when we met last month to discuss the upgrades."

"This isn't your fault."

"No, it's Luther's." Cross slammed his palm on the steering wheel. "I wouldn't have thought Bianchi's problems would follow his nephew across the country. What if all the kidnapper wants is to torture Luther Bianchi?"

I didn't have an answer, at least none that I wanted to voice for fear of facing future prosecution. "Mercer will know what to do, but there are a few things you ought to know. Mercer's team will do whatever it takes to get a positive recovery, even if it means making a mess."

"How big of a mess?"

"You might want to have an entire legal team waiting in the wings to assist Almeada and Ganz. And you should probably start searching for jury consultants now."

Cross scratched his chin. "Our contract is for work to be done at Barber Productions. I'll have Almeada review what we signed. That might be rock solid enough to insulate us."

I didn't see how, but I didn't waste my breath pointing it out. "Mercer will also expect to get paid."

"I'll cover it, if Brent can't. No one works for free. That's one lesson you should take to heart."

"I'll think about it. But if the kidnappers are operating locally and things go sideways, I don't have any sway with local law enforcement. Petrocelli doesn't seem the pliable, bendy type when it comes to filing charges or throwing the rulebook away. Mercer will have an exit strategy. You and I don't have that luxury."

"I'll see if anyone at the office has friends out here. Like you pointed out, I've hired investigators from a lot of different agencies. Surely, the LAPD owes one of my people a favor."

"There's one other thing that's bothering me."

"What's that?"

"Adrianna's also MIA. Everyone says she's away on a work trip, but most couples talk on the phone when one of them is traveling. By now, she should have expected a call or text from Brent. Why hasn't she texted him or left a voicemail? You've been monitoring his phone records. We know she hasn't reached out."

"I'll have Justin check into it. He can pull her call logs."

"Tell him to keep up-to-date on Sylvio's too."

"We've been monitoring his since Brent went missing. The reason we didn't know about the texts was because those were received through a gaming app. No one outside the game would have any record of it."

"Only someone who knows Sylvio would know to contact him that way."

"Unless whoever's responsible got close enough to check out Sylvio's phone."

"That could be anyone he met at a bar, went on a date with, encountered in the men's room, or who hung around his desk while he was off running an errand. I'll go over Barber Productions' sign-in sheet and appointment calendar and run everyone who's dropped by in the last six weeks."

"Don't forget, some of these people might travel with assistants and entourages."

"Right." This might be our first lead, but I couldn't shake Adrianna's lack of communication. "Don't you think Adrianna visited Brent at work at some point?"

"Sure."

"Couldn't she have gained access to Sylvio's phone or Brent told her what games his assistant plays and what his handle is? If they are best friends, like Sylvio insists, Adrianna would have access to all of that. The three of them must have socialized plenty of times."

"Do you think she has something to do with this?"

"Either that, or she could be another potential victim." I wondered why Petrocelli hadn't explored that option. But since he lacked proof Brent Barber was missing, he had no reason to go down that rabbit hole.

After pulling up Adrianna's information again, I tried calling her at work. "Hi," I said, "I'm looking for Adrianna

Keys."

"Have you tried her cell?"

"I have, but she didn't answer."

"She's not in right now. I can take a message."

"Do you know when she's expected back?"

"Anytime, really."

"She doesn't have set hours?"

The person on the other end of the line thought I was crazy. "Scouting talent doesn't run on a schedule. Only the show does."

"Right, sorry." I gave her my first name and phone number, hoping Adrianna would call me back, but I wasn't counting on it. According to Adrianna's coworker, no one had seen her since she left work Friday night. "Did she return to her hotel?" I asked.

"Probably."

"But you don't know?"

"I'm not her keeper. Girl can do whatever she wants."

"Do you know if she had plans to see her boyfriend?"

"Boyfriend? No, I don't think so." From her tone, I didn't think she knew Adrianna had a boyfriend.

After hanging up, I called the hotel. I spoke to someone different this time. It took less than five minutes to find out Adrianna had returned to her room Friday night and left Saturday morning after breakfast. But she hadn't gone back to the hotel since. "Are you sure she didn't check out?" I asked.

"Positive," the desk clerk said.

"Thanks." I gave her my phone number. "Have her call me when she returns." I put my phone down. "No one's seen Adrianna since Saturday morning. She might have gone missing around the same time Brent did."

"What are you thinking?" Cross pulled into the garage and parked beside my car.

"She's wrapped up in this somehow. That's the only explanation."

"Is anyone worried about her? Has she missed any appointments?"

"They said she's scouting talent and doesn't stick to a schedule." We already had four dead and one missing. Now it looked like it might be two missing. At this rate, there wouldn't be anyone left standing by dinnertime. "We need to find her. At the very least, we need to know if she figures into any of this."

"She's supposed to be out of town." Cross killed the engine and picked up his phone. After shooting off a few rapid-fire texts and getting responses equally as fast, he put the phone in his pocket. "She's in San Diego. Justin pinged her phone to verify it. He's narrowed her location down to a few blocks. It looks like she's in her hotel. Are you sure the desk clerk knows what she's talking about?"

"There's only one way to find out."

EIGHTEEN

Cross tried texting the kidnappers from Sylvio's account, hoping to open a line of communication. But the app said the message could not be sent; the user did not exist. While Amir and the techs worked to figure that out, Cross and I headed for San Diego, hoping to have better luck finding answers there.

We'd been on the road for almost twenty minutes when an unknown number called my phone. I put it on speaker. "Hello?"

"We'll be on the next flight to JFK," Julian Mercer said.

"LAX."

"What the bloody hell are you doing there?"

"The job's in Los Angeles."

Mercer barked the correction to Bastian. "What's your connection to the victim?"

"He's a Cross Security client."

"No emotional attachment then?"

I'd forgotten how succinct Mercer could be. Though, he did seem quite a bit chattier than what I remembered. I looked at Cross, who shook his head. "None."

"Good." Mercer waited a beat. "Tell me what you know so far." So I did. "Are you sure the shooters abducted your client?"

"Video surveillance proves it. Right after they escaped, they went to Brent's house and grabbed him."

"And he was alive?"

"As of Saturday afternoon."

"Four dead." He paused. "We need proof of life."

"That's easier said than done. We don't even have an open line of communication with the kidnappers."

"Do you know who they're targeting for the ransom?"

"We're guessing Luther Bianchi since Sylvio contacted him and he knew about the message beneath the mat."

"If Bianchi's the target, why would the kidnappers reach out to this Sylvio chap? Could he be who they are targeting for the ransom? He's the assistant. He has access to company assets. He could be in a position to provide them whatever they want, whatever they believe they are owed and warned Barber about."

"Possibly." I hadn't thought of that. I glanced at Cross.

"Negative," Cross said, sounding far more militaristic than I'd ever heard. "Bianchi told Sylvio to pick up the note. He must have made some sort of arrangement with the kidnappers since he knew it was getting delivered and where it would be. For all we know, they contacted him directly prior to Sylvio reaching out. We haven't nailed down the timeline yet."

"When will you?" Mercer asked.

"Once I meet with Luther Bianchi," Cross said.

"Unless Bianchi's responsible for the abduction," Mercer said.

"Nothing indicates that," Cross argued.

"Nothing disproves it. Send me what you have. We'll put together dossiers."

"I already have profiles for those involved," I said.

"They haven't helped."

I gritted my teeth. Mercer always knew how to push my buttons. "I'm also sending you the photos and video I took of the shooters on Saturday and the delivery guy who left the heads on our doorstep. They aren't amateurs, but we haven't found anything on them yet."

"I'll contact you once we land." Mercer hung up without

another word.

Lucien turned to me, taking his eyes off the road. "I thought you said he wouldn't show up without knowing the situation."

"I guess he's bored." I licked my lips. "Mercer made some valid points. Do you think Bianchi's behind this?"

"What's his motive?"

"I don't know, unless he's afraid Brent's going to inform on him to the Feds."

"That's possible. Brent isn't exactly a typical kidnap victim. He makes a decent salary, but nothing too exorbitant. He doesn't carry ransom insurance. He isn't a celebrity or high-profile personality. He lives in a nice enough house with his live-in girlfriend. She isn't independently wealthy, but like Brent, she makes an okay salary but not enough to make this a worthwhile payday. They have no known enemies. Outside of work, they keep a low-profile. They'd make lousy targets for someone who's just in this for a large payout."

"Still, if this is about Brent and Luther, why did the shooters-turned-abductors torture Roundtree and steal whatever was in his filing cabinet? Are you positive Barber Productions isn't involved in anything shady?" I asked.

"You've seen their financials, client list, and project calendar. Everything matches up."

"That doesn't mean they aren't cooking the books or hiding something."

"What did Jablonsky have to say about that?"

"The forensic accountants couldn't find anything to use against Brent."

"See?" Cross kept his eyes on the mirrors as he maneuvered through traffic. "This feels personal." He adjusted in his seat. "And while you make some good points, I don't think Luther would do this to his nephew. At the very least, why would he hire crisis negotiators and lead them to their deaths? That makes absolutely no sense. Why would Mercer even suggest that?"

"He's seen something similar happen before."

"I'm hoping that's the exception and not the rule."

"Let's go over it again from the top." I opened a blank

document on my laptop and made a list of bulleted points. "Whoever these men are, they knew Adrianna wasn't home. They disabled the cameras. They knew how to get inside Brent's house and get out without setting off any alarms. Everything about them reads like professionals, but they know things, private things, like what Roundtree keeps in his filing cabinet." I still didn't know what possessed Fenton Roundtree to go to the office that day, but there had to be a reason. If we could figure out what that was, we might be able to figure out who the shooters were or what they wanted. I made a note of that at the bottom of the page.

"Those weird occurrences at Barber Productions were probably the shooters testing the system to see how to bypass it. They were trial runs. Maybe that's how they created a master key. They unlocked one door at a time," Cross said.

"Sylvio said things went missing and were moved. That wasn't just a trial run. They were looking for something, probably whatever Roundtree had in his office."

Cross reached for his phone, keeping one eye on the road while he hit speed dial. "Nero, send your best tech wizard to Barber Productions and sweep for bugs. Leave whatever you find in place, but let Justin know how complicated it is. If we need a specialist to handle it, he'll assign someone to check it out."

"Mercer has a guy who can do that," I said.

Cross nodded. "Forget that. Just tell me the verdict. I want to know if the building's been compromised. Ignore the tech I planted." Cross placed the phone in the cupholder.

"Do you think the shooters planted devices inside the building to subvert security?" I asked.

"Possibly or they planted bugs to collect intel or comb the internal servers. Assuming Sylvio is correct in his assumption that a company laptop was taken, the kidnappers must be looking for something. I'm guessing they need Brent in order to find it or access it."

"They might need Sylvio to get whatever they don't have," I suggested. "Do you think they'd kidnap Adrianna to use as bait or to force Brent to comply with their demands?"

"Let's not jump to conclusions. We don't even know if she's missing. Justin spoke to Adrianna's boss. She's been busy all week, ever since she arrived to do some remote scouting. She might have left her phone on silent or she's taking some time to unplug and recharge before getting back to it."

"That sounds way too optimistic and highly unlikely."

"Perhaps, but as far as I can tell, the kidnappers never communicated with Brent prior to the note they left with his sushi. We checked every phone line he had access to. If they took Adrianna, they wouldn't have had to fight him in the house or force him into the trunk. He would have gone willingly. He loves her too much to do anything to jeopardize her safety."

"But the note said last chance. They must have made other threats. We just haven't found them."

"Something tells me we won't."

A million thoughts went through my head. "Harming negotiators breaks every rule in the book. The kidnappers can't be trusted, which means Brent's chances aren't great. They had no problem killing Roundtree and the guard. They would have killed me too. Their actions were perfectly orchestrated until I messed everything up."

"You've seen them. You're a loose end."

"The gas station surveillance feed got a look at them. The police have the photos on their website."

"Regardless, they haven't issued a notice or warning to the public. Do you find that odd?"

"I don't know how the LAPD operates. They might not want to cause a panic."

"Or they have some inkling about what's going on and don't want to show their hand just yet."

"How could they know what's going on?"

Cross stiffened, his grip tightening on the wheel. "I don't know. The crisis negotiators could have had files or intel the police have already seen. All I know is Petrocelli seemed awfully sure of himself."

"When Mercer arrives, the two of you can exchange

conspiracy theories. In the meantime, let's work with what we know."

"Which is?"

"The shooters didn't ransack any of the other offices, not even Brent's. They only wanted what was in Roundtree's filing cabinet. Whatever it was, it fit inside an aluminum briefcase. It could have been money, files, or some sort of documentation. If they just wanted the company laptop, they didn't have to wait for Roundtree to go to the office or torture him for intel. They could have taken it whenever they wanted." I watched another mile marker zoom by. "How do you think they lured him into the office?"

"I don't know, Alex. Sylvio says he had no idea Roundtree would be at work."

"Last night, when you told me you were working on it, did you know what was going on? What did Sylvio tell you?"

"The same things he said in the safe house. You heard him. He only gave me the bare minimum. He thought Luther was handling it. He didn't tell me anything else."

"Did you tell him about the shredder in the office and the threatening note we found with Brent's blood on it?"

He took his hands off the steering wheel for a moment to flex his fingers. "It was pertinent. Luther had a right to know."

I typed in the names of the crisis negotiators, making sure the internet hotspot I'd set up was connected. "Crisis negotiators shouldn't resort to violence as their first recovery attempt, but it looks like these two missed that memo. Did Luther hire them to conduct a negotiation or follow through on a hit?"

Cross stretched his neck from side to side. "I'm not sure. I haven't spoken to him about it, but when I do, I have no intention of asking that. Plausible deniability, have you heard of it?"

"Could that be the game the kidnappers were talking about?"

"I don't know. All I can say for certain is Sylvio never received a ransom demand or proof of life. He gave

Luther's associate the information to reach out to the kidnappers, but I can't access that account. However, if the kidnappers message Sylvio again, we'll know about it."

"You put spyware on his phone?" I chuckled. "Nice move. Bastian will be impressed."

"Bastian?"

"Mercer's righthand man."

I jotted down a few more notes concerning my encounter with the shooters. They didn't wear masks, and with the silenced weapons they carried, they didn't plan on letting anyone live. I saved the file and uploaded everything to Bastian's dropbox.

NINETEEN

San Diego wasn't that far away. We'd get there in two hours, figure out what was going on with Adrianna, and head back. But I couldn't help but wonder what Detective Petrocelli would do to me if he realized I'd left town. Perhaps he'd throw a party, but given his warning on Saturday, I had trouble believing that. Luckily, he never had to know about this.

I let out an exasperated sigh and continued digging up everything I could on Adrianna Keys. Her name alone had been enough to send my radar buzzing. Justin forwarded me the background checks Cross had already conducted. According to everything they'd found, Adrianna Melody Keys was her real name. How a music producer found a woman with that name to be his girlfriend was beyond believable. It was almost as if she'd been created exactly for him. The only way to make her more perfect would be if she changed her first name to Piano.

"Did you know she's a talent scout for one of those reality TV shows?" I asked.

"Uh-huh."

"They sent her to San Diego to look for contestants for one of those music competitions. I'm sure she must have signed a non-compete and some fancy NDAs, but I can't help but think the talent she doesn't sign might get passed along to Brent in the hopes they can assist him on his projects."

"That depends on how useful they'd be when it comes to digital sound production."

"Have you seen what they do at Barber Productions?" I asked. "Brent has an orchestra at his disposal, not to mention several different vocal talents. Everything about their relationship is perfect." Maybe we had the motive wrong. If they'd both been taken, this might not have anything to do with Brent, it could have to do with Adrianna and the music business.

"It makes sense. Music is how they connected online."

"I still don't see how online dating is a good idea."

Cross chuckled. "It worked for them."

"Does Brent know she used to strip?"

"I told him as soon as I discovered it. That was around the time Brent asked her to move in with him."

"He didn't care?"

"For most men, snagging a dancer comes with bragging rights."

I scanned the intel on my screen, but I didn't see any indication that she was involved in any illegal enterprises. "What about health implications?"

"She was never arrested for prostitution. Her medical records didn't show a series of STIs or the usual issues sex workers face. I don't think she ever turned tricks. She didn't work in one of those clubs."

"There aren't a lot of clubs that aren't like that. Who owned it?"

"I don't remember."

I scrolled up the page, pausing halfway through to close my eyes and take a deep breath. The last thing I needed was to get carsick. Reading while in motion wasn't a great way to avoid it. Sucking in another breath, I blew it out through my mouth. When I opened my eyes, the headache and nausea remained.

"Do you have any gum?" I asked.

Cross shifted in his seat and pulled a pack from his

pocket. "You look sweaty. You didn't look that bad when we opened the box. Are you feeling okay?"

I unwrapped a stick and put it in my mouth. Chewing would help. I wasn't sure why, but it always did. "I'm fine."

He gave me a sideways look before tucking the gum back into his pocket. "Don't ralph in the rental. Let me know if I need to pull over." We didn't speak for the next five miles. "Well?" he finally asked.

"I'm fine."

"No, not that. What did you find on Adrianna?"

"The club where she worked doesn't appear to be connected to Luther Bianchi or to anyone in Brent's sphere. Nothing connects her to Roundtree. I found several photos of her, Brent, and Sylvio online, but Sylvio said they were best friends. They all hung out together. She doesn't appear to be connected to whatever this is. She's a California girl, through and through, so if this is some sort of payback aimed at Luther Bianchi, the kidnappers would have no reason to target Adrianna, just like they'd have no reason to murder Roundtree."

"They met online before Brent relocated," Cross said. "But I agree."

"Is she the reason he moved here?"

"Not exactly. They dated long-distance for a while, but Brent always intended to move to L.A. He figured he might as well get a jump on the dating game by searching for matches in the area."

"Wow, someone planned ahead."

"He didn't want to be sucked into the Bianchi world and he definitely didn't want to spend his life fighting over political ideology and promising backers money in exchange for favors like his father. Los Angeles provided him with a lot more opportunities. It was a smart move, until now."

I thought about that for a moment while I stared out the windshield, focusing on the road ahead instead of the trees and signs which whipped past us. "If Brent and Adrianna have no secrets, the kidnappers might try to get whatever it is out of her if Brent doesn't cooperate."

"That's assuming they want intel or access to something.

We don't know what they want." Cross tapped the speed dial and hit the speaker button. "Justin, tell me you found something."

"Amir pinged Adrianna's phone, but it hasn't moved locations since the last time we checked. According to this, it's still in the vicinity of the hotel. We can't get an exact address, but I'm guessing it might be in her room."

"What about her work routine? Have you figured out where she's been hanging out during her off hours or who she's been seeing?"

"We've retraced her steps and spoken to several of her friends and colleagues. Her credit card records show charges at several different restaurants and bars, but none of them have been used since Friday night. Given the charges, it looks like she wasn't alone. Don't ask how, but I've seen surveillance footage from one particular restaurant. On Monday and Thursday, she was with the same man. He appears to be in his early to mid-thirties. They look cozy."

"Do you think she's having an affair?" I asked.

"Possibly, or he could be a honey trap the abductors used to lure her away without causing a commotion."

"We need an ID," Cross said. "That could be her kidnapper, if she's been kidnapped."

"I'm on it, boss."

"Thanks, Justin. What about Fenton Roundtree?"

"Nothing popped on him. He's clean. I spoke to his wife and combed through his phone and internet activity. As far as I can tell, he never received a threat. His wife was with him all night Friday. She said no one made any deliveries or dropped off any messages."

"What about game apps and encrypted texts?" Cross asked.

"Roundtree didn't waste his time with those things. He never behaved oddly or acted worried. I've already reviewed his business communications, his work e-mail, and the group chats the production teams at Barber used. Again, I found nothing."

"Does his wife know why he went to the office on Saturday?" I asked.

"He told her he forgot something at work and wanted to pick it up. While he was there, he figured he'd review the progress they'd made on a few projects in the hopes of ducking out early on Monday. That would have been their anniversary. He had made reservations at a Michelin-starred restaurant and promised her a trip to the jewelry store afterward. I contacted the store. Roundtree paid cash for a four carat diamond anniversary band. The store owner said Mrs. Roundtree had no idea."

"Damn," I said. "How much did that set him back?"

"Almost eight grand."

"At least we know why he went to work that day. Could the killers have taken that ring from his office?" Cross asked.

"No, sir. He hadn't picked it up yet. He wanted to wait until he took his wife to the store, so it could be properly sized."

"Did Roundtree tell his wife what he left behind at the office?" Cross asked.

"She has no idea. She thought that was just his excuse so he could put in the time in order to take half a day Monday."

"All right. Dig deeper into Sylvio and make sure everything he told us is true and keep an eye on his phone. The second he receives a call or message I want to know about it."

"I'm on it, boss."

Cross hit the end call button and put on his signal light when he saw the sign for our exit. "Hopefully, we'll find Adrianna and she can shed some light on this situation. Perhaps Brent told her to volunteer for this assignment because he knew it wasn't safe at home and didn't want her in danger. You're right. The threat left with his sushi delivery makes me think he knew what was going on. I just don't know why he didn't say anything about it to me."

TWENTY

Adrianna Keys wasn't hiding in her hotel room or chilling at the pool. Cross convinced the hotel to let us see the security footage. The last time she'd been caught on video surveillance was Saturday morning. She'd left her room, dressed in a stylish skirt and sleeveless top. She carried an oversized purse, which she'd filled with some fruit from the breakfast bar before leaving the hotel. From what I could tell, she didn't appear to be under any duress.

"Her car is parked in the hotel garage," Cross said. "Since she didn't use her credit cards, I don't think she called for a ride."

"She could have taken a taxi." I jerked my chin toward a yellow cab that dropped off a charge at the front entrance.

Cross leaned against the desk. "Could I get a look at her room charges?"

"I'm sorry, sir," the desk clerk said. "That's against hotel policy."

"Right." Cross peered down at the monitor. "Do you know if she called for a cab? We know she left Saturday morning and has yet to return. Her car is here." The clerk looked torn. "Please. Not to sound melodramatic, but lives are at stake."

She scratched her forehead. "Give me a second." The freshly manicured French tips clacked softly against the keyboard. "Ms. Keys didn't make or receive any calls to her room. She ordered room service several nights and a few movies. That was about it."

"Was anyone else staying in her room?" I asked.

The clerk bit her lip. "Occupancy is listed as one. We only gave her a single room key."

"Still, she might have had a dinner guest or an overnight visitor at some point."

"I'm sorry. I don't know anything about that."

Cross held out his phone with a frozen surveillance image of the man Adrianna met for dinner on Thursday night. "Have you seen him here?"

The clerk leaned closer. "No, sir. Do you think he did something to Ms. Keys?"

"We aren't sure."

She blew out a breath. "You saw the surveillance footage. Did you spot him anywhere on it?"

"No." Cross slipped her his card and a few folded bills. "Thank you for your help. Let me know if Adrianna returns. It's imperative I get in touch with her."

"Yes, sir."

Turning, I studied the lobby. It was like most mid-priced hotels. The surveillance footage hadn't shown any guests, invited or otherwise, entering Adrianna's room. "We could flash her photo around. But I'm not sure what good it'll do. Whatever happened to her didn't happen here."

"Check around the pool. I'll speak to the parking attendant and see if he remembers anything."

Cross and I split up. The pool didn't show any signs of foul play, so I wandered around the grounds. Security cameras only covered the doorways. The hotel had three entry points, one of which was inside the fenced in pool area. The other two were at the front and rear. With so many guests and staff coming and going, this wasn't the ideal place to stage an abduction.

Ten minutes later, I circled back to the valet stand.

Cross stood with his hands in his pockets, waiting for the parking attendant to bring the car around.

"Anything?" he asked.

"Nope. This was a waste of time."

"Only because hotel management wouldn't let us inside her room."

"We need to find out if her phone's there. Do you think she left it on purpose?" I asked. "You saw the footage. When she left Saturday morning, she looked like a tourist on vacation. She didn't look like she was in fear of her life or worried about her boyfriend."

Cross tipped the valet as I slid into the passenger seat. "Let's see what her coworkers can tell us."

I hoped our next stop wouldn't be a bust. Unfortunately, the woman I'd spoken to on the phone had already given me the highlights. However, visiting the office, which was a tiny, cramped conference room on the fifth floor of a television studio building, provided some insight into why Adrianna didn't have a set schedule and why she avoided the office as much as possible.

No one wanted to be squeezed inside, except the writers, who seemed to get a perverse pleasure out of the conflict the small space created, which only fueled their ideas for making the reality competition show more dramatic and entertaining. However, Bonnie, the production assistant, gave us a list of potential contestants Adrianna was supposed to interview and audition.

"Adrianna has a set schedule." I held the list out, pointing to the times and dates. "Britt Asani performed at the Blue Lagoon Café at nine o'clock Wednesday night. Dax Jefferson performed at open mic night at the Clamshell this past Monday." I scanned the rest of the sheet. Adrianna didn't have any auditions listed for Thursday.

A quick internet search revealed Dax Jefferson was the man she'd been cozying up to. As soon as we returned to the car, I ran a background check on him. He had a record for aggravated assault. He served all four years in Folsom state prison. Most offenders got released early for good behavior, but Jefferson served the max sentence.

"What did he do?" Cross leaned over the center console,

watching as I worked.

"He nearly beat a man to death." I zoomed in on the photo from the news article. It showed a slightly younger version of Adrianna's dining companion with a grin on his face as the cops hauled him toward the waiting cruiser in handcuffs. Blood spatter covered his face and chest. "He has gang tatts." I pointed to the one on his neck and the other on his forearm. I switched back to his criminal record. "I don't see any mention of it here or any other offenses listed." That was weird. I pulled up his last known address. "We should ask him about it."

It only took a few minutes to get to Dax's place. He had a studio apartment in one of the sketchier neighborhoods. A couple of corner boys eyed us as we stepped out of the sedan. One of them whistled at me.

"Yo," I called, "have either of you seen Dax around?"

"Dax who?"

"Jefferson." I took a step toward them, aware of my boss adjusting his jacket to allow easier access to his weapon.

"He just got home." The guy pointed to the building looming behind him. "Why? You got a beef with him or something?" He zeroed in on Cross's handgun.

"No, we just want to talk to him."

"You don't look like cops."

"That's because we're not." Cross kept his eyes on them. "My boss's girl has gone missing. She's been hanging around Dax for the last few days. Have you seen her around here?" Slowly, he held out his phone, flashing the surveillance photo at them.

"Naw, man. Dax's old lady lives with him. He wouldn't bring a side piece home unless he wanted his ass shot to bits."

Cross tucked the phone away. "You understand we still gotta make sure."

The corner boys made a hole, allowing us to pass. The one who whistled made an appreciative humming noise. Since he was probably close to ten years my junior, I decided to take it as a compliment instead of the insult it was.

"Having fun, Lucien?" I whispered once we entered the

building. "Are you trying to impersonate a mob hitter?"

"It worked, didn't it?"

"They didn't pose a threat."

"Did you see the elephant gun the one on the right had tucked behind his back? One wrong move, and he might have gotten an itchy trigger finger."

"Now you sound like Martin."

When we made it to Dax's apartment, Cross and I stood on either side of the doorway and knocked. A few seconds later, the door inched open.

"Can I help you?" Dax asked.

I smiled brightly. "We're following up on your audition for *Talented Musicians Across America*. May we speak inside?"

Dax opened the door wide. "You liked that, huh? Do you want to make another demo tape?"

"Actually, that's why we're here." I gave Cross a warning look to keep his mouth shut. "Adrianna never turned in the one you made."

"Are you serious? She made such a big deal on getting everything right. I can't believe she'd do that to me. She seemed so nice. I thought she was really into it."

"When's the last time you spoke to her?"

"Thursday. I met her at the studio. She gave me a tour."

"What time was that?" Cross asked.

"Like 5:30. It was after I got off work."

"Did you go anywhere afterward?" I asked.

"Yeah, she took me out to dinner. She said it was on the studio's dime. She said they wanted to woo me a little." He gave us a suspicious look. "I don't recognize either of you. Did you say you worked on the show?"

"We're here from L.A.," Cross said before I could tell him we were private investigators.

"So's Adrianna. She didn't mention you. What are your names?" He took a step back, noticing the concealed weapons we carried beneath our jackets. "Aww, damn. Not again."

"Take it easy." I held up my hands. I'd seen plenty of people rabbit. Right now, Dax was exhibiting all the signs he planned to make a break for it. "We're private investigators. Adrianna's missing. We need to find her."

Dax looked from me to Cross. "Is that true?"

I glanced at my boss, giving him a look. Cross raised his palms to elbow height. "It is."

Dax relaxed a little, his actions less twitchy, but his eyes continued to roam over the room while he determined the best escape routes. "Why are you asking me about this?"

"You might be one of the last people who spoke to her." I lowered my hands. "You hung out twice in the last seven days. She went to your performance at the Clamshell."

"Yeah, so? A lot of people were there. She heard plenty of other people sing. She told me she liked the way I sounded. That's why she invited me to tour the local studio. They had a sound booth. That's where I made the demo."

"Do you remember if anyone at the office made her nervous or uncomfortable?" I asked.

"We didn't really run into anyone. It was basically just Adrianna and me."

Cross looked around the room before taking a seat on the couch. He picked up the stack of magazines and flipped through them. I gave him a look, wondering why he had checked out of the conversation. He reorganized the magazines by date and replaced them on the coffee table before resting his outstretched arms along the back of the couch.

"What about at dinner? Or at the Clamshell? Did you notice anyone paying an inordinate amount of attention to her? Did anyone interrupt your dinner?" I asked.

Dax thought for a moment. "Not that I recall."

"Did you leave the restaurant together?"

"Yeah, she called for a rideshare."

"Did anyone follow you?"

"How would I know?"

"Given your history, it makes sense you'd pay attention to things like that." I nodded at the tattoo on his neck. "Have you done time?"

"What does that have to do with anything? I didn't hurt Adrianna. I wouldn't. She might be my ticket out of here."

"But you have a record." I waited.

He looked away. "I got into it with a rival a few years

back. The cops broke it up, arrested me, and didn't listen to a damn word I said. That's behind me now. I'm a free man. No parole. No nothing. I served my time."

"Did Adrianna know about that?"

Dax nodded. "That's part of the reason the show was so interested in having me compete. It'd be an underdog story, a tale of redemption, is what she called it. She was psyched. She said the audience would eat it up, and if the judges thought I had the talent to back it, I'd probably get a record deal and enough money to move somewhere nicer and safer. A place where I could raise a family."

"This is a waste of time," Cross muttered.

I gave him a stern look. *Zip it.* "Who got dropped off first?"

"She did." The light bulb flicked on above Dax's head. "A black four-door pulled past us while she was getting out of the car. They didn't go to the valet stand, but they idled a few feet past it. One guy got out. But the car didn't take off. It just stayed there. I thought that was weird."

"What time was this?"

"It was around midnight, I guess."

"Did you get a good look at the man?"

Dax shrugged.

I fished out my phone and found the photo I'd taken inside Barber Productions. "Do you recognize either of them?"

"That one, on the left, he might have been the guy who got out of the black car."

"Are you sure?"

"Not really." Dax rubbed his sweaty palms on his pant legs, leaving wet stains behind. "What's going to happen now? Adrianna's my contact. She scouted me. If something happened to her, I could lose my shot. You gotta find her. She has to be okay."

"Do you remember anything else? Did the man follow Adrianna inside? What happened to the black sedan?"

"He didn't follow her. He lit up a cigarette and moved away from the entrance, toward one of the benches since it's a smoke-free zone. As far as the car goes, it was still idling when we pulled away."

"Did Adrianna go inside the hotel?" Cross asked, climbing off the couch.

"Yeah, she said she had an early morning and planned to go straight to bed. She had to get to the office early to make sure her boss saw my demo."

"Have you seen the black car or either of these men since?" I asked.

"No."

Cross handed him a card. "Call us if you do."

TWENTY-ONE

"Why are you in such a rush?" I asked as Cross dragged me out of the apartment and down the stairs.

"Dax doesn't know anything."

"He saw the shooters. He recognized their car. If they were outside Adrianna's hotel, that means she didn't decide to go radio silent for a few days. They did something to her. For all we know, she's been taken or killed. We need answers. Dax might have them."

"He doesn't." Cross exhaled. "Think for a second, Alex. If he knew where she was, he would have told us. Given how much he has riding on this music competition, he didn't have anything to do with her disappearance."

"The shooters or kidnappers, whatever the hell they are, were here." I squinted as we emerged into the bright sunlight. "Adrianna left the hotel early Saturday morning. The timestamp on the security cams said it was before nine. She didn't look stressed or anxious. I don't think she expected trouble." That didn't explain why she and Brent hadn't talked or texted much that week. "Unfortunately, no one knows what she planned to do with her day. But whatever it was, she never made it there. The men must have done something to her before they went to Barber

Productions. The security guard might not have been their first kill that day."

"That isn't going to help us find Brent. We need proof. Facts. Evidence. Something."

I wondered if the San Diego PD would be more helpful or forthcoming than Detective Petrocelli. "I wonder if her body's been found."

"Her family or boss would have been notified. Justin would have heard about it." Cross cleared his throat. "We already reviewed the hotel's camera feed. We never saw a black sedan or the shooters. That means they didn't park in the hotel garage or enter the building. Continuing to search the hotel is pointless. That's a dead end. It doesn't matter what Dax saw. He didn't stick around long enough to see what happened after Adrianna went inside, and he never set foot inside the hotel either." Cross held up two ticket stubs. "I found these. Dax and his wife spent all day Saturday at the San Diego Zoo. They arrived a little after nine a.m. In case you had any lingering doubts, he isn't involved."

"He might have had more to tell us."

"Like what?" Cross checked his phone.

"I don't know. That's why we needed to ask more questions."

"Unlike you, I don't have time to waste."

I grumbled to myself and followed him to the car. I wasn't sure I'd survive putting up with my boss and Julian Mercer. One was bad enough.

"See ya, sugar," the corner boy called as I opened the door. "Next time you drop by, I hope it'll be to see me."

"You better hope not," I said under my breath.

Cross had yet to turn on the car. "Justin texted me. He arranged a meeting with Luther Bianchi first thing in the morning. I have to get back."

"So go." I noticed the corner boy who'd called out to me crouching down to see why we weren't moving. He took a few steps toward the car. Automatically, I hit the locks. "Now would be good."

Cross smirked and put the car in gear. "I thought you said they were harmless."

"Not harmless, but we could handle them. However, doing so would make a scene, which might involve a phone call to the police. Do you really have time for that? You said you have to get back. Where are you supposed to meet Bianchi?"

"For breakfast at one of his restaurants." Cross noted the time. "Justin booked me on a flight leaving from SAN in an hour and a half."

"You might just make it."

For the first time since he arrived in California, Cross looked torn. "You need backup. This isn't a background check or evaluation. We're looking into known killers turned kidnappers. This isn't the type of situation Cross Security usually handles. I don't want you doing anything alone."

"I'll be fine."

"I'm serious, Alex."

"So am I."

"Too bad. That's an order."

I laughed. "Are we going to have *that* conversation?"

"I mean it. Drop me off at the airport and drive my rental car back to Los Angeles. If you leave it at our office, I'll have someone pick it up and return it to the rental place. Wait until you hear from me before doing anything. When are the K&R specialists arriving?"

"Mercer didn't give me a time, but he'll find me once he sets up his base camp or whatever he calls it."

Cross pulled onto the freeway, keeping his eyes peeled for airport signs. "Nero's team is at your disposal. They can handle the situation with Sylvio and the sweep of Barber Productions without your input. If they find something, I'll let you know, and you can let Bastian take a look. Can I trust that you won't do anything without my say so?"

"Define anything."

"I'm serious, Ms. Parker."

"Clearly."

He worked his jaw for a moment, his fingers curling tighter around the wheel before releasing and repeating the process. I watched them move, realizing Cross was making fists while driving. "I'll have Justin book a second seat on the flight if this is too complicated a task."

"That won't be necessary, unless you want me to speak to Luther Bianchi for you." That was something I'd already been advised against and wasn't stupid enough to volunteer for, but I wanted to see what Cross would say. "That's probably much more dangerous than anything I'd do while you're gone."

"It might be a tossup."

"Then maybe you should reconsider giving me orders."

For the rest of the drive to the airport, he rehashed everything in the works, gave me the names and numbers for the lab he used, how to contact Nero, Omar, and several other teams he had operating in the area in case I couldn't wait for him or Justin to put me into contact with them, and reminded me to avoid the police at all costs, unless I found myself under fire or in an emergency situation. "If any trouble arises, don't hesitate to contact Jason Ganz. He'll handle whatever legal issues you have."

"No problem."

"And make sure you're at the office to supervise the phone installation. We need hardlines."

I gawked at him as he turned for the airport. "With everything going on, I don't see how that's a priority."

"Make it one." He pulled up behind a minivan. "Depending on how my meeting with Luther Bianchi goes, I should be back in L.A. sometime tomorrow. However, if something changes and I'm delayed, I'll have the hotel deliver my bag to your beach house. Is that okay?"

"Fine."

"All right." He tucked his weapon into the glove box and checked his pockets for his wallet, passport, and phone. "Watch your back."

"You too." I went around the car and got behind the wheel, adjusting the seat while Cross headed inside. The only good thing about this was I wouldn't have to worry about getting carsick on the return trip.

Except I wasn't ready to call it quits. We'd come all the way here to find Adrianna or figure out what happened to her. Instead, we were left with a giant question mark. She was gone, and the only thing I knew for sure was the shooters abducted her boyfriend and had been following her, possibly even staking out her hotel. Since they weren't responding to our attempts to negotiate Brent's release, I had to do something to figure out where they were. So I went back to the hotel.

By now, it was dark. The hotel and surrounding buildings had enough lights to make the streets seem safe, but with two shooters on the loose, I knew better. Hoping Justin wouldn't narc on me, I called and asked if he could ping Adrianna's phone again. It still hadn't moved, and it remained on.

They hadn't been able to pinpoint the exact location, but it had to be somewhere in or around the hotel. I'd start with her room and move outward. I entered the hotel and requested a room on the same floor as Adrianna's. The desk clerk from earlier remembered me.

"You still haven't found her?" she asked.

"No, but I want to stay close in case she returns." I slipped her a twenty, hoping that would be sufficient after Cross's generous contribution. "A connecting room would be even better."

She tapped the keyboard. "I'm sorry, Ms. Parker. Adrianna is in 503. There are no connecting rooms. I can put you in 507. It's two doors down or 508, if you'd rather be on the other side of the hallway. The other rooms are occupied."

"By whom?"

"I'm sorry I can't answer that. I shouldn't have even told you her room number."

Even if I stopped by the ATM, I didn't think her answer would change. "That's okay. Either room is fine."

"507 has a king. 508 has two doubles. The room rate is the same."

"507's fine." I handed her my credit card and license while she input my information.

With the room key in hand, I took the elevator up to the fifth floor. I didn't know Adrianna or her habits, but I hoped she had the ringer on her phone. When the elevator doors opened, I read the sign and scanned the room numbers until I found my way to 503.

After dialing her number, I pressed my ear against the door and waited, but I didn't hear any ringing. That didn't mean her phone wasn't there, but until I figured out how to get inside her room, I couldn't assume anything. The hallway remained empty, so I opened the app on my phone, but that had been designed specifically to thwart security systems. It did nothing to assist me in unlocking the hotel door.

After examining the handle and lock, I went to my room, slid the card through the reader, waited for the light to turn green, and depressed the handle. The room appeared just as expected. Aside from the bed, there was a small table and two chairs. Everything had been cleaned nicely. Adrianna's room would have the exact same setup.

I unlocked the door to the balcony and stepped outside. The exterior balconies didn't connect, but the gap between each one wasn't too far to navigate. Three feet, maybe four. But heights weren't my thing. And going splat from a fifth floor drop wasn't on my to-do list. So that would be plan B.

For plan A, I detoured to the ice machine and held down the button, allowing the ice to pour onto the floor. Then I wandered the halls until I found a courtesy phone. From there, I called the front desk and reported a large puddle on the fifth floor. I grabbed the ice bucket, slipped into one of the hotel provided robes, and waited outside 503.

Ten minutes later, two women in hotel uniforms pushed a cleaning cart past my room. "Dammit." I knocked harder on the door. "James, I left my key inside. Can you open the door?" I knocked again, turning to find the maids setting up wet floor signs around the mess I made. "Excuse me," I called.

"Yes, ma'am?" The closest one looked up while the other one pulled out a mop.

"I'm sorry to bother you." I peered around them. "I went to get ice, but I couldn't even get near the machine."

"We should have it cleaned up soon," she said.

"No, that's not what I was asking." I tried to look sheepish. "I locked myself out of my room, and my boyfriend's out on the balcony. I'd think by now he'd realize I never came back with the ice, but he's probably too busy checking sports highlights on his phone to notice I'm missing."

"That's not a problem." She stepped away from the mess, picking up the master key which hung from the side of the cleaning cart. She swiped it, unlocking the door. "There you go."

"Thank you so much."

She nodded before returning to the mess. I'd have to leave a nice tip for the trouble I caused. But that was neither here nor there. I pushed the door closed, flipped the lock, and engaged the security bar. Now to get down to business.

The first thing I did was call Adrianna's phone again. Nothing rang or buzzed. A suitcase had been propped open on top of the luggage rack while a hard-shelled rolling bag sat on the floor beneath it.

I started with the rolling bag, but it was empty. I checked for hidden compartments, but I didn't find any. The zippers on the other suitcase were fastened together with a tiny brass-colored lock. Since I hadn't thought to bring my lock picks or bolt cutters, I pulled out a pen, started near the end of the zipper, and shoved the writing end between the teeth. Once it was wedged in pretty good, I rocked the pen right and left until the teeth separated and I could slide the pen along the track, unzipping the suitcase.

Aside from her jewelry case, the locked bag contained paperwork and contracts relevant to her job and her laptop. I took that out and powered it on. Luckily, Adrianna had synced her devices. The missed calls and texts she received appeared on the side of her computer screen. Bingo.

Justin had already checked all of this, but I scanned everything again. Brent hadn't texted her since last Monday. His message was brief but encouraging with a few kissy face and heart emojis at the end. That was it.

Everything after that had to do with work. No one threatened her. She hadn't received any random or unknown calls.

I hit the locate device tool and waited for a pin to drop

on the map. After sending the precise location of Adrianna's phone to mine, I checked the rest of her computer. I didn't find any e-mails or dark web correspondence that indicated Adrianna was involved in whatever happened to Brent. Still, I couldn't be certain.

The photos I found on her hard drive and uploaded to the cloud made me think otherwise. Adrianna and Brent looked like the ideal couple. Two workaholics who bonded over their love of music.

After powering off her computer and returning it to her bag, I did my best to reseal it by sliding the locked double zippers along the track, pulling the unzippered teeth back together. A portion of the zipper remained open, bubbling out near the side, but it was better than nothing.

A quick search of the rest of her room didn't reveal anything. She traveled just like any other career woman. The only item of interest was a list of venues and attractions she wanted to explore. Included on this list was a whale watching cruise. Beside the cruise, she'd scrawled the day and time. *Saturday, 09:45.* That must have been her intended destination before she vanished.

The maids had left by the time I let myself out. I unlocked my door, took off the robe, left a tip on the dresser, and called Justin on my way down the stairs. He'd determine which whale watching cruise was scheduled for that time and get me the address and contact information, but at this time of night, the operation would have already shut down. It was too dark to see whales or dolphins. So that wasn't a priority. Finding her phone was.

The tracker led me down the sidewalk and across the street. I pushed open the door to the coffee shop and dialed her number. With the low hum of conversation and the hissing of the machines, I didn't hear any ringing. I hung up and went to the counter.

"Excuse me." Ignoring the dirty looks I received from the patrons waiting in line, I waved down the barista. "Do you have a lost and found?"

She reached beneath the counter and pulled out a basket. "What did you lose?"

"A cell phone."

She sifted through the items. "Sorry."

"No problem." I brought up a photo of Adrianna. "Did you happen to see this woman come in here?"

She squinted at my screen and shook her head.

"Were you here Saturday morning?" I asked.

"I was here all day Saturday." She tucked the basket beneath the counter and asked the next person in line for his order.

I dialed Adrianna's number one more time while I squeezed my way through the crowded coffee shop, past the condiment bar, and down the narrow hallway toward the bathrooms. Surprisingly, neither of them was in use, but Adrianna's phone wasn't there. The door at the end of the hallway had an emergency exit sign above it, but it had an alarm that would sound if I opened it.

Checking the pinned location again, I wandered outside. An athletic store stood on the other side of the coffee shop, but they were already closed. Maybe Adrianna's phone ended up in a dumpster. Perhaps she'd accidentally thrown it away while getting her morning coffee. I moved through the alleyway, aware of the long shadows cast by the discarded boxes and broken pallets.

I dialed her number again. A faint ringing sounded off to my left. I moved closer, wondering if I was hearing things. When I lifted the black lid off the green dumpster, the melodic chime grew louder. I leaned over the dumpster, praying I wouldn't find her body inside.

The glow of her phone shone through the refuse in the clear plastic trash bags. I bent over to move the bags out of the way, but there were too many. I tossed a few of them out of the dumpster. No body. At least not yet. I dug deeper, tossing more bags out. I could almost reach her phone when footsteps sounded behind me. I reached into my jacket just as something cold and hard pressed into the back of my neck.

"Hold it," a gruff voice warned. "Don't move."

I grasped the handle of my gun, but before I could clear leather, he pulled the trigger.

TWENTY-TWO

I hit the ground hard, a fire burning at the back of my neck. Pain shot down my back and through my extremities. My vision blurred before fading to black.

When I opened my eyes, the first thing I saw was a gray rat. He stood on his hind legs, his front paws near his face. He wiped his whiskers with them, his nose twitching as he tilted his head up and sniffed the air. Dropping back to all fours, he scampered beneath the dumpster, ran out the opening on the other side, and disappeared into the shadows.

My blood pounded against my temples, making my vision pulse with each of my heartbeats. The buzzing sounded again. A familiar tingling sensation remained that wasn't caused by my vibrating phone. I sat up, reaching for my holstered gun. It was gone.

"Keep your hands where I can see them. No sudden movements. Who are you?" the man asked. He wore an oversized camouflage jacket. He held a can of pepper spray in his outstretched hand, his finger itching to press down on the release. "What are you doing out here?"

I moved my hand away from my holster. "I'm Alex." I started to edge closer to the dumpster, stopping when I remembered my new friend with the whiskers and tail. "I'm looking for someone."

"In the dumpster?"

"No." I shook my head, feeling my nerves twitch and ache from the taser. "Well, maybe. I don't know."

"You don't know?"

"It's a long story."

He looked from side to side. "I got time."

That made one of us. "Good for you."

He jerked his chin toward the dumpster. "Who are you looking for?"

"Adrianna Keys."

The name meant nothing to him, so I described her. "A lot of women around here fit that description."

"I can show you a photo." I held up my palms. "Do you mind if I stand up? I don't want Rizzo to get any funny ideas."

"Rizzo?" He lowered the pepper spray a few inches in confusion.

If I kept this up, I'd be able to get away in no time. "The rat." I pointed in the direction it ran.

"You mean Hershel."

"You named him Hershel?"

"Why not? You named him Rizzo."

"Rizzo is a rat's name." I shook my head. "Never mind. Is he yours?"

The guy chuckled and tucked the pepper spray into his pocket beside the taser. "I'm not crazy." He eyed me carefully as I pulled myself off the ground. "You try anything, I'll put you on your ass again. Got it?"

I held up my palms. "Assaulting women in dark alleys isn't a wise move."

"Trespassing is illegal, lady. So is carrying a concealed weapon."

"I have a permit."

He flipped open my wallet, which he'd taken while I'd been incapacitated. "California doesn't recognize permits issued from anywhere else."

"My application's pending."

"Same with your P.I. license?"

"Who are you?" I asked.

"It's better if we don't go down that road. Where's that photo you wanted to show me?"

I tapped on my phone, seeing the message Justin had sent. He'd forwarded me the contact information for the cruise. For a split second, I thought about calling 9-1-1 or sending him an S.O.S. as a reply, but the weirdo with the taser didn't seem that threatening. If he wanted to hurt me, he would have done it while I was flat on the ground. I just hoped the electric shock hadn't scrambled my better judgment along with my nervous system.

"Here." I held out my phone. "That's her. She's staying at the hotel across the street. No one's seen her since she left Saturday morning."

"Were you hired to find her?"

"I work for her boyfriend." That was true enough.

He leaned a little closer, his jacket shifting to the side and revealing a flash of gold. "That doesn't explain why you're looking in the dumpster."

"I pinged her phone." I didn't want to turn my back on this guy again, but I didn't want him to take her phone after I dug it out. "It's in there."

He nodded, so I reached in and scooped it out. The screen wasn't cracked. Aside from some ooze which clung to the back, it didn't appear damaged.

"Now it's your turn. Do you want to tell me what you're doing back here, officer?" I asked.

"What gave it away? Was it my familiarity with the penal code?"

"Well, it sure as shit wasn't the unannounced and unprovoked use of a taser. That falls under unnecessary force and police brutality."

"Do you want to press the issue? I have more than enough reasons to arrest you."

Jason Ganz wouldn't want to make the drive to San Diego to deal with another arrest. And the news would likely get back to Detective Petrocelli, who might try to force me to leave the state. "Next time, announce first. I'm going to assume you're new since you don't have a gun."

"I'm off duty."

"Which makes this worse."

"You were rooting through the trash."

"That's not illegal."

"The concealed weapon is."

I didn't want to spend the rest of the night going in circles with him. "Don't do it again."

He narrowed his eyes. "Same."

"Agreed, if you help me with something. You said you had time."

"Have you filed a missing persons report?" he asked.

"No. We aren't sure she's missing." I didn't go into any of the surrounding details, believing in this instance Cross might be right. "A black sedan's been stalking her. The driver's been careful not to get caught on hotel surveillance, but I was hoping you might be able to find the car."

"Do you have a plate or know who it's registered to?"

"Both," I said. "It was stolen." I read the information to him while he made a call and repeated it to the person on the other end.

He listened intently. "Are you sure?" he asked before nodding a few times. "Okay."

"What?" I asked.

"The car was found late last night. It was torched and left on the side of the I-5 near Anaheim. Highway Patrol spotted it."

"Was anyone inside?"

"No. Why would you think that?"

"I get paid to think things like that. You do too." I tucked Adrianna's phone into my pocket and made sure I had my phone. "Was there anything in the car?"

"The torched car?" he asked.

"Point taken." I eyed my nine millimeter which was tucked behind his back. "Do you mind?"

He thought about it for a few seconds. "Paperwork's a bitch."

"That it is."

Reluctantly, he unloaded my weapon, pocketed the bullets, and handed me the gun. "Do you have any idea who these men in the car might be or why they're interested in Adrianna Keys?"

"I'm working on that part."

"Would you tell me if you had an answer?"

"I don't even know your name." I watched his expression carefully. "Are you afraid I'm going to report you for getting trigger happy? Actions like that are what give cops a bad reputation."

"The way I see it, I give you my name and things get official. That would mean I'd have an obligation to cite you, but this wouldn't just be a fine and citation. I'd be bound to bring you in for further questioning. And like I said, I'm off duty."

I wasn't sure I bought it, but I didn't have an entire night to waste just to see how far he'd take this. "All right, Mystery Man," I edged toward the mouth of the alley, "I'll be seeing you."

"Wait. You still don't know where she is. A tossed phone doesn't bode well. Don't you think you should make a report? She's been gone more than twenty-four hours. She doesn't have her phone. She could be anywhere by now."

"I gave you the information. Feel free to run with it." I backed toward the street, keeping an eye on Officer Trigger Happy. "You've got my name. If you find something, give me a call."

"You can't just walk away."

"Why not? You're off duty. You have no intention of doing anything about it."

He looked torn. "If I run into you again, things might be different. Don't walk around with a weapon until you get a permit, and stay out of dumpsters. A lot of shit's been popping off in alleys these last few weeks."

That froze me in my tracks. "What kind of shit?"

He looked up from where he'd been tossing the bags back into the dumpster. "A few homeless people have been beaten and locked inside dumpsters. One was nearly crushed when the garbage truck made a pick-up. Luckily, a sanitation worker heard his screams and pulled the emergency stop. It took the rescue squad an hour to get him out."

I grimaced. "That's terrible."

"Yeah."

"Any idea who might be behind it?"

The cop seemed surprised I asked that question. "They haven't said much to me. I'm sure the brass knows more, but all I've heard is they were beaten and forced into the dumpster at gunpoint. Then tonight, I find you making room inside a dumpster while holding a gun. You can see why I thought you posed a threat."

"Regardless, announce first and give your suspect time to comply." I gave him a final look and darted across the street. Unfortunately, the dumpster smell came with me.

TWENTY-THREE

The ocean breeze helped clear away some of the garbage smell. It didn't matter what city I visited. Alleyways always smelled the same, a combination of piss, hot garbage, and wet dirt. I never understood where the wet dirt smell came from, but it was always there, holding the rest of the odors in. Maybe it was more compost than wet dirt, but either way, it was gross.

The cruise ship remained docked. At this time of night, even the cleaning crew had gone home. The moored ship rocked gently from side to side. I scouted the area for surveillance cameras and found a few. The metal gate over the ticket booth was secured with a single lock.

After retrieving my picks from the car, I made fast work of that lock and moved the gate out of my way. The door wasn't any harder to crack. But the ticket booth contained nothing of value. It wasn't much larger than the interior of a carnival game. Beside the register was a monitor and hard drive. Glancing out, I made sure no one was coming and accessed the files from Saturday morning.

The footage played on the monitor. A flickering horizontal line appeared near the bottom of the screen. No wonder they hadn't invested in better locks, even their computer equipment wasn't worth stealing.

A crowd of twenty boarded the cruise ship. Adrianna wasn't among them. I'd call back during business hours just to make sure, but given the location of her missing phone, she'd been taken before she ever got a chance to whale watch. The footage gave me a timeline. She must have been on her way to grab a cup of coffee when the men in the black sedan rolled up on her. They could have been waiting in the alley. It was wide enough to conceal their car. They must have grabbed her, tossed her phone, and took off. So where did they go?

I let myself out of the booth, locked the door, and pulled down the metal gate, resecuring the lock in place. As I headed back to the car, I spotted a night watchman making the rounds. I approached him, flashing my credentials in his direction. "Excuse me, sir, I was hoping you could help me." I asked if he'd seen Adrianna, the shooters, or the car. I showed him photos, but he was no help. "Thanks, anyway."

When I got back to the car, I rolled down the windows, letting the ocean breeze remove the overpowering smell of garbage, while I perused her phone. I checked the tracking data and her call logs. From what I gathered, she hadn't missed a single audition or scouting opportunity prior to today. But since it was Monday, her absence would be noticed, especially after Cross and I planted the thought in people's heads. The only way they wouldn't give it a second thought was if she called in sick.

I wondered if the kidnappers had planned that far ahead. They had when it came to Brent, who told Sylvio he'd be out of town for a few days. Why hadn't they forced Adrianna to make a call like that? Had they grabbed her just so they could question and kill her, kind of like what they did to Roundtree?

"What do you people want?" I checked to see if the kidnappers had reached out, but they hadn't said a word since leaving the heads at our office. Would Brent's skull be waiting for me in the morning? Hoping I was wrong, I backed out of the space and headed for the freeway. It was time to go home.

* * *

I'd only been asleep for an hour when I heard rustling coming from the kitchen. "Martin," I mumbled, opening my eyes to glance at the clock. It was a little after four. By now, Cross should be on his way to meet Luther Bianchi. What a night.

I flopped onto my back, stretching out my arm and coming into contact with a warm lump. I nearly jumped in surprise. Martin wasn't in the kitchen. He was asleep beside me.

He shifted, letting out a low groan. "Alex, what's wrong?"

"Shh." I pressed my finger to his lips. "Someone's in the house."

The security system hadn't alerted us to any intruders, and the proximity alarm failed to inform us someone was approaching the front door. As silently as possible, I grabbed my nine millimeter and shoved my feet into a pair of shoes. Then I crept to the doorway, pressed my back against the wall, and peered around the jamb. The hallway was dark, but I could see light coming from the kitchen and living room. Had we left the lights on?

The rustling sounded again. It was more of a crinkling. Plastic, maybe. Thoughts of the shooters came to mind. Everything about them screamed professional. Were they laying down plastic sheeting before killing us to make for easier disposal of our bodies?

I leaned back against the wall. The beach house didn't have many escape options. Our room didn't have any windows in order to avoid unnecessary sunlight and the sound of crashing waves, which drove me insane. Now, I wished I hadn't been so picky.

The window in the bathroom wasn't particularly large. I'd fit, but I didn't think Martin would. I'd have to lure them into one of the other rooms while he escaped. The back door would be his best bet, except the beach didn't provide much cover. But he was fast. He could run in a zigzag. They might be professionals, but they weren't expert marksmen, not when it came to moving targets. I'd learned that firsthand during our previous encounter.

"You have to get out of here," I whispered. "I'll provide a distraction. Make sure the hallway's clear before you go out the back. Don't stop. Keep moving. Avoid running in a straight line."

"Who do you think is here?" Martin grabbed my backup piece from the nightstand and came up behind me. I put my hand on his shoulder when he attempted to move past me and shook my head.

"I don't know, but it could be the shooters from Saturday. They don't like leaving witnesses."

"I'm not going anywhere."

"Fine. Hide in the bathroom and call 9-1-1. Don't come out unless I tell you it's safe." This damn beach house had a lot of things, but it was sorely lacking in a panic room. "I can hold them off. That should give the cops time to arrive." Too bad they weren't still camped out front.

"Fuck that. We stick together."

"I liked it better when you listened when I told you to hide."

"Too bad." He exhaled. His hand steady. His grip strong.

"All right, but if I tell you to duck and cover, you better do it. And don't you dare get shot." That taser must have scrambled my good sense because allowing Martin to provide backup was unheard of.

"Ditto, sweetheart." He kissed me roughly. "I love you."

Now I knew we were doomed.

Slowly, we crept down the hallway, keeping our backs pinned to the wall. The bathroom, guest room, and laundry room were clear. When the hallway ended, I signaled to Martin to hold position while I crouched down and rolled to the next nearest cover position behind an armchair. The rustling in the kitchen grew louder. I peered around the side of the chair, but I couldn't see over the counter.

A sharp metallic snap sounded to my right. I spun, gun aimed in that direction. A man dressed entirely in black crouched over a rifle case. I motioned for Martin to cover me and moved toward the man in black.

I'd only made it two steps before I felt the muzzle of a handgun press against the side of my neck. "Easy," a familiar voice said, "we come in peace."

Martin came up behind him, his weapon trained on the man holding me at gunpoint. "Drop it," Martin warned, his voice deadly.

"Bugger." The rustling was joined by a banging, followed by the sound of several jars rolling across the tile floor. "Bloody hell," Bastian rubbed the back of his head, "don't shoot. I told Jules to call first. But he said there was no need since you were expecting us."

"Bastian?" I released my grip on the gun, letting it dangle from my pointer finger.

The man behind me grabbed the gun from my hand and lowered his weapon and mine to the coffee table. He held up his palms and turned to face Martin. "It's your turn, mate."

"Hans?" Martin asked.

Hans snickered. "In the flesh. I'm chuffed you remembered. I see you're packing a bit more of a punch these days. Impressive." He glanced toward me. "Who's protecting whom?"

I nodded to Martin, who put the gun on the table.

"James, no hard feelings about last time, I hope," Bastian said. "We were only following her orders by protecting you."

"Things are different now," Martin said, "but I appreciate the sentiment." Martin stared at me with such intensity, I looked away.

Bastian held up a container of peanut butter, getting my attention. "Do you mind, love? I'm absolutely famished."

"Help yourself." I didn't like the look in Martin's eyes.

"Why didn't you tell me you invited friends over?" Martin asked. "We could have had hors d'oeuvres and dinner waiting."

"I didn't know when they'd get here. This was Cross's idea."

Martin eyed the three men again. The last time I'd called Mercer's team for help, we nearly lost everything. Martin hadn't forgotten that. But his anger wasn't at them.

It was at me.

"I can make you something to eat," Martin offered, his friendly business tone replacing whatever feelings he actually had. "You must have had quite a long flight."

"No worries." Bastian shrugged it off, opening the fridge to find a bag of baby carrots. "It's afternoon for us, but it's the middle of the night for you. Go back to bed. I'm sorry we woke you. Jules thought if we snuck in, we wouldn't disturb you. I guess we did anyway. Again, apologies."

Martin focused on me. "Are you all right?"

"Yeah."

"Are you sure?"

I nodded. "Go back to sleep. We're good here."

"We'll talk about this in the morning." He turned to Hans and Bastian. "Good night, gentlemen."

After Martin left, Bastian cringed. "Sorry, love. We didn't mean to cause any friction."

"I'm just glad you're not here to murder us." I resisted the urge to drop into the chair. If I did, I'd never get up.

"That explains the artillery," Hans said. "Luckily, we brought plenty of our own. If someone intends to make a bloody mess, we'll be here to stop them."

"That's not why I called." I surveyed the room. "Where's Mercer?"

Donovan Mayes closed the rifle case and unzipped another bag, taking inventory of the flashbangs and zipties. He'd been the man I first spotted. "Julian's setting up in the other room. He wanted to get a jump on things before you woke up. He thought somewhere out of the way would be best."

"Sure, he did." I glanced at Hans who had joined Bastian in the kitchen and was making a massive peanut butter and jelly sandwich. "There are chips in the cupboard and a container of cookies in the pantry. If any of you know how to brew a cup of espresso, I'll tell you where I hide the candy jar."

"I'm on it," Bastian volunteered.

Hoping they wouldn't blow up the kitchen or the neighbor's house, I headed in the direction Donovan had pointed and found Mercer hanging a clear plastic sheet over the large wall in the game room. He had placed photos of Brent Barber, Adrianna Keys, Luther Bianchi, Fenton Roundtree, and Sylvio DePalma on top of the air hockey table.

"Mercer," I said.

"Parker." He didn't bother to turn around.

"You broke into my beach house."

"Yours? It's leased to James Martin."

"Still, you knew I'd be here." I picked up Roundtree's photo, finding a folder beneath it. "Did you search for his name when mine didn't pop up?"

"Do you want me to tell you how we bypassed the security measures too?"

"In fact, I would, very much."

"Another time."

"You should have knocked."

"Perhaps."

"How are you?" I asked.

"Brilliant." Mercer continued to work. "Any developments in the last twelve hours?"

I told him about my trip to San Diego and what I discovered.

"You should have nicked her laptop," he said.

"It didn't have anything on it."

"It might have."

"I know what I'm doing."

He glanced at me for the first time since I entered the room. "Very well."

"Do you think they killed her?"

Mercer picked up one of the photos and taped it to the plastic sheet. "Possibly."

Yep, still infuriating. "What do you think they want?"

"Have you IDed them yet?"

"No, but it's just a matter of time. The car they drove was torched, so they don't want to leave evidence behind, but they hadn't been expecting the firefight at the gas station or me to catch them in the act. I have their photos, but facial recognition is still working on it."

"Do you have any others besides the ones you sent?"

I retrieved my phone and handed it to Mercer. "I think I

sent you a copy of everything."

He ignored me, focusing on the video. "You're sure these are the same men who abducted Brent Barber?"

"Completely."

"Bollocks."

"What's wrong?"

"They're mercenaries, hired to do a job. Whatever it is, K&R isn't their end game. They wouldn't waste their time. This is something much bigger." He watched the car disappear off the screen.

"Is that why you hopped on a plane?"

"I was hoping I was mistaken."

My blood ran cold. "What are we looking at?"

"I don't know yet, but they'll take out anyone or anything that stands in the way of their mission. We should prepare accordingly."

TWENTY-FOUR

When I got tired of pacing, I rolled the cue ball back and forth over the felt. Since the hired guns weren't planning on a giant payday for the kidnapping, that explained the lack of ransom demand. "Why hasn't facial rec gotten any hits? If they're as bad as you say, shouldn't they be in the system?"

"They routinely scrub any record of their existence. Photos, fingerprints, dental records, DNA, everything imaginable. You may never get a hit," Mercer said.

"Great." I wondered if Bastian did the same thing for Mercer's team. "Do you know their names?"

"That one," he pointed to the man who'd left Barber Productions with the briefcase, "is Vincent Castillo. At least, that's what his passport said the last time we ran into him."

"What about his buddy?"

"Channing Irmine."

"Okay." The casual way in which Mercer said their names rubbed me the wrong way. "Do you hang out at the same Black Ops meetings?"

Mercer scowled at me. "No."

Bastian entered the room, espresso in one hand and tea

in the other. He handed me my drink and placed Mercer's on the table. "Did I hear you say Castillo and Irmine?"

"Yes."

"Bugger. I thought they were dead."

"Not yet." Mercer pinned up a map and rested his hips against the table, taking in his handiwork. "After this job, they might be."

"What do you know about them?" I asked.

Bastian grabbed a jar of mixed nuts off the bar and popped the top. He crunched down on a cashew. "Private military contractors. They're familiar with the K&R game, but they never showed much interest in it. They preferred more straight-forward missions. Retrieve intel and eliminate the target. In and out." He caught the look on my face. "That might not be the situation here."

"History dictates otherwise," Mercer mumbled.

"We can't rule anything out yet, Jules," Bastian insisted.

"Who do you think hired them?" I asked.

"Someone with deep pockets."

"Brent Barber isn't worth much. Neither is his girlfriend."

"His family connections complicate matters. His father controls a great deal of money and political power. The same could be said of his uncle." Mercer opened another file and continued hanging the intel on the plastic sheet. "Right now, we're dealing with too many possibilities."

"We're still compiling data," Bastian said. "Brent Barber Sr. has a lot of enemies, including the individuals who run powerful corporations. To be clear, very few of them are clean. Most have blood, in one form or fashion, on their hands. It'll take time to suss it out. Then there's Luther Bianchi."

"My boss should be meeting with him right about now," I said. "Brent's assistant forwarded the original threat to Bianchi, who attempted to handle the situation on his own. The team he hired was slaughtered."

"They must have been given a rendezvous point or dead drop location," Bastian said. "They wouldn't have known where to go otherwise. We need that location."

I sent a text to Cross. "Luther Bianchi hasn't been the

most cooperative."

"Let's hope he can shed some light on this matter." Mercer drew an X over the two crisis negotiators Bianchi had hired to deal with the situation. "Bianchi's a nutter for hiring a less skilled team to handle Castillo and Irmine."

Bastian chomped down on a Brazil nut. "How would he have known, Jules?"

"A man like him should know everything. It only took you a matter of minutes to figure out the crisis negotiation firm had done more 'fixing' than K&R work. Bianchi would have found the same thing."

"That's why he hired them," I said. "Bianchi doesn't believe in paying off the opposition." I sipped the espresso, but it'd take more than caffeine to keep me going. "We're not even sure Bianchi's the target." I stared at the intel Mercer's team had compiled. "Why do you think Brent and Adrianna were taken?"

"I don't know, love." Bastian screwed the lid back on the jar and placed the nuts on the bar. "I've only brushed the surface, but I read everything you sent and ran through the usual suspects. It isn't clear. Brent isn't worth enough for someone to put a hit out on him that would be worthy of Castillo's and Irmine's attention. That leads me to believe Brent possesses something they desperately want or he's being used as leverage to convince someone in his orbit to cooperate."

"Like his father or uncle," I said.

"That's the most reasonable assumption."

"What about the bird?" Mercer asked.

Bastian shook his head. "Ms. Keys is worth less than her boyfriend. Powerful people are not in her orbit. She isn't a high-value target."

"Then why take her?" Mercer stared at her photo, the lines around his eyes deepening. "She was removed from the situation. Away for business, seemingly safe."

"They grabbed her first," I said. "We're assuming they may have used her to incentivize Brent to comply."

"You're probably right," Mercer said. "She seems like a secondary target."

"We don't even know if she's still alive," Bastian said.

"No one even realized she'd been taken."

"They still haven't." I thought about the San Diego cop I'd run into. Maybe he knew more than he let on. In fact, he could be working with the kidnapping mercs. But if that were true, I didn't think he'd let me go.

"What is it?" Bastian eyed me curiously.

I shook the wayward thoughts away. "They tortured Roundtree. His fingers were broken. They wanted intel and whatever was inside his filing cabinet. No matter how I twist this, I keep coming to the same conclusion. This has to do with Barber Productions."

Hans joined us with a plate in hand. "I thought Roundtree worked at a sound studio."

"He does," Mercer said before I could.

Bastian perused the website for what must have been the tenth time. "The company looks clean. As far as we're aware, they're not a front for anything. Their projects look innocent enough. I don't think they're developing anything top secret or vital to national security. If they are, they're keeping a lid on it."

"National security?" I blinked, wondering how I missed the sharp turn the conversation had taken.

"Those are usually the kinds of missions Castillo and Irmine take," Hans said. "The kind governments are too afraid to send their own operatives to handle."

"What about building codes or security information?" Bastian asked. "They would have wanted to make a clean exit. No witnesses and no trail to follow, digital or otherwise. Roundtree might have been able to get them out unseen. That might have been all they wanted from him."

"I don't think Roundtree could have given them anything they didn't already have." I thought about the emptied drawer in his office. "They took something with them. We believe it's Roundtree's company laptop. We just don't know why."

"Fenton Roundtree doesn't fit the qualifications for an HVT." Bastian clicked another key. "Nothing in his background popped either."

Mercer glanced back at me. "Was anything else taken from Barber Productions? The laptop might be a misdirect."

"I don't know. I haven't been back to Barber Productions since the attack on Saturday. The police have everything locked up tight, and Cross has a policy about staying away from them."

"Brilliant policy," Mercer said, not a hint of sarcasm in his tone.

"What about a key or security access?" Bastian asked. "Surely, the company's vice president controlled those things."

"They already had the building codes. They knew the layout and had a master keycard," I said.

"How did they get that?" Mercer asked.

"I don't know yet. I've run checks on every employee, but everyone's keycard has been accounted for. The master key they used wasn't assigned to anyone."

"Look again," Mercer said to Bastian.

"Did anyone see them enter or leave?" Hans asked. "You mentioned a guard had been killed."

"I don't think he tried to stop them. I found his body near the vending machines. He might have been on break." I put the empty cup down. "I'm pretty sure I'm the only person who saw them leave."

"Where was the rest of security?" Mercer asked. "They have trained guards assigned to patrol the corridors. How did they miss two shooters?"

"I don't know."

"Convenient."

"More than likely, they flipped a guard for access and intel," Bastian said. "He probably kept the rest of his mates distracted."

"Actually, they might have been testing the system for weaknesses." I told them about the weird occurrences that happened inside the building over the last five weeks.

"Recon," Mercer said.

"Sounds like it." Hans took another bite of his sandwich. "The bird's right. They want something from that building."

"If that were the whole of it, they wouldn't have kidnapped the CEO and his girlfriend," Bastian said.

"There has to be more to it. Some sort of access that only Barber would have." He squinted. "Sound production. Odd."

"What are you thinking?" Mercer asked.

"Voice recognition or a passphrase, something like that. Barber could have special access coded to his unique vocal signature." Bastian worked the mouse with practiced ease while he typed one-handed. "I still don't know what they would hope to access. I'm not seeing anything on the company's servers."

"You've already hacked it?"

"It was a long plane ride, love."

"That still doesn't explain what they wanted from Roundtree." I hated not knowing. Too bad the dead couldn't speak. I bet Fenton and the guard would have plenty to say.

Hans finished his sandwich and wiped the crumbs off the bar and onto the plate. "So you decided to stop them on your own while unarmed? You're lucky to be alive."

"They could find her if they wanted," Mercer said. "They know where she works. I'm sure they know where she lives. Killing her isn't a priority. They have enough complications. They know they're blown. Covert is no longer feasible, so they'll return to the most basic mission objectives."

"Which are?" I asked.

"To be determined."

Hans put his plate beside Mercer's teacup and nudged me. "What's the deal with this Sylvio chap?"

"He's Brent's best friend and assistant. Before Brent was abducted, Sylvio received a call from Brent saying he had a family emergency and would be out of town for a few days. Then he received an anonymous text on a game app, contacted Bianchi, and you know the rest," I said.

"Where is Sylvio now?" Mercer asked.

"At one of Cross Security's safe houses. A security team is keeping an eye on him."

"If Castillo and Irmine wanted Sylvio dead, he would be." Mercer sipped his tea.

"I wonder why he isn't," Hans said.

From the way they talked, Castillo and Irmine could wipe out all of California if they felt like it, but I'd faced off against them. They weren't that good. After all, I lived to tell the tale.

"Why would the kidnappers contact Sylvio?" Bastian asked. "We don't think this is about a ransom, so they had no reason to announce their presence. That complicates their timetable."

"What exactly did the text say?" Mercer asked me.

"Tell him to pay up or Brent's dead."

Mercer frowned, the wheels turning in his head. "But it didn't include an actual demand. No amount was mentioned."

"No."

"This sounds like a deal gone wrong," Bastian said.

"Maybe Castillo and Irmine went to work in a pub. I hear shite like that quite frequently when my tab comes due," Hans mused. "Maybe Castillo fell on hard times and now busts kneecaps for a living."

"The text didn't specify who needs to pay up?" Bastian asked.

I shook my head. "That's when Sylvio reached out to Luther Bianchi."

"Why did he assume Bianchi was the person in question?" Bastian asked.

"I'm not sure he did, but Brent told him if anything ever happened, that he should contact his uncle."

"It sounds like Brent expected trouble." Mercer turned back to the photo array.

"What about Brent's house?" Hans asked. "You said that's where he was abducted."

I explained my theory and gave them information on the sushi delivery guy. "The home security system was wiped. I pulled what I could from the backup. The cameras and security system had been disabled."

"That's Castillo and Irmine," Bastian said. "I wouldn't have expected anything less. Every move they make is measured."

"Including taking Adrianna?" I asked.

Bastian's fingers drummed against the side of the table.

"I don't know how she figures into any of this."

"In a *we'll kill your entire family* kind of way," Hans suggested.

"She isn't family," Mercer said. "Adrianna Keys isn't married to Brent Barber. I don't see how taking her would further their agenda." He looked at me. "The same way I'm not sure what they hoped to learn by interrogating and killing Roundtree. We're missing something."

"No shit." I tried to see things from a different angle, but none of it made sense. "The police might know more, both here and in San Diego. The rest of the staff at Barber Productions should be questioned, starting with security. We need to retrace Brent and Adrianna's activities over the last two months and figure out what's going on. Something must have changed."

"Why haven't you done this yet?" Mercer asked.

"We're less than seventy-two hours in. There hasn't been time. This would be easier if we were working with the police, but Cross made it clear not to go near them."

"And you listened?"

I ignored that and returned to speculating. "If this is about extorting Bianchi or Brent Sr. or forcing one of them to make good on their debts, I don't think the shooters would have abducted Adrianna or made a detour to Barber Productions. In fact, it looks like they grabbed Adrianna and killed Roundtree before they went after Brent."

"Bas," Mercer turned to his second-in-command, "look into the possibility. Our objective is determining who's pulling the strings. Once we figure that out, we'll have a better grasp of what's going on. Hans, take Donovan and go back to Barber's house. Make sure Parker didn't miss anything."

"Do you want us to check out San Diego too?" Hans asked.

"See what the house reveals first. After that, pay Barber's security staff a visit. If that still doesn't lead anywhere, you'll have to make the trip. But that's a last resort. I'm not sure when we'll be ready to move. Things could pop off at any moment. I need you to remain close." Mercer peered into the living room. "Where's Donovan?"

"He's scouting the area," Hans said. "If you ask me, I think he's hoping to spot some beach bunnies."

"It's too early. They don't show up until sunrise." I yawned.

"Good to know." Hans grabbed his plate and left the room. I listened for the sound of the sliding door and the beep of the security system reengaging before relaxing.

"Get some sleep, love," Bastian said. "We'll need you sharp. Our entrance wasn't supposed to wake you."

"You know better than that."

Mercer continued to stare at the intel he'd pasted to the wall. "Where are your files?"

"Most things are on my computer." I glanced at Bastian. "I would log you in, but I'm guessing that's a waste of time."

"Not a waste."

Relenting, I retrieved my laptop from my bag and turned it on. After giving Bastian access to my dropbox, the bug Cross put on Sylvio's phone, and every file and search I'd conducted, I headed for the bedroom. With any luck, Martin had gone back to sleep and wouldn't wake up the moment I entered the room. But I didn't even make it to the bedroom before my phone rang.

TWENTY-FIVE

"Shit." I silenced the call, freezing in the middle of the hallway. I didn't hear Martin stir, so I crept back to the living room on my tiptoes, went into the game room, and hit answer. "Hello?"

"I was starting to think you were screening my calls," Cross said. "I don't have long to talk. Luther's conferring with someone. This is a fucking mess. He's ready to blow everything up. But I think I've convinced him to give Cross Security a chance to fix it."

Mercer turned at the sound of my voice, intrigue on his face. "Who is it?"

My boss, I mouthed. "How?"

"Through the usual methods."

"Which are?" I asked.

"Contracts." Cross cleared his throat, indicating just how anxious he was.

"Put it on speaker," Mercer said.

I hit the button and put the phone down on the green felt. "Mercer and his team arrived an hour ago. They're here now. You're on with them."

"Mr. Cross, any updates?" Mercer asked.

"Some. We're still in the middle of a meeting," Cross

said.

"Is this a kidnapping negotiation?" Mercer asked. "Has Bianchi received a demand or proof of life?"

"No."

"To which?" Mercer asked.

"Either. Luther doesn't know who's behind this. He says he doesn't know anything about a debt or repayment. However, if Brent got himself into hot water, Luther's willing to do whatever it takes to get him back alive. He'll give them whatever they want."

"Has he already told them that?" Mercer asked.

"Yes."

"Was that before or after Luther sent the headless horsemen to take care of the situation?" I asked.

"Before," Cross said. "That's why the kidnappers gave him an address to make the drop-off. They said if he gave them what they wanted, they'd release Brent. He sent the crisis negotiators to take Brent back by force. He thought they could handle it. He didn't realize the lengths to which the kidnappers would go."

"Bollocks," Mercer cursed. "It'll be hard to recover after that. Are they still open to negotiating?"

"I don't know." Cross blew out a breath. "They haven't made contact since."

"Has Luther tried contacting them?" I asked.

"No response."

"How are they communicating?" Mercer asked.

"The same game app. Different user name. Amir's already run it. It hasn't been deactivated yet, like the last one, but everything about it is bogus. The user's location is hidden behind a VPN. We haven't had any luck cracking it."

"What is the name?" Bastian asked.

Cross spelled it out.

"Assuming we can open a line of communication," Mercer said, "the first step will be rebuilding trust. We'll have to give up something as a show of good faith once we receive proof of life. That is the priority."

Cross lowered his voice. "Do whatever you have to. The kidnappers don't trust Luther. They won't deal with him.

His attempts to speak to them have gone unanswered. The last time they made contact, they sent the warning to Sylvio."

"No more games," I said.

"That was the last message, but it was on a different account. Maybe if Sylvio messages this new user, we can get the kidnappers talking again."

"Have you told Luther your plan?" I asked.

"The less he knows, the better."

"Agreed," Mercer said.

"Remind him the Feds are all over him. His hands are tied. He doesn't have a choice," I said. "Letting Cross Security take over is his only move."

Mercer muted my call. "Bas, what do we have?"

"Cross is right, commander. We can't pin the location. The account is new. It was created less than a day ago. The user is currently active, but his score is zero and he hasn't even begun the first level. He's not playing the game or participating in any way. But he's been online for the last fourteen hours. He's waiting for something."

"Message him." Mercer folded his arms across his chest and waited. "Tell him we want to talk about sound design." Mercer unmuted the call. "Cross, we'll take over the negotiation. Get copies of the communications Bianchi sent and received. I don't like surprises." Mercer looked at Bastian. "Anything else?"

"Negative," Bas said.

"I already sent the chat transcript to Amir. There isn't much. I'll have him forward it to you," Cross said.

"Great, now get the hell out of there," I said.

"All right." Cross sighed. "Luther's on his way back to the table. I'll finish up here and make sure he doesn't interfere again. We'll talk soon."

Once the call disconnected, Mercer raised an eyebrow in my direction. "Why couldn't he handle that over the phone?"

"Luther Bianchi's a paranoid prick." A moment later my phone chimed, notifying me the transcript had been received. "He's under federal investigation, so he won't use the phone."

"That's the misdirect," Bastian said, his eyes remained on the screen. "The file is in your dropbox, love. It looks like the kidnappers didn't have much to say. Bianchi bullied them into giving him a location to meet for the exchange. Castillo and Irmine had plenty of time to prepare an ambush."

"Did they hint at what they want?" Mercer asked.

"Negative. It's the same messages we've already seen. *Pay us what is ours.* That was the first communication, which was sent Saturday night." Bastian pointed to the timestamp. "Bianchi replied, requesting more information. They told him it'd be forthcoming. He could find it on Brent's doorstep." Bastian picked up a pen and gnawed on the cap. "He's lucky he didn't end up with a body part."

"That's when Luther sent Sylvio to pick up the message." The neighbor's doorbell footage had caught a messenger service arriving in the neighborhood around that time. That's who left the card beneath the mat. "Sylvio provided Luther with the details, which were a reiteration of the text."

"Except it demonstrated the kidnappers knew where Brent lived. It gave their claim legitimacy," Mercer said.

"Luther sent back this message." Bastian pointed to the screen where sixty percent of the words used were expletives. "He said he'd pay up. He just wanted Brent back." Bastian pointed to two more messages Luther sent immediately afterward. "He tells them he needs a location for them to make the exchange, payment for Brent."

"There it is." I pointed to the reply, confused by the string of numbers.

"Time and coordinates," Mercer said.

Bastian entered them into the computer. "That's in the middle of an industrial center." He entered a few search parameters. "It's also in a four-block blind zone with at least a dozen entry points."

"They don't want to be tracked," Mercer said.

"Could they be keeping Brent there?" I asked.

Mercer shook his head. "They wouldn't hand out coordinates to a real location."

"Still," Bastian reached for the comm and stuck it in his

ear, "it won't hurt to have Hans and Donovan swing by."

"The headless bodies haven't been found yet," I said. "They might be there."

"Doubtful," Mercer said.

Bastian had just relayed the location to Hans when a pop-up appeared on his screen. "Jules, we have contact. Should we introduce ourselves?"

"Not yet." Mercer read the screen. *What do you want?* "Tell them we need proof of life."

Bastian typed the response and hit enter. A moment later, the pop-up alert sounded again. "The kidnapper said proof would be forthcoming. In the meantime, he wants to know if we have what he is owed."

Mercer exhaled. "Not yet. Tell him we won't waste our time if Barber's dead."

Bastian sent the reply. The three of us waited with bated breath for an answer. This one was much slower, more deliberate.

I looked at Mercer. "What kind of negotiation technique is that?"

"It isn't one. That's a stall tactic." Mercer crouched down beside Bastian. "Any luck tracing their location?"

"Not with the protections they have in place. The damn app encryption makes it impossible." He connected my computer to his and was using both screens at once. When this was over, I'd need all new passwords and a new computer.

"They're going to make us wait." Mercer stepped away from the screen. "They know we can't give them what they want. I don't know why they are bothering with this charade."

"How would they know that?" I asked.

"Because whatever it is, is very specific. Something only a select few know about." Mercer went back to leafing through the dossiers. "Let me make a few calls."

"You mean you know how?" Bastian teased.

"Sod off."

A few seconds later, the phone rang. I turned, expecting it to be Mercer's, but he was in the midst of speaking to someone from military intelligence. Confused, I scooped my phone off the pool table and read the screen. *Cross.*

"Are you still alive?" I asked.

"Not funny. Luther's our newest client. He hired us to find his nephew. If we fail to follow through on the contract, he'll make my life unpleasant."

"Why did you agree to that?"

"We need his cooperation. Almeada said this was the safest way of working together without endangering the company."

"You shouldn't make deals with suspected gangsters."

Cross chuckled. "Remind me to keep you away from the client files."

I hoped that was a joke, but if it was, I didn't find it funny. Instead, I told him what had happened in the last twenty minutes. "We're waiting to hear back, but Mercer doesn't think it'll be anytime soon. They know we don't have access to what they want. But we still don't know what that is."

"What happened after I left San Diego?" Cross asked. "Justin tried to fill me in when I landed. But the story sounded impossible since you promised you'd head straight back to L.A."

"Promise is a strong word." I told him about my adventure inside the hotel, the search of Adrianna's room, finding her phone, and my trip to the docks. "The men who killed Roundtree and abducted Brent also took Adrianna. Actually, I'm guessing she was taken first."

"Did she have access to Barber Productions?" Mercer asked. "Castillo and Irmine wouldn't have wasted their time unless they had a reason."

"Castillo and Irmine?" Cross asked, hearing the question through the receiver.

"Mercer identified the shooters. They're mercs," I said.

Cross cursed. "Adrianna had no reason to have access to the building, but they might have figured she could get them Brent's keycard."

"Except the card used to enter the building wasn't coded to him. It was an unassigned master." I thought for a moment. "I guess it could have been hers."

"Why would she have a card?" Mercer asked.

"At one point, I had unfettered access to Martin Technologies until someone stole my ID card." I stared at Mercer, but I doubted he'd ever apologize for doing that. Kind of like the way he and his teammates made themselves at home without so much as knocking. "Do you think she would have kept it on her while she was traveling?"

"I don't see why it would be hers," Cross said.

"Really? You've never given anyone access to Cross Security? Not even Jade?"

Cross grunted. "Point taken. You should ask Sylvio about it. He would know for sure."

Mercer concluded his call, giving mine his complete attention. He rested his hands on the edge of the table while he stretched his back and hovered closer to me. I adjusted the volume and put my phone down so we could both hear.

"I'll have our techs run the names and see what they can find," Cross said. "After I catch up on a few things, I'll be on the next flight out." He hesitated. "Nero said they didn't find any bugs at Barber Productions."

"I'm not surprised," Mercer said. "Men like these don't leave a trail. They don't take any action that will compromise the mission."

"Are these the kinds of things you typically see?" Cross asked.

"These are the basic tenets of covert ops, not of a normal negotiation," Mercer said.

"Are there such things?" I asked.

Mercer looked at me, the slightest bit of amusement in his eyes. "Not really, but they usually follow a pattern. The kidnapper's goal is made clear and issued in the ransom demand. We have no known demand. No named ransom. It'll be harder to negotiate when we don't have an established starting place and a heaping dose of mistrust."

"How do you propose we proceed?" Cross asked.

"Carefully," Mercer said. "Like I told Parker, this doesn't feel like a kidnapping. It feels like an unsanctioned mission or a revenge play."

TWENTY-SIX

Revenge, a dish best served cold. That was the only thing that came to mind. Boy, did I need sleep.

Luther Bianchi insisted he never double-crossed anyone. I didn't believe it, but arguing wouldn't get us anywhere. And Cross didn't want to take a bullet for being obstinate and contrary, so he went along with what Bianchi said. After Cross left Luther, he paid Brent Sr. a visit, but he knew even less than Luther.

Meanwhile, Bastian should have rented scuba gear given how deep a dive he was performing. Mercer sat on top of one of the stools, resting his back against the bar and staring at the wall. He hadn't moved in five minutes. I wondered if he'd mastered the art of sleeping with his eyes open. Sure, he might be jet-lagged, but at least he got to sleep on the flight. I couldn't say the same, and after everything that happened, I never made it back to bed.

My phone beeped with a notification. I scooped it up and opened the attachment that had been forwarded from Sylvio's phone. A low-quality video played. The camera moved too quickly for the low resolution, making streaky blurs before becoming still. "Oh god."

Mercer appeared behind me, having crossed the room

with the same stealth as a jungle cat. "Brent Barber's alive."

"Seriously?" Bastian sounded surprised. He checked the pop-up box, but the kidnapper hadn't replied to us. Instead, he'd sent his delayed reply to Sylvio.

Mercer watched the video two more times before handing my phone to Bastian. "See what you can pull from this."

Bastian glanced back at me. "Now would be a good time for that candy stash you promised. Situations like this always make me peckish."

"Cupboard above the fridge. It's behind the all-purpose baking mix. Don't tell Martin."

"Right-o." Bastian winked.

Before I could say anything else, Mercer dialed Cross's number. "Yes, we received it. Did Sylvio receive further instructions?"

"Speaker," I hissed.

Mercer hit a button and put the phone down. We needed to find our rhythm before we stepped on each other's toes.

"The kidnapper wants what he's owed by tonight," Cross said. "That's all the message said."

Bastian returned with a lollipop hanging out of his mouth and the jar of candy in his hand. He put it down beside him and opened the clone of Sylvio's phone, along with the updated messages. "We've got it all right here," Bastian said. "We still don't know what it is they want."

"They think Sylvio has access to it." Mercer narrowed his eyes. "Message them again. Tell them now that we have proof, we can discuss terms."

Bastian sent the message, sucking on the end of the pop.

"They must think Sylvio can get them access," Cross said. "Brent shared everything with him."

The computer chimed. "They said they'd contact us again closer to the time they expect delivery. They don't want a repeat of yesterday morning or they'll deliver bits of Brent." Bastian looked up. "What should I reply?"

A good negotiator never lied. That's what I'd been told. Instead, it was better to make half-promises. But everything about this negotiation was a lie. The men who took Brent and Adrianna had no intention of releasing them. "Do they even need us to get them whatever they want? Or are they stalling, like with the delayed messages?" I asked.

Mercer inhaled slowly, almost as if he were counting. "Ask them what they want."

Bastian sent the message. Half a second later, the computer emitted a strange sound. "The account's been deleted."

"What?" Cross asked. "I thought you knew what you were doing."

"We do." Mercer exhaled just as slowly. "If they reach out to Sylvio again, we know they haven't completed their mission. Whatever they've been hired to do isn't done."

"And if they don't respond?" Cross asked.

"Then it's already too late."

"Fuck." Before Cross could go off on a tirade, my phone chimed. Mercer glanced at it, a smug look coming over him. "Hang on."

"The kidnappers reached out again to Sylvio. This is their third account. I'm sensing they're getting desperate." Mercer looked at Bastian. "This time, we make them wait."

Cross read the message which had also been forwarded to his phone. "They won't budge on telling us what they want. I'll have Nero and Omar speak to Sylvio. He might have failed to mention something pertinent."

"Or he's been lying to us," I said.

"Hans and Donovan should speak to him," Mercer said.

"My guys will go first," Cross said.

"Fine," Mercer wasn't pleased, "but we have a clock on this."

"I'm aware." Cross hung up without another word.

I moved closer to the computer and read over Bastian's shoulder. Three different user names on the game meant he was able to search for commonalities. The person on the other end was using the same VPN. Even though the actual location was cloaked and hidden, it provided a few points of reference.

"Do you think you might get enough to pull a MAC address?" I asked.

Bastian snorted. "You're asking for miracles."

"Only because I've seen you pull them off."

He smiled at me. "Only for you, love." He crunched down on the lollipop. "What do you say, Jules? Mind if I rattle their cages?"

Mercer gave us a look. "Carefully."

"Find out what the kidnapper has to say about Adrianna's disappearance," I said. "If she's alive, he has two bargaining chips."

"We'll need a second proof of life, once the kidnapper admits he has her too," Mercer said.

"That could lead to two more users being created." Bastian typed the message. "How do you think Cross will take this? He didn't seem pleased with the previous message."

"Don't worry about that," I said.

After we asked about Adrianna, the kidnappers stopped replying. But they didn't shut down the account or create a new user. They might have gotten wise or were wondering how we'd figured that out. Either way, it was time we waited them out.

I stared at the phone, waiting for something to happen. "Let's say someone hired Abbott and Costello to break into the Barber Productions building."

"Irmine and Castillo," Mercer corrected.

I waved a dismissive hand at him, ignoring the interruption. "They take their time running recon and figuring out building security. That could explain the strange occurrences Sylvio told us about. Castillo and Irmine realize the easiest way in is with a key. They figure out who has access, happen upon Adrianna, and figure she's an easy mark. She's out of town. They could make it look like a mugging, or they could break in to her hotel room."

"I hate to burst your bubble, love, but they didn't do either of those things," Bastian said.

"Which means they needed more than just the card. They needed her." I stared at her photo before turning my gaze to Bastian and finally Mercer. "Why did they take her? You said they're mercenaries. They like simple jobs. Clear mission parameters. Taking a non-target is sloppy and dangerous. It increases their chances of getting caught. Why would two mercenaries, not career kidnappers, go through the trouble?"

"Controlling her might make Barber more compliant," Bastian said.

"Agreed."

"But the scene at his house, the blood on the shredder, that doesn't read like someone who's complying," I said.

"Maybe you have it backwards, love."

"You think they took Brent to make Adrianna comply?" That didn't make sense since Mercer and his crew had already determined Adrianna wasn't worth enough to kidnap.

Mercer shook his head, reading his teammate's mind. "Adrianna couldn't get them into Barber Productions, but she could get them inside her house. You said the security system was disabled and the hard drive wiped. If Brent didn't tell them where the files backed up, Adrianna must have."

Lack of sleep made my mind a jumbled mess. "Fine, but they disabled the cameras before they took Adrianna."

"That's easy enough," Bastian said. "I could do that here if you wanted and leave the motion sensors and the rest of the lot alone."

"Don't you dare."

"They grabbed Adrianna first," Mercer said. "She knew Brent was at home. She had a key to the front door and the codes to get inside. That's why they needed her."

"So why did they waste their time going to Barber Productions?" I didn't need them to answer. I'd been saying it all along. "This has something to do with whatever goes on inside that building."

"They wanted the laptop," Bastian said. "And something else. Something they haven't gotten yet."

"Something Sylvio has or can get them," Mercer said. "At least, that's what's indicated."

"They planned to get inside that building. It wasn't a spur of the moment decision. This has been going on for over a month. They wanted whatever Roundtree kept in his office. We believe they took it since his drawer was empty, so what did they gain by interrogating him?" I asked.

Mercer watched me from the corner of his eye. "We'll find out."

* * *

Leaving Mercer and his team unsupervised wasn't something I wanted to do. But this was Cross's show. I was just along for the ride. And right now, the boss's biggest concern was getting the phone lines installed.

"You didn't look that bad inside the interrogation room," Detective Petrocelli said once I was within earshot. "Is there something I should know about?"

"I suffer from sleep disturbances." I eyed him as I unlocked the office door. "To what do I owe the pleasure, Detective?"

He peered into the office, as if he half-expected a body to drop from the ceiling or be lying on the ground behind the receptionist's desk. "I'm just following up."

"On?"

He remained glued to the doorframe. "Yesterday's events. I thought it'd help if I got a good look at the operation you've got going here. Where was the box?"

"It was left about six inches to your right. I'm sure the crime lab took photos. And even if they didn't, you pulled footage from building security. Remember? You showed me those photos of the delivery driver." I took a seat behind the desk and locked my bag which contained my gun inside the bottom drawer. I didn't need to give Petrocelli any other reasons to arrest me. "You must have seen where he put the box."

"I'm surprised it didn't leave a mark."

"I wasn't here. I don't know who cleaned up the mess." He continued to linger in the hallway. "Would you like to step into my office?" I asked.

He glanced down the hallway again before coming inside. "When's your boss expected to arrive?"

"He isn't."

"No?" Petrocelli didn't fool me.

"Nope."

"What exactly are you doing?"

"Working."

After wandering through the tiny reception area, Petrocelli pulled one of the chairs closer to my desk and sat down. "We've tracked down the getaway vehicle."

"Great."

"You don't seem surprised," Petrocelli said. "How come?"

"Do you know what surprises me? The fact that you thought you should share that tidbit of information. Didn't you make it clear you didn't want me anywhere near your investigation?"

"That hasn't changed."

"No?"

"I'm not here to ask for your help. I have a few more questions. Like I said, I'm following up."

I leaned back and folded my hands neatly on top of the desk. "Follow away."

"Did you notice if the car was already parked when you arrived at the Barber Productions building?"

"No."

"No it wasn't, or no you don't remember?"

"The second one. I didn't even drive past that service shop. I parked in a garage. Like I said, I've never seen the car before."

"What about the men?"

I shook my head. "Have you identified them yet? Maybe you found them with the car."

He maintained a poker face. "Where's Brent Barber?"

Ah, the real reason he came knocking on my door. "I don't know. I've tried contacting him, but he hasn't answered his phone. I believe it's turned off."

"Is that why you were desperately trying to contact his girlfriend?"

"According to Sylvio, Brent said he had a family emergency. It stands to reason she would know something about that."

"They haven't communicated with each other in over a week."

"Really?"

"Stop pretending. She's gone too."

"Don't you think you should be out looking for her instead of harassing me?"

"We just released the scene. Barber Productions is open for business. Brent's employees have been cleared to return to work. Sylvio wasn't among them."

"Maybe it's his day off."

"I went by his place. He wasn't there."

"Maybe he just didn't want to answer the door. He could have been in the shower. You could always call him."

Petrocelli narrowed his eyes and pulled out his phone. "Sure, let's do that."

While he dialed, the office door opened. A man in phone company garb, holding an equipment bag and clipboard, asked, "Cross Security?"

"Yes, sir." I stood, wondering if Petrocelli was going to be a dick and send him away due to pressing police business. If this service call got rescheduled again, I might ask Mercer to reconsider his stance on wet work. "We need a separate line in each office."

The phone guy examined the wall jack before turning his gaze skyward to the ceiling tiles. "Can I see inside the offices?"

"Absolutely." I opened each of the doors, catching Petrocelli leaning over in his chair to peer into the offices while he asked Sylvio rudimentary questions.

"I'll get started in here," the phone guy said. "You look busy."

"Thanks. Let me know if there's anything you need." I returned to the reception desk.

Petrocelli waited for me to sit down before he said, "Mr. DePalma, where is Brent Barber?"

I couldn't hear Sylvio's response, but from the look on Petrocelli's face, he gave the same vague answer he'd given Cross the first time we asked.

"After the shooting, the same men who killed Mr. Roundtree went to Mr. Barber's house and forced him into the trunk of their car. Do you know anything about this?" Petrocelli kept his eyes on me the entire time. "If you don't come to the station to answer questions, I will send officers to escort you. Do you understand? I expect to see you within the hour." He tucked the phone back into his pocket.

"You think the shooters killed Roundtree and kidnapped Brent Barber?" I asked.

"I didn't use the word kidnapped."

"One can only assume that's what happens when a person gets shoved into the trunk of a car. At least, that's what happened to me."

Petrocelli gave me a confused look. "Happened to you?"

"Yeah, long story. It has nothing to do with this."

He shook it away, assuming it was nothing but rhetoric. "Do you want to know what I find interesting? The two decapitations were local crisis negotiators. I find that an unlikely coincidence."

"It seems to me someone's trying his damnedest to ensure Brent Barber's safe return."

Petrocelli gave a few barely perceptible head nods. "Cross Security's website doesn't list negotiations as one of their services."

"That's because it isn't."

"Kidnappings require skilled professionals."

"Would you consider the men who were killed and left on my doorstep skilled professionals?"

Petrocelli tapped his knuckles on the desk and stood. "Tell whoever's in charge of the negotiation to turn this over to the police. We'll do our best to get Brent back alive."

But the detective's best wasn't going to cut it. "If you really mean that, you'd share what you know. Secrets are bound to lead to nothing more than misery and death."

"Something tells me you already know as much as I do." He wanted me to show him mine first. I just hoped afterward, he'd still show me his.

"Barber Productions has experienced a series of strange events in the last five weeks. Doors unlocked, the security system going crazy for no reason. I'm guessing the police must have responded to some of these calls from the security company. I don't think those were system glitches."

"You think the shooters were testing the building for weaknesses." Petrocelli nodded a few times. "I'm sure cyber division will be able to determine that after they review the security logs."

"You have them?"

"We have everything. I'm not in the business of prematurely releasing a scene."

"Then you must know plenty of things." I stared him down. "Why was Fenton Roundtree murdered? What did the shooters take from his office?"

Petrocelli didn't even acknowledge he heard the questions before walking out the door. So much for sharing intel.

TWENTY-SEVEN

As soon as the phone lines were installed, I locked up the office. Leaving Cross and Mercer to their own devices didn't seem like the best idea, but I didn't have anything solid. That's what we needed, a tighter grasp on reality. Then we could come up with a game plan.

Since Barber Productions was no longer crawling with cops, I decided it was worth a visit. Nero texted to let me know Sylvio had left the safe house. The Cross Security team followed him to the police station. As of yet, he hadn't left, but Jason Ganz showed up soon after. Since Nero texted me these details, I was sure he also informed Cross, which would explain Ganz's appearance. Once Petrocelli finished with Sylvio, I'd take my turn. Until then, I'd try to get answers to the rest of my questions.

The front door to Barber Productions wasn't locked. Four guards manned the check-in desk. Prior to the shooting, it had been two.

"I'm Alexis Parker." I showed them my ID and credentials. "I work for Cross Security. I was hired to evaluate building security. After what happened Saturday, I thought I should stop by."

The nearest guard entered my name into the computer.

"I wish you'd finished your evaluation sooner."

"Do you know what happened?" I asked, reading his name tag. *L. Jovon.*

"Our system was hacked. The cameras were looped. We had no idea anything was wrong."

"Were you in the building when it happened?"

"Yes." He pointed to one of the guards stationed beside the metal detector and the other sitting beside him. "All three of us were, except Scotty."

"Do you remember hearing anything?"

"No. The place was mostly shut down. The third floor was working on a project. Other than that, I didn't know anyone else was even in the building," Jovon said.

"What about you?" I asked the man beside him. *R. Drucker.*

"I didn't see or hear anything either, which I don't understand. I walked the entire building. I checked all the exits and made sure the doors were locked. I don't see how those men could have gotten inside."

"Do you have timed routes?" I knew the answer, but asking instead of telling usually encouraged people to open up.

"Yes, ma'am." Drucker rubbed the back of his head. "I don't know how anyone else would know that."

"Do you think the men who broke in could have been monitoring your movements?"

"The police think so since the shooters hacked into our system in order to bypass the security in place. But I hadn't considered they could have used our own feed against us until the cops brought it up. I didn't even think that was a thing that happened in real life."

"How do you think they accessed the system?" I'd done it remotely by gaining access to their wi-fi and burrowing in through there. "Did they tap into one of the hardlines?"

"I don't think so. The system runs daily diagnostics. A breach like that should have been uncovered."

"Do you mind if I ask why this place has more security than Fort Knox?"

"It doesn't. If it did, Jarrod and Mr. Roundtree wouldn't be dead right now."

I'd seen deflections before, and that was a good one. "Jarrod?" That was the guard who'd been killed. "Did he normally guard the executive floor?"

"No, ma'am," Drucker said. "He heard Mr. Roundtree was in the building and went up to keep him company."

I glanced at Jovon. "You said you didn't know anyone else was in the building besides the group on the third floor."

"I didn't get here until noon. Mr. Roundtree came in before that. I only found out after the fact. He wasn't scheduled to be here."

"Is there any reason Mr. Roundtree needed added security? Why do you think he was killed?"

Jovon blew through his pursed lips. "I don't know why anything happened the way it did."

"What goes on in this building?" I asked.

"Ma'am?" Drucker raised a confused eyebrow.

"Don't ma'am me." I exhaled. "You're licensed to carry firearms. You have advanced training. The security measures in this place are top of the line, and you have rotating patrols. I'll ask you one more time, what goes on inside this building?"

"Barber Productions specializes in creating music and sound effects." Jovon might have been reading from a brochure.

"I didn't realize that required maximum security."

"It doesn't, but that's Mr. Barber's decision. He wants his people and his company protected," Drucker said. He glanced around, making sure the other two guards were occupied. "It never made sense to me either. One day, I asked Mr. Barber why he took so many precautions. He said in this business a leak on a project could ruin his reputation and make studios less likely to hire us. I'm not sure if that's true, but Mr. Barber believes it. Hence, the security."

"We routinely make sure no one's taking company property off-site or posting anything on social media, texting away secrets, or contacting the trade publications," Jovon said. "That's why all these measures are in place."

I wasn't convinced, but I didn't want to argue. "The men

who broke in took something from Roundtree's office."

"What?" Drucker asked.

I watched Jovon. I couldn't be sure, but I suspected he knew something. "I don't know. It was kept in the middle drawer of Roundtree's filing cabinet. The men who took it tortured Mr. Roundtree. They shot Jarrod first, when he was stopping to get a drink from the vending machines. Then they questioned Roundtree, killed him, and took whatever he'd been hiding in the filing cabinet."

"That doesn't make any sense," Jovon said. "Are you sure about that?"

"Why? What's wrong?"

"Jarrod didn't drink soft drinks. No juice. No soda. He was a health nut. Quinoa bowls and green smoothies. Nothing with sugar or artificial sweeteners. You could sometimes convince him to put some honey in his green tea, but even that was an uphill battle."

"He'd just give it to Alyssa, anyway," Drucker said.

"Could he have been getting something for Roundtree?" I asked. "A snack or soda?"

"Probably. Jarrod was that kind of guy. He always went above and beyond."

"Who's Alyssa?"

"She's Mr. Roundtree's executive assistant. She and Jarrod had just started dating. He always brings her tea in the morning since she doesn't drink coffee."

"Is she here today?" I asked.

"I checked her in myself," Drucker said.

"Do you mind?" I pointed to the elevators.

Jovon and Drucker exchanged a meaningful look, carefully considering my request. "I guess it would be okay. After all, Mr. Barber hired you."

"Thanks."

Before I could take a single step, Jovon came around the desk with the wand. I held out my arms and waited for him to finish the sweep. "What's in the bag?" he asked.

"Handcuffs, a nine millimeter, extra ammunition, a nail file, clippers, a mini scissor. Wait, maybe I took that out." I gave him a sheepish look. "Tools of the trade."

"I can't let you walk around the building armed," he

said. "Not after Saturday, not with everyone on edge."

"Especially since the police have been scrutinizing us," Drucker added.

"All right." I took out my phone and wallet before handing them my bag. "Keep it safe."

"Yes, ma'am."

"What did I say about that, Mr. Drucker?"

"Sorry, Ms. Parker."

Considering everything that happened, the executive floor didn't look that different from the last time I was here. The woman behind the reception desk gasped when the elevator doors opened. I glanced behind me, afraid a giant spider or clown had been the cause of her fright. Apparently, I had triggered her anxiety.

"How may I help you?" She tucked a strand of dyed purple hair behind her ear. She had a stud in her nose, one in her eyebrow, and another in her lip.

"Alyssa?" I asked.

"Yes?" She looked like she wanted to hyperventilate.

I painted a reassuring smile on my face and held up my palms so she'd know I meant her no harm. "The security guards downstairs said I should speak to you. You were Fenton Roundtree's assistant."

"Uh-huh."

"I'm Alexis Parker. I was hired to evaluate building security. I just have a few questions, if that's okay."

"Uh-huh."

I ran through the basics, asking how long she worked there and if Roundtree ever received any threats or potentially dangerous visitors. She gave me the same answers everyone else did. Fenton Roundtree should have been a saint. "What about mishandled deals or projects that fell apart? Did anything like that happen recently?"

"Not that I'm aware. Fenton always had meetings with prospective clients and future investors, but most of those took place outside the office. He liked to wine and dine. He was really charismatic. Honestly, I used to tease him that this place was too drab for his personality, so he actively sought out new clients just so he'd have an excuse to get out of here. Lunch, dinner, drinks. Whatever. He loved it all."

"No one ever claimed he ripped them off or took something that didn't belong to him?"

"Um..." She opened a drawer and pulled out a binder. She flipped through the tabs with her dark purple nails. Tiny constellations dotted her ring fingers. "About ten months ago, one of the developers threw a hissy fit because Fenton showed the company's proprietary sound editing software to several investors during the course of a dinner meeting. The developer argued the IP belonged to him and only he had the right to share it, but since it had been created on company time, using company resources, for the company, it was work for hire. It belongs to Barber Productions."

"What does the software do?"

"It edits sounds. I think the developer hoped to sell it to an app designer or something. But Mr. Barber and Fenton made it worth his while not to press the issue."

"What's the developer's name?" I asked.

"Edwin Hardt."

"Do you have his contact information on file?" The name sounded familiar, but I'd run so many background checks I couldn't be sure.

Her face contorted in a 'duh' look. "You can go downstairs and talk to him, if you want."

"He still works here?"

"Yeah. Whatever the issue was, it got resolved."

Edwin Hardt would be my next stop, but since he still worked here, I doubted he hired mercenaries to kill Roundtree and kidnap Barber. It would have been flagged when I reviewed his financial statements. "I just have a few more questions."

"Uh-huh."

"Did Fenton have access to any sensitive materials?"

"Like what?"

"I don't know."

She shrugged. "Not that I know of."

"What about his relationship with Mr. Barber? How would you characterize that? Did they socialize outside of work?"

"I'd say they were friends. I don't know if they hung out or anything, but they worked well together. They had little inside jokes. Half the time, they'd say they were brainstorming or working on something but they'd just be standing in Mr. Barber's office playing with his little golf game."

"Golf game?"

"Yeah, he has one of those projectors and the ball on the string. You hit it with the club and it shows the ball flying, even though it's tethered to the ground. They'd do that for hours when they were working late."

"Do you think Mr. Barber gave Fenton access to his house or his home security system?"

"Why would he?"

"I don't know. In case he got locked out or something."

"Nah. They both have chicks." She frowned. "Sonya must be devastated. I'm really surprised Mr. Barber and Adrianna haven't stopped by to pay their respects. I've been organizing food deliveries and flowers and stuff for Sonya. Everyone here wants to do something. I don't know what's up with Mr. Barber. I figured he'd be the first in line to offer his sympathies."

"The police didn't mention anything to you?"

She shook her head.

Deciding it'd be best not to let the cat out of the bag, I switched back to my main question now that I'd gotten a feel for Alyssa and didn't think she was involved or intentionally trying to deceive me. "What did Fenton keep in his filing cabinet, specifically in the middle drawer?"

"Everything he'd take with him when he left at night. His keys. His thermos. His lunchbox."

"A laptop?" I asked.

"Uh-huh."

"Security said no one was allowed to leave the building with project information."

"That rule doesn't apply to the executives. Fenton needed to have the materials with him for his client meetings."

"Did Mr. Barber know about that?"

"Yeah." Her head bobbed. "Fenton never tried to keep

any secrets from Mr. Barber. They were in this together. Mr. Barber always said he'd run this place into the ground if Fenton wasn't around to help him." She peered down the empty hallway. "I can't help but wonder if that's what's going to happen now."

"One last question," I said. "The Roundtrees' anniversary was Monday. Do you know what Fenton had planned?"

She scanned the calendar. "He cleared his afternoon. He told me on Friday he hoped to duck out early. He said he wanted to surprise his wife with something special." She dabbed at her eyes. "It's so sad. Poor Sonya."

"Did he tell you what the surprise was?"

She shook her head. "He always seemed like a romantic guy. He probably had something amazing in mind."

"Like dropping a few thousand on some jewelry?"

"I don't know. Maybe. That seems like something he'd do."

"Any idea where he'd get the cash to do that?"

"He's an executive. I'm sure he had it, but with all the bonuses that have been handed out this past month, maybe he used that to splurge a little."

TWENTY-EIGHT

Edwin Hardt had started out as a programmer in Silicon Valley. He'd gotten an internship straight out of college, made good money, and left when the company changed owners. He'd put those skills to use at Barber Productions, creating a user-friendly interface for digital sound editing. He spent a great deal of time going into the specifics, which went way over my head but also made me doubt he was responsible for the murders and abduction. He might have been scary smart, but that didn't stop him from telling me everything he knew about his project and beyond. Unfortunately, he didn't know anything about a threat or problems inside Barber Productions.

"What about Fenton Roundtree's laptop?" I asked. "Word is you were angry about him showing off your program."

"I was, but I got over it. I just wanted some recognition. I already dealt with plenty of that bullshit before. But Mr. Roundtree was cool, and so's Mr. Barber. Once I aired my grievance, Mr. Barber called me into his office, personally thanked me, promoted me to project manager, gave me a nice pay bump, and offered me some stocks. I'm now part owner of the company. Isn't that cool?"

"How big of a chunk did you get?"

"Three percent."

"What does that translate to in dollars and cents?"

Hardt chuckled. "It translates to a hell of a lot if I design something incredible and we can use it to boost ourselves to the next level."

"But at the moment?"

"It's worth maybe a new car or a down payment on a house."

"Nothing that'll make you independently wealthy?" I asked.

"Nah, but that's what crypto's for."

Once I left Barber Productions, I pulled up everything on Jovon, but if he'd taken a bribe or been paid off, it didn't show in his financial records. I tossed his name over to Mercer, figuring if Hans and Donovan hadn't paid him a visit yet, they should. They'd be better at convincing him to talk. But more than likely, whatever he knew probably had nothing to do with Brent's abduction and more to do with Jarrod's love life.

My trip to Barber Productions hadn't revealed anything I didn't already know. Unless Fenton Roundtree had something else tucked away that no one knew about, the mercenaries must have wanted his company laptop badly enough to kill for it. According to building security, it remained unaccounted for, but Roundtree might have left it at home when he stopped by the office on Saturday, unless he'd locked it in the drawer before he left Friday night and that's why the mercenaries planned their strike for Saturday, not expecting to encounter any resistance inside the building. By all accounts, Roundtree shouldn't have been at the office. The poor man had the worst timing.

Unsure what to do, I drove to Fenton Roundtree's place. His wife would know what happened to the laptop, but I didn't get out of my car. A police cruiser remained parked out front. After checking with Nero, I was reassured that Detective Petrocelli and Sylvio remained at the station. So the annoying detective wasn't the one paying Sonya Roundtree a visit.

I didn't want to interrupt the police from questioning the grieving widow. I'd have to check back later. Maybe Mercer was having better luck.

I checked my messages, but the last message I received was from Cross saying he was heading to the office. Bianchi would get word to him if there were any additional developments, but it looked like we'd effectively cut him out of the negotiation. Instead of wasting my time playing phone tag with Cross, I dialed Bastian.

"How are things?" I asked.

"Nothing new since the last time you checked, love."

"No additional info on the ransom?"

"None."

"What about on Adrianna?"

"The kidnappers haven't responded."

"What did Mercer say?"

"Nothing."

"That sounds like Julian."

"Have the police finished with Sylvio yet? He's our best bet. We're itching to take a crack at him."

"No. Cross's team will let me know when the police release him. They didn't get anything useful out of him before Petrocelli intervened."

"I'm sure we'll have better luck."

"What are you planning on doing with him?"

"It depends on his level of chattiness."

"Great."

"Don't worry, love. We know where the line is."

That didn't mean they wouldn't cross it. It also didn't mean I wouldn't either. This situation was getting worse and worse. Lives hung in the balance. I couldn't wait for the police to finish asking their questions. I needed to know everything right now. It was the only way to throw the kidnappers off kilter and buy some time to figure out how to get Brent and Adrianna back, assuming they weren't dead yet.

I entered Sylvio DePalma's home address into the GPS and turned the car around. I had no idea what Cross was doing or what kind of bargain he'd struck with Luther Bianchi. But something told me if we didn't get Brent back alive, our biggest problem wouldn't be Luther Bianchi suing us.

Cross wasn't thinking straight. Brent was his friend. That clouded his judgement. Meeting Luther was supposed to help the situation, but all we'd managed to do was call off one set of dogs for another. Luther Bianchi had already made it clear he had no intention of cooperating with the kidnapper. Men like him didn't succumb to threats. Instead, he'd get even. At least Mercer would do everything he could to make a recovery possible. We just needed more information.

Sylvio knew something. He was the last person who spoke to Brent Barber. He received the first anonymous text from the kidnapper and also the last. Sylvio reached out to Luther Bianchi, which derailed our investigation. I just didn't know if that had been Sylvio's intention. Perhaps that was innocent enough, given his relationship with Brent, but the more I thought about it, the less I believed it. Nothing was ever that easy or that convenient. The kidnappers wanted Sylvio involved. That's why they reached out to him on multiple occasions. I just didn't know why he was so important.

I circled Sylvio's neighborhood twice before parking near a shade tree. Petrocelli had told Sylvio to come to the station, but the police weren't staking out his place or searching his apartment. Then again, they didn't know everything I did.

Sylvio's apartment building didn't have much in the way of security, so getting inside didn't take much effort. Regardless, I didn't want to risk getting identified if the police decided to perform a canvass or pull nearby surveillance footage, so I entered with my sunglasses on and leather gloves covering my hands. Another problem with California, the weather wasn't conducive to performing clandestine operations in broad daylight.

Above the door, Sylvio had hidden two keys. The first one unlocked the deadbolt. The second worked wonders on the doorknob lock. I put the keys back where I found them and pulled the door closed behind me.

The apartment was a mess. It looked like it had been

tossed, just like Brent's bedroom. I unzipped my jacket, resting my hand on my gun. What were the kidnappers looking for?

"Hello?" I waited, listening, but the only sound I heard was the hum of the air conditioner.

I stopped outside the bedroom door and peered into the room. The closet looked like it exploded. Clothing and accessories were strewn about. Every duffel bag and suitcase had been pulled out and left opened. A few appeared to be half-packed, but the clothes weren't folded. They were hanging over the sides. A sleeve here, a sock there.

A creaking came from the living room. Carefully, I approached the door and peered into the hallway. I watched and waited, but I didn't see or hear anything. Deciding to check it out, I moved into the living room.

It was just as messy as the rest of the apartment. The living room connected to the dining area and kitchen. Half the kitchen cabinets had been opened. A box of cereal lay sideways on the counter. Honey-coated circles had spilled out and scattered across the floor. Dishes were piled up in the sink. The couch cushions sat slightly askew, as if someone had been hunting for loose change.

The creaking sounded again. I turned, finding the refrigerator door cracked open. It swayed ever so slightly as the air blew from the nearby vent. Opening the door wider, I looked inside. Condensation had formed on the outside of the condiment bottles, nearest the opening. But nothing smelled like it had spoiled and the thermometer inside said the internal temperature was forty-two degrees. Sylvio relocated to the safe house yesterday. If he'd left the fridge open, the temperature inside should be much higher. Someone else had been here recently.

I searched the entire kitchen, finding the flour and sugar canisters had been emptied and every box had been opened and searched. I had to assume that was the work of the kidnappers. Unfortunately, it didn't give me any clue as to what they were so desperate to get their hands on.

Returning to the living room, I scanned the area. On the coffee table, behind a stack of magazines was a glass vial and two unused syringes. Picking up the vial, I found it nearly empty. Only a drop remained. The label told me it was a horse tranquilizer. The skin at the back of my neck prickled, and my blood ran cold.

I pulled out my camera and took a few snapshots of the vial and syringes. Could Sylvio be responsible for the kidnapping? We checked his background. He didn't have the resources necessary to hire professionals like Irmine and Castillo. But maybe we missed something. Maybe Sylvio wasn't who we thought he was, or he had what the kidnappers wanted. That would explain why he'd been so nervous at the safe house and why he'd gone to the police station when Petrocelli called. Sylvio was scared. How much did he know? Why wasn't he helping us?

I picked through the rest of the items on the coffee table. Nothing. I moved toward his desk. No computer. No tablet. The desk drawers contained printer supplies, power cords, and a collection of mouse pads and batteries. Had he taken his computer with him? I texted Nero, asking about it, but Sylvio hadn't brought any devices to the safe house except his cell phone, which Lucien had taken and replaced with a throwaway.

The dining room table was just as cluttered as everything else. Beneath some plastic takeout bags, I found his laptop. Since we couldn't question Sylvio until the police were finished with him, this would have to do.

Several framed photos caught my eye. They sat on top of the side table in the dining area. Two of the photos were of Sylvio's family. One was his parents' wedding photo. The other was a group shot of his entire family. A third frame contained Sylvio's graduation picture. The rest were of him and his friends. Sylvio and Brent stood next to each other in two of the pictures, smiling and laughing. Was that a lie?

I wasn't sure what I expected to find, but the vial and syringes told a very different story than what I found in the rest of the apartment. Despite his anxiety, I didn't think he was dosing himself with horse tranquilizers. Were they even his or had the kidnappers brought them, expecting to pull off another abduction?

Sylvio was involved. I just wasn't sure how. He could be

masterminding this or the kidnappers needed something from him, a final piece of the puzzle we had yet to solve. Maybe they came here, hoping to find that missing piece and figured they'd use the drugs to force Sylvio to comply. Depending on the dosage, animal tranquilizers could make him groggy and easy to question or they could kill him.

I returned the picture frame to its rightful spot, snapped a few more shots, and turned my attention to the pile of opened mail beside the picture frames. No outstanding bills. No final notices. Nothing indicated Sylvio was in financial crisis.

His parents and relatives had sent a few birthday cards. I skimmed the handwritten notes, but none of them sounded threatening or hostile. The rest of the mail was an assortment of magazines and junk. I was in the process of leafing through it when I heard a rustling in the kitchen.

I moved through the dining room and into the kitchen, my gun in my hand. The fallen cereal crunched beneath my shoes. No one had been in the kitchen. I would have noticed the stepped-on food. But where did the noise come from?

Going out the other opening, I moved down the hallway and back into the bedroom. The room looked like it had before. I checked the bathroom, which I hadn't gotten around to the first time. As I suspected, the medicine cabinet and linen closets were open. Even the hamper had been emptied. A pile of dirty clothes covered the floor beside the toilet.

For good measure, I checked the toilet tank. The cover sat askew, creaking as I slid it back into place. Still, I had no idea what made that rustling sound, but it was probably the air conditioner blowing some part of this mess around.

Tucking my gun away, I pulled out my phone to update Mercer on the situation while I went to finish up in the dining room. I noticed a black bag on top of the desk. It hadn't been there before.

I froze, sensing the trap, but I was too late. Someone shoved a white plastic bag over my head and pulled it tight. He hooked his ankle around mine, forcing me off balance and onto the ground. I landed hard, my shoulder taking the brunt of the impact. He pinned one arm behind my back. I threw an elbow with the other, hoping to get him to release his grip, but he shifted out of the way. The glancing blow did nothing but anger him.

He slammed down on the bend in my elbow, tugging it farther behind my back and locking it in place by looping his arm around both of mine while pulling the bag tighter around my neck. I bucked and rocked, but he held firm.

"Stop fighting. It's just like going to sleep."

I threw all of my weight from one side to the other, hoping to get loose. But he held tight. With every gasp, the bag pressed against my mouth and nose. The tiny amount of air that had been inside had already vanished. The plastic invaded my mouth, tasting vaguely of peanut sauce and bug spray. I tried kicking and twisting my way free, but he wrapped his other leg around mine, keeping me down and still. Whoever this bastard was, he was trained.

My pulse pounded in my ears. I tried holding my breath, but that didn't work. So I sucked the plastic into my mouth, attempting to gnaw my way through it as images of the headless crisis negotiators came to mind. I was getting dizzy. All I could hear was the crinkling of the plastic. My lungs burned for air.

Desperate, I pushed my tongue against the plastic, forcing as much space as possible between it and my mouth. I inhaled slowly around my tongue. The pressure in my chest eased ever so slightly. I pressed harder against the plastic. My vision dimming. I sucked in another breath, unable to keep the plastic from filling my mouth. As a last ditch effort, I bit down hard and jerked my head to the side.

He held the bag even tighter. The bottom edges dug into my flesh so deeply I couldn't even swallow. I jerked my head again, which only made him pull harder. Gripping the bag between my front teeth, I continued to jerk from left to right. He yanked the bag harder, attempting to keep me in place. This time, the thin plastic ripped.

I filled my lungs, my vision clearing. And then I stopped struggling. I let my taut muscles go slack. But he didn't fall for it.

With all my might, I threw myself backward against him. My legs knocked into the side table. The frames and other knickknacks crashed to the ground on top of us. The table went over to. The glass shattered around us, but he never let go. I'd trained specifically for scenarios like this, but successfully getting out of the hold was damn near impossible. So I screamed as loud as I could. The walls were thin. Someone would hear me.

That made him shift positions. I anticipated he'd cover my mouth. Instead, he dropped his grip on the bag and released my arms. I pushed myself up just as something sharp jabbed into the back of my neck. I knocked it away, seeing a thin stream of liquid squirt over my shoulder. But I had been half a second too late.

My scream turned into a dull hum. My muscles went slack. My vision went wobbly, my eyelids becoming too heavy. He left me on the ground amidst the broken glass.

I tried to sit up, to move away, but I only slid a few inches on my shoulder. My legs moving but not gaining any traction. He tried to ziptie my hands, but I rolled onto my back, allowing my head to loll to the side. I recognized him. He delivered the heads to the office.

"You," I slurred.

He muttered something I couldn't quite hear before securing my ankle to the table leg. Removing my gun, he unloaded it and placed it on the dining room table. I stared up at it, struggling to keep my lids from closing. He watched me, debating if he should finish the job or shackle me further. Instead, I closed my eyes and remained still.

Once he walked away, I opened my eyes, but between the torn bag still over my head and whatever he jabbed into me, I couldn't see much. The angle didn't help either.

He moved back and forth, opening cabinets and searching compartments. He wore black combat boots with the laces tucked into the tops, just like his pant legs. He didn't even pause when the floor shook.

Earthquake? I wondered. As if this situation wasn't bad enough. He pulled out the desk drawers, dumping each one out on the floor and sifting through the items before examining the bottoms and sides. Whatever he wanted, it wasn't here.

How did he get inside? Did I miss him? The only room I hadn't checked when I first entered was the attached bathroom. But the apartment was so small, I couldn't figure out how he snuck around me or where he hid.

Unable to make sense out of any of it, I watched him for what felt like an eternity. He went into the kitchen, the cereal crunching beneath his feet. The cabinets slammed. "Dammit."

While he slid underneath the sink, searching the inside of the cabinets, I rolled off my arms, took the bag off my head, and fumbled for my gun. I couldn't exactly reach it from here, and sitting up seemed beyond my current capabilities. So I pulled on the tablecloth. My gun and ammo landed beside me with two consecutive thunks. But he didn't notice. Quickly, I reloaded my weapon and aimed with both hands.

"Freeze," I said.

He crawled out from under the sink and cocked his head at me. "What are you going to do with that?"

"Hands up." My arms shook, my aim wavering. I blinked a few times, forcing the two identical versions of him to shift into one.

"Fine." He raised his hands and climbed onto his knees. "You got me. Now what are you going to do with me?"

"Where's Brent Barber?"

"Who?"

"What do you want? Tell me. We'll get it for you, but you have to let Brent and Adrianna go. Fair exchange. The ransom for their lives. Everyone walks away. We all win."

"You're starting to feel it, aren't you?" He grinned wickedly. "You've been poisoned."

It's not poison. It was the damn horse tranq. He wanted to get in my head. I couldn't let him. I squeezed my eyes closed and shook it off. Why was everything so hazy?

He laughed. "And to think, I was considering letting you live." He leapt toward me, grabbing a knife from the drawer.

I squeezed the trigger. The shot went high and to the left, shattering the window. Pounding sounded at the front door, like a battering ram smashing against it.

He hesitated for a moment, keeping an eye on me while he strained to hear what was happening in the hallway. The wood splintered, the door buckling under the pressure. Desperately, I tried to steady my aim. Before I could fire again, he grabbed the black bag off the table and crashed through what remained of the window and disappeared.

I stared at the broken glass and dropped the gun, afraid the police would see it and open fire. I flopped back onto the ground, feeling the glass fragments crush beneath me. Why did he jump out a window? Did he kill himself? Did he break a leg? How high were we? We needed him alive. He could take us to Brent and Adrianna.

I couldn't remember what floor this was. But I felt more rumbling and shaking. I closed my eyes, hoping to convince whoever had entered I didn't pose a threat. The floor creaked, but I didn't move. I didn't even breathe.

Donovan rubbed his knuckles against my sternum. "Parker?"

I opened my eyes and took a deep breath. "He jumped." I turned my gaze toward the window.

"We know. Hans went out after him."

"Hans jumped out the window?"

"It's not exactly the first time." He helped me sit up, gently brushing the glass shards away and picking a syringe out of the rubble. Blood coated the needle and a few drops had spattered onto the pen. "Any idea what this was?"

"He said poison. I don't believe it."

Donovan examined the puncture at the back of my neck. "Okay."

"Feels like a sedative or tranquilizer, not enough to knock me out, but enough to shut me up. I'm guessing it's the horse tranq from the table."

He tucked the syringe away, giving the floor an uncertain look. "You all right to move?" I nodded, and he cut me free and helped me up, grabbing my arm before I toppled over. "I'll take that as a no." He ducked underneath one of my arms and tapped the comm in his ear. "How much time?" He frowned. "Copy."

"What are you doing here?"

"Later." He propped me against the wall while he picked up my shell casing and tucked it into his pocket. "Anything else?"

I spotted a crumpled hundred dollar bill beside the desk. "That." I stepped away from the wall. The ground didn't seem quite as sturdy, but I remained upright and moving under my own power. Scooping up the bill, I pointed to the vial on the table. "Grab that too." I moved toward the broken-down door, but Donovan grabbed my arm.

"Not that way." He redirected me away from the door and toward the destroyed window. "Fire escape's our best bet, even if it's a bit dodgy. The bobbies are on the way. Neighbors reported screams and gunfire. It's time we take our leave. The coppers will just have to sort through this rubbish for us." He climbed through the window, offering me his arm for support as I followed after him. When we reached the bottom rung of the rusted ladder, we spotted Hans waiting near a black SUV. "You get him?"

"No." Hans eyed me. "Is the bird okay?"

"She will be. Hopefully."

"I can answer for myself," I said. "And I'm not a bird."

Hans grinned. "Apologies, milady." He rolled his wrist in the air, performing a royal wave of sorts. "But that is a term of endearment."

Sirens sounded in the distance. Donovan grabbed the keys from my pocket and tossed them to Hans. "Time to regroup."

TWENTY-NINE

Bastian had been glancing in my direction every few minutes. "All right, love?" he asked.

"Fine." I retracted my fingers from the blisters on my neck.

"You shouldn't be." Mercer studied the photos I'd taken. "Why didn't you clear the apartment first?"

I'd asked myself that a hundred times since I got jumped. "The door was locked. The main room was clear, so was the bedroom. When I spotted the vial and syringe, I got distracted. I don't know. It was stupid."

Mercer put my phone down and went to the wall and stuck a pin in the map, marking Sylvio's apartment. Beside it, he wrote the time and date and hung another photo of the alleged delivery guy. This one had been taken from a nearby surveillance camera. "Taran Heuzen. We don't have much besides a name, which is probably an alias. What did he say to you?"

"Besides threatening my life and claiming he poisoned me, not much."

Mercer waited for me to elaborate, the impatience obvious on his face.

"He had training of some sort, but he's sloppy. He didn't

bind my hands." I thought about the fight. "He underestimated me or overestimated the amount of tranquilizer he shot into my neck."

"Don't make the same mistake. He and his teammates are ruthless and deadly."

"Teammates? Besides the two you've identified, how many more could there be?"

"There's no telling. Depending on mission parameters, we could be looking at an entire unit." Mercer continued to wait me out, but I didn't know what he wanted me to say. Finally, he asked, "Do you know what he was looking for?"

"No. I offered to get whatever he wants in exchange for Brent and Adrianna, but he didn't bite. He left with a bag." I pulled the crumpled hundred out of my pocket. "I think this was inside it."

"So this is about money." Mercer took the bill and held it up to the light. It wasn't counterfeit. I'd already checked.

"I don't know. Whatever he hoped to find in Sylvio's apartment, he didn't get. The money might have been a consolation prize."

"How can you be sure?" Bastian asked.

"He was still searching when I pulled the gun on him. He'd still be there now if Donovan and Hans hadn't knocked down the door. He tore the place apart. I'm pretty sure whatever he wants isn't there, or he would have found it."

"I'm surprised he was on his own. I'd imagine they'd work in teams," Bastian said.

"Depends." Mercer pointed to the photos of Brent and Adrianna. "We don't know if they have her or if they are keeping the two of them together. If they separated their hostages, even with additional assets, they might not have the manpower to cover everything. Heuzen makes the runs. Pick-up and delivery. That's his job."

Bastian added a few more drops of solution to the glass and gave it a gentle shake before lifting the glass beside it and comparing the two liquids.

"Poison?" Mercer asked.

I scowled at him. "Wouldn't I feel worse instead of better if I'd been poisoned?"

He shrugged, but I saw the smile in his eyes. Julian Mercer liked busting my chops.

"It doesn't look like you got dosed with anything more than a mild tranquilizer. You should be tip-top in no time," Bastian said.

"Great." But I'd been reckless. I knew better than to make a basic mistake like that, but I'd been preoccupied and rushed. I was too focused on how Sylvio fit into this to even think the kidnappers might still be inside.

"Regardless, it's probably best you didn't let too much of that get into your bloodstream. A higher dosage could have killed you."

I thought about what Heuzen had said about letting me live. "He behaved strangely for a mercenary. The two who killed Roundtree wouldn't have hesitated to put a bullet in me. Why did he?"

"Maybe he thought he could use you to find what he wants," Mercer said. "You made the offer. Perhaps he's thinking about it."

"Sylvio must know what they want. We have to speak to him, but the police aren't letting him out of their sight. Do we know if he's been arrested?"

"I don't think they've filed charges, but he's still in the police station." Bastian clicked a few keys. "No charges from what I can see."

"We have to get him out," Mercer said.

"Jules, if we can't touch him, neither can they. This gives us time. If they're on a clock, they might get desperate and reach out."

"Or they'll find an alternative solution." Mercer dropped into a chair. "Heuzen should have bloody well killed you. That would have been the smart move. Castillo and Irmine used silencers on Roundtree. That would have worked here. One shot, execution style, no screams, no commotion, no hurrying."

"Jules," Bastian scolded, "don't say shite like that."

"Any professional would have done it. Why not him?" He nodded to Heuzen's photo.

"He's new," I suggested, but Mercer was right. "I don't think he had a gun with him."

Mercer squinted. "He could be our weak link. The one they don't trust."

"It fits with the tasks he's been given." Bastian rocked in his chair, the pen dangling from the corner of his mouth. "How do we exploit that?"

"I have no bloody idea. Figure it out, Bas."

Bastian glared at Mercer, muttering something under his breath.

"Do we know if Heuzen has ever been inside Barber Productions?" I asked.

"Facial rec's checking the security footage for the last six weeks." Bastian glanced at another screen. "No hits yet, but it'll take time."

Mercer turned. "Bas, have the headless bodies been located yet?"

"No. I've been listening to the police scanner and monitoring their intake system. No reports have been made." Bastian reached for the open box of licorice pieces and spit out the pen before popping a piece of candy into his mouth. Based on his exaggerated chewing, the strawberry twists were stale. "Hans and Donovan scoured every inch of the meet site. No blood. No expelled casings. Nothing to indicate an ambush or two murders took place there."

"But they left a mess inside Sylvio's apartment and Brent's bedroom. Why?" I asked.

"That wasn't a crime scene until you showed up. Heuzen didn't know his search would be compromised," Mercer said. "Is your DNA in the system?"

"Probably," I said.

"Your blood was on the syringe. Droplets must be on the floor too," Mercer said.

"The police won't bother with that. They have too much to do, and even if they run it, by the time they get the results, it'll be months from now."

"I still don't like it."

"I didn't like getting stabbed in the neck or suffocated, but I can't do anything about that now." The thought made me rub my neck again.

"A chokehold would have worked better than the bag,"

Mercer said. "Cleaner, easier to control, less time consuming." Bastian shot the commander another death glare. "He could have left you alive because he didn't feel like performing more unpaid work." Mercer might have been cynical, but he made a valid point.

"We know this has to do with Barber Productions. They took Roundtree's laptop, but they didn't want him. They wanted Brent and something Sylvio has. Could this really be about some million-dollar project?"

"Castillo doesn't work like that," Mercer said. "It'll be about the money, but he doesn't do corporate sabotage."

"People change," Bastian said.

"Not that much. His unsanctioned missions have caused him to only associate with war lords and traffickers. He'd never cross paths with a rival sound studio, unless this links back to some form of organized crime."

"Could we be wrong about the laptop?" Bastian asked. "Maybe they didn't take Roundtree's. Maybe that's what they are hunting for and they think Sylvio has it."

"Donovan grabbed Sylvio's laptop." I pointed to the device Bastian had already searched. "I didn't find any other computers or devices at his place." I rubbed my face and sent a text to Ganz, asking for an update on when Sylvio would be released.

He's a person of interest. They can hold him a full forty-eight hours before they charge him, he replied.

Would Petrocelli do that? I asked.

He made a name for himself by doing shit like this.

"The cops don't want to let Sylvio go," I said. "Until charges are filed, I don't think there's anything we can do." I tried to think of a solution, but nothing came to mind.

Bastian pulled me from my reverie. "What were you hoping to find by going to Sylvio's?"

"Evidence of the kidnapping. A threat. A ransom note. Other communications. Proof he's been withholding information or that he's involved in Brent and Adrianna's abductions. Something that would bring us one step closer to finding them."

"Do you think he's involved?" Bastian asked. "I haven't found any indication of it."

"Before this afternoon, I thought he might be. Now, I have my doubts, but I don't trust him. He's misled us. Frankly, I'm starting to think everything he's said might be a lie." I zoomed in on the photo I'd taken of the vial and syringes, but besides the drug name, no other information had been available. "Do you think they drugged Brent or Adrianna when they were taken?"

"That's one way to ensure they didn't attract any undue attention. Depending on the dosage, Castillo and Irmine could have dragged Brent out to the car without him making a peep," Bastian said. "That fits with the footage we've seen. No one reported screams. Brent might have struggled a little, given the marks on the stairs and the blood on the shredder, but they might have been afraid of overdosing him since he appears to be the primary target."

"Any idea where they got the tranquilizers? Could they be Sylvio's? He takes anti-anxiety medication."

"For humans, not animals," Mercer said.

"I'll leave the detecting up to you," Bastian said. "But I'd say they probably came from a vet's office. Someplace that specializes in farm animals and equines."

"That'll take too long to run down," Mercer said. "They could have already had a supply from their last mission."

"What about Sylvio?" I asked. "Does he have any connection to vets or horse farms?"

Bastian shook his head. "Sorry, love."

"What about Jovon? He gave me strange vibes," I said.

"Hans and Donovan are speaking to him now. They will assess the situation," Mercer said.

"I've seen what happens to the people you question. They usually come out of things worse for wear."

"Donovan and Hans are simply having a friendly chat," Mercer said. "That's all. Jovon won't be harmed if he abides by the rules and cooperates."

"Are you planning on abiding by the rules?"

Mercer challenged me with his eyes, but I didn't back down. His gaze softened and he smiled. "For now."

I eased into a chair and drank some water. I'd gotten so close to one of the kidnappers today, but we hadn't been able to track his whereabouts after he fled Sylvio's apartment. And it hadn't brought us any closer to figuring out what the kidnappers wanted or where they might be keeping Brent and Adrianna.

"You should rest, love," Bastian said.

"In a minute. How did Hans and Donovan know where I was or that I was in trouble?"

"Luck," Mercer said. "After revisiting Brent's house and questioning several Barber Productions employees who hadn't bothered to show up for work today, they made the round trip to San Diego, searched the hotel and the alleyway, and returned with Adrianna's belongings. After that, we picked up reports of a disturbance at Sylvio's address and thought it best to check it out."

"Did you find anything on Adrianna's computer?" I asked.

Bastian shook his head.

"From what I gather, the mercs were hired to retrieve something. They must have thought it was held on Roundtree's company laptop and that they needed Brent Barber to access it. But they still don't have it, and now it looks like Sylvio might. Adrianna's just collateral damage or an end to a means." I frowned. "I meant means to an end. Talk to Nero and Omar. They questioned Sylvio. They might be able to help."

"We have, but they didn't ask the right questions," Mercer said. "I told Cross he should have let us handle it."

"He's stubborn like that." I sighed. "I should have mentioned it sooner, but this is personal for my boss. He and Brent are friends. He feels responsible."

Mercer eyed me. "I know. I've known all along."

"I wanted to say something. I should have."

He shook it away. "No matter. It doesn't change the mission. Before this afternoon, questioning Sylvio would have been harder, more abstract. Now it'll be concrete."

I wasn't sure I liked the way he said that either. Thoughts of concrete shoes came to mind, and I wondered if that's how Luther Bianchi had made his rivals disappear all those years ago. "We're so screwed," I mumbled.

"Get some sleep, love," Bastian insisted. "You're no good to us like this."

"What if the kidnappers try something else? We have to figure out what they want."

"We will," Bastian said.

"How?" I asked. "How are we going to figure that out?"

"We don't have to," Mercer said, "if we get them to tell us."

Either that was brilliant or the most ridiculous thing I'd ever heard. But since I wasn't sure which, it was time to call it quits. Lack of sleep led to delayed reaction times, poor impulse control, and impaired decision-making, all of which had contributed to my potentially near-fatal encounter.

"What about Sylvio?" I asked.

"As soon as he gets released, we'll pick him up and keep him safe." Bastian gave me a reassuring smile. "Lucien Cross has two of his best guys parked outside the police station. Keeping watch is their job. It doesn't have to be yours too."

"Let me know when we're ready to move," I said. "And Julian, make sure someone's here at all times, okay?"

"Aye."

"What's wrong, love? Are you spooked?" Bastian asked.

"It's not for her." Mercer nodded, understanding. "She's afraid if they come looking, they'll find him."

"James?" Bastian asked.

I nodded. "I already warned his bodyguard of the potential threat and told him to keep his eyes peeled. But I'm not sure it's enough."

"We got him," Mercer said.

"Just don't tell him. He's forgiven me for last time, but I don't know if he'll ever completely get over what happened. I promised him no repeats. This feels a bit too much like one."

THIRTY

"Sweetheart," Martin whispered, "are you okay? Let me see."

I rolled over, throwing one arm over my eyes to shield them from the overhead light. "Who told you?"

"Bastian." Martin tossed his jacket and tie onto the chair.

"Did he tell you the guy jumped out a window to get away from me?"

Martin smiled, but it never reached his eyes. "He left that part out."

"What did he say?"

"That you needed to catch up on some sleep." He sat down beside me, gently brushing my hair back before pressing his lips to my forehead. "You never came back to bed last night. We never got a chance to talk this morning. Was that intentional?"

"No. I had to unlock the office for the phone guy."

"Good excuse."

"It isn't. Not entirely." I sat up. "I didn't know Mercer would show up in the middle of the night or that they'd come straight here. Our client and his girlfriend have been taken. Cross couldn't find any locals to handle it. He doesn't usually deal with these types of cases."

"Why the exception?" Martin ran his thumb across my cheek, his eyes finding something below my ear disconcerting.

"Brent Barber's one of his friends. I don't think Lucien has many of them. He just wants to make sure the guy survives this."

"It has to be serious if you called for a British invasion." He placed his fingertips on my chin and gently urged me to lift my head.

"Martin, no." I grabbed his hand and pressed it to my lips. "I'm okay. That's it. End of story."

"The last time you had marks like that..." Fire burned in his eyes. "Are you sure you're okay?"

"Uh-huh. But don't grab me from behind, unless you want to risk an elbow to the solar plexus."

He leaned down and kissed me before picking up a change of clothes and heading for the bathroom. When he came out, he left the light on the lowest setting, so I wouldn't have to deal with the dark. He climbed into bed beside me with a cool compress in his hand. "Here, this should help."

I adjusted until I was comfortable against his shoulder before letting him spread the cloth out against the bruises and blisters. It eased the sting, which felt like a nasty rug burn. "Are you mad?"

"No."

I looked at him. "Bullshit."

"I'm not." He kissed me again before stretching an arm out beneath my pillow and tilting his head so it rested against mine. "For once, I'd like to take you someplace where shit like this doesn't happen. Three thousand miles isn't far enough when you're working for Cross."

"Shit happens everywhere."

He exhaled. "No wonder billionaires want to go to space."

"That wouldn't help. Have you heard of alien abductions?"

"I'm not sure I buy into that. With the abduction stories you hear, aliens would have to be a race of rogue proctologists, and that'd just be weird."

"What?"

"Think about it. If you found a new species, would you stick something up its ass during your first encounter?"

"I wouldn't stick anything anywhere. But I'm not male. Your kind thinks differently."

"I take offense to that."

"So do I."

"Alex?"

"I don't mean you, handsome. I'm just basing that on statistics. Maybe the aliens thought they had consent. Perhaps that's how they say hello."

"Ass-play doesn't seem like a first encounter activity unless that was previously agreed upon." He laughed. "Stop distracting me. I have an actual point I'm trying to make here."

"You brought it up."

"I want you somewhere safe, away from killers and crazed kidnappers. Is that too much to ask? Because it shouldn't be."

"I know."

"That's why I'm putting the idea of space travel out there. If this project of mine were to take off, really take off, the sky's the limit. We could get a nice little planet to ourselves."

I laughed, finding the playful grin on his face the most attractive thing I'd ever seen. Instead of fighting, he was being downright adorable. "Martin, I don't want to go to space." I ran my hand along his forearm when he wrapped it around my waist. "I like breathing. You can't do that in space."

"In that case, I'll make sure wherever we are, you never stop breathing."

"Ditto." I snuggled against him. "So based on this conversation, should I assume you had a good day at work?"

"It wasn't terrible." He ran his thumb across my cheek, catching a strand of hair and tucking it behind my ear. "I wish you could say the same."

"It's fine. I'm okay."

He raised an eyebrow in disbelief. "Really?"

"Ask me again tomorrow. Right now, I'm just glad one of us had a good day."

We talked about his project and the meetings he had and the ones he lined up. We talked about letting Bastian make a grocery list for Marcal since he'd eaten us out of house and home. Martin made sure I stayed focused on him and not on Sylvio DePalma. I couldn't think about that now, or I'd barge into the police station or knock down Petrocelli's door. And we couldn't afford that. I just didn't know if Brent and Adrianna could afford for me not to do it.

Eventually, I yawned. Martin put his phone on do not disturb and turned the TV on. He resisted the urge to envelop me fully in his arms, knowing that would cause me to panic. Instead, he let me use his shoulder like a pillow. Within a few minutes, I'd fallen asleep.

Noise outside the bedroom woke me. I opened my eyes, feeling clearer and less fuzzy. It was just after four. I'd slept on and off for most of the night, regretting every second as time Brent and Adrianna couldn't get back.

A gentle rapping sounded against the bedroom door. "Love?" Bastian whispered. "You have a call."

"Who?"

"Hmm?" Martin snuggled closer, the bridge of his nose rubbing against my temple.

Before I could disentangle myself from him, Mercer barged into the room and handed me the phone. "Answer it."

I looked at the caller ID. *Unknown.*

Martin sat up, eyeing the man in our bedroom like an alpha prepared to mark his territory. "What's going on, sweetheart?"

"I don't know."

"Answer it." Mercer put his hands on his hips. "It could be them."

"Alex," Martin warned, but I pressed the green button and held it to my ear.

"Hello?"

"I thought you'd want to know Adrianna was dropped

off an hour ago. She didn't have any ID, so that's led to some delays. Lucky for you, I have friends at most of the major hospitals, so I got the first call. If you want to talk to her, I suggest you hurry. By dawn, the LAPD will have gotten word, and you won't be able to get near her."

"Who is this?" I asked.

"Rizzo's buddy."

"Hershel?"

"You can call me that for now."

It's okay, I mouthed to Martin before getting out of bed. Mercer followed me out of the bedroom. I pressed my finger to my lips so he'd remain silent. Then I hit the speaker button. "Where is Adrianna?"

"She was picked up just outside L.A. by a truck driver. He dropped her off at the nearest hospital. Mercy Gen. They got his information on file, but I already ran it. He runs long-hauls. He was across the country when she was taken. He's only been in the area these last eight hours. He couldn't have grabbed her from the hotel."

"What's his name?" I asked.

"Don't waste your time. I said I checked, and I did."

Mercer shook his head. Since the hospital had the information on file, his team would find a way to get it.

"Why are you calling me with this?" I asked.

"It's simple. Kidnappings are federal. You used to be a Fed."

"You looked into me?"

"Damn straight. For all I knew, you were a fucking serial killer."

"Women usually aren't."

"Usually, not always."

Mercer snapped his fingers, waiting to see if Bastian could get a location for the caller. Bastian held up three fingers before making a zero with his hand. Thirty seconds.

"Is Adrianna okay?" I asked.

"She took quite the beating, but she's stable for now. A word of advice. If you want to talk to her, claim to be family. If not, you won't get past the double doors."

"Has she spoken to anyone? Have the police questioned her yet?"

"Look, the spread of this information through the police database is slow. But it's not that slow. You're wasting time. It'd be easier if you asked Adrianna these questions. She's in room 323. I told my contact to expect Adrianna's sister. It just so happens, she has the same name as you, so your ID should work. Good luck. I'll be in touch."

The call ended, and I stared at the screen, more confused now than before. "Anything?" I asked.

"One sec," Bastian said.

"Who was that?" Martin pulled a t-shirt on over his head as he came down the hallway.

"A San Diego cop," I said.

Bastian nodded, his jaw dropping a little. "The bobby made the call from the station."

"What does he have to do with the kidnapping?" Mercer asked, suspicious. "Bas, find out which copper made the call and pull up everything you can on him. Is he on the take? Is he dirty? Find his skeletons."

"Alex?" Martin's eyes showed concern. "Why does tonight feel like we're reliving several of your nightmare cases at the same time?"

"We aren't. Mercer's wrong. This guy isn't dirty. I'm not sure what his deal is, probably white knight syndrome." He was trigger happy, which could translate to dirty if he had to cover something up. "But he's helping."

"That remains to be seen," Mercer said.

I looked around, wondering why it was always four a.m. "What happened with Sylvio?" I asked. "Is he still in custody?"

"Affirmative. Donovan will stay here. Hans will scout ahead. Bas, grab what you need to be mobile. This probably isn't a trap, but we can't be too careful. We move out in five." Mercer unzipped one of the bags in the corner of the living room to check the gear.

I went into the bedroom to change with Martin at my heels. When I turned around, I let out a sigh of relief. "She's alive. She's the first one who's survived."

"You're wrong, sweetheart. You did. Twice."

I kissed him. "Don't worry. I'll update Cross from the road. But this is good. We have a chance of finding Brent."

Martin returned my smile. "Just be safe. No more close calls or near-misses. If I have to leave for work before you get home, call me and let me know that you've made it back alive."

"I will." I went into the bathroom to brush my hair and teeth, surprised when I came out to find him in workout gear. "It's early. You should go back to sleep."

"I will when you do."

Martin filled several thermoses with coffee which he handed out as we left the beach house. Once we were safely inside Mercer's armored SUV, I let the smile drop. "She was picked up on the side of the road. What does that mean?"

"She might have escaped," Bastian suggested.

"Or Heuzen heard what you said. They may have let her go because they want her to deliver a message or get something for them," Mercer said. "Either way, I've alerted Cross. A development like this should result in some sort of noise, possibly a demand. If the kidnappers gave us something, they'll want something in return."

THIRTY-ONE

Mercer glanced down the hallway, his posture rigid.

"I don't like hospitals either," I said.

"It's not that."

I turned to get a better look at his expression. I couldn't tell if he was uncomfortable or in tactical mode. Overworked interns and nurses had already started making the morning rounds. Very few visitors were on the floor. He narrowed his eyes at the lone security guard drinking coffee near the elevator.

"Pointless," he mumbled. Tapping the comm, he whispered to Hans, "Maintain eyes."

I didn't hear Hans reply, but I assumed it was in the affirmative. I hadn't asked Mercer for my own earbud since I had enough voices in my head, but I probably should have.

"Here we are." The nurse opened the door to Adrianna's room. "I'm sure she'll be relieved to see family when she wakes up."

"Has she said anything? Do you know what happened to her?" I asked.

The nurse looked grim. "Someone attacked her. She refused a rape kit, but whatever happened must have been brutal. She hasn't said much. She wouldn't even tell us her name. It took almost an hour to coax it out of her. It's probably due to the trauma. She's scared. An officer tried to take her statement, but she wouldn't talk to him either. He fingerprinted her, but we'd already been alerted to her disappearance. We knew who she was. You're family, so I'm sure that's why you were notified so quickly. A detective hasn't even gotten here yet, but he should be arriving shortly. I'm guessing you were worried."

"Terrified."

The nurse squeezed my hand, noticing the marks on my neck for the first time. "She's safe now. We're waiting on some test results, but we'll take good care of her, I promise."

"Thank you. Do you mind if we sit with her?"

"Not at all."

I crept toward the bed. Emergency lighting above the sink gave the room a greenish-blue glow which mixed with the neon yellow and orange coming from the window where a fast-food sign lit up the otherwise dark sky.

Mercer went to the window and peered outside. He removed a penlight from his pocket and clicked the switch twice. "Affirmative."

"What are you doing?" I whispered.

"Making sure Hans knows our location. It'll make it easier for him to determine the best position for sniper's nests."

"Snipers?"

"We can't be too careful."

The woman in the bed let out a startled gasp, sitting up and pushing herself into the uppermost corner of the bed. The heart monitor increased, letting out a warning beep.

"Adrianna, it's okay." I held up my palms. "I'm Alex. This is Julian. We're here to help."

"Are you with the police? The nurse said they'd be here in a few hours to question me." She reached for the call button, but she didn't push it. Instead, she held the tiny controller in her hand. "Let me see your badges."

Mercer stepped away from the window, producing one of his business cards. "Personal security specialists, madam. Lucien Cross hired me to negotiate Brent Barber's safe release. I can do what the police cannot, if you allow us to assist."

"You know Lucien?" She swallowed, his name catching in her throat.

I poured a cup of water from the pitcher on the table and held it out to her. "It's a long, complicated story. He's actually my boss. Julian works freelance."

She relaxed a little, the look of distrust fading. "I know Lucien. Brent's talked a lot about him over the years. He's come up in conversation recently. Brent said he needed Cross Security to help him with some issues, but he never told me what they were."

"He didn't tell Lucien very much either. We know Brent was taken from his home Saturday afternoon. Before the two men grabbed him, they shot and killed a security guard and Fenton Roundtree."

Tears formed in her eyes. "It's true? I thought they were lying. I thought..." Her hands trembled. "I hoped it was a lie. Fenton was a good man." She gulped down some air. "These psychos still have Brent." The tears ran down her cheeks. "They're going to kill him."

"Not if we can stop them," I said.

Mercer gave me a warning look. *Don't make promises you can't keep.* "Madam, we need your help. Who are these men? What do they want?"

She swallowed again before taking another sip of water. Her face was bruised. Her lip and eyebrow had been split. The gash on her eyebrow had scabbed, but the one on her lip looked fresh. Her cheek was swollen, the veins around it had burst in spiderweb patterns, making the bluish bruise purple and red in areas.

I glanced at the chart at the bottom of the bed. A few small bones in her left foot were fractured, along with two ribs and her cheekbone. Her wrist was sprained, and three of her fingers had been broken. Bruises covered thirty percent of her body.

"I just...I don't. Everything. It was just so much." She sucked in a shaky breath. "Oh, Brent." The tears fell with renewed vigor, a few sobs escaping.

I passed the clipboard to Julian and sat on the edge of the bed beside her. The lines around his eyes and mouth deepened. She'd been tortured. Getting answers would not be easy. We couldn't push. She'd already been through too much.

"You're strong. You're a survivor. That's good. They probably weren't counting on that. I'm guessing Brent's just as strong. How did you get free?" I asked.

"Brent distracted them. He told them he'd tell them everything, but he needed the computer. When the taller one went to get it, Brent started yelling that he couldn't breathe or see. He jerked so violently he knocked his chair over. They thought he was having a seizure." Her lip twitched before her chin started trembling. "I always hated when Brent did that. He had this whole routine down."

"He faked seizures often?" I asked.

"Only at Halloween. It was a stupid gag about a poison apple. But he'd done it so much, they believed him." She fought to stop crying, which only made it worse.

I reached for her uninjured hand. She gripped mine tightly before leaning forward and hugging me, burying her face against my shoulder while she cried uncontrollably. "I'm sorry this happened to you. I know you don't want to talk about this, but we have to."

"Where were you kept?" Mercer asked.

"I don't know." She fought to regain control of her breathing.

"Do you remember any street signs or landmarks? What did the surrounding buildings look like?"

She shook in my arms. "I don't... I can't..."

"It's okay. We'll go slow. We'll figure it out together." I gave him a look. "What did you do after Brent faked a seizure?"

She drew back, her entire body quaking. "I ran. I shouldn't have. I should have stayed. I shouldn't have tried to get away. He told me to go. To get help. I should have been stronger. I should have..."

"Shh," Mercer soothed, "it's okay."

She wiped at her eyes, wincing when she touched her cheek. "They caught me before I made it to the stairs. They threatened to kill me for trying to escape. They made Brent watch while they beat me. While they..." She sucked in another deep breath and swallowed away the words. "They tied me up and blindfolded me. They didn't trust us to stay together, not after that. They told Brent if he ever wanted to see me again, he better stop screwing around and cooperate."

Mercer opened his mouth to ask a question, but I gave him a sharp look. She'd get there. Asking wouldn't make the story come any faster.

She held out her hand for the cup. I refilled it and gave it to her. She took another sip. "One of them put me in back of a covered pick-up. It smelled kind of like skunks and rotting meat. I thought I was going to be sick. Someone was next to me. Two someones. They had killed them and dumped me back there with the bodies. I knew they weren't taking me somewhere else. They were done putting up with me. I was too much trouble. They told me from the beginning not to cause trouble. I just...I didn't...I was so scared. Brent's still there. They're going to kill him too." She started to hyperventilate.

Mercer took the pulse monitor off her finger and stuck it on his, not wanting to give the nurses any reason to interrupt us. "Where is Brent?"

"I. Don't. Know." She said in between gasps.

"Breathe with me." I took deep, measured breaths, guiding her by example. A few seconds later, she inhaled and started to hiccup. "Continue your story."

"We hit so many bumps and took so many turns, the bag they put over my head started to ride up. I wiggled out of it." Her haunted expression appeared magnified in the dim light. "Those men beside me, the dead ones, they didn't have heads. Who does that? Were they going to do that to me? Were they going to dig a hole and throw us in?"

"No. They weren't. And we're not going to let them do that to Brent either." I glanced at Mercer who kept eyeing the wall clock.

"How did you get away from them?" he asked.

"The rear window rattled, and I realized I could push it open. I couldn't get the back gate to release, but I kicked open the window and hoisted myself over the gate and somehow squeezed through the opening. I was sure they'd seen me in the rearview. But the truck didn't stop. I hid in the ditch, near the side of the road, sure they'd come back to get me."

"When was this?" Mercer asked. "What time of day?"

"I don't know. It wasn't completely dark yet, but it was getting hard to see. I remember watching the taillights on the truck fade and being afraid the brake lights would turn on next, but they didn't."

"That might be how they missed you," I said. "Did any other motorists stop to help?"

"We weren't on a main road. I'm not sure where we were."

"Did you see any signs?"

She shook her head. "Once I was sure they weren't turning around, I crawled along the side of the road. I don't know how long. It was so dark. These bright lights stopped in front of me. A guy in a big rig got out and asked if he could help. He untied me and wanted to know what happened."

"Did you tell him?" I asked.

She shook her head. "I was afraid he could be working with them. I never saw anyone else on that road except him."

"Where was this?" I asked.

"I don't know. It looked like the middle of nowhere. I've never seen so much nothingness before. Even when I go hiking, there are always people around. This was so remote. So desolate."

"You're safe now. They can't hurt you. No one can."

"Why didn't you speak to the police officer?" Mercer asked. "I'm sure he offered to help."

"I don't know." A fresh round of tears joined the trail which had already soaked through the collar of her hospital gown. "A few hours after they grabbed me, I heard them talking about the police. They kept saying they'd been close. That they'd have to kill us if the cops showed up."

"You're afraid if the cops get involved they'll kill Brent?" I asked.

She nodded.

"When were you taken?" Mercer asked, placing the pulse monitor back on her finger. The look in his eyes told me not to interfere. "Tell us every detail you remember."

"It was Saturday morning. I'd left the hotel. I wanted to get coffee." She snorted and choked. I handed her a tissue, and she blew her nose. "That feels like so long ago."

"How did they approach you? Did you see them? Do you think you can recognize them?"

"I called for a taxi and was waiting for it outside the coffee shop. A black car pulled into the alley beside me. The next thing I know, I'm waking up in this drafty room." She described the men in great detail. Mercer took out his phone and showed her a few images. Her heart rate increased. "Him," she said, "and him," pointing to Castillo and Irmine, "are the men who took me, who hurt me, who hurt Brent." She bit her lip. "That one," she pointed to Heuzen, "he put the bag over my head and carried me out to the truck."

"You're sure?" Mercer asked.

"Ye-yeah."

"Did the other two know he was letting you go?"

She looked confused. "He didn't let me go. He was taking me somewhere else to kill me."

"Did they know?" Mercer asked. "Did they tell him to do it?"

"I don't remember."

"It's okay. It doesn't matter," I said.

Mercer glared at me over her head, but when she looked at him, his expression softened. "All that matters is you got away."

"Who are they?" She nodded toward his phone.

"Mercenaries," Mercer said.

"Why did they do this to us?"

"They didn't tell you?"

"They wanted to know about Brent, about our house, the layout, the security system. They wanted to know where Brent was and when he'd be home. They said he had something that didn't belong to him and they wanted it back. That they'd waited long enough, and they couldn't wait any more."

"Did they say what it was?"

"No." She blinked. "I told them they had it wrong. Brent would never steal anything. They didn't care. They said if I told them how to get into our house, they'd get it and leave us alone." Her lips formed a scowl. "I didn't believe them. I wouldn't cooperate, so they twisted my wrist backward. They said they'd snap it if I didn't tell them. But I wouldn't, so they broke my fingers until I answered."

"How much did you tell them?" Mercer asked.

"I gave them the security code and Brent's computer password. Everything they wanted. They already had my house keys. I figured they wanted to rob us. I hoped that was it. I didn't know where I was, but I thought I could escape once they left. Except they chained me to the chair and locked me in the room. Hours later, they came back with Brent." Her chin quivered, but she'd nearly cried herself out. "It's my fault they have him. It's all my fault."

"Do not blame yourself." Mercer looked into her eyes. "You couldn't have stopped them. They would have gotten in without your help. It might have been worse." Mercer slid the tray table closer, took one of the pages from the back of her chart, and flipped it over. "Was that room the only place they kept you?"

"Yes."

"Were you and Brent together the entire time?"

"Until I tried to escape."

"How many kidnappers were there?"

"Three," she said.

"Think," Mercer insisted, "did they have comms?" He took out his earbud to show her. "Do you remember them speaking on the phone or taking orders from anyone?"

"I never saw anyone, but they kept referring to the boss. I overheard one of them on the phone. I guess it might have been Sunday night or Monday morning. Time lost all meaning in that hellhole. Something happened. They were told to be on alert. They left us alone inside, maybe for an hour or two. But they chained us to the chairs. We couldn't get free."

"Did you ever see the boss? Did they ever refer to him by

name?" Mercer asked.

She shook her head. "No one came or went except those three men."

"Did they wear masks or bring anything with them?"

"No masks. They had gloves. They always had gloves. And they brought all sorts of things with them. The worst was the car battery." She cringed, a sudden desperation coming over her. "You have to find Brent."

"You have my word. We will do everything we can to bring him back to you." Mercer gently wiped her tears with a tissue. "Do you want to take a break?"

She shook her head. "I want this done. I want everything to go back to the way it was. I want to wake up and find out this is just a stupid nightmare. The sooner we go through it, the sooner it'll be over, and Brent will be back."

"Do you know how long it took to get from San Diego to that room?"

"No, they knocked me out. They injected me with something." She reached toward the back of her neck where a small red welt remained. "Everything happened inside that room. They beat us, tortured us, they made us watch the other suffer."

"Tell me about the room." Mercer held the pen in her direction. "And the building. Whatever you can remember."

She took the pen in her uninjured hand. "I don't know. It was drafty and cold, like a basement. No windows and only one door."

"Where was the door?"

She drew a rectangle on the page and sketched the door in the center of the wall. She drew the chair where she'd been tied up and where they'd kept Brent. "They'd unchain only one of us at a time." She rubbed her cheek. "I remember laying my head on his leg and crying."

"Did they feed you? Let you use a bathroom? Anything like that?"

"They gave us two meals a day. Always in cardboard containers from a takeout place." She continued sketching on the paper, drawing an odd balloon shape next to a smaller square inside a larger square. "They let us use the bathroom. It was walled off on one side, but mostly open on the other. It was weird. Like half the wall was missing on the one side. The taller one watched me sit on the pot while he stood at the door. It was humiliating."

"Perverts," I muttered.

"What about a shower?" Mercer asked.

She shook her head. "We were lucky to use the bathroom, but we had to go on their schedule. Brent peed himself when they were hurting him with the jumper cables. They punished him even more for that."

I studied her drawing. The lines were all jagged from her shaking hand. "Did you hear any noises? Traffic? Kids playing? Trains? Buses? Anything like that?"

"No sounds." She shuddered. "They said no one could hear us scream."

"Why did they torture you?" Mercer asked. "What did they want from you?"

"Julian," I gave him a look, "careful."

Adrianna leaned back against the pillow, drained. "Hurting Brent didn't work. He couldn't tell them what they wanted to know. So they thought doing those things to me would change his mind. They said if he really loved me, he would stop them. But he didn't know anything. He begged them not to hurt me. They wanted to know the code. That's all they kept saying, over and over. *Give us the code.* That one," she scrolled back on Mercer's phone, stopping on Castillo, "said it was a zero sum game. One person wins. One loses. Someone had to pay for what Brent had done. It could either be him or me. Brent told them this didn't have to be like that. Brent said he'd give them anything, do anything, if they'd just let us go. But that man said Brent had to lose. He had to pay."

"Did they say anything specific about the code?" I asked. "What was the code for?"

"Who knows? They acted like Brent was a spy or something. He's a sound geek. He plays with digital music all day. None of it makes any sense. That's why he couldn't give it to them. He told them that, but they wouldn't listen. They didn't believe him." She let out a miserable whimper.

"I'm even more afraid of what they'll do once they find out he's telling the truth."

"When you attempted to escape, Brent said he'd give them what they wanted, but he needed a laptop. Whose laptop?" I asked.

"When they first grabbed him, they told Brent they killed his partner and took his laptop. They wanted Brent to log on to it. I think they wanted Fenton's password, but I don't know why they'd think Brent would know that." Her eyes fluttered, her pressure and heart rate decreasing. I watched the numbers decline before spiking upward again. She inhaled sharply.

"Do you know if Fenton was involved in anything clandestine?" Mercer asked.

"I don't think so. All he and Brent ever talked about was sound design and implementation. Those are the only programs Fenton had on his computer. He showed them to us a million times. He didn't even have solitaire. Who doesn't play solitaire?"

"I don't know," I said.

"That's how much they loved their work. The last time Fenton showed us his computer, he was demonstrating how the new programs worked and how he'd improved or tweaked things for the perfect sound design, how the algorithm could incorporate the right thematic expectations into each individual scene, and how each sound wave functioned on the different frequency spectrums. They'd been so excited about it. That's all they talked about, but I don't see why anyone else would care."

I'd heard similar things from Edwin Hardt about his program's capabilities. "Could that be what they wanted Brent to unlock?"

"I doubt it. The program runs when you click on it. It's not password protected." Her eyelids fluttered, her voice weaker. "They kept saying they wanted the code. Brent said he'd give it to them once he could see the laptop, but I think it was a lie to buy me time."

"Could this have anything to do with Brent's family?" Mercer asked. "A code could grant them access to a bank account or sensitive material. It might have nothing to do with the laptop, but rather something on the internet."

"Brent's family is garbage. He avoids them as much as he can."

"What about Sylvio DePalma?" I asked. "Do you think he knows what they want?"

"I don't know."

"Did they ever mention him?" I asked.

She squinted, the numbers on the monitor rising and falling in unsettling patterns. Sweat broke out on her forehead. "I don't feel so good. Something's not right." She convulsed. The machine emitted a warning beep before the alarm sounded.

THIRTY-TWO

I stared out the windshield, watching the sky brighten as we returned to Malibu. Bastian turned around to look at me, giving me a reassuring smile.

"The doctors said she'll be fine, love. Stop worrying."

"I'm not worried about that."

Mercer's eyes roamed from the mirrors to the road, stopping briefly to get my attention in the rearview. "Do you believe her story?"

"She's terrified. You saw her stats. She can't fake that kind of heart rhythm."

Mercer's gaze returned to the road. "I'd say they were kept in an abandoned basement. Someplace remote. No one heard their screams or reported it. It could be a private residence."

"The neighbors would have heard," I said.

Bastian turned back to the rough sketch Adrianna had made. "Could it be an unfinished basement?"

"Most likely," Mercer said. "No interior windows usually means subterranean. The holes in the bathroom wall and rudimentary fixtures could mean it's being demolished."

"Or remodeled," Bastian said.

"What about a new building under construction?" I

asked.

"No." Mercer checked the side mirrors again, but we weren't followed. "Adrianna would have heard men at work. She said they didn't hear anything."

"What about soundproofing?" Bastian suggested.

"Possibly." Mercer drove past Martin's beach house and circled the entire neighborhood. Several surfers were already out, catching the morning waves. They wore wetsuits and traveled in groups of two to three. I didn't spot Martin and wondered if he'd already gone to the office.

By the time we parked, Hans had pulled up. He hefted the oddly shaped duffel, which doubled as a rifle case, over his shoulder as he headed for the front door. "Nothing to report. I waited until the bobbies arrived before pulling out. Do you think she'll tell them what's going on?"

"It'd be hard for her not to." I thought about her injuries. "Even if she keeps her mouth shut, they know she was assaulted. Her only emergency contact is Brent. They won't be able to get in touch with him. They'll figure it out."

"Let's just hope that doesn't interfere with what we're doing." But it already had. "What about vantage points?" Mercer asked.

"Nothing within a hundred meters. Best chance would be from inside. Up close and personal." Hans scratched his eyebrow. "Do you think they have the balls to do it?"

"Do what?" I asked, regretting my words almost immediately.

"Complete the kill." Hans gave me an apologetic look. "I'm guessing Taran Heuzen let her live, just like you. Maybe he has a fondness for birds."

"Shh." I didn't need anyone to put more thoughts like that into Martin's head or mine.

"I've already hacked into the trucking company's database." Bastian followed us inside. "I know precisely where the driver's truck stopped before he rerouted to Mercy Gen. Assuming that's where he found her, we can narrow down our search grid. I'll get it on the map."

"Adrianna said the pick-up made a lot of turns. They could have been driving for hours," I said.

"Not that long," Mercer corrected. "They drugged her and took her to an undisclosed location before questioning her about accessing Brent's house. She was taken around nine. They abducted Brent immediately after leaving Barber Productions. That gives us, at most, a five-hour window. With Saturday traffic, they can't be that far from the city."

"I'll narrow our search radius and lay the truck driver's path on top of it. That should help tremendously." Bastian grabbed a marker and pulled the cap off with his teeth.

"Now that she's escaped, they'll want to move Brent somewhere more secure." Mercer stretched out his arm, making his shoulder pop. "Even if we find their base, it may be too late." He went into the kitchen and filled the kettle with water. "Whoever hired Castillo and Irmine to carry out this mission has no intention of letting Brent Barber live. You heard what Adrianna said. Zero sum game. One side wins. One side loses. No matter what, Brent's on the wrong side."

"We have to change that." I grabbed a notepad and jotted down the facts, then I called Cross. "Adrianna's alive. She had a cardiac episode, but the doctors expect her to make a full recovery."

"What about Brent?"

"They still have him. You should know, they tortured her. They're torturing him. They want what he took and some kind of code. We think it has something to do with Roundtree's laptop, but that's not enough. They broke in to Sylvio's apartment. They think he has it. That's probably why they reached out to him. They must think he has whatever it is they want or he knows where it is on account of his close ties to Brent. Do you have any idea what Brent might have taken or what this code could be?"

Cross thought for a moment. "Have you spoken to the widow? She might have some idea."

"Not yet. The police were there when I stopped by. And after what happened at Sylvio's apartment, I—"

"Understandable." Cross exhaled. "Sylvio convinced us this had to do with Brent's uncle. He dumped all of this into Luther Bianchi's lap and got everything jumbled. I wish we hadn't wasted so much time."

"Is Sylvio still in custody?"

"Yes. Omar and Nero are monitoring the situation, but I don't think the cops plan on letting him go."

"What are they planning on charging him with?"

"I don't know. Petrocelli doesn't have a case. There's no evidence of anything. Maybe obstruction or conspiracy. After all, obstruction and interference are Petrocelli's two favorite crimes. Ganz was reluctant to breach attorney-client privilege, but Almeada spoke to him. Thankfully, he doesn't have the same hang-ups. It sounds like Petrocelli realized Brent and Adrianna have vanished. He's hoping to sweat Sylvio for answers."

"We don't have time for this. We're supposed to be sweating him for answers."

"No shit. Nero took Sylvio's phone before he went to the station. It's still hooked up so Amir and the other techs have remote access in case of anything, but even the best techs I know haven't been able to determine where the messages originated. We still don't know who's behind the kidnapping or why."

"Bastian's working on it too, but it doesn't look promising. Adrianna mentioned Brent's been talking about you a lot lately. Whatever this is has been building for a while."

"I'm assuming it ties in with the security issues and the request for a building evaluation."

"Probably."

"What about the master key? Was it Adrianna's?"

"I don't think so. I didn't get a chance to ask her directly, but she said she gave the kidnappers info on the house, not on Barber Productions. Do you think Sylvio had an all-access card made?" Perhaps Petrocelli had a reason to keep Sylvio on ice. "I found tranquilizers and syringes inside his apartment. The same ones that were used to subdue Adrianna and knock the wind out of my sails. I think Taran Heuzen may have brought it with him, but maybe not."

"What does Mercer think?"

"We're running out of time."

"I agree." Cross cleared his throat. "I'm heading to the airport now. I'll see you in a few hours."

"Safe travels."

When I stepped out of the game room to update the team on what Cross had said and ask Bastian about the phone, I spotted Martin and Donovan sparring near the pool. They wore boxing gloves as they danced back and forth. I'd seen Martin fight, but this morning, he looked like he wanted to kill. Donovan had the same calm expression he always did, but he moved with practiced ease. They bounced on the balls of their feet, moving faster than most prize-fighters.

Donovan threw a right jab. Martin barely blocked it, the force knocking his own glove closer to his chin. Instead of faltering, he followed through with a right hook, which Donovan couldn't block with his arm extended. It connected.

Donovan reacted, ducking to the side before retaliating with an uppercut. Martin stepped back, both gloves down to block, and Donovan popped him with a right cross. Martin stumbled a little, shaking his head. I moved toward the door, but Hans clucked his tongue at me.

"James can hold his own. And if Donnie gets his arse beaten, I'll tease him until our dying day. Don't spoil my fun." He glanced at his teammates who weren't paying a bit of attention. "Does anyone want to put a wager on this?"

"You're insane." I studied Hans. "Martin's a civilian. The fight's rigged."

"Possibly in his favor." Hans rolled his eyes. "He's a ringer. The suit and tie and gym-toned muscles sell him as a fraud, but he isn't. I know that for a fact. Who do you think sparred with him most days in London? Back then, he was fucking pissed half the time and spitting angry the rest of the time. He might have been sloppy and drunk, but he's got the muscle memory and technique to fall back on. Did you teach him that?"

I watched the love of my life continue to box, partially in awe and partially terrified that I had turned him into a beast. But he always had that fire. Normally, it was a lash of the tongue or well-timed quip. His brawn matched his brain. I'd known it for some time, but it had been a while since I'd seen it demonstrated.

Martin didn't do anything he wasn't passionate about, and he threw all of his energy and effort into the things that mattered most. Right now, that was reassuring everyone involved that he didn't need protecting, that he wasn't dead weight or a liability, and that, if push came to shove, he could protect me too. "No, that's all him."

They went another ten minutes, longer than most professional bouts, the sweat drenching their shirts. Martin's forearms glistened with perspiration. When they were done, they bumped gloves, and Martin tossed Donovan a towel. The long-range tactician slid open the door, the smile evaporating from his face when he found the rest of us waiting inside.

"Are we ready to move, commander?" Donovan asked, out of breath.

Mercer glanced back at Bastian who'd been buried behind the screen since the moment we entered the house. "Not yet."

"I'm gonna shower and catch a few z's."

"Aye." Mercer rubbed his eyes, probably just as exhausted as the rest of his team. But he'd power through.

I settled onto one of the island stools, my notepad and laptop in front of me. Bastian would do everything in his power to figure out where Adrianna and Brent were held, so I could focus on something else. Anything else.

Instead of looking at this from the same angle, I hit it from the other side. What was Barber Productions involved in six weeks ago that would have gotten them onto the radar of some powerful entity? What could sound design have to do with mercenaries?

I started on the company's website, checking the list of recently completed projects. But I didn't find anything controversial or political. Six weeks ago, Brent Barber, Fenton Roundtree, and Sylvio DePalma had returned from an award festival, where they'd been honored for the sound effects in a movie. Before returning home, they'd taken several meetings and signed tons of new clients. Business was good. That trip had done wonders, but the problems started soon after. Were they connected? I didn't see how, unless this was corporate sabotage. And Mercer had already nixed that idea.

Since Barber had granted us access to most things as part of our evaluation, I skimmed the internal data, checking the contact forms for anything threatening in the last six months, but I didn't find a single thing. No one had tried to shut down any projects. So this shouldn't be about that.

The glass door slid open a few minutes later, but I didn't bother to turn. Martin reset the alarm and came over, his skin and hair damp from his dip in the pool. "Hey, gorgeous." He planted a chaste kiss on my cheek. "How did it go? Is Adrianna okay?"

"She's been through hell. They did terrible things to her. She said they made Brent watch."

Martin swallowed, his hand moving to the bend in my hip. He gave my side a squeeze and kissed me again. "Did he crack?"

"She said no."

"I would have. I'd do anything for you."

My heart ached. "He can't give them what they want. He doesn't have it."

"What do they want?"

"A code, something to do with accessing Roundtree's laptop. Something Sylvio might have or know about." I thought about the crumpled hundred dollar bill and the ransacked apartment. I felt that familiar twinge at the back of my brain. It was right there. But what was it? What wasn't I seeing?

Martin frowned, his eyes studying something on my computer screen. "Like a password?"

"That'd be my guess."

"Are you sure they didn't mean code, like programmer's code?" He pointed to a line on my screen. "Barber Productions, that's sound production. They have a studio. They make sound recordings."

"Music, voice, and effects," I said.

"Huh."

I knew that huh. Martin had a thought. He went to the

coffeemaker, filled it with enough water and grounds to keep the six of us awake until the next century and placed the first cup under the spout. Once it brewed, he handed it to me and put a second mug underneath it. He put it on the counter for Bastian and went to make a third cup.

"What are you thinking?" I asked.

"I'm not sure." Martin turned but Hans had bunked down in the living room, and Mercer had retreated to the game room to strategize. After taking a sip, he opened the refrigerator door, took out a few ingredients, and went to the pantry. "A lot of chatter's been going around about advances in AI technology. Image, video, text, and even sound creation. It's a huge thing everywhere, but with the cluster of nearby tech companies, I hear a lot more about it now than I did at home. It's interesting stuff. Based on the number of programmers Barber Productions has on the payroll, I'm guessing he's working on creating his own program."

"They developed something. It's proprietary, but I spoke to the designer. He didn't think it was advanced enough to be worth much at this stage. But it saves the sound editors time."

"Do you have the specs on it?"

I scanned the database, but they weren't listed. "No."

Bastian shifted in his chair. He continued working on narrowing locations, but he had a knack for multitasking. "That could be it. Technology already exists, but if they made some sort of advancement, possibly accidentally, that could be what Castillo and Irmine were hired to retrieve." He glanced over his shoulder. "I hadn't considered that before because everything's very Hollywood here, but broken down to the basics, sounds have been used to create next-generation weapons or disrupt societies, even through such simple means as manipulating news stories."

"You mean like deep fakes?" I asked. "Those rely on previous recordings of people's voices. The different sounds are pulled out and extrapolated to make new sentences and phrases. That's not new technology."

"No, but if Barber Productions has an AI, which can fill in gaps, mimicking tone and all the right things, it might be able to overcome voice recognition and voice pattern signatures. That would grant whoever controlled the program access to all sorts of classified information or get them one step closer to unlocking such information." Bastian put the pen cap down, sipping his espresso before resuming his gnawing.

"You're talking about top secret applications. Governments and weapons and all sorts of things far beyond my comprehension." I looked back at my computer screen. "Barber Productions is in the entertainment biz. That's too farfetched, and even if it isn't, wouldn't the kidnappers have grabbed the programmer instead?"

"Is there just one?" Martin asked. "It looks like this was a team project which Brent Barber personally oversaw. The original programmer probably didn't make all the tweaks. He must have turned in the bare bones, and others weighed in. Brent would have offered input. He has unique sounds recorded. He fed the program data. It might be someone else's baby, but he taught it what to do. He made it learn all these tricks."

"That's the program on Roundtree's computer. But if they have that, what else could they want?" I asked.

Martin opened the box and grabbed a measuring cup. "Pancakes?"

"No need to ask, mate." Bastian slid closer to me, abandoning his computer for a moment. "Barber Productions might not have unlocked the program's full potential, but if the kidnappers had the modified source code with the added bells and whistles and access to the database and all these other sound databases, there's no telling the implications such things could have. They could do everything and anything, from taking over voice-controlled virtual assistants to ordering military strikes and altering troop movements."

"You're telling me this could cause wars?" I found that hard to believe.

"Possibly." Bastian reached for my computer, searching for information on the program, but besides the project name, none of the information or code was stored on Barber Productions' servers. He checked the cloud.

Nothing.

"What about plain old chaos?" Martin checked the temperature on the griddle before ladling the batter onto the surface, forming six perfect circles. "A majority of people have voice-operated virtual assistants. They control the temperature in their homes, their lights, their cars, what they order online, food delivery, the list could go on forever. Having someone else control that remotely using a program which could sound like you or some other voice that the device would react to could result in all sorts of things. Think about the water temperature in the shower. Some people have voice controls for that."

"Or gas ranges. It'd be an easy way to maim or kill from afar while making it appear entirely accidental. It'd be the perfect way to eliminate targets without ever lifting a finger or firing a shot." Bastian went back to his computer screen. "I think you're on to something."

"Am I the only one who finds this way out there, like the plot of a B-rated technothriller?" But despite my personal opinion on the viability of such an operation and the practicality of its uses for covert actions, a tiny bit of it made logical sense. This was the type of thing that mercenaries would be hired to recover. It would be worthy of killing and kidnapping over. I just wasn't buying into it. The right answers were usually the simplest, and this was too damn complicated. "But the kidnappers made it clear they wanted back what Brent Barber took. That he'd been warned to return it. How does that fit with some doomsday program?"

"It doesn't, I guess," Bastian admitted.

"There are probably safeguards in place to prevent such things from happening, anyway," Martin said. "I doubt the CEO of a production company would know how to bypass those."

"True, but if someone could, the potential for a program like that is limitless." Bastian reached for a fork as the first pancake hit his plate. "It is something to keep one up at night."

THIRTY-THREE

I wasn't sure what I found more unsettling, the possibility that Bastian and Martin were right and some doomsday program had been created by a sound production studio working for the entertainment industry or that Brent Barber could die because someone believed it. Despite what Bastian and Martin had discussed at breakfast, I wasn't ready to jump on the bandwagon. We had no proof that's the code the kidnappers wanted, and if it was, there wasn't a chance in hell we could risk letting them get their hands on it. Maybe I should call in the FBI, DHS, NSA, and every other alphabet soup agency to intervene. But that would be premature, especially if we were wrong and the code turned out to be a password to access an overseas bank account. So I went back to the drawing board.

With Martin at work and Mercer's team working on determining where Adrianna had been held, I didn't see any reason to hang around the beach house. More than anything, I wanted to go back to the hospital and speak to Adrianna. I spoke to the nurse who'd been kind enough to give me access. She said Adrianna was sedated and the police were keeping her under armed guard.

I drove to the Roundtrees' residence. A police cruiser

remained out front. Two officers were seated inside. They weren't questioning Sonya. They were protecting her.

Nero told me Sylvio remained inside the precinct. Ganz had left the night before, and he hadn't shown up today. If the police wanted to question Sylvio, they wouldn't be able to do so without his attorney present. Something told me Detective Petrocelli might be running out the clock, but it wasn't for the reason we thought.

Against my better judgment, I went to the station. A rookie was working the front desk, fielding walk-ins and answering the phone. I waited my turn. Someone filed a report. Another man had to pick up a copy for his insurance claim.

"Ma'am?"

I studied the layout. Conference rooms were off to the side. The door at the back required a code to enter. Beyond that was the roll-call room, booking, holding cells, access to the garage, stairs, and elevators which led to the other floors and divisions.

"Ma'am?"

I glanced to my right, seeing a fresh-faced guy in an over-starched uniform waving at me. I pointed to my chest, and he smiled, nodding.

"How can I help you?" he asked.

"Is Detective Petrocelli around? I need to speak to him."

"I'll check." He slid the sign-in sheet toward me. I wrote my name legibly and slid the clipboard back to him. "Let me see if I can track him down."

He picked up the phone and dialed an extension. "Is Petrocelli available?" He paused. "Alexis Parker." He glanced back at me. "No." He waited. "Okay, I'll let her know." After putting the phone down, he gave me that practiced smile, which was meant to keep people calm. "He'll be right down."

"Great."

I took a seat in one of the chairs, studying the rest of the people in the waiting area. At least two of them were armed, but given their wilted white t-shirts and uniform pants, I'd say those were cops who'd just gotten off shift.

They were probably waiting for a friend. A woman with a too-large purse, oversized hat, and sunglasses remained near the door. Clearly, she didn't want to be identified. When she reached into her bag, I tensed. But she didn't pull out a weapon. Instead, she grabbed a hard candy and unwrapped it.

A few minutes later, the door near the back opened. Detective Petrocelli stepped out. "Ida," he nodded to her, "what are you doing here?"

"You told me to stop by sometime this week." The woman adjusted her hat. "I thought I should see what kind of progress you made."

"Still working on it." Petrocelli smiled warmly at her, an expression I didn't believe he was capable of. "I might have found someone who has more time to dedicate to it. How about I call you in a couple of days and we'll talk about it?"

"You can't do anything before then? You know how important this is."

"I know. Give me three days."

"Fine, Dean." She stood with a flourish. Even though she didn't have a boa, I imagined her flinging it around her neck as she turned and headed out the door.

He exhaled, rubbing the top of his head while staring at the floor. "Must be a full moon." He didn't even bother looking in my direction. "Shouldn't you have brought your shadow with you, Ms. Parker?"

I approached while he held the door open, waiting for me to follow him. "I heard Adrianna Keys is in the hospital."

"You didn't hear shit." The door slammed behind me when he let it go. "You were at the hospital this morning. Do you want to tell me what's going on?"

"What did she say?"

He glanced at me as he led the way up the stairs to RHD. "I'm not playing that game. Answer the question."

I wasn't playing that game either, so I changed topics. "I see a unit's keeping an eye on Sonya Roundtree."

He stopped at the top of the stairs, turning on me. "What the hell's going on?"

"You have Sylvio DePalma in custody. As far as I know,

he hasn't committed a crime."

"Were you inside his apartment yesterday?"

"No."

"Lying to a police officer is a crime."

"That's debatable."

He looked like he wanted to throw me over the railing. Somehow, he resisted. "You have ten seconds to tell me why I shouldn't charge you with obstruction. Nine. Eight."

"Are you protecting Sylvio?"

"Seven. Six." He reached for his handcuffs.

Yep, coming here was stupid. "Brent Barber's been abducted."

A satisfied smirk tugged at his upper lip. "Now we're getting somewhere." He pushed the door open to robbery-homicide division and crossed to his desk. I hurried to keep up, eyeing the desks we passed. Half of them were unoccupied.

He grabbed a straight-back chair and put it down beside his desk, which was wedged in the center of a row. I took a seat, wondering if Sylvio was locked in one of the holding cells or camped out on a couch in a break room somewhere.

Opening the middle drawer, he pulled out a notepad and a binder. "Have the kidnappers contacted you?"

"No."

"What does Cross Security have to do with the murdered crisis negotiators?"

"Nothing," I said, surprised he'd even give that much away. "We didn't hire them. We didn't know anything about the meet until after the heads were delivered to our door."

"Who has the kidnapper contacted? What are his demands?"

"No one and nothing."

"That's bullshit. Negotiators wouldn't have been hired or killed if no demands had been made."

I snorted. "Yeah, you'd think so, but that's not been the case. This isn't a ransom. It's a rendition."

"Rendition?" He frowned. "What do you mean?" He opened the binder, which contained details on Roundtree's murder. "You asked if he was tortured. What do you know?" He saw the hesitation and uncertainty on my face. "I can help."

"Actually, you can't. Kidnappings are an entirely different beast. They're federal, so I can have my friends take this away from you at a moment's notice. I don't want to do that. You have a homicide to solve and innocents to protect."

He pushed the desk phone toward me. "Fine, let's see your so-called friends take over this investigation. I don't need this shit. I have plenty of other cases to work on."

"Like Ida's?"

His eyes went cold. "Why are you wasting my time?"

"I have to speak to Sylvio."

"No."

"Brent Barber is running out of time. Please."

"You're not a cop. The state of California doesn't recognize you as a private eye."

"The paperwork is pending. I'm sure my license is in the mail."

"Not if I make a call."

"Regardless, I'm a security consultant. I was hired to evaluate Barber Productions' security and I'm doing everything in my power to protect Brent Barber. You are standing in my way. When his body turns up, that's on you. Not me. You." I shoved the chair backward as I stood.

Petrocelli grabbed my wrist, his eyes on the blisters and bruises that wrapped around my neck. "I told you from the start to stay away from this."

"That's not how I'm wired."

He pushed away from the desk and dragged me into an empty conference room, slamming the door behind us. "You have one minute. Off the record. Fucking talk. Now." He looked at his watch and then at me. This was the closest thing he'd give me to a free pass or a collaboration. I didn't trust him not to use every bit against me and blow everything up, but I had to speak to Sylvio and I couldn't wait for the clock to run out.

"The same men who killed Roundtree and the guard abducted Brent Barber from his home. Hours before, they drove to San Diego and grabbed his girlfriend outside her hotel. They used her to gain access to Barber's house. That's why the security system wasn't tripped. That's why there were no signs of a break-in. The kidnappers forced Brent to call Sylvio and tell him he'd be out of town. Hours later, they contacted Sylvio again, telling him they'd kill Brent if they didn't get what they were owed. Sylvio reached out to Brent's family, who hired the negotiators. By the time Cross Security learned about any of this, it was already too late."

"What about Adrianna? Why didn't they kill her?"

"They would have, but she escaped." I tried to gauge his reaction, but he made the effort not to give anything away. "She heard the kidnappers say if they spotted the cops, they'd kill Brent. She's afraid to say anything to anyone. You need to assign a protection detail to her hospital room." The nurse said that had already been done, but Petrocelli refused to confirm it.

"Tell me what happened at Sylvio's apartment yesterday."

"The delivery guy who left the heads on my doorstep was there. He was looking for something. I don't know what, but if he finds it, they'll have no reason to keep Brent Barber alive."

"What makes you think they won't let Barber go once they realize they don't need him anymore?" Petrocelli cocked his head to the side. "They let Adrianna go."

"She escaped. Did you not hear me say that?"

"Maybe they let her escape. Did you ever think of that?"

"We aren't dealing with career kidnappers. We're dealing with killers who don't leave loose ends. She needs protection."

Petrocelli lowered his wrist. Time was up. He'd given me nothing, but the look in his eyes told me he already knew most of what I'd told him. "So do you." He jerked his chin toward my neck. "You've seen them. They know who you are and where you work. Like you said, they don't like loose ends. You're a loose end, unless there's something else you've failed to mention."

"I'm not working with them."

"So you keep saying, but you know a lot of things you shouldn't. I'm still wondering how you knew Adrianna was in the hospital. No one had any idea."

"A friend called and told me."

"What friend?"

I honestly had no idea, but I didn't want to get into that. "Are you going to arrest me?"

"I should." He exhaled. "Sylvio's in the break room. Second door on the right. Don't be here when I get back, or I will arrest you."

THIRTY-FOUR

Sylvio nearly jumped out of his chair when I pushed the door open to the break room. His shirt was stiff from dried perspiration. He wiped his palms on his pant legs, both knees jittering up and down.

"Are you okay?" I asked.

"Fine."

"You don't look it." I picked up the coffeepot and turned over one of the ceramic mugs. It looked clean enough, so I poured myself a cup. "What's the deal?"

"Deal?" His Adam's apple bobbed.

"With Petrocelli?" I jerked my chin toward the hallway. "If you aren't under arrest, you can walk out anytime you want."

He nodded a few times before pulling out his anti-anxiety medication and dry-swallowing one of the pills. "Uh-huh."

Dammit. I should have seen it before. Rubbing my eyes, I opened the fridge, finding a brown paper bag labeled *Dean*. He would mind, but I didn't care. "Here." I peeled off the top of the yogurt cup and grabbed a spoon. "Eat something. You shouldn't take those on an empty stomach."

"You can't just steal people's food."

"It's a community fridge." I pulled out the chair in front of him. "The yogurt's for everyone."

He eyed the container skeptically. "Do they have any granola?"

"Let me check." I opened Petrocelli's lunch bag and took out a small container of unappetizing bits. "Here."

Sylvio sprinkled the granola on top of the yogurt and took a bite.

I waited for him to swallow before asking, "Why didn't you have the same qualms about stealing something far more substantial?"

"What are you talking about? I never stole anything in my life."

I gave him my hardened glare, watching him shrink in on himself. "Did Petrocelli tell you what happened at your apartment yesterday?"

His eyes went wide. "No."

"The men who have Brent ransacked the place. Any idea why that might be?"

"Nuh-no."

"Dammit." I slammed my palm on the table, making Sylvio jump. "They're looking for something. And for some reason, they think you have it. I'm guessing that's why they contacted you after they took Brent and killed Fenton. What did Brent say to you when they forced him to contact you? Did you even speak to him? Or did they give you instructions on what to do?"

"No. I talked to Brent. I didn't know anyone had him or he was in danger. I didn't know anything was wrong until the police told me about Fenton. All Brent said was something came up and he was going out of town. That was it. I don't know anything about anything." Beads of sweat erupted at his temples and ran down the sides of his neck. Sylvio might have several reasons to be anxious, but one of them was because he was lying through his teeth.

"Brent doesn't know what's going on. Did Fenton? Were the two of you in cahoots? Is that why they tortured and killed him?"

Sylvio put the spoon down and leaned over, hurling into

the trash can.

"I told you not to take pills on an empty stomach." I also knew nerves and eating didn't always mix.

"Ms. Parker, please."

"Four men are dead. Jarrod the security guard had nothing to do with anything. He was a good guy who happened to be in the wrong place at the wrong time. Maybe you knew him, maybe not, but he had nothing to do with this. I don't think Adrianna or Brent do either. After the things the kidnappers have done to him, to her, he would have given them anything to make them stop. But he couldn't. You're the only one who can stop them. You have to tell me what you did, who you ripped off. It's Brent's only chance."

"I don't know." He swallowed a sob. "I didn't do anything. I swear."

"You keep insisting Brent's your best friend. Do you know what they are doing to him as we speak? If your positions were switched, wouldn't he do everything in his power to save you?"

Sylvio shivered, leaning back and pulling his knees to his chest. "I thought you and Lucien were going to rescue him. Lucien said he had a plan. He would take care of this."

"How?" I wanted to scream. "The kidnappers won't talk to us. They won't even tell us what they want. The deadlines they've sent to your phone have come and gone, and nothing has changed. They expect us to know what was taken and how to get it back. Until we have what they want, they won't negotiate. Truthfully, they have no use for us. They've decided to get it back on their own. That means Brent's as good as dead."

"No."

"They threw Adrianna into the back of a pick-up with the bodies of the two crisis negotiators. I'm guessing they have a dumpsite, but she managed to get away. A nice man found her and brought her to the hospital. She's in rough shape. They beat her, broke her bones, and forced themselves on her as a means of breaking Brent. He had to watch them hurt her and listen to her scream. And when that didn't work, they turned their attention to him. She said they had jumper cables and a car battery. Do you have any idea how excruciating that is? How fucked up this is?"

"Brent," his chin quivered, "no. They wouldn't. They can't hurt him. They won't get what they want if he's dead."

"He doesn't have it. He would have broken, given it up, if he did. They know that. That's why you've gotten their attention. If Petrocelli hadn't been in a dick of a mood yesterday, you would have been home when they broke in. You would be the asshole hooked to the car battery right now." I exhaled. "You know it's true. That's why you haven't left the police station. Petrocelli made you the same offer he made me. He said he'd protect you, right?"

"He told me I can't leave."

I didn't believe that. "That protection he promised isn't going to get Brent back. If anything, it's going to get Brent killed. The kidnappers know he can't or won't help them, which means they are upping the torture until it kills him. He's already convinced Adrianna's dead. He doesn't have anything left. He will succumb unless you tell me what they want." I stared at him, hoping I hadn't made a giant mistake by jumping to these conclusions. "What happened on that trip to the award ceremony six weeks ago? What did you take?"

"I didn't take anything," he screamed. "It was an accident, a fluke. One of those one in a million, crazy mix-ups. I didn't realize it until I got home, and I didn't know what to do after that. I tried calling Brent, but we'd just gotten back. He was too busy with Adrianna." Again, I sensed the jealousy. "He didn't answer the phone, so I called Fenton. He found the same thing in one of his bags. We figured Brent must have too, but he never said a word to either of us. I kept trying to feel him out, but he never even hinted. I know Brent. After a few drinks, he would have spilled the beans." Sylvio rocked violently, swinging his leg back and forth. Any moment, he'd get up to pace, or he'd knock his chair over. "He really doesn't know anything about it. I thought for sure he did."

"What is it? The kidnappers searched your suitcases and Brent's. Did you find a stash of drugs? Pills? Tranquilizers?"

"No. Money. A shit ton of money." He pushed away from the table, practically climbing the walls. I didn't think he was claustrophobic, but he acted like it.

"How much is a shit ton?"

"4.2 million, give or take."

"Dollars?" I wondered if I heard that right. "How did you find 4.2 million dollars?"

"It was in our luggage. Okay, not our luggage. It turned out our bags got switched. I don't know how, probably something with the airlines. But when I got home from that film festival where we got the award, everything I had packed was gone and inside my bag were a few shirts and cash. All in hundreds. They weren't counterfeit or sequential. No one reported their bags missing. The airlines never contacted me to say they made a mistake. They never returned my bag or Fenton's either, so we figured that made the money ours."

"I don't think the person who lost that much money would agree."

"Maybe the guy's rich and wouldn't miss it."

"People with that kind of wealth don't travel with suitcases full of cash. The only ones who do are involved in illegal enterprises. They wouldn't be able to report it. But that doesn't mean they'd just chalk it up to some fluke and let it go. We're talking about four million dollars. Do you understand that?"

"I didn't think–"

"Shit started happening at Barber Productions the week after, and you didn't connect the two?"

Sylvio's face drew into an *oh shit* expression.

"You didn't make the connection?" I repeated.

"How would they have known who found the money? I didn't know whose money it was. How would they know who got it by mistake? We figured we were free and clear."

"They probably got your bag since you had theirs. Did you have a tag on the outside?"

"No, that was the weird thing. The tag on the outside of the bag was mine. The bag itself looked just like mine, but the contents weren't."

I had no idea if TSA had accidentally switched them or if

something odd had happened when the bags were being loaded and unloaded or if the owner of the four million had found two identical bags to switch because he feared being searched or stopped. "Whoever's money that is knows where it is. He knows you have it. He knows Fenton had it. But that doesn't explain why they grabbed Brent. They should have taken you."

A lightbulb came on over Sylvio's head. "Oh god."

"What?"

"I just remembered, my luggage tag broke. Brent gave me one of his spares to use. It had his name and address on it." He placed his fingertips against his lips and stared at me for a long time, the blood draining from his face. "This is all my fault."

"What did you do with the money?" I asked. "They've searched Brent's house and your apartment. They emptied Fenton's filing cabinets. Where's the cash?" That much would have to weigh upwards of forty pounds, if my math was right. It wouldn't be easy to conceal or transport.

"I don't have it. I mean, I have some. It's in a box beneath my dresser."

"I'm sure they found that." I thought about the bag Taran Heuzen grabbed before jumping out the window and the crumpled hundred he'd left behind. "Where's the rest of it?"

"We deposited it." He blinked a few times. "Fenton knows a lot of guys who can do accounting things. We got an offshore numbered account to put the cash into until we figured out what to do with it. Fenton thought we should filter it through the company, but I knew Brent had a lot of issues with doing stuff like that. So we were just sitting on it. Mostly. We kept a little for rainy day funds."

"Did Fenton keep the money in his office?" I asked.

Sylvio shrugged, but the guilt was written on his face. I had half a mind to contact the kidnappers and offer a trade, Sylvio for Brent, but that wouldn't fix the problem. It'd make it worse, and I wouldn't be able to live with myself, even if I wouldn't have minded sticking sharpened bamboo beneath his fingernails or performing some amateur dental surgery on him.

"That explains the ring Fenton bought for his wife," I said. "How much did he keep?"

"I don't know. Ten grand, maybe."

"How much did you keep?"

"A hundred."

"Thousand?"

Sylvio nodded. "The rest is secure. But I thought it'd be nice to have some spending money."

That might have been enough to buy us some time and negotiate. "Did you keep it all in one place?"

"Yeah, in my apartment."

That was gone now. So much for a good faith gesture. "Shit."

"You said Adrianna escaped. Has she said anything about where they were kept or who has them?" Sylvio asked. "Maybe she can help. Then Lucien can send a team to negotiate and rescue Brent. You can still fix this, right?" He licked his lips, his eyes shining. "Brent has to be okay. Surely, his uncle Luther or his father can do something to save him."

"We can't do anything because we don't know where they are. Adrianna doesn't know where they were being held. The men behind the kidnapping are hired guns. They aren't pulling the strings. This is a job for them. When it's over, they'll take their cut and disappear. The person you pissed off, the one who hired them and is masterminding this whole thing, that's who you need to be afraid of. He won't stop until he gets his money back, and he wants to make an example so no one else will ever steal from him again. The kidnappers want a code. That's our only chance at negotiating. It's Brent's only chance. Do you know anything about that?"

"It's for the account. Fenton must have told them about it." Sylvio stared into my eyes. "I want you to know I never meant for any of this to happen."

"You should have come to that conclusion four days ago. The crisis negotiators would still be alive. Adrianna and Brent would be in a lot better shape."

He reached for a pen, hesitating before writing anything down. "What happens if they get this? You said they'd kill

Brent."

"They're going to kill him anyway. This is our only chance to lure them out. Frankly, it's your only chance too. They went to your apartment and found the cash. They know you're involved. They might even know you're responsible." I looked around the room. "At some point, Detective Petrocelli's going to kick you out the door or put you in lockup. Either way, your chances of survival will be greatly diminished when you aren't surrounded by L.A.'s finest."

"What about witness protection?"

"Witness protection for what?" I stared at him. "What did you witness? Did you see a crime take place? Do you know whose money this is or where they got it? Can you help the state or federal government prosecute a crime?"

"Nuh-no."

"So that's out." I glanced at the door, sensing my five minutes were up. "Cross Security's still your best chance of getting Brent back alive. Do you want your best friend to die?" I nodded down at the pad and pen near his hand. "Give me something I can use to bargain with."

"What about me?"

"Once Brent's safe, we'll figure out who's behind it and make sure he ends up behind bars where he can't hurt anyone else. It's the best I can do."

Reluctantly, Sylvio wrote down the code to access the account. I nodded, wondering if this was too little, too late. When I pushed open the door, Petrocelli and two uniformed officers stood on the other side.

I froze, afraid he'd follow through and arrest me. Instead, he pretended not to notice me and pushed his way into the room. "Mr. DePalma, I have a few more questions for you. These men will escort you to the interview room." Petrocelli looked up at the surveillance camera. "I'd like to remind you that you've already been read your rights."

That was my cue to leave. Petrocelli had used me to get more information out of Sylvio, but I'd seen the camera. I knew it was there, and I took the risk anyway. Some things were more important.

"Parker," Petrocelli called before I could make it

through the double doors, "you owe me a yogurt."

THIRTY-FIVE

I bounced on the balls of my feet, watching Bastian pull up the flight manifest from Brent Barber's return trip six weeks ago. He separated the flight crew from the passenger manifest and forwarded them to me. "I might be able to run it faster, love."

"You have enough to do." I slid behind my computer and started at the top of the list. "Have you narrowed down possible locations as to where Brent is being held?"

"Still working on it. I've narrowed it to a twelve kilometer radius. This would be easier if Adrianna knew the direction she traveled."

"Didn't the twists and turns help?"

"A lot of these roads twist and turn." Bastian spun the lollipop stick in his mouth while he worked. "Donovan and Hans are scouting ahead. They'll report back as soon as they narrow the list of possibilities. But you ought to prepare yourself, love. If they realize Adrianna's alive and talking, they'll cut ties."

"With 4.2 million on the line?"

"It depends."

"On?"

"On whose money it is and how much of a cut they're

getting."

I continued running checks. Halfway down the list, a red alert popped up. "How did TSA miss this?"

"It's a domestic flight. They don't worry as much with those." Bastian peered at my screen. "Bugger, the wanker's a bleeding plaza boss. No wonder they had so much cash stuffed in those bags. He must have been in charge of smuggling it back into Mexico from the Northwest. Instead of flying it in, where customs would seize it or he'd have to pay them off, he had it sent to Los Angeles. He must have planned to get it across the border another way, probably through the tunnels."

"TSA should have stopped him."

"Why? His travel papers are in order. They had no reason to question them." He pointed to the date. "The FBI only added that alias a month ago. They didn't know about it before then."

Alejandro Gonzalez, just another in the long list of aliases used by the cartel leader. "Something spooked him. That's why he switched bags or tags." I narrowed my eyes at the screen. "The group from Barber Productions must have gotten off the plane before he did."

"The lot flew first class," Bastian pointed out. "They deplaned first."

"By the time he made it to baggage claim, Fenton and Sylvio had already claimed their bags." I continued running the rest of the passenger list, finding two cartel hitmen had also been on the flight. They'd been arrested at the airport and were currently awaiting trial. That must have been what caused the delay and why Gonzalez had gotten spooked and switched luggage tags.

"The op went tits up," Bastian said. "Two of Gonzalez's guys were taken down by undercover DEA agents. He must have figured it was safer to let Barber's lot take the money than risk having it confiscated. He must have figured it'd be easy enough to recover it at a later date."

"He didn't count on Sylvio and Fenton hiding it in an offshore account." I flopped back in my chair. "Gonzalez is only a plaza boss. His boss must not know about this. That's why he outsourced the kidnapping. He'd probably be decapitated for screwing up. Can we use that to our advantage?"

"Possibly." Bastian stared at the blinking cursor on the game app. "Jules?"

Mercer grunted from his spot on the couch. He'd heard every word we said but had yet to offer an opinion. Dragging himself upright, he crossed the room and stared at the screen. "We still need their location. Without it, we can't guarantee Barber's recovery."

"Do we have time to wait?" I asked. "They could kill him at any moment."

Mercer glanced at me, exhaling. "Fine." Placing his fingers on the keys, he wrote a simple message. *We have the code. We're willing to hand it over in exchange for Brent Barber. Send proof of life.*

I opened the window on my computer which had a direct connection to Sylvio's cell phone. But when the chime sounded, it didn't pop up on my screen. It went to Mercer's.

"How do we know you're not lying?" he read.

"Because we're the good guys," Bastian muttered.

"What's the flight number?" Mercer asked. After I read it to him, he input it into the screen.

A few seconds later, another chime sounded.

"They're rather chatty this afternoon." Bastian plugged something into the side of the computer. "If they keep this up, we might finally have something."

"What's it say?" I asked.

"Brent Barber stole from us. He has to pay," Mercer read.

"Tell them the truth."

"This is my negotiation. Let me handle it."

"Tell them," I hissed.

Mercer pulled his shoulders back and typed a response. A moment later, another chime sounded. "Stubborn tosser." Mercer typed more furiously. Another chime, followed by more typing. "Bloody bastards."

"Keep it up," Bastian urged. "We're close. Just a few more messages and I might be able to crack through their VPN."

Mercer nodded. I stood behind him, reading as he went. He hadn't given much away on our end, just what we'd already learned about them, their mission, and what they wanted. "Sod off, you fucking wankers," Mercer mumbled. But he didn't type that. Instead, he wrote the one thing I knew he would. *Brent Barber's life for the money. Otherwise, you won't see a dime. He is not responsible. You are punishing the wrong man.*

Prove it. Tell us who's responsible.

Mercer glanced up at me. "No. It's too dangerous." *I want to see Brent in the next five minutes,* Mercer typed.

"Jules, I've gotten as close as I can. You can wrap it up," Bastian said.

Mercer ended the transmission by listing a secure e-mail address and phone number. *Tick tick.* "Where are they hiding, Bas?"

Bastian pulled up a grid that covered southern and central California. "It isn't much, but it cut our search radius in half. Unless they switch user accounts again, I doubt we'll be able to track them remotely."

"Update Hans and Donovan on the situation. Tell them which direction to move."

"Aye." Bastian picked up the radio and spoke into it.

"Haven't you ever heard of cell phones?" I asked.

"Radio communications are easier. We keep a secure channel," Mercer said.

I bit my lip, but no matter how hard I tried to keep my mouth shut, I couldn't help but to ask the question, "Do you think Brent's dead?"

"Possibly." Mercer stared at the screen, his entire focus on it and not me. "They would have told him she was dead. After that, he wouldn't want to go on."

"That's how they hoped to break him since nothing else worked."

"It might have been too much between that and the advanced interrogation tactics. Weaker men would have succumbed much sooner."

"I hope you're wrong."

Three minutes later, he received an e-mail notification. A photo appeared on the screen. It could have been doctored, but five minutes didn't give the kidnappers much time to pull off a convincing photo manipulation.

Brent Barber looked like he'd been in a horrible accident. His shirt looked wet and was tinged red. A scab had formed over his left eyebrow, which I assumed might have been from the hit he took from the shredder. His clothes clung to him, but he looked too thin. Dark circles made his eyes appear hollowed out. One blue eye stared at us from the other side of the screen. The other was swollen shut.

"Are those cigarette burns?" I pointed to the marks peppering his arms and the middle of his chest, where his shirt was torn open.

"Possibly, or marks from the jumper cables." Mercer scanned the photo, pointing to the watch the kidnappers showed in the photo with the time and date. It wasn't exactly a newspaper, but those were a little hard to come by. Mercer zoomed in on the wall behind Brent Barber. "Concrete walls. That has to be a basement. Maybe they haven't moved locations yet. Bas, I'm sending it to you."

"On it."

A second notification popped up. *Your turn. We want the code and the name.*

I pulled up the bank information that Sylvio had given me. The account he and Fenton shared had just over four million in it. The initial deposit had been slightly less than that, but in the last month, a few thousand in interest had accumulated. I read the total to Mercer, who typed it into the reply, followed by, *We make the exchange in person. Do we have a deal?*

This time, the ding wasn't an e-mail notification, it was a video chat request.

"Wait." Bastian made sure everything was running. "Good to go."

"Parker, out." Mercer pointed to the door.

"Hell no."

"I've seen you conduct negotiations. This is a sensitive matter. You need not be here."

"My house, my rules."

Mercer didn't have time to argue. "Fine. Stay off the

screen and keep your mouth shut, or you'll botch the whole thing." He gave me a warning look, which might have been cold enough to refreeze the polar icecaps.

From Bastian's computer, I could watch the exchange in the upper right corner. Bastian recorded the call while attempting to conduct a trace. But we both knew it would be fruitless. So I kept my eyes on the kidnapper, hoping to spot something useful in the background.

Despite the mask, I'd spent enough time staring at the photos of the men to know the one on screen was Vincent Castillo, even though he didn't remove his mask.

"We've been burned once," Castillo said.

"That was before I took over the negotiation. It won't happen again. Allow me to introduce myself. I'm Julian Mercer. And you are?"

"I know who you are." Castillo didn't give his name, but he wasn't stupid enough to think Mercer hadn't figured out who he was. They'd met before. "Who hired you?"

"That's irrelevant. I represent Brent Barber's interests."

"That's not a name. My employer wants to know who he's dealing with this time."

"Tell Gonzalez he's dealing with a concerned third party, who'd prefer remaining anonymous. Luther Bianchi will not cause him any more trouble, unless Brent is not returned."

"Aren't you supposed to be more discreet, Mr. Mercer?"

Mercer wouldn't be goaded that easily. "How much is Gonzalez paying you?"

I raised a questioning eyebrow, wondering how things had gotten derailed, but Bastian nodded encouragingly, spreading his hands wider, hoping Mercer could keep the conversation going for a while.

"A flat fee, plus a percentage of the recovery," Castillo said.

"Any chance we could buy out your contract?" Mercer asked. "You could walk away an even richer man."

Castillo shook his head. "You don't fuck with the cartel, mate. Even you should know that."

"Barber didn't fuck with them," Mercer said. "It wasn't his bag that got switched."

"It had his luggage tag."

"You know it wasn't his. You searched his house. You stalked his girlfriend. He never had Gonzalez's money. Fenton Roundtree did."

"That doesn't account for the second bag. We'll make the exchange, but someone has to pay. You deliver the money and the person responsible, and you'll get Barber back alive. That's the only way."

"What about Adrianna?" Mercer asked.

"What about her?"

"You abducted her. We'd like her released. She, like Brent, has nothing to do with this."

"She's gone. You waited too long. You should have gotten what we wanted sooner. Maybe then you could have saved the girl."

Mercer scowled. "We had nothing to go on. You didn't say what was missing."

"Yet, you figured it out." Castillo laughed. "I bet it has something to do with that little run-in that took place at Sylvio DePalma's apartment yesterday between my associate and yours. DePalma has Mr. Gonzalez's money, doesn't he?"

"That is of no concern to you."

"It's of great concern. You're going to bring us the cash and the man responsible. What harm could it do for you to tell me who to expect at the meet?"

"No name, not until the exchange."

"Fine. I'll bring Barber and you bring whoever. But I'm guessing it's DePalma. He's Barber's righthand man." Castillo snickered. "Are you sure they aren't in on this together?"

Mercer ignored the question. "Barber looks half-dead. What guarantees do I have that he'll survive long enough to make the meet?"

"None, but if you don't bring me what I want, I can guarantee his demise. The longer we wait, the lower his chances are of making a full recovery."

I hated this part. What was stopping these mercenaries from getting bored and putting one in Brent's head?

Mercer sighed. "Then let's not wait. I'll bring the bank

account information and the man who deserves to be punished. You bring Brent. Once I know he's safe, I'll give you what you want, just tell me when and where."

"Let me confer with the boss. I'll get back to you."

THIRTY-SIX

I studied the maps and blueprints. "This has to be the place."

"Not necessarily," Mercer said.

"It's within the search radius. It's old and remote. No one's lived there in nearly a decade. When the owner died, the estate went to a distant relative. She hasn't found a buyer for the house or the land. Everything is overgrown. The houses aren't even that close together since it's in the middle of farmland and vineyards. It's unlikely the neighbors would have seen anything, and even if they did, they might have figured someone was surveying the land or planning to clear out some of the overgrowth. This is fire country, after all."

"They'd suspect something was up if they see people coming and going all of a sudden, especially at all hours of the day and night," Bastian argued.

"The kidnappers moved Adrianna out after dark. No one would have seen anything except lights. They might have figured those were movers or potential buyers, if they even noticed."

"These other locations also fit." Mercer pointed to four other spots on the map. They'd been built around the same time by the same builder. The basement layouts were identical on the blueprints. Each one looked exactly like what Adrianna had drawn.

"Gut instinct," I said. "The road leading up to this property curves and twists the most. To get back to a main fare from here would require several turns, just like she described." I pointed to the map. "The truck driver stopped here. This is the closest house to that stop."

"She was on the road for hours," Mercer said. "She might have traveled farther than she realized."

"With her hands tied and fractured bones in her feet? No way. Not after everything else she endured."

"You were a dancer, love," Bastian pointed out. "I'm sure you did plenty of things with broken bones."

"Not after an ordeal like that. She wasn't walking. She was crawling, remember? This is where she was kept."

Mercer gave me a long look before relaying the information to Hans and Donovan. "Keep your distance but maintain eyes. Report any movement."

"Do you think they've already cleared out?" Bastian asked.

"That would be the smart move." Mercer glanced at the computer. "Castillo wants me to think Adrianna's dead. I don't think he knows she escaped."

"How can he not know?" I asked. "Taran Heuzen loaded up the truck with the dead and decapitated and soon-to-be dead. When he arrived at the dumpsite, he would have realized she was missing."

"Heuzen is our weak link," Mercer said. "According to Adrianna, he didn't participate in the abuse. He runs errands. He doesn't want blood on his hands. Perhaps he let her go, or he didn't want to face the consequences for allowing her to escape. Either way, Castillo doesn't know she's alive. I'd wager Irmine doesn't either. Heuzen might be an asset, if we can turn him."

"Asset?" I choked. "He tried to kill me."

"We've been over this. He didn't. He let you live," Mercer said.

"He wanted information," Bastian said.

"Or he doesn't kill women." Mercer glanced at the

computer screen. "We could use him, force them to turn on their own, create a distraction."

"Brilliant," Bastian said, "except we don't know how to reach him."

"They've been very careful about that," Mercer said. "He runs errands. They don't loop him in. He's an outsider. They probably plan to kill him when this is over."

"The cartel doesn't usually let anyone keep their phones." My fingers drummed a beat on the table. "They use burners, mostly." That wouldn't help us find him. "What about the car? They had that black sedan, but Heuzen drove the crisis negotiators' van. It might be able to tell us where Heuzen's been. Then we'd know for sure where Brent and Adrianna were held and possibly figure out a way to reach out to him or plant some seeds of distrust with his cohorts."

"That's a long shot," Bastian said. "But I'll see if I can pull up any GPS tracking information and I'll contact MI6. They owe us. Might as well cash in before they change their minds. I'll see if they have any satellite feed from the last few days that might reveal something."

I checked the time. It had been ninety minutes since the last communication with the kidnappers. I wondered what was taking them so long. Hopefully, they stopped the torture now that Mercer promised to give them what they wanted. But that was only if they believed him, and I wasn't sure they did.

Lucien Cross should be landing at any moment. He'd have a waiting voicemail which would catch him up on the important stuff, namely how Sylvio had played us and we'd fallen into his trap. Given everything that was happening, I was sure my boss would meet us here.

I circled the game room a few times. "Do you think they've changed their minds about the exchange?"

"They want the money. They have no other way of getting it, unless they move directly on Sylvio, and he's still in police custody." Mercer watched as I circled the air hockey table, making a figure eight by going around the pool table in the opposite direction. "The bobbies have actually proved useful, for once."

"I should have confronted Sylvio sooner. I knew something wasn't right. That trip they went on, the timing of the security glitches at Barber Productions, the ring Roundtree bought, it all added up to this."

"Don't beat yourself up, love." Bastian stuck his hand into the candy jar, finding it empty. "Sylvio made the effort to misdirect your focus. He wanted you to think this had to do with Brent and his family."

Still, I knew something wasn't right. "What did you find on the San Diego cop?" I asked, needing a distraction.

"Nothing yet." Bastian glanced at Mercer. "I can—"

"Bas, stop. We're in limbo. The intel on the van is being compiled by your bots, and it'll be at least an hour before MI6 gets back to us. This might be the only downtime you get. Get some sleep. I'll need you combat ready once the call comes in."

"What about you?" Bastian asked.

"That's an order," Mercer said, ending the discussion.

Bastian muttered a few things under his breath, but he didn't argue.

I pointed. "Bedroom to the right has fresh sheets."

"Thanks, love."

Once we were alone, Mercer turned on the air hockey table and pulled the disc out of the basket. "Parker." He nodded to the other side of the table.

"You mean Julian Mercer does something besides bark orders and work?"

"Not often." He placed the disc in the center of the table. "Ready?"

I leaned forward, hitting the disc with my blue mover. Mercer knocked it back with his red and it went flying across the table, ricocheting off the sides before I launched it back in his direction.

"Shouldn't you be getting some sleep too?" I asked.

"Can't." He kept his eyes glued to the puck. "I have to wait for their response."

"But air hockey?"

He chuckled. "You didn't leave me much of a choice. If I had to watch you circle the room one more time, I was going to tie you to the chair. Would you prefer that?"

"Not in the least." I scored a goal, and Mercer placed the disc back in the center of the table.

"While you were out, James spoke to me about what happened when you were taken. We would have been here. I should have been here."

"It doesn't matter. I survived."

"For future reference, I've told him how to get in touch, should he ever require it. Things had popped off at that point, but I'm sorry we weren't around to assist."

"Bastian mentioned Hans nearly lost his arm, and you lost a chunk of lung." I tried to deflect the disc away from my goal and accidentally knocked it in. "Are you sure you're combat ready?"

"Aye." When the game ended, Mercer had beaten me by one, which was my own fault. "Again?"

"Sure." I pressed the reset button when the proximity alarm went off. By the time I scooped up the tablet to check the exterior cameras, Mercer was already behind me, his Sig at his side. "It's Cross."

Before I made it to the front door, the familiar chime sounded at the computer. Talk about timing. Opening the door, I held my finger to my lips, not letting my boss inside the house until he acknowledged that he understood. Then we returned to the game room.

"Bring the access code and that thieving bastard to these coordinates in forty-five minutes. If I spot anyone else, Brent Barber's dead. No cops. No nothing. I know you, Mercer. Tell your team to stay home." Castillo held up his watch again and set the timer.

"That's cutting it close," Mercer said.

"Then hurry. Tick tick."

"Bollocks." Mercer squeezed the bridge of his nose.

"You've negotiated Brent's release?" Cross asked. "What are the terms?"

"They want the money and Sylvio," I said, "but we can't turn him over. Even if we wanted to, he's in police custody. If we tried to spring him, Petrocelli would send SWAT to go with us."

"Not us," Mercer said. "Me." He moved down the hallway and knocked on Bastian's door. "Get ready to move."

"Shortest nap in the history of naps," Bastian mumbled from the other side.

"What's the play?" I asked while Mercer reached for the radio.

"I'll take Donovan, put a bag over his head, and hope they don't catch on until it's too late."

"He's not close enough," I said. "You'll never make it in time."

"Fine, I'll take Bas."

"You need him to work overwatch."

"Bloody hell." Mercer glared at me. "What do you propose? You can't go. They'd know immediately you're not Sylvio DePalma."

"I'll go," Cross said. "Brent's my friend. Whatever I can do to help."

Mercer gave me a look, the unasked question evident on his face. I wasn't sure sending my boss into this situation was a good idea. But Cross and I had been in several scrapes and survived. I had to assume he'd make it through this one too.

"You can't shoot your way out of this," I said. "We're dealing with the cartel. Even if you survive and get Brent out of there alive, they won't stop coming for him. Not without the money."

"I'll give them the money," Mercer said. "It's the second part that's causing the problem."

"I'll go," Cross repeated.

Mercer gave my boss a look. "You do what I say when I say it. You follow my orders. Do you understand?"

Cross studied Mercer carefully. "As long as your primary objective is getting Brent out alive."

"It is."

"Then we're in agreement," Cross said. "I'll follow your lead."

Bastian entered the room, his hair wet from where he'd splashed water on his face. He raised an eyebrow at my boss. "Nice to finally meet in person."

"Likewise." Cross held out his hand. "Lucien."

"Bastian."

Mercer tapped the mouse a few times, pulling up whatever new data had arrived. "Enough with the pleasantries. Bas, get Cross outfitted. He's coming with me."

"I thought I was." Bastian eyed Mercer. "Are you sure that's wise, Jules?"

"No, but we don't have a choice."

Mercer pulled up the satellite imagery MI6 had forwarded to Bastian. "This could be a trap, just like the one they set for the crisis negotiators. Once they get the code, they'll probably kill us. In the meantime, they may move Brent or kill him and cover their tracks." He pointed to a photo from three days ago. "Parker's right. That's the house. The black sedan had been parked outside. The van never went there. The crisis negotiators drove it to this meet point." He marked it on the map. "From there, the kidnappers drove it to a blind spot, near the L.A. River. They must have met up, packed up the heads, and put the bodies into the pick-up. After that, Heuzen drove the van to Cross Security, and then proceeded to dump it soon after." He picked up the radio. "Hans, Donovan, any updates?"

"Negative, commander," Donovan said.

"Hans, report," Mercer barked.

"Nothing's happening," Hans said.

"Hold position for now, but be warned, we're set to meet in just under forty minutes."

"Copy. We'll reroute," Donovan said.

"Negative. Hold position."

"Commander?" Donovan asked.

Mercer looked at Bas. "Why aren't you getting ready?"

"Right-o." Bastian led Cross from the room.

"What's up?" I asked.

"Cross is emotionally invested. I didn't want to say this in front of him, but there's a good chance Castillo won't bring Brent to the meet. More bodies equal a bigger mess. From what I've seen, they have no intention of cooperating. Since they haven't abandoned the house, Brent must be inside. Hans and Donovan can do this on their own. But it'll get loud and messy, and it won't stop the cartel from retaliating. They want their money. It's always about money. I have to make sure they take the money before things pop off. Cross's presence will buy me some time."

"You want me to try to reason with Heuzen." I exhaled. "We don't know if he's at the house. Even if he is, what makes you think he'll be receptive to what I have to say?"

"He let you live." This was a bad play. The look on Mercer's face told me he didn't like it any more than I did, but we were out of options. "Hans and Donovan will have your back. Nothing will happen to you. You have my word."

"It's not your word I'm worried about." I cracked a smile. "But how can I say no to an invitation like that? After all, you knew damn well I was going, regardless of what you said."

Mercer snickered. "Indeed." He picked up the radio and updated the rest of the team on the situation.

Bastian entered the room in combat gear with Cross at his heels. "They want blood to spill, mate. No amount of money is going to change that. That's why you can't make a peep. We never confirmed Sylvio took the money. We might be able to convince them it was you, but it could backfire. They might kill you on the spot."

"Either way, we get Brent back." Cross looked at the spot circled on the map. "You're planning a raid."

"In case they renege on the deal," Mercer said.

"I can have a few of my teams assist. They can provide support and set up a perimeter."

Mercer thought for a moment. "Tell them to run silent, keep their distance, and hold position unless my people tell them otherwise."

THIRTY-SEVEN

Donovan lay on the dirt beside me, binoculars pressed to his eyes as we watched the dilapidated house. The windows had been boarded up, the shutters hung askew. Nero and Omar had checked in from half a mile away to say they were in position, but per Mercer's orders, they didn't approach.

"Hans, anything?" Donovan asked into the radio.

"Twenty minutes ago, Castillo left the house. We haven't gotten a visual on Heuzen or Irmine yet," Hans said in my ear.

"What about Brent?" I asked.

"Negative," Hans said. "We haven't seen him. Castillo took off in an SUV. I've already sent the details to Jules, but as far as I can tell, he was alone, unless Brent's body was already loaded into the back."

I hoped that wasn't the case. "Do you think he's still inside the house?"

"Possibly, or they moved him after they took Adrianna. The proof of life could have come from any room with concrete walls."

"More than likely, they'll wait to see what happens at the exchange before executing Brent, now that he's their bargaining chip," Donovan said. "Castillo won't trust Mercer to follow through because he doesn't intend to follow his own set of rules either. The stakes are too high. They'll need to renegotiate in person."

I looked at my watch. Twelve minutes until the exchange. "We move in once Mercer arrives."

"That's right. We don't want to tip them off," Donovan said. "How do you think Cross will hold up in a firefight?"

"He can hold his own," I said.

"Brilliant."

I fiddled with the microphone. "Do you think they're going to fall for it? That Cross took their money and not Sylvio?"

"Not a chance. The cartel will send a hit squad to eliminate Sylvio unless Jules can work some magic." Donovan gave me an encouraging look. "Lucky for you, we do this sort of thing for a living."

"After all this, Brent might send a hit squad to eliminate him."

"Not that anyone could blame him," Hans said in my ear.

I looked at my watch. Four minutes. On the bright side, my carry permit arrived this morning. That would be one less thing Petrocelli could hold against me. After making sure I had a few spare magazines, I got up, brushing the dirt off my palms, and pulled a vest from the trunk of the rental.

"You should prepare yourself. Brent won't be in good shape, if we find him," Donovan warned.

Two minutes later, I heard voices in my head. Mercer had arrived at the exchange. Bastian had gone ahead, setting up to provide cover fire if the situation turned deadly. Neither had spotted Castillo yet.

When the deadline arrived, I turned to Donovan. "Do you think Castillo changed his mind? Maybe they were made."

Before Donovan could reply, Mercer's voice came over the comm. "SUV just pulled up."

"Showtime." I crept along the outer perimeter of the house, figuring they probably had motion sensors and cameras keeping an eye out.

Donovan circled around the other side, scanning for radio signals and surveillance devices. "Clear."

"Where's Barber?" Mercer asked, his voice booming over the radio in my ear.

"You'll get Barber soon. I want access to the account first," Castillo said.

"The money's yours. We want no part of it. Brent Barber had nothing to do with taking it. I want Gonzalez to know that."

"So you keep saying."

Donovan waved at me from the other side. He was ready to move in, but I held up a fist. *Not yet.*

He gestured again, giving me a countdown. I nodded, hoping our actions wouldn't jeopardize our friends' lives.

"Here's the account information and access code," Mercer said.

Silence. I waited, imagining the kidnapper entering it into a computer. Finally, he said, "My boss has been waiting for this."

"Had you told us what you wanted, we would have gotten it to you sooner."

"Where's the thief?" Castillo asked.

"Not yet. You've gotten enough," Mercer said. "Where's Barber?"

"I knew you wouldn't deliver. Professionals would never sacrifice one life for another."

"I didn't say that," Mercer said. "But I'm no fool. Your SUV's empty. You didn't bring Barber. Once you give me his location, we'll make the trade."

Castillo laughed. "I can see the man in your back seat. It seems you held up your end. I should applaud you for being a man of your word. Unfortunately, the deal's off. I'll take him and go," Castillo said.

"Incoming, commander," Bastian warned. "Irmine's—"

Booming gunfire sounded in my ear, nearly making me deaf and cutting off the rest of Bastian's warning.

"Now." Donovan bashed in the front door with a battering ram.

The old wood splintered. I tossed a flashbang into the

opening and ducked against the house, waiting for the deafening boom. Once it exploded, we entered the house.

FBI tactical training took over. "Clear," I announced as I moved swiftly through the living room and into the dining room, sweeping my flashlight in every direction while I aimed my gun with the other hand. Cobwebs and dust motes floated in the patches of light.

"No movement outside," Hans called. "Moving to your location."

"Breaching the basement," Donovan said.

The padlock hanging from the outside was no match for the butt of Donovan's rifle. After two good hits, it broke off. He removed it from the lock, eyeing me. I nodded, and he threw open the door.

I crouched, spinning around the doorframe and aiming down the stairs. No one was in sight. He took point, moving swiftly down the steps. His heavy boots barely making a sound on the creaky steps.

The dingy, dimly lit room looked exactly as Adrianna described. From the staircase, I could see into the bathroom through the hole in the wall. This is where he'd watched her.

Not letting that thought get into my head, I met Donovan at the bottom of the stairs, tapping his shoulder to let him know I was behind him. He motioned to the left, so I moved in that direction while he went right.

Reddish-brown specks dotted the wall and floor. A larger puddle had spread over a portion of the floor, beside the wooden chair. I didn't want to think what they'd done to Adrianna to cause that, but they'd pay for it.

Donovan whistled. I turned, heading in the direction he'd gone. My flashlight caught sight of him crouching on the ground. He'd found Brent, still shackled to the chair the same way Adrianna had described. Beside him was a metal tub, several batteries, a blowtorch, and barbeque forks.

Donovan pressed his fingers against Brent's neck. "He's alive."

"Brent, hey, wake up." I knelt beside him, gently easing his head off his chest while Donovan cut his bindings.

Gunfire echoed in my ear, along with a few curses and Mercer's orders. But I'd tuned most of that out. Suddenly, the blasts were replaced with total silence.

"Mercer, report," Hans said.

"Two down. No sign of Barber."

"We got him," I said. "Brent's here. He's alive."

"He's in bad shape," Donovan said.

Hans came down the stairs, finding us easily. "Thought you might need some help with the extraction."

"It's about time you got off your lazy arse," Donovan teased.

"Where's Heuzen?" Mercer asked.

"I don't know. He's in the wind." I helped Donovan untie Brent, who let out a gurgling gasp. "Help me get him on the ground," I said. "He's having trouble breathing."

Hans slung his gun over his shoulder, taking over as they eased Brent off the chair and onto the floor.

"Brent, can you hear me?" I asked. "We're here to help you."

"Alex," Cross's voice cut in on the comms, "I have a medical team on standby beyond the perimeter. They can be there in two minutes."

"Send them," Donovan said.

I placed my face near Brent's chest, but I didn't see it rise or fall. He hadn't made a sound since that one gurgle. Opening his shirt, I saw the burns, cuts, and bruises. His ribs were broken. I didn't know if his lung was punctured. All I knew was he was in a great deal of pain every time his chest expanded, which would explain why he didn't want to breathe.

"Brent, look at me." But he didn't open his eyes.

"He's not breathing," Donovan said. "Let's get him out of here."

Hans and Donovan carried him up the stairs and out of the house just as the private ambulance pulled up.

The EMTs checked Brent's vitals. "He has fluid around his lungs. The pressure is preventing his chest from expanding." They loaded him into the back of the rig. One of them grabbed a large syringe. "This will buy him some time, but he needs a hospital."

"Go," I said, relaying the information over the comms.

"I'm on my way," Cross said. "I'll pull the teams and have them provide protection for Brent and Adrianna."

"Good idea." I pulled the comm out of my ear and sucked in a breath. Hans and Donovan continued to converse with the other half of their team, but I needed a moment without five other voices in my head. I stared down the road, watching two sedans fall into line behind the ambulance as they made a few more turns and finally disappeared from view. With any luck, Brent would live.

Hans nodded to me as I slipped the earpiece back in. "No word on Heuzen. He could be anywhere."

"We need him," Mercer said. "He's the only one left."

I grabbed a marker and a copy of the blueprints. "I have an idea."

* * *

"This is a bad idea," Mercer said.

"Do you have a better one?" I asked.

He glared at me.

"Exactly." I moved through the basement, photographing everything. "Heuzen was kept in the dark. He won't know his team was killed. When he doesn't hear from them, he'll think they've gone radio silent. But he'll come back. He thinks Brent is still here."

"He might know more than that. They could have a contingency. He may know to go to ground."

"He won't do it, not with this mess." I'd been cataloging everything, just in case law enforcement needed some help building their case. More than likely, Petrocelli would see this as another reason why I should be charged with obstruction. But I couldn't worry about that now. "Adrianna said they got fed twice a day. Pick-ups were Heuzen's job. He'll be here with Brent's dinner. Just be patient."

After what felt like hours, Hans' voice sounded over the comms. "Jules, a car's approaching."

"Copy."

Mercer moved into the bathroom and hid beneath the

partial wall. We didn't want to scare off the guest of honor.

A moment later, Donovan confirmed the driver was Heuzen. He had just parked outside the house. As predicted, he had a takeout bag with him.

"Make sure he doesn't escape," Mercer said.

"Affirmative," Hans said. "I'll pop his tires."

"He got your note. He's entering the house now," Donovan said.

I took a breath and braced myself. Mercer wouldn't let Taran Heuzen kill me. But he'd been right that this plan was insane. However, we needed to have a sit-down with Gonzalez, and Heuzen was the only one left standing who could take us to him.

The steps creaked as Heuzen slowly came down. He'd left the takeout bag upstairs, which filled me with relief. At least we wouldn't have a repeat of the bag trick. The last time had been a little too close for comfort.

"Show yourself," Heuzen ordered.

I flipped on the light and raised my hands. "I just want to talk. I believe we can help each other."

The first thing he noticed was Brent's empty chair. "How?" He jerked his gun at me, waiting for me to put my weapon on the floor.

Slowly, I removed my gun and placed it on the ground beside me before giving it a gentle kick. Heuzen's attention was entirely on me. He had no idea Mercer was in the room. That would help if things went south.

Heuzen grabbed my shoulder and spun me against the wall. After a quick pat down, he turned me back around, keeping a hand on my forearm. The barrel of his gun aimed at my mouth. From this distance, he wouldn't miss and I wouldn't survive. "Shut up and give me your radio."

I took it out of my ear, watching as he smashed it beneath his boot. Mercer better not make me pay for that. "That wasn't very nice."

"I said shut up."

"You tried to make me once. You're going to have to shoot me if you want it to stick."

He looked at me like I was crazy. "Don't tempt me. Where's Brent?"

"I'm confused. Do you want me to shut up or answer your questions?"

His eyes narrowed. "Where's Brent?"

"He's alive. He's safe. Just like Adrianna." I studied him. "But you already knew she escaped. They're going to be okay. However, your buddies, Castillo and Irmine, they didn't make it. That's why I wanted to talk to you. The money's been returned. It was transferred out of the account and back to your boss. Mission accomplished."

"I don't believe you." He flipped the safety off his gun. But before he could do anything else, Mercer came up behind him.

"You don't want to do that," Mercer said. "We still want to negotiate. Castillo wouldn't consider it. I hope you will."

"Be smart," I said.

Heuzen released my arm and let Mercer take his weapon. "None of this was supposed to happen. This was supposed to be an easy two fifty. We grab a guy, scare him into telling us where the money is, collect it, and call it a day. That's not what happened. That's not what those lunatics did."

Mercer said Heuzen was the weak link. I just hoped he was right. "You let Adrianna go," I said.

"What they did," he shook his head, "that was unforgivable. There are rules to war. But they broke them all."

"The war's not over yet," Mercer said. "Gonzalez wants blood. But enough has already been shed. I'd like to speak with him, discuss these matters, make sure he sees reason. Take us to him."

"You're insane. He'll kill you on the spot." Heuzen looked from Mercer to me. "Don't you understand who you're dealing with?"

"There's a tactical team outside, and the police are on the way. We're not asking."

"You're bluffing."

"I'm not," Mercer said. "We know you haven't been paid yet. With Castillo gone, Gonzalez will require an explanation. You have to meet with him. Either introduce us, or let us follow you. We'll wait until you're clear before making the approach, if you prefer to remain uninvolved. He won't know you're responsible. You have my word. But either way, you will take us to him, or you'll be held responsible for everything. Once you're behind bars, Gonzalez will send someone to kill you before you can talk. You know it's true. This way, you still get paid and you have a chance to escape. You have two minutes to decide. I suggest you hurry."

THIRTY-EIGHT

Mercer and I remained across the street from the cantina. Hans was inside, keeping an eye out while he flirted with the waitress. Bastian had found a nearby table and was monitoring the conversation closely. So far, Heuzen hadn't mentioned anything about us. He'd stuck to the truth, telling Gonzalez how Castillo and Irmine had gone off the rails and compromised the mission.

Gonzalez's expressions didn't give anything away, but he listened intently while he ate his dinner and downed several tequilas. When he asked about punishing the man responsible for absconding with his cash, Heuzen told him Roundtree had masterminded it and had already paid the ultimate price.

Seemingly satisfied, Gonzalez slid an envelope underneath one of the napkins and pushed it over to Heuzen. They drank a shot, and then Heuzen took off. He never looked back.

"Hold position," Mercer said. "Is the tracker working?"

"Affirmative," Donovan said. "Heuzen didn't notice when Alex switched his burner phone for hers. We'll be able to monitor his movements."

"Keep on that. We don't want any surprises." Mercer

and I remained outside the bar until most of the patrons had left. "I can handle this. You don't need the exposure."

"I have to know this is settled."

"It will be." Mercer eyed me. "It's best to remain anonymous."

"They know Cross Security. That's me."

"No, it's not," Cross said, nearly causing me to draw on him. "It's my company. Don't think because you're in charge of this branch that I'm handing you the keys. You can forget that."

"I thought you were with Brent."

"He's still asleep. Nero's keeping watch." Cross pulled me aside. "I can't let you go in there. James would kill me."

"He's not the one we should be worried about."

"Let me handle this, Alex. It's my mess. I'll clean it up."

I glanced at Mercer. "Don't screw up this negotiation. No repeats, remember?"

Mercer nodded.

"Call Petrocelli," Cross said. "We need to get ahead of this."

"Yes, sir." I just hoped they knew what they were doing.

* * *

Detective Petrocelli cleared the house before stepping outside, calling for a crime scene unit, and barking orders to the patrol units to secure the area. He took my statement, his face contorting in disbelief. When he was finished, he clicked the back of his pen and returned it to his pocket.

"You look shaken," he said. "Are you sure that's what happened?"

"Nerves." I tucked my hands into my pockets. No matter how much training and prep went into it, I still couldn't control the aftereffects of the adrenaline dump. "You saw the basement. Brent Barber's in bad shape. Have you heard anything? A private ambulance took him to the hospital, but I haven't been given any updates on his condition."

Petrocelli didn't believe a word I'd said, but he made a call. "He's out of surgery. I'll be questioning him as soon as the anesthesia wears off. So if there's anything you failed to mention, you might want to bring it up now. No reason to be caught in a lie."

"No lie," I said. "Adrianna described the place where she'd been kept. We used our skills to narrow down the possibilities. We noticed the front door was open, even though the house is boarded up, and we found him in the basement."

Petrocelli didn't believe it, but he couldn't disprove it either. "What about the kidnappers? Where are they?"

"Like I told you, someone fled the scene."

"We're not fucking doing this again. I'll give you a ride to the station. It's up to you if you'll come willingly or if you'd prefer handcuffs. Tell your boss he better meet us there."

"He'll want to contact his attorney," I said.

"I don't care, just as long as he's waiting for us when we arrive."

Once we made it to the station, Petrocelli put us in two separate interrogation rooms. But he didn't waste his time with Cross. My boss wouldn't speak without counsel. Instead, Petrocelli took a seat across from me.

"DePalma ripped off a cartel. He claims it was a mistake, that it happened by accident, but he never turned in the money. He and Fenton Roundtree put it into an account. Before you ran out of here, he gave you the account information. Where is it?"

"I lost it."

"You paid the ransom," Petrocelli said. "That's how you knew where Brent Barber was being held."

"Kidnapping victims have the right to hire whoever they choose to negotiate their release."

"That's not an answer."

"It's the only one I'm prepared to give."

Petrocelli rubbed his temples. "Since you're versed in the law, you can fill in the blanks on the crimes I can charge you with."

"Pretty sure none of that will hold up, and I'm even more certain the DA wouldn't prosecute under these circumstances."

"You're new around here. You have no idea how things work."

"I have some idea, but feel free to prove me wrong."

He leaned back, putting his feet up on the edge of the table. "Here's what I know. Sylvio DePalma's afraid the cartel will put a hit out on him. Even if the money was returned, the problem won't go away. Not if they want to make an example out of him."

"How long can you keep him in protective custody?" I asked.

"It depends on what kind of information he can provide. So far, he hasn't given us anything to work with. I have no reason to hold him, let alone offer him protection."

"Two kidnappers remain at large. Channing Irmine and Vincent Castillo. They were hired by Alejandro Gonzalez to retrieve his money and find the person who took it. Other than that, I don't know anything."

Petrocelli dropped his feet to the floor. "Stay put."

When I got tired of waiting, I put my feet up on the table, but I didn't find it particularly comfortable. Deciding Petrocelli only did it for show, I dropped my feet back to the floor and rested my head in my arms. By the time I opened my eyes again, the sun was shining in through the window.

Getting up, I went to the door, finding an officer stationed outside. "Bathroom break?" I asked.

"Yes, ma'am." He walked me down the hallway and waited outside.

After splashing some water on my face and checking the time, I went back into the hallway. "How about a cup of coffee and something to eat?"

"I'll bring you something." He placed me back inside the interrogation room. "Wait here." Two minutes later, he returned with a sandwich, bag of chips, apple, and a cup of coffee.

"Where's Detective Petrocelli?" I asked.

"He's on his way back."

For a moment, I thought of taking a play out of Cross's book, but I stuck it out for another twenty minutes. Finally, Petrocelli returned, appearing annoyed I'd been fed. He sat down beside me, picked up the chip bag, and helped himself to the rest of them.

"Doesn't quite make up for the yogurt," he said.

"You can't hold me indefinitely. I could walk. You didn't arrest me, but I stayed put out of professional courtesy. Where were you?"

"Speaking to Brent and Adrianna. What you said checks out."

"No shit."

"That has me worried."

"Why? You'd prefer if I were a pathological liar?"

"The heads were delivered to your office. The cartel knows who you are. Gonzalez knows who you are. What do you think he's going to do?"

"Send me a thank you card for taking care of business."

Petrocelli stared at me. "I can't decide if you're brave or delusional."

"Both."

"I just hope the next homicide that crosses my desk isn't yours."

"Well, if it is, you already have a suspect. Congratulations." I jerked my chin toward the door. "Am I free to go?"

"Careful, and don't give away any more yogurts that aren't yours."

* * *

When I returned home, Mercer and his team were already there. Cross had detoured to the hospital to be with Brent and Adrianna. He assigned Nero and a team of bodyguards to watch over them both. Mercer had updated the intel on the wall. Large Xs had been drawn over Castillo's and Irmine's faces.

"I feared we'd have to plan a prison break," Hans said.

"You all right, love?" Bastian asked.

"Never better."

Mercer arched an eyebrow but didn't comment. "It's a good thing we had all the necessary information to track your burner. Heuzen ditched the rental in the first parking garage he found and switched vehicles. He's in the process of disappearing, but he didn't find the phone. Donovan picked up his trail. He's at a pub now. It doesn't look like he has any intention of retaliating against you, but it's too soon to say. We'll keep an eye on him."

"How's Brent?" I asked. "Lucien said he was out of surgery, but I haven't heard anything since."

"They drained his pleural cavity. He's breathing much easier now. They're hopeful he'll make a full recovery. But he has to take it easy for a while, same as Adrianna." Bastian smiled. "I might have hacked into the hospital's database."

"For some reason, when I know you're the one doing it, it isn't nearly as unsettling," I said. "How did things go on your end? What did Gonzalez say?"

"He'll listen to reason. He got his money and enough revenge to satisfy his bloodlust. Castillo transferred the funds out of the account. After that, he and Irmine tried to kill us. He understood why we had to take action. It was just business. The police haven't found the bodies yet, but it's just a matter of time." Mercer gave me a look. "It won't trace back to us. We've already dumped our weapons."

"Do you know where the funds went?" I asked.

"Gonzalez has already moved them to another account. The cartel is careful. They don't trust easily." Mercer stared at the maps. "He's still missing a hundred thousand, which Heuzen never handed over, which means we have one more drop to make before business is complete."

"You're planning another sit-down with a plaza boss?"

Mercer shrugged. "This isn't the first time I've brokered deals with drug dealers. Large portions of the Middle East were controlled by the men who ran the opium trade. In order to operate in the area, sometimes we had to get their approval. Other times, our mission was to eliminate them. It all depended on our orders."

"Julian, you don't have to do this. I didn't call you for this."

"You called with a job. We see it through until completion. We won't kill him unless there is no other option. That will only anger the higher-ups, and we don't want to start a war we can't win." Mercer slipped on his jacket, appearing more relaxed and at ease than he'd been in days. Firefights always brought that out in him. But even my grief counseling group wouldn't try to figure that one out. "Hans will remain here. But I don't think you'll be targeted. If the cartel wants blood, they'll move against Sylvio. I'll make sure to impress that point upon them, as well."

"Where are you getting the money?" I asked.

"Cross."

* * *

When Martin returned home that night, I asked Bruiser, his bodyguard, to stick around. Martin didn't ask why. Hans crashed in the guest bedroom, but something told me he slept with one eye open. Bruiser made himself comfortable in the living room.

After Martin finished prepping for tomorrow's meetings, he climbed into bed beside me. I wrapped my arms around him and kissed a path along his chest.

"I love you more than anything," I said. "No matter what, I want you to know that."

"I do." He pulled me away from him, taking my face in his hands. "What happened?"

"Nothing. I just wanted to say that."

He kissed me gently before combing his fingers through my hair and playing with the ends. "Do we need to go home?"

The cartel could get to us anywhere, but if this was Gonzalez's vendetta, I wasn't sure he'd go through the trouble to order a long-distance hit. I also believed Mercer when he said he'd take care of this. "I don't think so."

"Are you ever going to tell me the extent of what this was?"

"I will if you want me to, but can it wait until the morning?"

Martin nodded, kissing me. "Do you expect anyone to burst into our bedroom if we lock the door?"

"Only if they hear one of us scream."

"Then try not to scream, sweetheart."

THIRTY-NINE

When I woke up, I didn't believe the clock. 12:21. I flopped back against the pillow, wondering what the day would bring. Jablonsky warned me not to piss off any organized crime bosses. The last thing I wanted to do was tell him I screwed up again.

After taking a shower, dressing, and drying my hair deliberately slow, wanting to enjoy as much of this ignorant bliss as possible, I went into the kitchen. Mercer's team had already packed their bags. The plastic sheet he'd hung on the wall in the game room, which he'd covered with intel, had been taken down. The printed files had been shredded.

"Are you going to burn those?" I asked.

"We could have a bonfire," Hans deadpanned, "and invite some of those bikini babes to join us." He stared out the sliding door, watching the people on the beach.

"I don't think your girlfriend would be particularly pleased," Donovan said.

"What she doesn't know," Hans said.

"Will bite you in the arse, mate." Donovan nodded to me. "We'll be taking our leave of you shortly. Everything's been handled. Jules doesn't anticipate any problems, but you know how to reach us."

"Thanks. What happened last night?"

"Best to let the commander tell you." Donovan glanced around the room, but everything was packed and ready to move. "We're going to do a little sightseeing while we have the chance. Maybe go for a swim."

"Sure, whatever you want."

"Toodles," Hans called as they headed out the back door.

I found a pitcher of iced coffee in the fridge, poured myself a glass, added milk and sugar, and gave it a stir. "Julian?" I stepped into the game room, surprised to find him at one of the arcade machines. Based on the score and the level, he must have been playing for over an hour.

"Martin set a plate aside for you. It's in the fridge." He paused the game, turning to look at me. "Are you ready to talk?"

"Whenever you're finished saving the earth from space invaders."

"I'll meet you in the kitchen." By the time I'd reheated breakfast, Mercer had joined me. He sat at the counter across from me. "We met Gonzalez at the cantina to hand over the rest of the money. Bas and I explained exactly what happened and why it took so long to return his money. I also mentioned the man they'd tortured was the nephew of a powerful crime boss, one who might start telling his associates to look elsewhere for the services the cartel provides."

"Luther Bianchi isn't in the drug business."

"I wouldn't be so sure about that, but even if that's the case, he has a lot of friends. Some of them are. I also went on to explain enough blood has been shed. Fenton paid the price, and that's enough. Sylvio made a mistake, but he didn't mastermind the theft. Whether that's true or not is irrelevant. All that matters is Gonzalez believes it. I also impressed upon him that Brent thinks of Sylvio as a brother, or he did before this, and if something were to happen to Sylvio, it should be at Brent's hand, not the cartel's."

"They understood that?" I asked.

"Of course. It's about revenge and honor. Gonzalez got what he wanted. He's ready to wash his hands of this."

"What about Heuzen?"

"He's already left the country. He is no longer your concern. You're safe, and so is Cross Security."

"Has Lucien paid you yet?"

"He said he'll be by this afternoon. We'll work out payment, and then we'll be on our way."

"Another job?" I asked.

"Best if you don't ask those questions."

I couldn't quite read the expression on his face. "Are you in trouble?"

"No, just trying to stay one step ahead of it."

"Is there anything I should know?"

"Bas tracked down the name of that copper from San Diego, the one who's been harassing you. Sergeant William Russo. Bas e-mailed you a copy of his personnel record. I don't know what he wants from you, but I'd suggest you steer clear. There was an incident. Ever since, he hasn't been cleared to carry a weapon, so he's working a desk."

"Sergeant? What happened?" I asked. "What did he do?"

"He was investigated for a fatal shooting that resulted in the deaths of two of his mates. The records are muddled. The investigation made it sound like one of them took friendly fire, but Russo was cleared of wrongdoing." Mercer scowled at the computer. "Another bloody cover-up, I'm sure. The next time he contacts you, tell him to sod off."

"Thanks for the tip."

*   *   *

Cross examined every inch of the office before nodding. "It looks good. We're finally ready to hire some staff."

"Don't you dare put me in charge of that."

"Why not? You're running this branch of Cross Security."

"Temporarily." The last thing I wanted was to be an office manager. "Remember, you didn't want to put me in charge of anything."

Cross laughed. "You're right about that, but you can handle this."

"I'll quit."

"Fine, but I need you to hire a replacement first."

"I hate you."

He grinned. "On a more serious note, Brent wants a full security detail. We're not shorthanded yet, but you might have to do some juggling."

"Isn't that the kind of thing Justin handles?"

"It is, which is why you need to find someone who can do that here. Applications have been forwarded to your inbox. We've already vetted every one of them. You just need to conduct the interviews. Once you find a worthy candidate, pass the details on to legal, and they'll handle the rest."

"It's your company. You should conduct the interviews."

"I thought you'd want to choose since you'll be working with them every day."

"Fine. Whatever." I looked at the calendar, counting the days until I could go home. "When's your flight?"

"In three hours. I didn't want to leave until I knew everything was set."

"Phone, internet, food delivery, Cross Security is ready to go."

"If only we had a receptionist." He slipped into his jacket. "If any legal issues arise, contact Jason Ganz."

"Yep."

"Alex." Cross hesitated at the door.

"I know. Trouble follows me around."

"I was going to say thank you. Is there any chance Mercer and his crew would be open to discussing a permanent position at Cross Security?"

"I believe his exact sentiment would be sod off. Would you like me to translate?"

"That's okay. I got the gist."

A few minutes after Cross left, the bell above the door chimed. "What did you forget?" I asked.

"Nothing," an unfamiliar voice said.

I looked up. "Hershel."

"My name's not really Hershel."

"No, it's not." I gestured to the chair. "What brings you so far out of your jurisdiction, Sergeant?"

He licked his lips. "You looked into me."

"It seemed fair. You have to keep in mind, Rizzo's a rat. He had some pretty unkind things to say about you. I'm wondering if they're all true."

"Don't believe everything you hear."

"I'd like to hear the story from you."

"Maybe one of these days." He looked around the office. "Cross Security has a reputation for being full of cops who fell from grace."

"Not just cops."

He nodded a few times before taking a seat in front of my desk. "I heard Brent Barber's going to make a full recovery. How's Adrianna?"

"Also set to make a full recovery, at least physically."

"That's usually the easier part."

"Yeah." I reached behind me and filled a second cup with coffee and slid it toward him. "Thanks for the assist."

"Anytime."

"Sergeant," I said.

He shook his head. "It's just Will." He sipped the coffee. "This isn't half bad."

"Perks of the private sector."

He looked around the office. "Y'know, I was thinking it might be time for a change."

DON'T MISS BURIED ALIVE, THE NEXT ALEXIS PARKER NOVEL

COMING TO PAPERBACK AND AVAILABLE AS AN E-BOOK

ABOUT THE AUTHOR

G.K. Parks is the author of the Alexis Parker series. The first novel, *Likely Suspects,* tells the story of Alexis' first foray into the private sector.

G.K. Parks received a Bachelor of Arts in Political Science and History. After spending some time in law school, G.K. changed paths and earned a Master of Arts in Criminology/Criminal Justice. Now all that education is being put to use creating a fictional world based upon years of study and research.

You can find additional information on G.K. Parks and the Alexis Parker series by visiting our website at www.alexisparkerseries.com